THRONE
BREAKERS

Also by Rebecca Coffindaffer

Crownchasers

THRONE BREAKERS

REBECCA COFFINDAFFER

An Imprint of HarperCollinsPublishers

HarperTeen is an imprint of HarperCollins Publishers.

Thronebreakers
Copyright © 2021 by Full Fathom Five, LLC

Library of Congress Control Number: 2021939638
ISBN 978-0-06-284519-1

Typography by Chris Kwon
21 22 23 24 25   PC/LSCH   10 9 8 7 6 5 4 3 2 1
❖
First Edition

To my big damn hero. So say we all.

THRONE
BREAKERS

PROLOGUE

Seventeen years ago . . .

NL7 HOLDS PERFECTLY STILL AS THREE FLOATING tablets circle the alloy frame of its body. The only other sentient presence in the room—a woman, human, Helixian—moves from one tablet to the next, her hands touching lightly across the surfaces, her eyes scanning the readouts.

Diagnostic outputs. It is the fifth time she has scanned NL7's functions in the past twenty-four hours alone. Far more frequent than usual.

The woman stumbles a little and catches herself on the edge of a nearby desk. She leans against it, her breathing heavy.

NL7 has noted recent changes in the woman's performance and appearance. A loss of body mass. A greater probability of instability. Slurred or inarticulate speech patterns.

"You are experiencing physiological malfunctions," it says to her.

"Yes. Yes, I am." She looks up at it and smiles. "That reminds me. I need to tweak those speech patterns a little more."

Pushing off the desk, she waves one of the tablets over to her. NL7 observes as she taps and swipes along the screen. It has another question, but it cannot ask her until she has finished adjusting its dialogue algorithms.

When she finally waves the tablet away, it takes NL7 a fraction of a second to adjust to its new functionality, and then it asks, "Is it serious?"

She smiles again. NL7 notes that this one differs from the previous one in small ways—shape, intensity, and something else it cannot quantify.

"Brain stem degeneration. So yes, NL7. It's very serious."

"Rest would be the preferred course of action for someone in your condition."

At a gesture from her, the tablets return to their docking ports, and the woman pats NL7 on the equivalent of its shoulder joint. "Not quite yet. I will soon."

She leaves the room and comes back a moment later carrying another, much smaller creature. NL7 analyzes its face—human, similar in genetic makeup to the woman, approximately two years old. A child, then. The woman's offspring.

She steps over to NL7. The child stares up at it, and it stares back.

"NL7, I'd like you to meet my son, Edgar," the woman says. "Edgar, this is NL7. It's going to take care of you."

ONE

STARDATE: 0.06.03 in the Year 4031, under the reign of the Empress Who Never Was, Nathalia Matilda Coyenne, long may she rest in glory
LOCATION: Playing the waiting game on a spaceport called Pal

SOMETHING JAGGED AND METAL ON THIS CHAIR IS digging into my back, right near my spine, and it's gonna leave a bruise. I just know it.

Fuck it. It can join all the other injuries I've collected recently. I've been shot, dislocated my shoulder, thrown myself off a cliff, blown up the best spaceship in the galaxy, crash-landed on a planet that poured acid rain, and had fifty thousand volts jammed into my body. It's been a week, is what I'm saying. Or more than a week, I guess. It's all kind of running together. There are really just two points in time for me right now.

Before Coy died.

And after.

There's this itching deep inside my muscles. It's been there for hours and hours, and it makes me want to snarl and snap at things like an Ekarsian saber rat. I want long, sharp teeth. I want fangs I can bare to tell everyone around me right now to get the hell away from me.

Instead, I'm on a spaceport called Pal.

Its official name is Palaxindromedaxardian, but pretty much no one wants to say that more than once so everyone just calls it Pal. As in, buddy. As in, friend. As in, I'll bump into someone and they'll apologize to me. It's that kind of place. Which doesn't really sound like something to complain about except that my head right now is filled with this primal, from-the-gut screaming and all the politeness around me just makes it louder. I'm too aware of the anger radiating off my skin. Is there a spaceport somewhere where no one talks and everyone gets around by shoving and using their elbows? Maybe that's the place I should've gone to.

I didn't choose Pal, though. And I only have to stay here long enough to find the person Hell Monkey and I are looking for and then bug out. I've got business on Apex that can't wait.

I shift in my seat, trying to see if there's a way to sit in the godsdamned thing without getting a blunted stab in the back. Who the hell made this thing anyway? Or better yet, who bought it and set it outside of a spaceport cantina like they thought it'd be great fucking relaxation?

I catch Hell Monkey watching me from across the little metal table between us, his eyebrows way up near his hairline. "You okay over there?"

"Sure." I try to sound casual, but it comes out like a growl. "Who doesn't love the feeling of being skewered to death very,

very slowly? Your contact is gonna be here, right?"

He nods and leans back, totally relaxed, looking like someone who hasn't been attacked by furniture his entire life. What must that be like? "They'll be here. It's early yet. I told them to meet us on the twelve and we're still ten minutes out from that."

Ten minutes. Hand to the stars, it sounds like he said ten hours. I squirm and try not to let my gaze drift over to the big display of media feeds streaming silently on the wall beside the cantina. Edgar Voles is expected to land on the kingship within the hour. His worldcruiser has already been spotted in the Apex system, gliding victoriously home, and dozens of correspondents surrounded by three times as many camera drones are swarming the kingship hangars, waiting to get the first glorious shot of the so-called winner of the crownchase. The new emperor of the United Sovereign Empire.

My face twists with disgust, and I taste sourness and bile on my tongue.

"And you're sure about them?" I ask. "They can get us what we need? Because the work Drinn is doing is not gonna be enough—"

"They're good, I promise. They've come through for me several times. Alyssa . . ." His hand lands on mine where it rests on the table. Heavy and warm as a magna-clamp. It's solid enough that I still and bring my eyes back over to his. "It'll work. You just need to be a little patient."

I turn my hand underneath his so we're palm to palm and my fingertips curl against the underside of his wrist. "Me? Patient? You must be new here."

His lips quirk a little, just for a second. But his expression sobers quickly. "You still wanna go through with this?"

I stiffen, and my mouth pinches into a thin line. I don't take my hand back, but I ball it into a fist under his grip. "You know I do. If there'd been any way for us to overtake Edgar before he reached the kingship, I'd have a blaster shoved right up against his stupid head already."

He drops his gaze to the table, and his words come out slow and careful. "Don't get me wrong—it's not like I don't think he deserves it—"

"Good, because he definitely, definitely does."

"—and you know how I feel about the Voles family—"

"A bunch of manipulative shitheels, the whole lot of them."

"—but whether this plan is the plan, though—"

"Nuh-uh, it's the only plan." I scoop my hand out and over his, squeezing my fingers tight around his knuckles. "He doesn't get to keep the throne. He doesn't get to play emperor. He doesn't get to sit up there on high and make decisions for you and me and a thousand planets' worth of people."

That makes Hell Monkey raise his eyebrows again. Skeptical. Or maybe worried. "Who does, then? You?"

"No. No no no. That's still a big pass." As soon as the words are out of my mouth, I see his shoulders relax just a fraction. "That's up to the other prime families to figure out, but I refuse to let him steal what Coy was supposed to have and not pay for it."

He stares at me for a second, and I can see a whole lot of something clicking away behind his hazel eyes, but I can't read what it is. Which is weird. Almost two and a half years side by side means I've usually got a pretty direct line into his thoughts, but this . . . must be way down deep. He opens his mouth, closes it, opens it again—

A figure drops heavily into one of the other chairs at our table, and I just about jump out of my skin, my hand dropping onto the butt of my blaster.

It's a Ravakian, tall and broad with four arms and four legs and a double row of iridescent plates protruding from their spine. They make the chair underneath them look like a toy, and their expression is one that a lot of cultures would interpret as amused—eyes crinkled, wide sharp-toothed mouth turned upward at the corners. I don't know Ravakian society as well as I'd like, though, so I can't tell for sure that this is amusement and not, say, something more murderous. I flick a look over at Hell Monkey.

He grins and touches his hands to the sides of his face and then to his shoulders, the best those of us with less than four hands can do for the traditional Ravakian greeting. "Oorva. You're looking shiny."

She—the *oor* designates female—chuckles and mimics the greeting. "Hell Monkey. You're looking like trouble." Her voice sounds like rocks tumbling against each other, and her eyes slide over to me, bright yellow and slit-pupiled. "So, crownchaser, I hear you're looking to sneak onto the kingship."

TWO

I MAKE A QUICK SCAN OF THE PEOPLE MOVING around the spaceport, seeing if anyone is listening or might have overheard, but we seem to be in the clear. Still, I shoot Hell Monkey a seriously weaponized glare. "Are we just straight-up telling everyone what we're up to?"

Oorva lets out a gravelly chuckle and gets to her feet. "Relax. He said only what he needed to say. I put together the rest. Come. Follow me. Let's get somewhere where we can sort this out."

I step up right behind her, that itch back in my muscles, ready to move, ready to get something—anything—done that might get me back on the ship and into the stars. Hell Monkey follows on my heels, hands in the pockets of his jumpsuit, not touching me but there all the same. I want to reach for him—I know he'll reach back if I just try—but I can't bring myself to do it. I don't entirely trust myself. It's like I'm covered in spikes and teeth lately. One second I want to be held and the next I just want to taste blood.

Oorva takes us through the polite, crowded corridors of Pal, passing by open shops and vendors selling everything from clothes and food to ship upgrades and virtual reality experiences. All of it is pretty standard for an active spaceport, and mostly I'm trying to make sure I'm not recognized. I've got an old jumpsuit on, with gloves and a hood to keep me from being too easy to spot by crownchase aficionados. That's pretty much all we had on hand by way of disguises, though, so I just try to look like I belong. Nothing to see here. Move along.

We follow Oorva to the far edges, where the traffic is less and the shops are quieter, and she quickly sweeps us inside a little vendor cubby that looks like it sells replacement parts for common bots. It's fairly unassuming, a little disorganized—and definitely not the real business that she does here. Which is confirmed when she takes us into a back storage room and then down a hidden floor hatch into a sublevel room that's crammed with less-than-legal items, as well as a workbench and an impressive display of tools. Unlike the shop above, everything down here is polished, shining, and organized with vicious efficiency.

"Welcome to my workshop, lambs." She's such a huge presence in this little space, but she moves through it as easily as I can fly a ship through a meteor shower. Lights come up across the ceiling, gleaming off her iridescent plating. Her hands are all moving at once, selecting a few items here, snatching up a tool or two there, arranging everything on the workbench in front of us. "I've got several things already prepared based off Hell Monkey's communication, but there are some finishing touches to put on."

It takes some godsdamned willpower not to tap my feet. "Will it take very long?"

Oorva tilts her head at me, her arms going still. "You won't get very far in the vengeance game with that lack of patience."

A cold feeling fills my chest, and I cross my arms in front of me. "I'm not in the vengeance game. I'm in the justice game."

Oorva shrugs. "I suppose that's a matter of perspective, crown-chaser."

I'm on the verge of responding—with something very clever and devastating, for sure—but Hell Monkey gives me a warning look. Because we need what she's got. We're back to square one otherwise.

Come on, Alyssa. Put the spikes away.

"What do you need from us, Oorva?" Hell Monkey asks as he steps over to the bench.

The Ravakian picks up one of the items and starts fiddling with it. "Well, the credits we talked about would be a nice start." She reaches out a massive arm and taps Hell Monkey in the middle of his forehead. "You're sweet, little lamb, but this is expensive work."

I reach into my pockets and fish out three high-capacity credit chips, plunking them down. "I'll give you the last three once we have all our stuff." I'd drained my account just the day before, pouring it all onto credit chips I could take with me anywhere. She's not wrong about this being expensive—my pockets will be substantially lighter walking out of here—but it'll be worth it.

It'll all be worth it.

I'm gonna fix this, Coy. I swear to the stars.

Oorva picks up the cred chips, examines them, and then grins at me, her teeth glittering. "Let's do business, then." The credits disappear into her pocket, and she scoops a series of bright-colored irregular-shaped data cards up, holding them out. "First things first: your new ship identity. This green one gives you your new identification code and registration. The blue one changes your radiation signature and energy output so you're not leaving any tracks that look like your old self. I'm assuming you two already thought about the ship's exterior . . . ?"

Her yellow eyes flick between us, and Hell Monkey nods. "We've got a friend working on it. She's a standardized design—no customizations—so it shouldn't be too hard."

"Good." She taps the last data card, a violently pink one. "This one goes in last, directly into the AI system. Only caveat is that since this is an unauthorized override, it can sometimes cause . . . quirks."

I squint down at the bright card. I think I took a medicine that was this color one time. "What kinds of quirks?"

"It depends on the AI," Oorva says with a shrug. "Generally nothing functional. More like . . . in attitude."

Hell Monkey gives me a side look, but I don't know anywhere else we can get a comprehensive overhaul like this, so I say, "Consider us forewarned. Are they ready?"

"Almost. I just need to finalize your ship's name."

Ah. Yeah, that. The thing is, I'd already planned on renaming the ship *Nathalia*, after her fallen captain, but you can't really pull up to the kingship flashing the name of the crownchaser the new boss in charge murdered and not have it set off a few red flags. I try to come up with something neutral and unconnected to me or the crownchase in the slightest, and I'm floundering. . . .

"*Verity*," Hell Monkey says suddenly, and then he looks over at me. "That okay with you, Captain?"

I nod, grateful, and as Oorva bends low over the data cards, finishing the encoding, I catch his hand in mine. "Thank you," I mutter under my breath.

His grip is warm and firm. He keeps his eyes locked on what Oorva is doing as he says, really quietly, "It was my mother's name."

Fuck. That hits me right in the sternum like a fist and knocks all the words out of my mouth. All I can do is squeeze his hand harder and press my arm against his, although it seems pretty paltry as far as sympathy goes.

"All right!" Oorva straightens so suddenly that I flinch a little. Gods, I must be losing my nerve. "That gets you lambs into the hangar. But these are what you'll need to get through the ship." She holds out three thin metallic patches, each one about two and a half centimeters square. They're all totally unique from one another, from how their metallic threads lie together to the swirls and imperfections in the designs. My breath catches a little as I hold one up to the lights.

Glamour keys.

"I can't believe you have these." Excitement tightens my voice. "I've heard of glamour keys before but never gotten the chance to see one."

Oorva snorts. "If you were curious where all your credits are going—there's your answer. Those sons of bitches cost a lot, both in social collateral and actual collateral. Luckily you know someone who has both. You get how they work?"

I nod as I take all three of them and tuck them into an inner pocket of my jumpsuit. "In theory, yeah. Unless you've got any hot tips to pass along?"

Oorva laughs, low and gravelly. "Hot tips are only offered upon receipt of final payment."

She holds out one of her hands, and I roll my eyes and slap the last three cred chips into it as Hell Monkey collects the data cards and pockets them. Oorva grins as she checks the totals on all six chips. Then she cuts her sharp yellow eyes back over to us. Her face is half gleaming teeth.

"Walk soft and watch your ass, crownchaser. If you're doing what I think you're doing, you're gonna need every advantage you can get."

THREE

Our luck runs out on our way back to the docking bays.

We come out of Oorva's shop, working our way back into the flow of people, and we're about halfway across the spaceport when a figure blocks my way and I stop short, looking up.

It's actually two people—one is definitely axeeli, the other has some of the spiked features of a deonite. The deonite clutches the axeeli's arm and bounces on their toes (they tend to have a lot of toes, as a species). The axeeli has a personal tablet gripped tightly in their hands, and their eyes shift color rapidly—from a dark gray to a vivid red-orange—as they take in my face.

"It's you!" Their voice is a little breathless. "I mean, you're you! The Alyssa Farshot!"

The deonite smacks them on the arm. "I told you!" They grin at me. "I told them. I saw you from across the port, and I said, 'That's a crownchaser,' and they said, 'No way is a crownchaser on Pal,' but I was right! Here you are!"

"I am very much here," I say, mainly because I don't see how I'll get out of this encounter without saying *something*. I'm not sure

14

what else to do, so I paste a smile onto my face. It feels weird and stiff. I cut a glance over at Hell Monkey, who's drifting backward and looks like he's tempted to make a break for it, but they spot him, too.

"Stars and gods!" The deonite might be looking a little swoony. Not that I blame them. Obviously, I've got no place to judge when it comes to swooning over Hell Monkey. "What are the chances of meeting both of you?"

Hell Monkey clears his throat uncomfortably. "Pretty good, actually. We're basically joined at the hip most days."

"Can I take your picture?" the axeeli asks, holding up their tablet. "I mean, can we take a picture with both of you? I hate to be a bother, but you were our absolute favorite crownchaser. We really wanted you to win."

Were. Wanted. Past-tense verbs, of course. Because the crownchase is technically over. Edgar Voles won. And the rest of us are nothing more than also-rans.

At least, that seems to be the official story if you're interested in buying it. Which I'm absolutely not. None of this shit is over in my book. We're still a long way from the end.

The axeeli and deonite are staring at us, excited expressions on their faces. Waiting for a response. I nod, because I don't really trust myself to use words right now, and grab Hell Monkey by the arm, hauling him over next to me. The axeeli sets their tablet to hover at eye level, and then they and the deonite rush over and sandwich us, grinning widely at the tiny lens. I'm pretty sure my own expression looks more pained than pleased, but it's the best I can do for them right now.

After a second, the axeeli darts back over to grab their tablet, making sure they got that good shot. I'm looking for an opportunity to extract myself from this whole situation when the deonite fixes their wide, round eyes on me and says, "We believe you, you know. About Edgar Voles murdering Nathalia. We're on your side."

I feel Hell Monkey go real still next to me, and I slice a look at them, trying to figure out if they're being sincere or not. But I can't get a read on their face. My *side*? What the hell does that mean? There isn't a side here. There's just those of us who want Edgar to pay for killing Coy, and anyone who's not on that team is wrong.

I try to keep my voice very even as I say, "Because it's the truth."

"Exactly!" The deonite nods enthusiastically. "We know what really happened. It doesn't matter what anyone else says."

A cold, curdled feeling fills my gut, and it's a fight to keep my face blank. I've been too focused on everything else to check in with the noisy sea of media feeds, but something is telling me I'm about to pay for that blind spot.

Fantastic.

I give the deonite and the axeeli a tight smile. "It's been great— really awesome—but if you'll excuse us, we have to . . . see to our ship."

I fast-walk it away before they can answer, rushing but, y'know, trying not to look like I'm rushing. Hell Monkey follows in my wake, and when I glance back at him, he's got that little crinkle between his eyebrows that tells me he's worried. Either about me or about what the two crownchase fans just told us—I'm not sure which. I lead the way, cutting through streams of people, and then break into a run down the corridor that leads to the docking bays. By the time I tear around a corner and punch open the temporary access code for our spot, my heart is pounding against my sternum and my breath rasps out of my lungs. The heavy bay doors beep and slide open, and Hell Monkey and I dash inside.

We immediately stop, and Hell Monkey whistles in appreciation as we look over our worldcruiser.

The Nathalia. Or, I guess, the Verity now. We put in for "major repairs" and got a fully enclosed landing space instead of having to post up at an airlock, and Coy's former engineer Drinn took on the job of altering her exterior so she doesn't look like her old self.

He's done a hell of a job with it, too. Especially for a guy who was shot only forty-eight hours ago.

The plating details around the prow and along the dorsal have been altered and resoldered, and he's repainted it from nose to aft in vibrant shades of orange. He's putting the finishing touches on the ship's belly, his enormous vilkjing body crammed into the meter and a half of space between the hull and the floor. The treatment cuff in the med bay fixed him up pretty well, although he's still favoring his left side a bit.

He pauses his stream of spray paint as he sees me hauling ass toward the aft and grunts. "Trouble?"

I shake my head as my boots hit the onboarding ramp. "No, keep going. Hell Monkey, can you get started with those data cards? I just . . . need to check on something."

I leave them behind, scrambling down the corridors, up a

ladder to the first level and into the navigator's quarters. I swipe on the display screen embedded in the wall and go to the media feeds first, flipping to the *Daily Worlds* to skim their headlines.

I only need to read the first one.

COYENNE FAMILY RELEASES OFFICIAL STATEMENT CONCEDING CROWNCHASE, OTHER FAMILIES EXPECTED TO FOLLOW WITHIN THE DAY

It feels like a fist grabbed my ribs and is just *squeezing* them together. That itch deep down in my muscles intensifies until I'm pacing and I want to scream, but instead I lash out with a fist, slamming it into the wall.

I get an aching hand and a scraped knuckle for my effort. It just makes me even madder.

I stomp over to the display screen again and call out to the ship's AI. "Nova! I need an open comms channel to Cheery Coyenne. Tell me you can do that for me."

In the heartbeat before I get a response, I almost expect to hear Rose's voice—my old AI from the best ship ever that's now blasted into space detritus. But I don't. Instead it's Nova who says, "Understood, Captain Farshot. Connecting now."

I don't expect Cheery to answer. I figure she'll just ignore me. Maybe even block me. But suddenly there she is, coming to me live from the other side of my screen. Her foarian horns are tight spirals of silver, like her daughter's were, but her eyes are obsidian-black and her skin is a lot lighter gray. She uses a single long finger to sweep a strand of hair from her face and tilts her head back. So she's looking down her nose at me a little.

Shit. Cheery's in full matriarch mode. She's never been the biggest fan of me, per se (see, I can do that fancy royal talk), but we haven't crossed wires too often because I was almost always on her daughter's side. So we were good enough.

But I'm not so sure now.

"Miss Faroshti," she says. "This is a surprise."

I don't know what gets my hackles up more—the way she says that surname or how she's acting like she doesn't know why I'm calling. "The hell it is, after the news that just broke! What the fuck, Cheery?"

She narrows her eyes to slits. "May I remind you, Alyssa, that you are talking to the head of a prime family, not one of your backwater, asteroid-trash buddies."

I take a deep breath, look down at my feet. Chastened. "You're right. I'm sorry." And then I bring my gaze back up, burning a hole in the screen with my glare. "What the fuck, Primor Coyenne? You conceded? To the Voles family?! Edgar killed Nathalia! I put him on blast to the whole godsdamned quadrant!"

Her lips are so pinched together they're basically nonexistent. There's a shine of emotion in her eyes, but she's got it pinned down so well I can't get a read on what all is happening in her head. "Yes, I heard your . . . explanation as to what happened."

"My exp— Cheery, I was there! I saw it all happen! You can't concede to your daughter's murderer!"

That cool, political mask slips back into place. "You are not the arbiter of what I can and can't do, Alyssa. The Coyenne family council gave these matters our full consideration, and the facts are these: we are legally bound to uphold the winner of the crown-chase, and as soon as Edgar Voles sets foot on the kingship, he will be that winner."

I flail my arms, wildly, angrily. "Oh, yeah, sure, we should definitely handcuff ourselves to some archaic pissing contest instead of bringing justice down where it belongs!"

There's movement in the corner of my eye—the door slides open and a figure steps inside, but I don't have to turn my head to know it's Hell Monkey. I can tell by the way he moves through the space. The way he lounges just inside the door, one arm propped up against the wall, the other hand in the pocket of his jumpsuit. I can feel his eyes on me, but I don't turn to look at him. I run my hands down my face, pressing hard against my eyeballs. Cheery Coyenne watches me with nothing in her expression, not even a spark of actual feeling.

"The Voleses are murderers." My voice is quieter now. The yell has gone right out of me. "They don't belong on that throne."

There's a pause, and something softens in Cheery's eyes, dropping her shoulders just this fraction of a centimeter. She sighs. "Alyssa, you're not very well versed in imperial politics, so out of respect for your childhood friendship with my daughter, allow me to give you some free insight. Your mere accusation of something this serious, however passionately delivered, does not automatically make it true. The truth is we have no evidence that Edgar Voles was ever on Nathalia's ship. No footage from onboard cameras or drones. No transmissions from mediabots."

"But what about—"

"In fact, the only crownchaser who we know for sure boarded Nathalia's ship after the battle over Calm is . . . you."

Her eyes are like twin black holes, tearing into me. There's a cold weight in my stomach. "What are you saying, Cheery?"

"I'm saying tread carefully, Alyssa. There are hardly any Faroshtis left as it is."

She waves a hand, and the channel goes dead.

FOUR

I SIT DOWN HARD ON MY BUNK.

The silence in my quarters lies heavily on me, and all of a sudden my jumpsuit feels too hot, too tight around my neck. It's trying to choke me. I unzip it with shaking fingers and yank my arms free of the sleeves, pushing the top down till it hangs around my waist, leaving me in just the tank top underneath. It helps. A little. My skin feels cooler. A little less like it's slowly squeezing me to death.

The only crownchaser who we know for sure boarded Nathalia's ship is you. . . .

There's burning in the back of my throat, and I think for a hot second that I might puke all over the floor. That they think that I might . . . That I would . . . I swallow hard. *Don't throw up, Farshot. You've got enough of a mess to clean up already.*

Something else has to be going on. I can't believe that even Cheery Coyenne would ignore her daughter's murder to . . . what, play nice with the Voles family? I mean, everyone who heads up these prime families has always been pretty cutthroat about power and politics and all that, but there's gotta be limits to that, right? A hard stop at which they go, "Hey, maybe doing what's right is more important than doing whatever the hell benefits us. . . ."

My eyes find Hell Monkey, still standing there, watching me with those worried lines around his big hazel eyes. He doesn't say anything, and he doesn't have to. I know what he's thinking, and that kick-starts the anger in my chest again.

It's always there now. That fury. It sits right on top of me. It's like I'm this burning sun, lashing out with solar flares every few minutes.

"I don't want to hear it," I tell him, pushing back onto my feet. "The plan stands. We're doing it."

His inhale is so sharp and so deep that I can hear it. "Alyssa—"

"No! No . . ." I stomp past him, ducking under his arm to get to the door. "We literally just talked about this. The decision is made."

He spins, following me down the corridor like the tail on a comet. "You know what? It's a bad godsdamned decision. And I'm tired of tiptoeing around you and pretending like it isn't."

"Wow! How burdensome for you! Please accept my condolences." I slide down the ladder and swing into the aft bay, which is all shut up and locked down now. Drinn is over by the walls, securing crates to the floor. "We good?" I call to him.

Drinn grunts and nods, tapping his chest in a vilkjing salute. I can't tell if he's mocking me or not, but I don't have time to figure it out. I turn on my heel—

—and Hell Monkey is there. Blocking my way. He tilts his chin down, looking me steadily in the eye.

"It was one thing to pursue this idea in the beginning, but now you have the head of a prime family—the one prime family that should *definitely* be on your side—telling you to stand the fuck down. And you're gonna play this like business as usual?"

"Cheery Coyenne changes nothing. I've got a narrow window *right now*. Another few days and Edgar will be so integrated with the kingship that getting to him will be impossible. I'm doing it." I shoulder past him and head back up the ship, calling out to the ceiling as I go, "Nova! Get this rust bucket warmed up and ready for go-time!"

"Don't do it, Nova!" Hell Monkey's footsteps are like thunder in the corridor behind me. "You're better than this. You don't have to listen to her."

"Nova, prime the engines. That's an order."

A beat. And then the walls of the *Nathal*—no, the *Verity*—hum to life. I smile. A little smug. Good to be the captain.

"Forget the narrow window, Alyssa. Cheery Coyenne changes everything, and you know it." He's still storming along behind me, undeterred. "You're not going in there as some kind of righteous deliverer of justice. You're going in there looking like an asshole who doesn't know how to lose."

"That's ridiculous! I never even wanted to win!"

"That's not the point! You've got nothing—no backup. We need to be smarter about this."

My feet hit the bridge, and I stop, turning back to Hell Monkey. "Look, it's gonna be fine. I know all the corners of the kingship. I know how to get in, get it done, and get out. You don't have any-thing to worry about! You and Drinn will be safe on the ship the whole time, completely out of harm's way."

Hell Monkey stills, and his expression goes flat and hard. "I can't believe that that's what you think I'm most worried about right now."

I try not to let it show, but part of me stumbles a little. I've seen Hell Monkey get this look on his face before plenty of times, when he's truly and deeply angry, but he's never pointed it at me. Not once. Not even during that mess on Divinius IX. But he's mad at me now. Beyond mad. And it cools my anger more than anything else—to realize that I didn't just piss him off. I hurt him. He's less than half a meter away from me in a technical, physical sense, but I think if I tried to touch him right now, I wouldn't be able to actually reach him.

"I'm sorry," I say, but not like how I said it to Cheery Coyenne. An actual apology this time. "I shouldn't have said that. It was shitty of me. But I'm not backing down on this. I have to go."

His jaw loosens a little bit. He takes a deep breath, rubbing a hand over his buzzed brown hair. "You don't think I understand this feeling? That I don't remember what it's like? It's like a fireball right here"—he brushes his fingers across the bare skin just below my collarbone, and a little shiver goes down my spine—"and you want to take it and throw it at the whole universe."

I shrug. "I mean . . . not the whole universe. There's a few places I'd probably save."

"No jokes, Alyssa," he says, shaking his head. "I know this look. I wanted to burn everything down after my family died. I was just a kid, but it didn't matter. I threw myself at the universe for years, trying to make a dent in it, but all I got were bruises." He edges a little closer to me. Our noses are only centimeters apart, and he skims his fingers down my arm, taking the hand I hit the wall with earlier and running his thumb over my still-aching knuckles. "You're basically trying to burn sublight engines in atmo right now, and it's not gonna turn out good. Not for you. Not for anyone else around you. This isn't the crownchase anymore. This isn't something you can out-talk or out-fly."

His touch is soft and cool, which is nice because I feel like I'm just radiating heat. That fireball, I guess. That sun flare. The most logical parts of my brain are listening to him, giving off those signals of *this makes sense* and *you need to slow down*. My gaze drifts down to his hand, gently holding mine, and I realize with a little jolt that I'm standing in *that* spot. The spot where I stood, helpless, and watched Coy die and forever stain the decks of this ship with her blood.

Well. Logic has never been my strong suit anyway.

I lean in and press my lips against his, taking three or four seconds to just savor him. How he tastes like salt and coffee. How he smells of sweat and coolant oil. How his breath hitches in this little gasp when I flick my tongue against his.

Then I step back, smile a little, and say, "Just watch me."

VOLES SHIP SPOTTED ENTERING APEX'S ATMOSPHERE

Kingship officials await his landing in order to confirm
authenticity of the royal seal

MORE PRIME FAMILIES FALL IN BEHIND THE COYENNES

The Orsos and Megas both declare they will also concede the
crownchase should the seal be declared valid; Roys remain undecided

ALYSSA FARSHOT OFFICIALLY DECLARED PERSON OF INTEREST IN THE MURDER OF NATHALIA COYENNE

Sources inside the kingship say officials are taking a second look at
the actions and motivations of the Faroshti crownchaser

FAYE ORSO AND SETTER ROY RELEASED FROM MEDICAL CARE ON VIOLA

Neither the crownchasers nor their official companions provided public
statements about the battle over Calm or the race's final result

THE KINGSHIP, APEX, THE KYRA SYSTEM

UNTIL THIS MOMENT, EDGAR VOLES HAD NEVER LIKED the kingship.

He'd appreciated its prestige and construction. He'd respected it for the power and symbolism it held for the empire. But he'd never liked it. Never liked visiting it or coming to it. He had, in fact, not set foot on this ship since he was close to thirteen years old and his father finally decided it wasn't necessary to drag him everywhere like a disliked and untrustworthy pet.

He'd thought he'd never come back here, but he has to admit the ship is not as bad as he remembers. Perhaps it's the complement of crownsguards and diplomats, all in their finest clothes, trailing behind him in a stately processional. Or the small fleet of camera drones circling him dramatically, trying to catch every angle of his face.

The face of their new emperor.

He squeezes his fingers tight around the royal seal clutched to his chest. It was officially authenticated by a five-person panel of kingship and crownchase officials, and now media correspondents throng all around the hangar bay, yelling questions at him and congratulating him on his success. Calling him "Imperial Majesty." People bow low and murmur, "Long live our new emperor," as he passes.

It's better than he could've ever hoped.

And also more terrifying.

He keeps his chin up, his eyes straight ahead as he walks to the transport waiting for him. Pretending to be unbothered and undistracted by the noise and chaos, as is befitting an emperor. But his mind spins.

Is his posture correct? Is his expression sufficiently regal? Did he select the right clothes for this moment?

Is he . . . enough?

The transport doors slide closed behind him and all is quiet. The select otari crownsguards there to protect him are too well-trained to try to chitchat, and the only other person Edgar has with him is NL7, still in the body of the mediabot and trying not to draw any attention to itself. Neither of them wanted to provoke any questions about why Edgar Voles's mediabot no longer seemed quite like a standard mediabot, but Edgar had refused to face this moment—this achievement—without NL7 by his side.

The transport stops outside the tall, finely detailed doors of the throne room, and Edgar steps out, his heart in his throat. They open automatically as he walks toward them, as if recognizing his true authority, and then they swing shut in his wake, leaving all the crownsguards outside. The throne room stretches before him, long and elegant, with polished floors and walls of windows showing the blue sky outside slowly fading into a watercolor dusk. At the far end, up on a dais, sits the throne, crafted with geodesic patterns and the crests of the six families, just waiting for him. And in between him and it are an array of people, almost all of whom he recognizes—important, powerful figures from around the empire, the leaders of several key systems, the primors from the other prime families, including Radha and Jaya Roy and Charles Viqtorial dressed in the colors of the decimated Faroshti house.

His father is here too, over near the wall, scowling at him through all the people. William Voles had made multiple attempts to communicate with him after his win had hit the media feeds. Edgar had refused all of them.

Steward Ilysium Wythe comes toward him, arms spread in welcome.

"Edgar Voles, the illustrious victor!" The Solari enkindler places his hands on Edgar's shoulders, and Edgar almost flinches, so unused to physical contact. "Welcome home. Your empire awaits."

He takes Edgar by the arm and guides him up the dais, gently steering him to sit on the edge of the throne. When he gestures for the royal seal, Edgar hesitates, suspicious. He knows what is supposed to come next, but somehow that doesn't make it any easier to relax his grip.

Wythe smiles kindly and says, "Not to worry, Imperial Majesty. I will return it to you shortly."

Edgar hands it over, and the steward takes a second, staring down at it in a way that almost seems loving. Then he turns to the assembled audience and holds the seal above his head, calling out in a loud voice, "Kneel and bear witness as your emperor ascends."

Everyone present drops to their knees, and Wythe presses the cool, shining platinum of the seal into Edgar's chest. Edgar holds his breath, waiting, waiting—and then the metal liquefies, sinking into his skin, threading itself throughout his body and then down into the construct of the kingship itself. Edgar's vision goes white, bright and blinding, as the seal's connections spread farther and farther, connecting him to the room, to the ship, to everything. His head is filled with noise, his skin burns, and he opens his mouth to scream—

—and then he blinks and he can see again. His skin feels cool. His head is clear.

A deep AI voice speaks, and it sounds like it comes from inside him.

CONGRATULATIONS, EMPEROR EDGAR MARIUS TYCHO VOLES. THE EMPIRE IS YOURS.

FROM THE PERSONAL FILES OF ATAR VELRYN FAROSHTI, ACCESSED BY NL734014 ON STARDATE 0.06.03 IN THE YEAR 4031

Audio transcript of a personal long-range communication from Atar to Charles Viqtorial on 0.08.06.3988

"IT SEEMS YOU WERE RIGHT, CHARLES, AND MY HOPES that Emperor Roy's final wish would be accepted and supported on the event of his passing were unfounded. Saya has just informed me that Justus's eldest son, Aldius, has submitted a formal declaration of war on the Faroshti family and all of our allies. He will not accept Saya on the throne. He claims now that Saya manipulated his ailing father into selecting her as his heir and that her acceptance would be illegitimate.

"I do not know if any of the other prime families will join him. In truth, I have no idea what to expect at all. I know so little about the other primors and their heirs and who they are as people. How far will they take this? How bad will it get? I am scared for us and for the empire. I am scared for all the many trillions of people who might get caught between us.

"Saya, as you might already expect, has been extraordinary. I suppose as her brother I am biased, but while the news of war dragged at my soul, she bore up with a fierceness and a fire not often seen anymore among hallüdraens. She will not submit. She knows she is in the right, and she will not abandon her dreams for a better future for the quadrant. I take strength in that.

"I will feel even better once you're back. I'm glad to hear you're on your way. We will need each other more than ever in the days to come."

FIVE

STARDATE: 0.06.04 in the Year 4031, under the reign of the Empress Who Never Was, Nathalia Matilda Coyenne, long may she rest in glory

LOCATION: Apex. And here's hoping this is the last time I have to come here for a long while.

BY THE TIME WE DROP OUT OF HYPERLIGHT NEAR Apex, Hell Monkey and I have reached a cease-fire of sorts. Basically, he's still frustrated at me for staying the course, but not so much that he's abandoned his copilot seat and left me to fly us in solo. He's here. He's present and functioning. But he's laying the salt on pretty thick.

"Course plotted for direct approach to the kingship." I look up at the three-dimensional map of Apex projected in front of me, double-checking our descent vectors. "Can you transmit our request for docking?"

"Yes, sir, Captain, sir."

I roll my eyes at him. "Hey, do you need a napkin or something over there? You're dripping a little sarcasm."

"My *sincerest* apologies, Captain." He keeps his gaze down at the navcomm dashboard in front of him. "What do you want me to put for this part where they ask for the reason behind our visit? Would 'self-destructive tendencies' cover it?"

I lean way out of my seat and flick him in the earlobe. He swats me away, and I grab his hand, holding it until he finally looks me in the eye.

"I know you don't like this," I tell him, serious enough that his scowl softens a little. "Thank you for being here anyway."

He holds my gaze. And then he says, completely salt-free, "Can't think of anywhere else I'd rather be."

Son of a bitch. This guy. I squeeze his hand and nod because there's suddenly this big clog in my throat that's making it tough to speak.

Nova's voice breaks in, "NOT THAT EITHER OF YOU ASKED, BUT WE'RE ENTERING APEX'S UPPER ATMOSPHERE."

This, by the way, would be the "quirks" Oorva mentioned on Pal. Not long after Hell Monkey inserted the new data card into the system, Nova underwent a major personality shift, with extra doses of volume and petulance. I catch Hell Monkey's eye and press my lips together hard to keep from laughing, even a little. If Nova hears anything like that, she'll lay into us.

"Thank you, Nova," I say, reaching for the manual controls. "I'll take it from here."

"FINE. HAVE IT YOUR WAY."

I burn the *Verity* through the upper layers and drop her down into the atmosphere proper, the wide, sweeping blue of Apex filling the windows of the prow. It's almost ninety percent ocean on this planet, and the kingship is anchored in the middle of one of the biggest stretches of sea on the whole sphere. The closest land masses are a series of small islands about a hundred kilometers to the northeast, and I bounce a signal off their navigation tower, using it to double-check our coordinates as we draw closer, slipping down to an altitude of just fifteen hundred meters.

We're gonna be on top of the kingship in a matter of minutes. And it's gonna be a real short trip if we don't have clearance to dock.

"H.M.? Anything?"

He grumbles something to his console that I can't make out and then says, "Nothing. I'm checking. Give me a second."

Seconds are about all I can give him. I try to run through every-thing—new ship registration, totally new look, I even put together a stellar (if I do say so myself) imperial calling card dropping the kind of name and fuss that ought to hold weight for those check-ing IDs at the door. We should be good. It shouldn't be taking this long. . . .

Something moves in the corner of my eye, and I take my gaze off the skyline for just a second.

Coy leans against the captain's chair. The chair that used to be hers. Her eyes are glazed white and fixed on the view outside the windows. Her chest is covered in blood and scalded flesh.

My pulse pounds in my ears. All I can do is stare.

She tilts her head down suddenly and looks right at me. A smile curls her lips up, and I sink down, unable to look away, unable to see anything else but—

"Alyssa!"

Hell Monkey's yell shakes me out of it, and I jerk my head forward, heartbeat stuttering in my chest, the ship wavering a little as I right my hands on the controls.

Nova's voice blares overhead. "ARE YOU SURE YOU DON'T WANT A SUPERIOR INTELLIGENCE TO TAKE OVER?"

I let out a shaky laugh. My hands are trembling. "I'm fine, Nova. Everything's fine."

I chance a quick glance at Hell Monkey, and he's staring at me with narrowed eyes. "What the hell, Alyssa? I had to yell your name like three times. What were you staring at?"

"Oh, nothing." I shrug. "I just spaced out."

"You *spaced out*? Is the incredibly complex stealth mission you concocted somehow boring you?"

"It's not a big deal, okay? It's fine—we all turned out fine. How's our status over there?"

Hell Monkey frowns at me for another three full seconds, but then he waves a hand at his console. "We're good. Just got cleared. Park her in the western hangar bay, section B7."

"Excellent. I like the number seven. See? This is all gonna work out."

He snorts but manages to not say anything, which I'm betting takes an awful lot out of him. I'm tempted to ask if he needs to lie down after that kind of effort, but I really have to concentrate now as we glide down closer to the towering waves of the Eastern Sea. My hands are still shaking a little—it's like I'm cold all over, even though I feel burning hot from the inside out.

The kingship appears on the horizon, slowly filling the windows as we get closer and closer. It's never seemed so mammoth. So unfriendly. It doesn't look like quite the same ship now that Uncle Atar isn't the emperor ruling it. I know nothing has changed, really, but still. Staring out at it leaves a cold, crawling feeling in my chest.

When we're about fifty meters out, I switch all visuals to the digital viewscreen and pull the blast shields down over the prow so no one can get a peek at who's flying this thing. We imperial nobility like our privacy and all that.

At the sound of our landing gear settling onto the hangar floor with a quiet thud, I'm up and out of my seat, striding off the bridge and heading toward the gear lockers in the aft of the ship. Drinn's back there waiting for me, sitting on a bench with two blasters, a grappling gun, and a handful of suppressor globes—these spheres about the size of my palm that'll zap most humanoids into unconsciousness. I start strapping all of it onto the belt around my jumpsuit.

"You good?" I ask him quietly.

He nods once, his expression steady. "You sure about this?"

I take a deep breath and fish out the glamour key I'd stowed in my pocket, looking at the tiny metallic square in my palm. "I'm sure. You don't have to be, though. We've got a couple extra of these—you could take one and sneak out of here. Blend in with the crowds and all that."

Drinn frowns at the key in my hand and then shrugs. "Coyenne was solid people. She deserved better. You should take Hell Monkey with you, though."

I shake my head, double-checking that I've got everything I need, but I don't get the chance to respond before I hear the sound of footsteps behind me.

Speak of the stardevil. Hell Monkey appears in the doorway, hands in his pockets, his eyebrows still drawn low.

"Stay on the ship," I tell him as I tilt my chin up and bring the glamour key to the base of my throat, pressing it into my skin. "They'll keep the bay doors open all night during a fancy soiree like this, so if there are any signs of trouble, just head for the stars. I'll find my own way off this monster."

Hell Monkey lets out a short, loud laugh. "You don't get to order me around on this one, Farshot." He steps up to me and drops his forehead to touch mine. "Just make it back, okay?"

I run a hand along his scruffy jaw and breathe in the scent of him. "No problem. This'll be a piece of cake."

I step back and double-tap the glamour key to turn it on, feeling the little square of metal warm against my skin as it starts to work. Then I sweep past Hell Monkey, down the corridor to the docking port, and disembark the ship.

SIX

THERE ARE TWO CROWNSGUARDS WAITING OUTSIDE
the *Verity*, and I leave them hanging for exactly five minutes—just
long enough that they're starting to get itchy about going about
their business, but not long enough that they're beginning to get
pissed off. That's the moment when I swan off the ship.

I've read a lot—*a lot*—about glamour keys in preparation for this
moment. (Well, not this moment *exactly*, of course, but you get the
idea.) The thing about them is, at their core, they're the same basic
concept as a hologram or a 3D projection, functioning as a full-out
disguise and controlled by the mental image constructed by the
wearer. Whatever I imagine, that's what I'll look like. And it's such
an advanced energy signature that it can mimic right down to the
sense of touch. So if someone reaches for me, they'll actually feel
the glamoured skin, clothes, hair, whatever. That's how high-end
this tech is. It's not one hundred percent perfect. There's a limit on
how long they last. Usually not much longer than an hour, so you'd
better get your business done before it shuts down. Also it's not
universal—there are several races and species whose visual spectra
aren't fooled by the glamour key's illusionary technology.

But otari aren't one of those species. And neither are any of the prime families.

I sweep off the ship, waving the door closed behind me, and start talking before the crownsguards have fully realized that I'm there, the key stuck to my throat altering the sound of my voice.

". . . will not, absolutely will not be any later to the most important event in decades because my staff cannot get their shit together—"

By the time the two of them manage to react, I'm already past them, striding down the hangar toward the doors on the far end. They fall into my wake, and I think I actually hear one of them stutter as they try to stop me.

"Ma'am—if you could just—"

I make a hard stop and whirl on them. I was very careful about the identity I selected—I homed in on the Coyenne family because it's big and sprawling and almost all of them like to horn in on high-society functions wherever possible. Plus, thanks to years of friendship with Coy, I know more about her extended relations than I do about any of the other families. So I've made myself up as a foarian—tall, gangly, metallic horns, enormous eyes—complete with dramatic layers of brightly colored clothing, jewelry that's heavy on the most currently fashionable foarian designs, and a big gleaming pin of the Coyenne family seal on the collar. Very unsubtle. I've set myself up as a third cousin of Cheery's husband, and while Cheery herself could probably pick this lie apart with a few minutes of scrutiny, most everyone else who's used to imperial life on this ship—including all the guards—won't be too shocked at a distantly related Coyenne crashing the party. I'm betting I'm not the only third cousin Coyenne they've fielded today.

I wield my fake-height now with all the self-importance I can muster. "Excuse me. *Excuse* me. I am not a *ma'am*. I am a *lady* of the prime family of *Coyenne*. Do you understand what that *means*? Do you know what that makes me?"

The otari both square their shoulders, frowning at me. Too well-trained to be bowled over by just stage presence. Bastards. How dare they be so professional.

"My lady, we unfortunately are required to check the identification of every person entering or leaving the hangar. That goes doubly for coronation guests. If you could just . . ." He gestures at me—or, more accurately, at the illusionary wristband my glamour wears—asking for me to transmit my information.

Sure. No problem, buddy. Just let me put on some righteous indignation first. Gotta sell the performance.

I straighten my shoulders a little, and in response, my foarian hologram pulls herself so tall and upright that she's looking down on everything in here, even the ships. I know how to do this song and dance. I've seen it plenty of times. I used to live this life and watch folks just like my current persona move around the kingship and attend fancy soirees and talk all sorts of nonsense, and sure, yeah, I vehemently disliked all of it. But that doesn't mean I didn't take notes.

And I'm hauling all that old homework out now.

"The fact . . . that you have to ask . . ." I keep my voice quiet and low but let that rage-tremble creep into it. "That *no one* on staff here, not *one* person, had the appropriate awareness and foresight to *educate* you about the people you should *know on sight* just shows that the level of *decorum* on this ship has plummeted." I sniff, brushing imaginary dust off my imaginary sleeves. "I can only *hope* that the new emperor makes it a *priority* moving forward to ensure those who give the *most* to this empire are recognized *accordingly*."

I wave a hand over my wristband, transmitting to them the imperial calling card I cooked up on our way over.

MARICA GUSA OF THE PRIME FAMILY COYENNE

There are extra flourishes on it. It's a little more over the top than is fashionable. Basically, it screams, *Hey, I'm high-maintenance. Ask me how.*

The otari crownsguard looks it over, his partner leaning in to see it too, and at the point where they start to squint and bring it in closer to truly analyze it, I pull out my proverbial cannons and make the metaphorical kill shot.

"Cheery will be absolutely *livid* when she hears how I've been treated. I'm going to have to *call her* immediately. Both of you need to give me your names."

Their heads shoot up. The calling card is forgotten. And less than a minute later, they're escorting me onto a multiperson transport and directing me up to the top of the kingship.

Not bad, if I do say so myself.

Damn, I wish Coy could've seen that. She would've loved it.

SEVEN

THE HIGHEST LEVEL OF THE KINGSHIP IS THE IMPE-
rial floor. All of the specialized rooms and areas that the emperor
most often frequents—the throne room, the bridge, the imperial
quarters, the official meeting rooms of the Imperial Council—
they're all kept on one level so as to make day-to-day security issues
a little easier. Gods know that whenever the emperor comes down
to visit other levels or—stars forbid—gets off the planet for a little
while, it's a big deal with a thousand issues to manage. And the
imperial floor has the best damn views on the whole ship save for
the towers, so why would you want to leave, right?

Or better question: Why would you want to come back?

We take the transport all the way up, and I watch out the windows as we go, noting that there have already been some changes
as to who's walking the halls of the kingship. Definitely more Solari
enkindlers than I've seen in the past, which I kind of expected.
More humans, too, wearing the kinds of clothes currently in fashion on Helix. Which also makes sense. And there are some new
droids clanking around that have that distinctive Manufactured
by Voles™ look to them. Intimidating things with giant feet like

43

docking clamps and what looks like multiple automatic weapon attachments integrated into their arms.

I think back to that time I wound up at Voles Enterprises and saw the public suppression droids Edgar had been enthusiastically designing. These look similar. A little meaner, though. More streamlined.

It makes the hackles on the back of my neck stand up.

I'm still flanked by the two otari from the hangar as we step off the transport. They're eager to make sure that Cheery's best third cousin—I embellished a little on the way up—feels well taken care of, and they're especially useful in getting me through the guards at the door to the throne room itself, where the coronation reception is under way. As soon as I'm waved through, I magnanimously thank them for their assistance and then sweep regally inside the serpents' nest.

I'm lucky. The reception is packed with close to two hundred people, all chattering at top volume, probably without even listening to each other. Just as I suspected, too, there's a disparate number of foarians here flashing Coyenne family seals on their lapels and sleeves and necks, so I manage to slip into the crowds without anyone taking much notice of me. I work my way around the edges of the room, vaguely heading toward the refreshments table but really scanning to try to get a clear angle on one person.

Edgar Fucking Voles.

I'm not as tall as a foarian, unfortunately, so I'm mostly trying to scout between everyone's fluttering forms. I see a few of the prime family primors, including Cheery, and quickly duck away. Definitely don't want any of them looking at me too long. There's William Voles, lurking on the far wall and nursing a very large drink. I kinda thought he'd be in the thick of it, vindicated at finally getting his family on the throne, ready to wield all his newfound proximity to power. But then again . . . maybe you don't get any of that if you've been such a grade-A professional asshole for so long that you and your kid hate each other now.

Speaking of his kid . . . I catch sight of Edgar near the dais, just for a second, through the throng. He's surrounded by people, and I can't spot any easy way to get to him right off the bat.

I check my wristband display and the timer currently clocking how long my glamour key has been functioning.

Fifteen minutes, thirty-seven seconds.

Okay. It's okay. There's time yet. I just need to be patient and work my way a little closer.

Patience is easier said than done, though. Edgar's coronation was sixteen hours ago—that's sixteen hours since he absorbed the royal seal and began connecting with the kingship. The way I understand it, it'll take a few more days before he's able to do next-level stuff like track onboard life forms, mentally tap into security features, or telepathically command the crownsguard, but I'm not interested in cutting it any closer than this. It's got to happen now.

The glamour key on my throat zaps me with a little shock—a signal to me that someone has bumped into my illusionary form—and I look up into the smug, beaming face of Enkindler Wythe. He waves a hand apologetically, his eyes fixed on the spot where my hologram's head is.

"My sincerest apologies, my lady," he says. "I didn't see you there."

It's a real battle not to shudder. Wythe's voice just goes right through me every time I hear it. I take half a step back—no sense in pushing my luck, even with a fancy glamour key—and bow my head just a little. Not enough to signal submission—a Coyenne family member would never—but enough to demonstrate respect to Wythe's position. It makes my jaw ache, but I do it.

"The apology is certainly *mine* to make, Steward Wythe." I wave vaguely about the room. "I must've been *distracted* because I was so *parched* from enjoying the lovely reception. I was on my way to get a *refreshment*. If you'll excuse me . . ."

I start to turn away, expecting him to do the usual perfunctory response that releases me from the conversation, but Wythe nods and says, "Yes, yes, I've had many people tell me it's even better than Atar Faroshti's was. Not that you should compare these things, but, well . . . you know . . ." He smiles at me, like we're sharing an inside joke.

I want to punch that joke right off his face. But I smile and nod instead. Hopefully my hologram's face is less pained than it feels like mine is.

Wythe's eyes are drawn to something that might be vaguely in my neck area—this is a definite downside to this tech, not being really sure what he's looking at. He gestures toward it and says, "I do wish your family all of my condolences at the loss of your heir. Entirely unfortunate. I'm curious how everyone in your circles is handling this horrific loss."

It's like someone dumped cold water into my chest cavity. At least now I know what he was looking at: the big garish pin on my fake clothes. But I'm having a hard time coming up with an in-character response because his face doesn't match his words at all. He doesn't look remorseful. If anything, I'd say he looks pumped, like he just can't wait to hear my answer. Like the idea of the whole Coyenne family mourning Nathalia is the best entertainment he could've hoped for this week.

I take a deep breath and look down, stalling for time and trying to play up that sadness angle. I've got five more seconds, max, before the silence gets suspicious.

"Your thoughts are *so* appreciated, Steward Wythe." Marica's voice comes out just dripping with over-the-top sincerity, and I breathe a little sigh of relief that the tone is just right. "It is *such* a tragedy. We are simply *devastated*, of course. You know the Coyenne family—we are sure to *recover*—but it is nice to know that we have *friends* in *high places* thinking about us."

I smile at him, bowing again, and from what I can read by his expression, I seem to have hit the right notes. Wythe's smugness triples, and he folds his long hands together in that way he always did when he felt he'd won something over on me. So I feel like I've nailed it well enough to get the hell out of this conversation.

"My apologies, Steward, to have to step away when I'm *so* enjoying our conversation, but like I said, I am absolutely *dying* of thirst and I believe I saw *Socrates champagne* over there that I simply *must* get a glass of. There is no other *respectable* drink at functions like *these*, in my opinion."

He tilts his head in some half-ass acknowledgment that I'd be pretty offended by if I were actually Marica Gursa of Coyenne, but whatever because I'm at least able to slip by him and put some distance between us. That ridiculous exchange probably ate up close to five minutes of my remaining time, and I need to start making a serious move if I'm going to do this. I smooth my hands over my clothes so I can check for my blasters without it looking like Marica is checking for blasters. Both present and accounted for. All I need is an opportunity to use them.

I swing around a big loud cluster of people as I draw near the refreshments table and almost slam right into someone as I come up on the other side.

A tall, freckled someone with thinning hair.

My uncle. Charles Viqtorial.

EIGHT

UNCLE CHARLIE STANDS UP AGAINST THE WALL, right by the refreshment table, both hands wrapped around the flute glass in front of him. His eyes are fixed on the crowds, but it doesn't really look like he's seeing them. He definitely doesn't see me, although I'm just about on top of him.

Just slip by, Alyssa. Keep walking. You've got business to take care of.

But . . . it's Charlie.

Standing.

By himself.

At an official imperial function.

The same guy who knows the names of every diplomat and representative and planet leader in the entire quadrant off the top of his head. The same guy who could strike up a conversation with a toaster and sound completely engaged in it. That same guy—and he's standing silently over here without saying a word. He's dressed the part, in extremely nice and tailored clothes decorated with his sash and old medals collected over years of service as chief envoy.

But his face is gaunt. His eyes are so ringed with dark circles that it kinda looks like it might be makeup. The bones on his face are more pronounced, and there's no spark to his eyes.

I can't . . . quite bring myself to walk away from him. Not without saying . . . I dunno. Something.

I make a big show of scooting by right in front of his face as I reach for a flute glass on the table next to him. "So sorry, I've just been *desperate* trying to get over here."

Charlie blinks and looks around like a droid powering up. "Yes, of course. Apologies for being in your way."

"No, it's *no* trouble at all really, Envoy Viqtorial. To be honest, it is just *such* a pleasure to meet you."

It takes Charlie a second to react, but he finally puts on a pained smile. "The pleasure is mine," he says, although it sounds like there's zero pleasure in it. His attention drifts away again, back to the crowds, and I scramble for something to say.

"We are *so* sorry about your recent loss. I mean, of course, *all* of us in the empire *lost* something when Atar passed, but I recognize *just* how hard it must be for *you* as well."

Charlie's face twists a little, but he manages the tiniest nod and says, "Thank you. I appreciate it."

I slide into place next to him, also looking out over the people as we stand shoulder to shoulder. "I must confess myself a bit *surprised* to see anyone representing the *Faroshti* here, especially with all that *horrid* business recently."

"Yes, well . . ." Charlie shrugs. "There aren't many Faroshti family members left in the empire, and those who are living are too far removed to want to travel all this way. It seemed . . . appropriate to function as their representative."

I clear my throat, nodding. "Of course, of course. I mean no offense."

I try to get a read on what he's feeling underneath those words, but Charlie being Charlie, his Official Diplomatic Functions mask is on pretty tight. Even for me. Even in a situation like this.

I fidget and flick a glance at his profile as he surveys the extravagant trappings of Edgar Voles's coronation, and that heat and anger I'm carrying around right now flare up hot and sharp. Suddenly I have so many questions I want to ask him. Like . . .

Why are you even here, Charlie?

Why is *anyone* from my family here at this sham?

How could you show them any support?

How could you do this to Uncle Atar?

How could you do this to me?

But there's no way I can ask him any of that. Not without giving myself away. And not even Charlie can know what's going on here.

So I nod at him—a gesture he doesn't even notice—and keep moving, working my way closer and closer to the dais. I've got a second glamour key primed and ready in my pocket if I need it, but I'm hoping I won't need to use it—

—which is why I'm so ecstatic when I see Edgar step away from the tight knot of his newest fans and move through the reception toward a corner exit that leads to the observation deck. He actually walks within centimeters of me, flanked on either side by an otari crownsguard, and I wait five pulse-pounding heartbeats after that before I slip into their wake and follow them.

The observation deck is a long, curving corridor that connects the throne room with the Gold Room, where the Imperial Council holds the majority of their meetings. It continues the throne room's theme of "we like a lot of windows and never get tired of the ocean," with bonus alcoves where you can step out onto clear glass and feel like you're floating right in the middle of sea and sky. Even better, I can think of four or five ways at least to make a break for it from here and try to disappear into the inner workings of the kingship. Y'know, in the aftermath of the chaos I'm about to wreak. It's not what you would really call a foolproof exit strategy, but if there's one thing I'm good at, it's improvisation.

I see the backs of Edgar and his guards disappearing around the gentle curve of the corridor, and I try to maintain a real casual, just-seeing-the-sights pace as I pursue them. Most everyone else is still in the reception and not quite exhausted with hearing themselves talk yet. It seems the new emperor, though, needs a break, and I lurk a little at the curve, watching as the guards come to a halt and Edgar steps cautiously into one of those alcoves, staring down at the optical illusion of nothing but hundreds of feet of open air between him and thundering waves.

I take a half step back and close my eyes, breathing calmly as my hands go to my belt.

Last chance to back out. Last chance to change my mind. *What do you say, Farshot—are we doing this?*

I picture Coy, standing in front of me. I see her so clearly—her green eyes, her smile brighter than the light glinting off her horns and sharper than her tongue. It's so achingly vivid that for a second I swear she's actually going to be there when I open my eyes again.

But she's not. There's just an empty spot where I wish she was.

I storm around the corner and throw two suppressor globes from my belt—hitting one guard and then the other. They go down as a web of electricity wraps around them and zaps them unconscious. Edgar turns, startled, and I step over the downed guards and aim my blaster right at his nose.

Do it, Farshot. Come on. Do it—now. This is the best chance you're gonna get.

I've imagined this moment a million times in the past few days. The muscles in my hand are so tight they're trembling. All I have to do is squeeze the trigger just a little more, and it'll be done.

And I'll be a murderer.

My mind flashes to Charlie. Standing in the throne room only a few dozen meters away. I imagine what he will think of me when he finds out about this. About what I've done. How he'll probably never be able to look at me in quite the same way ever again.

Godsdammit.

I drop the angle of my blaster and shoot, hitting Edgar in the knee. He cries out as he falls to the glass floor inside the alcove, and I stand over him, my whole body shaking. Blood roars in my ears. I can't even hear my own damn thoughts.

What the hell am I *doing*?

"Who are you?" Edgar's face is scrunched with pain, and he winces as he props himself up on his hands, his injured leg stretched out in front of him. "You're not a Coyenne."

I laugh, dark and angry. It tastes like blood. "You don't think a Coyenne would have a reason to want to kill you?"

"I think a true Coyenne would've done it already." He frowns and shakes his head, looking for all the universe like a disappointed parent instead of the worst asshole alive. "What could you possibly want from me? I don't have the seal to give you."

I edge a little closer. The blaster sits warm in my palms, hot as the anger underneath my skin. "I don't want the seal. I want you to *pay* for what you did to Coy. I want you to give back that throne that you *stole*."

"I didn't steal anything. By all the written rules of the crown-chase as they stand, I won." He lifts his chin with that insufferable, distinctly arrogant expression that I've seen so often on his dad's face. All condescension and *this sounds like a you problem.* "I'm sorry if that's difficult for you to accept, Alyssa."

I freeze at the sound of my name. The glamour key itches at the base of my throat, and it hasn't been an hour—I know it hasn't been an hour—but Edgar Voles lies there looking straight at me. Not at my glamour—at *me.*

But he's human. Humans can't see through glamour keys. He should still only be able to see the foarian form of Marica Gusa, unless . . .

Unless he's fully integrated with the kingship. Way ahead of schedule.

Shit.

Shit shit shit.

That roaring in my brain gets even louder. I have to get out of here. Not now, like five minutes ago. I whirl around—

—but it's too late. A soft whine fills the air as a dozen blaster rifles held by a dozen crownsguards heat up, and behind them, another dozen of those brand-new security droids clank into place. The whole corridor is suddenly filled with blasters running hot and pointed right at my head. I didn't even hear any of them coming.

One of the droids helps Edgar to his feet, and he reaches a hand toward me and plucks the glamour key off my skin. The illusion around me falls away, and I hear a murmur go through some of the crownsguards. But I don't look at them. I keep my glare fixed right on Edgar and tilt my chin up. Unapologetic. Unafraid.

(Well, maybe a little afraid.)

Edgar looks down at the glamour key in his palm, then back up at me, and for a second, it looks like he's going to say something. His mouth opens, I hear the start of my name on his breath—

—and then the voice of Enkindler Wythe calls out over the rows of heavily armored bodies, "Defend your Imperial Majesty! Secure that traitor by any means necessary!"

One of the security droids stomps forward, and I only have half a second to register the electrified baton attachment on its arm and think, *Well, crap, not again*, before it jams it into my stomach and everything goes white.

ASSASSINATION ATTEMPT ON NEW EMPEROR FOILED

Kingship confirms that an as-yet-unnamed assailant attacked Emperor Voles but was quickly apprehended

WYTHE TO RETAIN HIGH-LEVEL POSITION IN KINGSHIP, REJECTING CALLS FROM IMPERIAL COUNCIL TO RETURN TO AMBASSADORIAL ROLE

The Solari enkindler points to recent chaos and unrest as reason for maintaining his post

IS THE FAROSHTI PRIME FAMILY FINISHED?

With Atar Faroshti passed and no confirmed reports on the whereabouts of Alyssa Faroshti, Atar's husband remains the only representative of a once-powerful family

RUMORS CIRCULATE THAT THE SOLARI RELIGION MIGHT BE GIVEN PREFERRED STATUS IN THE EMPIRE

Official preference toward the Solari would break with centuries of tradition and likely be a major boost in their efforts to expand across the empire

THE KINGSHIP, APEX, THE KYRA SYSTEM

EDGAR SITS ON A BENCH AGAINST THE WALL, STARing out at the wide expanses of sea and sky and waiting for the medbot to finish fixing the blaster wound in his leg. He's never actually been shot before. It was an excruciating experience—bright and searing.

And yet all he finds himself thinking about right now is Alyssa Farshot. Her defiant face after he took her glamour key. The look in her eyes after she shot him.

All the anger in it.

All the conviction in it.

She had wanted to shoot him right through the heart, to turn him into nothing more than a bloody smear on the glass floor. She hadn't done it, but she had *wanted* to. He had seen that want all over her face.

It rattled him. Far more than he thought it could. After all the years spent under the disdain of his father, he would've thought he'd be better inoculated than this against someone else's dislike. But this is beyond anything he'd ever felt before. She *hates* him.

He looks down at his hands and sees them covered in Nathalia Coyenne's dark green blood all over again. He wipes them roughly against the heavily embellished fabric he's draped in for the coronation reception, and he knows the blood is not there, but he swears he can see it and feel it between his fingers anyway.

There's a tickle at the back of his mind, this little sensation that he's starting to recognize as his new connection to the kingship. It had allowed him to see through Alyssa's disguise. To reach out to his security forces for help without tipping her off. It isn't supposed to be strong enough to do any of that yet, but it was, and that thought steadies him. Enkindler Wythe tells him it will get even stronger as it continues to grow and integrate inside him. The thought of it folding itself into his biological systems isn't as concerning as he would've thought. He's spent too long designing and building and studying artificial intelligence systems to fear them, and after all, it never seemed to do any of the previous emperors harm.

Edgar straightens as a familiar figure ticks down the corridor toward him. He relaxes a little to see NL7, even though it's still in its modified mediabot casing instead of its proper form. It draws close, its face swiveling from the medbot to Edgar's face and back again.

"You are hurt, Edgar Voles."

He nods, his face softening a little. It's not that NL7 sounds concerned—it doesn't really have or express emotions like that—but the form and manner of its inquiry tells him a lot. "It's minor. Easily fixed."

NL7 shifts a little closer to him. "If we had been there, there is a high likelihood we could have prevented this."

Edgar raises his eyebrows, a little taken aback. It's such a strange thing for the android to say. It doesn't fit within any of its normal protocols, per se, and Edgar finds he's quite touched. But before he can respond, that tickling sensation comes back—and a sudden flood of noise makes him clutch at his ears, like every voice in the kingship is in his head, all talking at once—

—and then it's gone, and Enkindler Wythe is striding up to him, smiling big, his long hands clasped in front of him. ". . . could not have planned it better myself, Imperial Majesty. Really, this worked out in every fashion."

Edgar blinks up at him and waves a hand at his injured leg as the medbot finishes up. "In every fashion, Enkindler? Surely you're not serious."

Wythe's eyes slide over NL7, where it waits at Edgar's elbow, and then the enkindler turns to him. "My sincerest apologies, Imperial Majesty. Of course the fact that you got injured is unconscionable and your attacker will be held accountable for her violence to the severest degree."

The medbot chirps out a noise and floats away, and NL7 puts a spindly metal hand under Edgar's elbow as he pushes onto his feet, testing his weight. He looks out again, at the wall of blue seas, blue skies, but he can see only Alyssa's face. "I ought to see her. Talk to her. Where is she now?"

NL7 is the one who answers. "The sublevel brig, under watch of a rotating guard."

Wythe slinks close to him. "You are, of course, welcome to go speak with her if you choose. I just can't stop thinking about how bold, how entitled she must be to try to unseat you at your moment of triumph. These other prime families really do believe they are owed everything without even having to work for it."

Edgar's gaze breaks and drops a little at the enkindler's words. "It's true. . . . I can't imagine what she was thinking. . . ."

"Hubris," Wythe scoffs. "Unadulterated hubris. She must take us all for fools—you most of all."

Something about that word—*fool*—sours in Edgar's chest. It curls, acidic, at the back of his throat, pulling at dozens of memories of interacting with Alyssa over the years, always with her holding him at a distance, always with her looking at him like he was lesser, something to be pitied. Poor, pathetic Edgar.

"Edgar Voles," NL7 says. "Will you go down to the brig?"

Edgar lets go of the droid and takes Enkindler Wythe's proffered arm. "No. Leave her down there. It's time to set the tone for my reign."

Personal log of Atar Faroshti, recorded on 0.08.06.4001.

TODAY MARKS THIRTEEN YEARS OF WAR.

I never, in all my youth, in all my travels, thought I would see one day of war, let alone thousands.

Thousands of days. Millions of casualties. What has this empire become?

The brutality and mercilessness only seem to increase as the war drags on. Aldius Roy and his allies, especially those of the Mega family, have reduced the Faroshti to ashes, and the Voles family leadership still refuses to take meaningful action to come to our aid. We had hoped our long-standing relationship as the oldest two prime families would mean something, but they have stood back and played in rhetoric. Even the Coyennes, who are notoriously neutral, and the rising Orso family have done more to support us of late, albeit indirectly.

I would say it is a miracle we have not been overwhelmed already, but in truth, it's diplomacy. Saya is tireless, going out again and again to the people of the empire, making her case for why we continue to fight, telling them about her vision for an empire that listens and lifts up all their voices. And Charles and I take the same message planet to planet, city to city. It has helped us stave off defeat so far, and Saya maintains her conviction that it will be the foundation of our victory.

There is more good news, too. Radha and Jaya have finally gathered enough numbers within the Roy family to break ranks and openly declare their support for the Faroshti claim. They hope to strengthen their position even further to overtake Aldius in family leadership. If anyone can do it, it is Radha and Jaya.

And perhaps then we can finally have peace.

NINE

STARDATE: 0.06.05 in the Year 4031, under the reign of the Empress Who Never Was, Nathalia Matilda Coyenne, long may she rest in glory
LOCATION: You ready for this? Locked up. Again.

I'VE DEFINITELY BEEN IN WORSE PLACES THAN THE brig of the imperial kingship. Not that it's super comfortable in here, but there's a wide, padded bench to stretch out on, and there's enough space to walk around a little. Three of the walls are solid alloy, smooth and metallic, but the fourth one facing the corridor is a force field. It's kept transparent, so I don't feel like I'm trapped inside a terrible cube. Not the worst situation I could be in while I figure out my next move.

The doors down at the end of the corridor slide open and there's the sound of a bunch of crownsguard boots clunking and droid feet clanking. I'm too far down to see anything very well. But I hear it. That voice I know so well.

"Watch it with the face. I've got a major following on the feeds—you do not want to piss off my fans."

Hell Monkey.

My heart does this weird thing where it both leaps upward into my sternum and sinks down into my stomach, so I think it actually just ripped itself into two pieces. I'm glad that he's here. I hate that he's here. I'm grateful that he didn't leave me behind and also seriously pissed that he didn't do what I told him to and leave me behind. I actually have to bend in half and take several deep breaths because I'm having too many feelings all at once. Story of my life lately. Too many godsdamned feelings.

There are only four containment units in the sublevel section, but they have enough smarts not to put Hell Monkey right across from me where we could see each other. They put him next to me instead, that thick wall of alloy in between us, and Drinn gets dumped right across from him. I can kind of get an angle on his big vilkjing form from the far corner of my cell, and when he spots me frantically moving around, he just raises his giant bound hands and nods. Then he retreats farther in, out of my line of sight.

I go to the front corner of the cell, where it butts up to Hell Monkey's, and knock a rhythm on the wall with my fist. Our secret knock. Because we're high-tech like that.

There's a long pause, and then . . . he knocks back. I let out a slow breath.

"Hell Monkey?" I call. I try to keep my voice low, but the force fields also give off a kind of low, deep hum so you can't exactly whisper either.

"Hell Monkey's not here right now—he's busy on the other side of the cell. Can you call back later?"

He's trying to keep his voice light, teasing, but I can hear an edge underneath it. I let my forehead drop against the wall. "What happened? You were supposed to get clear. You and Drinn."

A dark laugh ricochets off the walls. "Yeah. That definitely sounds like me, Farshot. Cut and run—that's my motto."

"I just . . ." I turn my head toward the force field, edging as close as I dare. "I didn't want you caught up in this. It was my business to settle."

There's the sound of shifting and then Hell Monkey's voice comes again, a little closer, like he's matched my position near the corner. "There was never a moment I *wasn't* a part of this, Alyssa. I don't know why you think you've got to separate the two things. You think I signed on for just Explorer Alyssa?"

"It's only that . . . I know how you feel about the empire, Eliot." I pause, and his name—his real name—hangs in the air between us. I don't use it very often, but it feels important to use it now. So he knows that I really see him. Not just who he is now, but where he came from. "All this back-and-forth with a bunch of rich-ass prime families. I didn't want to drag you deeper in."

"There's nothing but deep water around here now." His voice is as quiet as it can get and still be heard, but somehow it rumbles through me all the same. "We're not going to make it clear of all this if you can't trust me to swim on my own. I'll fall back if I need to."

I press my hand against the wall, right at the spot where he seems to be standing. I know he's right, but I still don't like it. Not because I don't think he can take care of himself—the guy definitely knows how to handle his shit. It's more that I don't want him to . . . see all this. It was one thing to drag him along on a crownchase where there was supposed to be a clear winner, a clear ending, and it was mostly a lot of dangerous high jinks. But this is something brand-new. An ass-deep mire of imperial politics. Centuries of muck and anger and grudges left behind by the same families that let his parents and siblings burn and covered up the evidence afterward.

I know he cares about me. I know he's loyal to a fault. But everyone has their limit, right? At what point does even someone like Hell Monkey figure out that I'm not worth this level of trouble?

At what point does he stop seeing Alyssa Farshot and just see another prime family heir screwing up his life?

I thought I could dip one boot back into this mess and jump right back out again. Stars and gods, what an idiot.

"So what's the plan?" he asks at last. "How do we break out of this nicely carpeted hellhole?"

I grunt. "Ah, yeah. That. I'm definitely working on a plan. An epic plan. It's going to be one of our best yet."

"You have no idea, do you?"

"None. I'm currently entertaining any and all flashes of brilliance. Maybe Drinn has some deep thoughts on this?"

Hell Monkey snorts. "Drinn's asleep."

"Are you serious?!"

"I mean, I'm looking at him right now and he's curled up in a corner over there with his eyes closed."

I sigh and slide down the wall onto my butt. "Well, with this kind of crack team, we'll be off this ship in no time."

The door at the end of the corridor cranks open, and I hear movement again—low voices, scuffling boots—that makes me scramble back onto my feet. "H.M.?"

"Someone's coming," he mutters. "Can't see who. I don't think the guards wanted to let them through, but they look like they're headed for you, Farshot."

Footsteps start coming down the hall, and I back up, up, up until I'm standing in the center of the room. Don't want to be too close to the entrance to this cell, but I don't want to find myself pinned up against a wall either. I bounce on my toes, ready for them—whoever they are. I'm honestly not much as a hand-to-hand fighter, but I'm great at throwing myself teeth-first into danger, so here we go, baby, light it up.

A pair of otari crownsguards step out on the other side of the force field, flanking a hooded figure who looks to be wearing some pretty fancy gear underneath. I spot a sash. The glitter of medals pinned in neat, particular rows. And my breath catches in my chest.

Charles Viqtorial pulls the hood down off his thinning red hair and gives me a sad smile. "Hello, Alyssa."

TEN

I RUSH FORWARD, STOPPING JUST SHY OF THE force field. "Uncle Charlie! What are you doing here?"

His eyebrows shoot upward, wrinkling the white freckled skin of his forehead. "That seems like a strange question. It would be odder, I think, for me not to visit my only niece when she's arrested for treason, don't you think?"

I step back a little, eying him. The tone of his voice is more on the amused side than sounding disappointed or angry or anything, but it's hard to get a read on Charlie's face beyond that. He's still got his diplomat mask welded on at this point.

I flick a look at the two crownsguards. One of them is completely unfamiliar to me, but the other one, the taller one with skin and scars the color of slate, I recognize as Ko, one of the crownsguard most often assigned to keep an eye on me when I was a kid. Once, when I'd teased her about being stuck with me, she'd scooped me up onto her massive shoulders and said, "I actually volunteer for this post, little empress."

She refuses to look at me now, though, staring off at some middle distance, straight-backed and stoic, like I'm not even here.

I square off to Charlie, clenching my teeth. "It wasn't treason. Edgar is the traitor. He doesn't belong on that throne."

Charlie sighs. "I understand that you believe that, Alyssa, but just because you declare it, doesn't make it so."

That sounds almost exactly like what Cheery Coyenne told me, and hearing those words come out of Charlie's mouth—my uncle Charlie—sends a sick feeling crawling over my skin. I step back a little more and cross my arms over my chest.

"Let me guess," I say. "'There's no evidence he was on the ship. Everything he did was within the rules. The only person suspect here is me.' Did I get the words right? Or did I miss a verse?"

Charlie shakes his head sadly, holding out his hands. "It's over, Alyssa. You have to stand down."

I laugh right in his face because he of all people should know better. "I don't 'have to' do anything, and I won't either, Charlie."

"You're only making this worse. On yourself. On the family. Everyone has conceded."

"I don't concede. The Faroshtis don't concede."

He tilts his chin up, lifting his nose in the air. Like he's proud. He's proud of all of this. "You didn't have to. I accepted on the family's behalf."

I stalk back up to the force field, fists clenched at my sides. "You had no right."

He shrugs. "You never really wanted the name of Faroshti anyway."

That is too far. I can't even form a response that isn't just a scream, so I swing at him. My hand connects with the containment field and sends volts of electricity buzzing through my arm. I jump back, shaking out my hand as little angry waves zigzag over my skin.

There. That'll show him.

"I'm not trying to upset you, Alyssa. I know this probably isn't what you want to hear. Or what you expected to hear. I suppose we all disappoint our family at some point or another."

He leans on the word *disappoint*, and I hesitate. Something about the way he says it makes me remember the last conversation we had, when I was on Station Shisso, hiding, ready to walk away from Coy and the crownchase. I'd been certain that Uncle Atar would have been disappointed in me, that I had let him down. I'd said as much to Charlie, and he'd said . . .

If he were with me right now, seeing what I'm seeing, he would be proud of you. You've never failed either of us.

Annnnnnd now I feel like a moron.

Because honestly? The very first thing I should've considered here is: Am I falling for the old misdirection trick by Charlie? Here I am, getting my hackles all up, feeling betrayed, and man, it didn't even cross my mind? *Come on, Farshot.* It's not like I haven't seen this trick before. It's not like I haven't *done* this trick before. You're an ally, but you pretend to be a person's enemy so that you can get closer or position things how you need them to be in order to make your big move.

And seriously, what makes more sense here? That buttoned-up, always-on-protocol Charles Viqtorial married my uncle Atar thirty-one years ago, was loving and loyal all that time, even through war and death and illness, and spent a decade and a half raising a hellion child like me with the patience of a saint—all of it to turn on his heel now and decide he's throwing in against me?

Or that he's putting on an act.

I look over at Ko again, and her eyes flick down to meet mine for a fraction of a second before she looks away again.

For an otari, that's basically a wink.

Damn. All right—if they're aiming for trouble, I'm in. But the question is, what's their plan here? Because there's a whole other otari next to Charlie, plus the two by the door. Charlie's not much of a fighter, which means it's one crownsguard against three. Not the best odds. I glare at all three of them and make a show of pacing the doorway. Acting like just your everyday enraged prisoner, but really I'm scanning all around the corridor, trying to catch any kind of clue about what game Charlie is playing.

I catch his eye as I put venom into my voice and say, "Disappointment isn't exactly the term I'd use here. Let's try rage. Or maybe bitter vengeance. I think that's going to be more along the lines of what we're talking about."

Charlie lifts a shoulder, all casual. "I certainly hope all of that is good company for you while you are stuck in the brig."

I edge right up to the force field until I can feel its energy pattern vibrating against my face, and I bare my teeth. "I'm not gonna be stuck in here forever. You should consider this a head start to get halfway across the quadrant before I bust out."

Charlie's wristband beeps a notification, and he sighs and shakes his sleeve back so he can see the screen. I watch him closely, but his face stays exactly the same. Practically expressionless. Like he's negotiating a trade deal instead of discussing treason and death with his niece.

"Well, then." He pulls his sleeve back down and folds his hands inside his robes. "I think that's all there is to say about this matter."

Then he pulls out a stun blaster, turns to the unfamiliar crownsguard next to him, and shoots them straight in the chest.

ELEVEN

KO SPRINGS INTO ACTION BEFORE CHARLIE EVEN pulls the trigger, charging down the hall and bowling into the crownsguards on duty. I can't see what happens next—I can only hear what sounds like several brutal, bone-crunching thuds, and then Ko is back, almost before the stunned guard hits the floor.

I stare at them—Ko with her shoulders squared, barely winded, and Charlie with his robes thrown back and the stun gun in his hand like he's some renegade in an adventure vid or something.

I hear Hell Monkey laugh a little from the cell next to me. "This is the kind of plot twist I can get behind."

I raise an eyebrow at Charlie as Ko gets to work on the security panel beside my cell door. "Going full action hero now, are we?"

He clears his throat and drops the stun blaster back inside his robes. "It's not usually how I like to solve a problem, but there are a time and place for everything, as they say."

Ko steps back from the security panel as the force field in front of me disappears. I don't even hesitate. I jump into the hall and throw my arms around my uncle hard enough that he grunts and stumbles back half a step. I know this probably isn't the best time to have a teary reunion or anything, but I don't have much in the way of family left and godsdammit I just want a little emotional support right now. Charlie himself has never been much of a hugger, but after a beat, he puts his arms tight around me, which is how I know that (a) he super missed me; and (b) things aren't looking great for us at all.

It's that last part that makes me step out of the hug well before I want to. I squat down by the stunned guard and relieve him of the blaster at his hip and the long blaster rifle strapped to his back. I toss the rifle to Hell Monkey just as Ko brings down his force field, and he catches it without even flinching. Fucking teamwork. I love it.

"What's our next move, Chaz?" Hell Monkey asks as he checks the charge and the safety on his brand-new weapon.

"We need to get you all back to your ship. Preferably with as little fuss as possible so they can't lock down the hangar bay."

"We have a window," Ko adds as she moves on to the security panel outside Drinn's cell. "Our people inside security can run interference, but our time is limited."

"How limited?" asks Hell Monkey.

She grunts, but doesn't look away from the panel. "Minutes, not hours."

I shake my head, my stomach sinking. "It's no good. Charlie, I seriously love this whole revolution energy, but there's no way we're going to make it very far. Edgar is already integrated with the kingship. He's going to know."

Charlie takes me by the elbow and swings me around so he can look me right in the eye. "You're sure about this, Alyssa?"

"Pretty damn sure. He saw through my glamour key up on the observation deck, and he definitely shouldn't be able to do that."

Charlie hums to himself, thinking. "Definitely much farther along than we'd hoped, but maybe . . ." He looks over his shoulder at Ko. "We need to alert the—"

"I'm on it," says Ko as the last force field drops and she steps away. "I think your vilkjing is dead, little empress."

Hell Monkey's eyes shoot straight over to me when he hears that nickname, a smile creeping across his face. His mouth is open, ready to snark, but I cut him off, pointing a finger at him as I stomp by.

"Not a single word out of you, buddy." I sweep into Drinn's cell and see him curled up on the bench in the corner, one massive arm thrown over his face. I nudge his foot with my boot. "Rise and shine, gearhead."

He slides his arm down to his chest and peers out at me with his sharp yellow eyes. "Prison break?"

I snort. "Yeah, it's prison break time. Think you can stay awake for it?"

He shrugs. "Your friends took too long." Then he rises and ambles past me into the hall, looking as excited about this whole situation as if I'd told him we were going to the button market on Ilra IV.

Ko is addressing Charlie again as I step back out. "Rex is in position. Five minutes and counting. We need to get moving or we're never gonna get them back on their ship."

"No way our ship is still flight-ready," I say. "They probably locked down the AI system as soon as they took H.M. and Drinn into custody."

"They probably *tried*," Hell Monkey says with a little smile. "But I locked it down first when I saw them coming. And not to brag, but I did a really good job at it."

Drinn grumbles. "Still gotta make it down there. How many decks between the brig and there?"

"Ten," Charlie says. "But we've got a plan to get you all onto a personnel transport that will take us down to the hangar level. After that, we'll just need to be very, very quick."

I raise an eyebrow at him. "And Edgar?"

"We're working on it." He squeezes my hand. "You didn't exactly give us a lot of notice for planning a jailbreak."

Another of those little beep notifications. Ko and Charlie both glance at their wristbands, and then Charlie looks up. "Ko, get them ready. Three minutes."

Ko nods and retrieves a standard-issue crownsguard pack from back near the door. They usually use them to hold official gear, charge packs for weapons, cuffs, med kits—that kind of thing. But Ko pulls out three long, blindingly yellow hooded robes . . . and three old, beat-up hoverdiscs.

My face goes slack. "Enkindlers? You want to disguise us as enkindlers? No one is going to buy that."

Drinn's already tugging his robe on—it's a tight fit across his shoulders, but not completely impossible. Most enkindlers are taller than even him, though, so the hem drags at his feet. On Hell

Monkey, it's practically a pool of citrus color on the floor around him. I hold mine up at a safe distance, wrinkling my nose. Everything about this fabric—the look of it, the feel of it, the smell of it—makes my skin crawl.

"Do I gotta?"

"Yes." Ko towers over me, her face stern. "Time is wasting. Get a move on, little empress."

I scowl as I bunch up the robe and pull it on over my head. "We gotta have a talk about the nickname."

TWELVE

HAND TO THE STARS, I DON'T REALLY THINK WE'LL
get that far in these disguises.

I mean, the robes are one thing, but Solari as a people are
extremely tall, too, and we had to make up that height differ-
ence with these extremely questionable hoverdiscs. Like, there
are professional-grade versions of these that are pretty sweet and
really useful as a mobility assist, but that's not what we have. Ko
apparently dug up the toy hoverdiscs I used to play on with the
other prime family heirs when we were all kids. Mine still has the
remnants of the old decals I stuck all over it.

So here we are, three escaped prisoners draped in one of the
brightest colors imaginable, hoods over our faces, hands tucked
into our sleeves, floating around on mediocre tech and trying to
look like we're gliding about in a glow of righteousness or something like that. It's a little touchy to start because Drinn's hoverdisc
sputters, shorts out, almost drops him on his ass, but he manages
to recover, even if it's not the most elegant move ever seen. When
we finally get ourselves more or less together, Charlie leads the
way in front of us, and Ko follows behind. I'm sweating before we

even step out into the corridor. I mean, you try keeping your balance and steering a hoverdisc—something I haven't ridden in *years*, for the record—all while being slowly suffocated by aggressively cheerful fabric. It's terrible.

Two seconds after the doors to the brig slide closed behind us, yellow warning lights snap on all along the corridor, and my heart slams into my throat. I start to flinch, to go for the blaster at my belt, but Charlie puts a steadying hand on my arm as a cool, automated voice echoes throughout the kingship.

"This is a safety alert. Fire has been reported in the northwest quadrant of the ship. Security personnel, please report. Evacuating sections fifteen, nineteen, twenty-three—"

Charlie tugs me forward. "Come, *enkindler*. We have someplace to be."

"Is this what Rex was in position for?" I mutter to him as we move down the hall. "Do you really think it's gonna be enough to distract Edgar?"

He falls silent as a knot of crownsguards jog by and then checks that they're well past us before answering. "I oversaw Atar's transition. Integration with the kingship can be spotty and overwhelming in the early days. Even if Edgar is advancing faster than usual, a security distraction in a separate part of the ship should give us cover for a few minutes at least." He takes a deep breath as we step into a more heavily trafficked area of the ship. "Hopefully it'll be enough."

We take a winding (read: slow because none of us can hoverdisc very fast) course toward the transport platform, keeping some distance between us and most concentrations of people. Flying casual. I can hear Ko's heavy step just behind me, and the sound of her so close by, watching over me, makes me feel like I'm seven years old again.

When the kingship felt big and magical and friendly. When it felt like a home.

We actually make it to the transports—color me shocked—and there's only one person there when we step on. Kalia Sharn—human, very dark brown skin, wearing a beautiful green high-collared suit. She worked on the throne room level as one of Atar's closest advisers. Or, I guess, one of his closest friends, really. She came to visit us often in our personal family quarters for dinner and sometimes even for holidays.

When she sees Charlie, she meets his eyes and nods. Then she gets up and swipes a passcode into the transport keypad. It pings in acknowledgment and turns red, and the transport whooshes off.

"Counselor Sharn," Charlie says, like they're at a cocktail party instead of committing high treason.

"Envoy." Her lips press together with the barest hint of a smile. "I hope you don't mind me using a priority passcode—I have urgent business down on the lower decks that I can't be late for."

"Completely understandable. We're happy to go along for the ride."

Only those at a high enough clearance level are given priority passcodes to use, a way to get wherever they need to go without being held up by additional stops or the in-and-out of other passengers. Kalia puts out a hand out to steady me as I wobble. Sweat drips down my nose, and I'm pretty sure not even the hallüdraen blue shading the contours of my skin can cover how flushed I am right now.

"Hey, Kalia."

She bites off another smile, but keeps her eyes focused on the kingship whizzing by the transport windows in a blur. "It's good to see you again, Alyssa."

"I'm surprised you all still have this much access around here. I figured Edgar Voles would have booted everyone out for his beloved droids on minute one."

Charlie's mouth pinches in a frown. "There's been too much happening with his coronation and ascension over the past two days. And Wythe hasn't gotten around to sorting out everyone's loyalties yet."

"Which means if you know how to play the game right," Kalia adds, "then you can maintain a lot of anonymity."

The transport starts to slow, and outside I can see the familiar corridors that converge onto the hangar deck. I take a shaky breath. Almost there. "I hope you don't get in trouble on our account," I tell Kalia.

"I'm smarter than that, Alyssa." She looks over at my uncle and nods. "Whenever you're ready, Charles."

Without looking at her, Charlie reaches out and squeezes her hand.

Then Ko hits her with a shot from the stun gun.

She catches Kalia as she falls and sets her down gently, which is a nice touch—I'd definitely like to wake up with as few bruises as possible after taking one for the team. It makes me feel weird, though, and a little light-headed. Like I've just stepped, without warning, off the edge of a cliff.

Ko tucks Kalia out of sight as we finally come to a stop and step off the transport. We make it off the platform and into the corridors . . .

. . . and that's when the lights flicker out.

There's a moment where everything is darkness—and then the red emergency lighting flips on.

The kingship's voice comes on over the sound system again. "Attention. This is an emergency security alert. Shipwide lockdown commencing."

Shit.

Ko whips out a knife and slices my robe from the neck all the way down to the hem. "Time to make a break for it."

I shrug out of the robe and jump off the hoverdisc, more than happy to feel solid ground under my feet and fresh air on my sweaty face and neck. Hell Monkey hops down beside me as I pull out my blaster, and we book it for the hangar bay, tearing down the hall stride for stride. I know it's close—how many times did I walk these decks as a kid?—but it feels dozens of kilometers away. I can hear Drinn's footsteps heavy behind me, Charlie's lighter ones, Ko somewhere behind them. I'm trying to calculate how long it will take them to scramble everyone back into the bay and seal the doors. A minute? Two? Maybe more if someone is farther out?

We can make it.

We. Can. Make it.

I round a corner, half a step ahead of everyone else. It's just a straight dash across this access hall to the hangar bay beyond, but something in my peripheral vision catches my eye and I turn.

Edgar stands in the access tunnel, pale and furious, surrounded by crownsguards with their weapons up.

I throw myself backward, into Hell Monkey, as a blaster shot rips past my ear and slams into the wall. We land in a heap, more blaster fire peppering the area behind me.

Hell Monkey squeezes my arms as he pushes us back onto our feet. "This place is so friendly. I love it. I'm so glad we came here."

Drinn peeks around the corner and grumbles as several blasts zing past his face. "That's a lot of guns. And they're circling around to cut us off. We're gonna miss our shot."

"No!" Charlie's voice is so sharp and urgent that I snap my head around to look at him. He grabs Ko by the shoulder and pulls her down to mutter something into her ear. I can't hear what he says, but I see Ko nod—and then everything starts moving at once.

Drinn heats up his blaster and swings around the corner, opening up suppressing fire, and I don't like it—he's too exposed, he's gonna get hurt—but Charlie puts a hand on my cheek just as I'm readying my blaster.

"Alyssa." He drops his chin to look straight into my eyes. His face is even more serious than usual. "You need to get out of here. Hell Monkey?" Hell Monkey straightens and meets my uncle's gaze. "Keep each other safe. Understand?"

"Whoa, whoa!" I wave my hands at both of them. "We do not have time to go into how much we're not doing this right now. Okay? Just—"

I look away from Charlie over to Hell Monkey for just a second, and in that heartbeat-quick span, Charlie steps past me out into the corridor with Drinn, blasters up.

"Charlie! Don't—"

Ko plants a big hand around the back of my neck and starts pushing me forward. "Time to go, little empress."

"No—I'm not—Eliot—" I reach for Hell Monkey and he's there, right behind me as Ko drags me past the others out into the hail of blaster fire, her big body a full-out shield as we run. The hangar bay entrance is ten meters away. It's so close.

I crane my head and look under my arm as we near the far side, trying to catch a glimpse.

Drinn leans against the wall, a raw wound covering his shoulder, still shooting with his good arm. And just as I'm watching, a blaster shot hits Charlie and he cries out and falls, bright red blood spattering his robes and his neck, shiny medals scattering on the floor.

"CHARLIE!"

I scream, twisting in Ko's grip, but she's too quick for me. She loops an arm around my waist and throws me bodily into Hell Monkey as we reach the doorway into the hangar bay. We stumble backward, and I hit the ground hard on my ass, coughing as the wind gets knocked out of my lungs. I suck in a desperate breath, and then I'm on my feet, running back toward the corridor where Charlie is, where my only family is—

—Ko hits the wall panel.

The doors slam shut in my face.

KINGSHIP UNDER ATTACK?
Troubling reports of blaster fire, injuries, and security breaches leak to the media, only hours after coronation festivities

WILLIAM VOLES OUSTED AS PRIMOR, FORCED TO STEP DOWN FROM VOLES ENTERPRISES
Voles is expected to leave the kingship and return to Helix in the wake of losing both leadership positions in favor of his son, Emperor Edgar Voles

SOLARI ENKINDLERS ANNOUNCE NEW EXPANSION INITIATIVE
Their plans include utilizing their new preferred status to establish conversion and evangelization centers in systems where they had previously not been welcome

HOW SECURE IS THE REIGN OF EDGAR VOLES?
The possibility of a kingship security breach so soon after taking the throne could fuel speculation that the new emperor is not up to taking the place of Atar Faroshti

THE KINGSHIP, APEX, THE KYRA SYSTEM

IT WAS EDGAR WHO HAD FIGURED OUT THAT THE prisoners had escaped.

He'd gone straight to his quarters after Alyssa's arrest, struck with exhaustion after everything that had happened, and fallen into a deep sleep.

He'd dreamed of Atar Faroshti. And Justus Roy. And all the other emperors before them. He'd recognized them not by sight, but by neural patterns. Their faces had been nothing compared to the complex individualized network of their brains. It had been fascinating. Like exploring a brand-new information database.

And then he'd felt a tremor go through him and woken with a start.

At first, it had seemed like nothing. A fire in the northwest quadrant, security personnel already on their way to control it, no apparent injuries so far . . .

But Edgar could feel it. There was something else happening on his kingship. The connection had been a noisy jumble inside him, unfocused, but he'd reached out, searching, until he'd found it.

Unconscious crownsguards in the brig. And three empty cells.

He can't help but feel pleased about it. Not about the fact that his guards and his brig failed to hold one angry girl and a couple of rough engineers—that obviously is enraging—but the fact that the royal seal AI is integrating so quickly and so effectively with his body. It'll be a matter of days, not weeks, before he's fully linked with the kingship—the fastest integration in two hundred years. It makes him feel . . . special somehow. Chosen. Like he was always meant for this throne.

He'd known it, deep in his heart. But now he had proof.

He stands in the corridor, watching his crownsguard detail as they finally manage to secure the otari and disarm the vilkjing. They are stabilizing Charles Viqtorial and securing compression cuffs around the other two when Enkindler Wythe arrives with NL7 following behind him.

"I told you we should've gotten rid of Viqtorial," Edgar says before Wythe manages to get a word out. His voice sounds firm, commanding. Imperial, even.

"There was no one else who could represent that Faroshtis at your coronation." Wythe's words are tinged with irritation. "We needed him and his support. Disposing of him so quickly would hurt public perception—"

"I control public perception now." Edgar steps over to a display panel on the wall and calls up footage of the hangar bay. Alyssa Farshot pounds her fists against the doors. Her companion—that *Hell Monkey*—brings his blaster rifle up and drops the three crownsguards who had been trying to flank them. He's saying something to Alyssa, but Edgar can't hear what it is. "She's made it to the hangar. Recommendations?"

NL7 moves up close to him. "Seal it off, Edgar Voles. Eliminate the threat before it eliminates you."

"She's not unsympathetic in many sectors of the empire," Wythe cuts in sharply. "If you obliterate her right now, it will look like an overpowered move by a distant new emperor. We need to completely change the story around Alyssa Faroshti."

Edgar looks over at him, his eyebrows raised. "What did you have in mind, Enkindler?"

Wythe folds his hands in front of him. "Nothing unites people like a new and intimidating threat."

Personal log of Atar Faroshti, recorded on 0.07.22.4013

MY LITTLE ALYSSA. I'VE BEEN HOLDING YOU FOR hours now, watching you sleep in my arms. No cares, no worries. Just the deep, undisturbed sleep of a baby who knows nothing of sadness or loss.

But those two things, I'm afraid, seem to go hand in hand with our family these days.

Tomorrow we lay your mother to rest. I painted her oseberg ship with the symbols of her life and our family myself, and even though I still have paint beneath my fingernails, it doesn't seem real. It seems like it is all happening to someone else.

Because how can this galaxy still be turning without Saya in it?

To survive two and a half decades of war, the decimation of our lands and our family, only to lose her now, in a senseless accident like this . . .

There now, I've gotten tears on your head. Poor thing.

That you didn't get to share this life with your mother for even six months, that you will never truly know her or what she meant to so many—this is my greatest sorrow. You deserve so much better than to start your life with this weight. All she wanted was a better, more peaceful, more equitable universe. For you and for everyone.

Sleep, Alyssa. It is my job now to carry your sorrows for as long as I can.

THIRTEEN

STARDATE: 0.06.05 in the Year 4031, under the reign of the Empress Who Never Was, Nathalia Matilda Coyenne, long may she rest in glory
LOCATION: Having the worst godsdamned day, I gotta tell ya

I THROW MYSELF AT THE SEALED DOOR OF THE HANgar bay, punching at the metal and getting two sets of scraped and bleeding knuckles in the process. Tears clog up my eyes, and my heart is clogging up my throat, and I wanna scream it all down but I'd probably vomit—just fucking vomit—all over the deck. I keep thinking, *There's gotta be another way into this corridor,* and I know this ship, I should have the answer, but it's like my brain is filled with this horrible buzzing sound and I can't piece anything together or even remember what I'm doing here, let alone all the paths through the intersecting hallways of a massive palatial ship.

"Alyssa." Hell Monkey grabs me by the shoulders and spins me around to face him. His face is blurry with all these stupid tears running everywhere. "We've gotta go—we—"

A high-pitched siren cuts through the air, and we whip around in unison as the metal hangar bay doors screech in protest and then start to edge shut. Far off on the other side of this cavernous space, another set of doors slides open, and I can hear the delightful clomping and clanking of more crownsguards and those shiny new security droids coming toward us. We've probably got a matter of seconds to get our asses out of here before we're target practice.

I look back at the sealed doors just for a second—

I'm coming back for you, Charlie.

—and then I take Hell Monkey's hand and bolt for the *Verity*.

She sits there, surrounded by waveskimmers and short-range liftships, dark and quiet, a giant anchor chain latched onto the bottom of her hull. Hell Monkey shoves his big-ass gun into my hands, and I get to work on blasting away at the chain links as he bolts for the engine room. By the time the anchor chain falls away, the *Verity's* main power is on and her systems light up all over the ship.

"Nova?" I call out as I clamber on board and make a mad dash toward the bridge. "You awake?"

"WHY DO YOU EVEN CARE? EVEN IF I WASN'T, I'M AWAKE NOW. WHAT DO YOU WANT?"

Wow. Kinda forgot we'd "upgraded" to the brattiest AI ever conceived. I wonder when that attitude is gonna wear off. "Get this ship ready to fly, Nova, and fast. I want engines hot by the time my ass hits the captain's chair."

"SURE, SURE, WHATEVER YOU WANT, *CAPTAIN*."

A second later, the engines rev so hard the ship shifts a little and I stumble, cracking my shoulder against the wall. Like I needed another excuse to cuss right now. Rubbing at my new sore spot, I barrel onto the bridge and just about face-plant on the navcomm as I throw myself into my seat. Swiping my fingers across the touch screens, I pull up everything—propulsion, weapons, sensors—so it's all in easy reach, and wrench the ship up off the deck, retracting her landing gear as I swing her around to the western hangar bay door.

The one that's almost totally shut now.

Hell Monkey drops into the copilot's seat, breathing hard. "Engines look good. No locks or clamps that I could spot. Let's do this."

"YOU REALIZE THIS SHIP CAN'T ACTUALLY FIT THROUGH THERE," Nova says.

"Yet. It can't fit there *yet*," I say as I adjust the controls. "That's what the cannons are for. H.M.?"

"My pleasure, Captain."

He hauls on the trigger and one, two, three, four shots blast out of both forward-facing cannons and slam into the hinges of the bay doors, exploding in balls of fire. Scorch marks streak black across the hulls of the row of waveskimmers just under my prow, and I'm pretty sure I hear a crash as one or two of the other littler ships get blown backward by my engine draft. Dammit. The hangar supervisor is gonna be so pissed at me. Pretty sure I can't do chores to make up for this one. I squint through the smoke, trying to get a clear peek at the door status.

Definitely damaged, but still intact. Shit.

"YOU PROBABLY SHOULD KNOW THAT THERE'S A BUNCH OF PEOPLE COMING UP BEHIND US. SOME OF THEM DROIDS.

SOME OF THEM NOT DROIDS. IF YOU WERE INTERESTED IN DOING ANYTHING ABOUT THAT AT ALL."

"One crisis at a time, Nova." I nod at Hell Monkey, and he unleashes more hell, throwing in an extra shot this time, and we get our reward as the hinges screech and bend and then the whole hangar door starts to list open. Now it's only a few meters wide, now it's ten meters, now it's twenty. Wind whips inside, swirling the smoke into nothing, giving me a clear line of sight to the midnight-dark sky beyond.

"Just what I like to see," I mutter. "H.M., how far away are all those persons Nova was talking about?"

He pulls up the rear cameras. "About fifteen meters, give or take."

"Fantastic. Give me some outside speakers so I can talk to those assholes."

His hands move quickly across the dashboard. "Speakers are live."

I lean a little closer to the navcomm. "Listen up, dingbats. I'm about to blast off, so either you duck or you lose your face parts. First and final warning, assholes."

Speakers off, I grip the controls, the feel of them soothing some of the emotions rolling around in my stomach, and I punch the *Verity* forward, feeling her leap underneath me. There's a horrific scream of metal on metal as the belly of the ship scrapes against the dangling bay door, and I cringe—oh, man, so much cringing, I don't think that's gonna buff out—but then, in another second, it's done. We're clear, and I spiral the ship down and out of the kingship, the open air all around me, bright moonlight fracturing on the rough waves below. I push the worldcruiser low, but not that low. Can't exactly skim the waves in this one. Ships like her are mostly meant for interstellar jet setting, not zigzagging around in atmosphere.

But I'm going to have to think of some tricks fast because there are some brand-new blips on our sensors.

"Gunships approaching," Hell Monkey announces, his voice tight, "taking off from the eastern hangar bay. One hundred sixty degrees off starboard. Two hundred degrees off port. One hundred meters and closing."

A shiver of adrenaline and anxiety crawls through me. "Awesome. Just awesome. I'm excited about this."

Hell Monkey snorts. "What's not to be excited about? Everything's going according to plan."

I smile a little. It's grim and pretty shallow, but it's still a smile of some kind because I'm glad Hell Monkey is here if nothing else. We've gotten out of tougher situations. We can handle this.

Come on, Farshot. Think. Think. You can't do anything for anyone if a gunship shoots you into the sea.

Nova's voice breaks in. "THOSE SHIPS JUST FIRED AT US. YOU TWO ARE DEFINITELY WAY MORE LIKELY TO DIE FROM THE IMPACT THAN I AM."

"Countermeasures!" I spin the *Verity* right, taking her up in a tight spiral. I hear three muffled booms as the blasts go off several meters from our aft. Not close enough to singe, but gods, it's too close. The shields on this thing are still a bit shifty after the crash landing on Calm.

Think, think, think.

I yank the ship's nose around, trying to lose them while I frantically scan the surface, and that's when I spot it.

A localized power generator. Sitting on one of the nearby land masses.

All power generators on Apex are equipped with anti-aerial protections to keep any ships from crashing into them and taking out the grid for a bunch of folks. They're coded to pick up on the particular energy signatures given off by thrusters and other propulsion systems that are cleared for use inside planet atmospheres. If you get too close and they pick you up, you're gonna find yourself caught in a containment field and staring down hours of bureaucratic red tape before you can get out again.

I point at it through the windows along the prow. "H.M.—"

He's already nodding. "I see it, I see it. You think these gunship pilots would know, though?"

"Let's find out. Fire up the aft cannons on this thing, aim for just above each of those bad boys. Make 'em move toward the deck."

"Consider it done."

I lean back, shaking out my fingers, taking a deep breath. And then I exhale, grab on, and push this junky worldcruiser through the ride of its life. Up, down, swinging wide around the island below, dipping close to the waves, cutting back in again. All I can hear are the engines and my racing pulse and the distant steady booms of the aft cannons. Sweat beads on my upper lip. I keep an eye on the sensors, watching those little blips, making sure they're flying low, letting them stay right on my tail.

I flick a quick glance over at Hell Monkey. "Ready to get weird?"

His hands are steady on the dashboard, and his expression is almost relaxed. "Always."

I swing us closer to the land mass. Closer . . . "On my mark, burn the sublight engines for two seconds and then cut all propulsion power." The gunships are right where I need them to be. It's go-time.

I dip low, so low, to the far side of the island, using a big tower to block sight line to the power generator. And then, at the last second, I take a sharp left, swinging around the tower.

"Do it, H.M.!"

The *Verity* surges forward, slamming me back against my seat. And then I jerk forward again as the engines cut, thrusters cut, nothing keeping us going but momentum as we coast into the space over the generator. I hold my breath, teeth clenched together, willing us to keep going forward, forward, as gravity starts to pull at the ship's big body. We just have to make it another four hundred meters . . .

The *Verity* drops a little in the air.

. . . three hundred meters . . .

I can feel us slowing down. Come on, baby, almost there.

. . . two hundred meters . . .

She starts to list starboard.

. . . one hundred meters . . .

We hit the safety range, and I holler, "Light it up!" and we throw everything into gear, full power to thrusters, the belly of the *Verity* breaking the tops off a couple of tall trees before I get her pointed up and away and clear of the surface.

Breathing hard, heart racing, I finally dare to look back at the gunships.

Trapped. Both of them. Suspended above the power generator, which has warning lights flashing and a crew running out the doors to assess the threat and deal with the situation.

Congratulations, power folks. Those assholes are your problem now.

I pull the *Verity's* prow up and aim her for the stars.

FOURTEEN

As soon as we clear Apex, I punch in coordinates and jump into a hyperlight lane. The pinpricked blackness of space all around us disappears, replaced by a color-streaked tunnel of light, and I just sit there for a long, quiet moment. Staring at it.

"Hey." Hell Monkey's voice pulls me back onto the bridge, and I swivel around to face him. He's already squared to me, his elbows propped on his knees. "You with me, Farshot?"

No, I'm not. I'm picturing Charlie falling in that spray of blood. Drinn, with a wound covering half his arm. Ko slamming the door closed between us. There aren't words big enough for this painful explosion of emotion pressing against the inside of my sternum. I don't know where to start, and I'm pretty sure if I started, I'd never finish.

So I just shake my head. And get to my feet.

"I need a second. Can you hold course? I'm just gonna take a walk, clear my head so I can figure out what the hell we do next."

He catches my fingers as I start to step away and holds them, his grip warm and light. "There's a way out of this. We'll find it."

I nod, but mostly because that seems like the thing you're

supposed to do when someone's trying to give you a pep talk. Honestly, now that the whole immediate, gunships-trying-to-smoke-our-asses danger has passed, I'm not totally sure there is a way out. Hyperlight maybe. Just stay in this lane and ride it until we run out of fuel or run out of universe. Whichever comes first.

I step off the bridge and pace down the port-side corridor. I said I wanted to take a walk, but there's actually just one place I plan to go: the captain's quarters.

Coy's old quarters. And where she sleeps still.

Her old stuff still hangs on the walls and covers the bunk, but most of what takes up this space is the stasis chamber that holds her body. I meant to deliver it back to Cheery as soon as I took care of Edgar, but now . . . well, that's not really an option.

I stand over it, looking through the clear glass at the body inside. Coy's wrapped in a blanket of her family colors, which covers the horrific chest wound and almost gives the illusion that she really is sleeping. I press a hand to the glass right above her face.

"You're gonna have to wait a little longer," I whisper to her. "I'm sorry."

I pause, like she might respond, which of course is well outside the realm of possibility. But gods, I wish she could. The desire to hear her voice, to have her sit up, right now, and tease me or scold me or laugh just completely swamps me, and this ache opens up in my chest, like a star going supernova. It collapses and I collapse with it, sinking down to the floor with my back against the chamber. Cold metal underneath me, cold metal at my back. Just cold all over inside and out.

I put my head down between my knees, threading my fingers together across the back of my neck. My old tutor, Mr. Odo, told me once this was helpful when you felt like the world was too big and out of control, and the entire universe feels too big and too out of control right now and all I can picture is me floating in the middle of it, tiny and lost and no docking clamps to keep me in place. So I close my eyes, tuck my elbows against my ears, and wrap my hands against the back of my head until I can't see anything or hear anything except my own ragged breath and that weird little swish of your blood zooming through your veins.

I stay like this for a long while. Until I open my eyes and see floor instead of stars. Until I can sit back and feel the metal and the walls around me instead of just nothingness.

"I really screwed up, Coy," I tell her, my voice breaking a little against the words. "I didn't make Edgar pay for what he did. I didn't manage to do anything but get Charlie and a whole bunch of other people in trouble, and I don't even know if Charlie . . . if he's still . . . Shit, I really, really cocked this whole thing all to hell."

I jump back onto my feet, pacing a tight circle around the chamber. "None of this should even be happening. You should be here. You should BE HERE." A bright streak of anger sizzles through me like lightning, and I bring a hand slamming down onto the glass. I kick it, too, my boot thudding against the base. And then I do it again. And again. And again. Until I'm wailing on this impervious coffin as I rant at my dead best friend's face. "Why the hell did you have to fight him for that seal?! Why couldn't you have just not been so fucking proud for ONCE in your life? Why? WHY?!"

By the time I'm done, the skin of my hands stings from the impacts, and I've got a big scrape across one of my palms. I stare down at it, shaking all over, watching tiny drops of blood bead to the surface.

There's a beep at the door and then it slides open. Hell Monkey takes in the room and the stasis chamber and me all in one sweeping look, and then he steps back, grabs a wall-mounted med kit from the corridor, and comes in and starts cleaning up my injured hand without a word.

"It was an accident," I tell him, defensive for some reason, the words all thick and half stuck in my mouth.

He nods but doesn't say anything.

"It *was.*"

"You don't owe me an explanation, Alyssa." He says it so quiet, with not even a hint of an edge in his voice, and it takes the teeth right out of me. His fingertips brush my knuckles, my wrist, as he presses the patch against my skin, sealing the wound so it can heal. "I came to tell you I'm having Nova do an intensive scan. Like, microscopic-level-type stuff. Anything foreign, any piece of tech that doesn't belong, she'll flag us."

I press my lips together, mind gearing up as I try to jump onto his train of thinking. "You think they let us go? Are you disparaging our dramatic escape?"

"You mean that daring escape where we managed to get past zero shields or barriers of any kind? The dramatic escape where there were no shots fired from the kingship, one of the biggest warships in the quadrant, and the only pursuit were the two measly gunners that gave us the runaround? Is that the dramatic escape you're referring to?"

I flex my hand, feeling the patch stretch and tighten against my skin. I know he's right—an important prisoner escaping and no one up top on the kingship authorized a single shot? No one scrambled additional fighters to come after us?

It does seem a little hard to believe. In a definite, stomach-sinking, not-so-good way.

I meet Hell Monkey's gaze, and we head toward the door at the same time, moving like a unit down the corridor and onto the bridge. I step up to the strategic operations table and use it to pull up the media feeds in a big projected display that fills the space between us.

And there it is. Or, I guess, there we are.

Security footage of me on the observation deck shooting Edgar and him pulling off my glamour key. Security footage of the prison breakout. Security footage of us blasting out of the hangar, blowing crownsguards off their feet, and leaving destroyed waveskimmers in our wake.

One by one, the repeating footage minimizes, and a livestream from the imperial throne room fills the center space. Edgar sits in Uncle Atar's chair, stoic, staring straight into the camera drone filming him. In front of him stands Enkindler Wythe, with his hands folded all pious in front of him. I turn up the volume so we can hear what he's saying.

". . . demonstrating a complete lack of moral character and a flagrant disregard for our sacred institutions—"

Hell Monkey raises an eyebrow. "Uh-oh. This doesn't sound like it's going anywhere good. . . ."

"—a growing threat that threw out centuries of tradition for her own ego," Wythe continues. "Alyssa Faroshti has proved herself to be a far cry from the noble, dignified Atar Faroshti, may he rest in the light of the sun. Invading the kingship and attempting an assassination and a coup on this throne and our newly crowned emperor is an act that defies belief. I have counseled our Imperial Majesty that even the grace of Solarus cannot be extended to such a soul."

Edgar Voles rises and steps forward, the camera drone zooming slowly in on his face as he speaks. He's holding himself differently—in a way that takes up more space and commands more attention.

"Alyssa Charlemagne Farshot, née Faroshti, is henceforth declared a traitor to the crown of the United Sovereign Empire. She must either surrender herself to answer for her crimes or forfeit her life. In our imperial mercy, her accomplice, Eliot Flynn, also known as Hell Monkey, is offered amnesty in exchange for turning himself and this traitor in to our custody. If he refuses, he will be branded a traitor as well."

My breath catches in my throat, and I shoot a look over at Hell Monkey. His face is very blank, very still, but he's gone two shades paler than normal under his dark stubble.

"All legal authorities throughout the empire are authorized to detain her, utilizing force if necessary. We will offer a substantial reward for her capture." Edgar hesitates, just for half a second, and then adds, "Preferably alive." He straightens his shoulders, his jaw hardening as he continues, "We will not allow enemies of our throne to take advantage of this period of transition to destabilize this glorious empire. In order to maintain security and assist in the capture of Alyssa Faroshti and any other highly dangerous persons, we have instituted the immediate and expansive deployment of security droids across the quadrant to ensure public safety. We will be working with all leaders to make this implementation as seamless as possible."

Wythe steps forward to speak again, but I shut it off. We don't need to hear any more.

I look at Hell Monkey across the strategic-ops table. He's staring at the surface, his fingers wrapped so tight around the edges that his knuckles have gone completely white. I'm trying to find something to say to him, but I can't think of a damn thing. He buried his real name after his family died, erased it from everywhere he could find so that it could be a secret, protected piece of them he carried with him. And now here it is, ripped away from him and put on blast to the entire quadrant.

Because of me.

"H.M., I—I'm so sorr—"

"Don't." His voice grates across the silence, and I flinch, cut by the sharpness of it.

I hesitate. I don't want to ask this question, but I kinda think I have to. "Is the water getting too deep?"

A not-small part of me expects him to answer immediately, to tell me I'm being an idiot and of course it's not, of course he's still with me. Because that's always been his response before. Always.

But he doesn't say anything. And the silence stretches until it pulls me down into my captain's chair. I spin around, staring out at the blur of hyperlight so I don't have to stare at him and the complete lack of words coming out of his mouth. I feel every beat of my heart, leaden inside my chest.

It's okay. He just needs time. We both need time to process and figure out a new plan. But we can't actually ride a hyperlight lane forever, and our safe havens just dropped to close to zero. I flip through the options, whittling them down to one long shot: a person who's got the ability to hide and defend us, the connections to keep us in the know on what's going on, and just enough of a moral center that I think—I think—they won't turn us in.

I pull up the communication controls. "Nova, I need a secure comms channel. Like, triple-secure. Bury it a few levels deep."

"THAT'S EXTRA WORK FOR ME, BUT FINE, I GUESS," Nova blurts out. "WHO ARE YOU TRYING TO TALK TO?"

I can feel Hell Monkey's eyes on the back of my head, but I keep my gaze forward. "Faye Orso."

FIFTEEN

STARDATE: 0.06.08 in the Year 4031, under the reign of the Empress Who Never Was, Nathalia Matilda Coyenne, long may she rest in glory
LOCATION: The Frevid system, on the farthest edge of the Outer Wastes. Right in the middle of prime "piss off and leave me alone forever" territory.

WHEN FAYE AND I WERE TOGETHER, THERE WERE TWO things we did really well: make out and get into trouble. Communication wasn't really a high priority for me at the time—Faye was just overwhelmingly too hot for my brain—but there were a few times when we'd go to one of the towers, way up at the very top of the kingship, and lie there looking up at the sky and talking about what we would do once we got older.

I, of course, wanted desperately to take off into the stars. Faye had already seen a lot of our stars, though. She'd wanted something more. She'd told me how she wanted to establish her own crew, out from under her dad's shadow, and "take them right off the edge of the universe." Leave the empire entirely. Set off into the vastness of intergalactic space and discover whole new galaxies.

So when I send her the secure message, I keep it simple: *Meet me at the edge of the universe.*

It's a calculated risk. The Frevid system is the farthest point in the empire and right on the edge of our known galaxy—exactly where you'd want to go if your next goal was to jump into intergalactic space. But this conversation happened four years ago, and we're both different people than we were back then, so I'm really, really hoping she got what I was trying to say.

Especially since it's been a few days and she's not here yet.

I'm trying hard not to be anxious, but the truth is, I don't have much to do but get anxious. I set us down on a small moon of ice and rock that satellites around the fifth planet in orbit. The information available on this place is pretty sparse—the planet is called Maeve, the moon is Pendra, it's got a survivable atmosphere but nothing you'd really call hospitable. Frevid as a whole doesn't seem to have much in the way of settlements or cities or other organizing elements to the life-forms, and according to our sensors, there's nothing alive at all on Pendra.

Which is fine. It's great. It's exactly what we need from a place. But our supplies are gonna run low pretty quick. And distractions are already in short supply.

I could use a few. The only real thing I've had on my to-do list since landing here has been recoding our ship's registration with a name that isn't known and wanted across the quadrant. I chose the *Serendipity* because who doesn't appreciate a little irony, right? Also, it's one of the most popular ship names in the empire, so one more worldcruiser with that name won't really make much of an impact.

But even that only took me an hour.

I've been checking the feeds pretty constantly, digging for information on Charlie and Drinn. There was a story about an hour after we hit hyperlight that they'd been captured while helping in our escape and were being treated for serious injuries and held on counts of treason. But there's been nothing since then. Which is honestly a good thing, because if the Charles Viqtorial had died from his wounds or been sentenced to death, that would've been a major headline.

It's a small comfort, though. And it doesn't stop me from scrolling deep into the feeds, like maybe if I just look hard enough, I can discover a secret hint about how my uncle is doing.

As for Hell Monkey . . . he's been quiet. And distant. He tells me there's just still a lot of work to do on the ship to get it in top shape, but it's a lie that sits between us like one of the massive rocky boulders all over this moon. Because he's back to sleeping in the engineer's quarters instead of cramming into my bunk with me. And I really didn't think it'd bother me that much—fine, whatever, more space for me—but I keep having a hard time falling asleep. And I wake up cold.

It's strange and lonely and I hate it, so I've resorted to convincing Nova to play a virtual form of the strategy game bagautchi with me. We've been at it for hours. That's how bad it is.

"ARE YOU CHEATING AGAIN? YOU HAVE TO TELL ME IF I ASK YOU."

I sigh, kicking off the navcomm so my captain's chair spins me around and around. "No, I don't. That's not how cheating works, Nova."

"I CAN'T CONCEIVABLY BE EXPECTED TO WIN IF YOU ARE NOT PLAYING BY THE RULES."

"You're thinking of this in the totally wrong way, Nova. It's about being creative. It's about thinking outside the box."

A beat of silence. And then: "FINE."

I stop spinning and wait, staring at the projected game. I expect to see a piece move or something to shift in the display, but instead emergency lighting floods the bridge and the navcomm screen blares out a message:

ALERT: AIR VENTS OPEN. OXYGEN LEVELS DROPPING.

Uh-oh. That's not good.

I feel it a second later—the thinness of the air as I try to pull it into my lungs and come back gasping and light-headed. I brace myself against the dashboard and suck in a desperate breath.

"Stop . . . Nova . . . you win . . . you . . . win. . . ."

My head spins—I can't *breathe*—and I tilt, the chair slipping away from me as the floor rises up to meet my face.

There's a beep, and then Nova says, "I ACCEPT YOUR DEFEAT."

Emergency lighting shuts off. There's a faint, whispering hiss as air floods back into the ship. My next inhale is deep and ragged, and I stay pressed into the floor while my brain and my heart rate and my lungs all steady. It definitely takes a second. Like, you'd probably expect that half suffocating might knock you down for a minute and—surprise—you'd be absolutely right. In fact, it's probably a solid two or three minutes before I right myself and haul my ass back into the captain's chair.

I drop into it gratefully, panting. "That's definitely one way to win a game, Nova."

The starboard-side bridge door slides open, and Hell Monkey barrels in, his face looking like a nebula storm.

"What the hell was that?"

I wave a dismissive hand, barely turning around. "I was teaching Nova how to cheat at bagautchi. She's a natural, obviously."

There's silence after my comment. I spin around to face him, still slouched down in my chair, feet and arms dangling. I probably look like a petulant kid, but hey, this is the first time he's walked his ass across the ship to talk to me in *days*, so he takes what he gets.

His face is that stoic type of livid he gets, and his big broad-shouldered form is all hunched together like he's just looking for a reason to explode outward into a thousand pieces.

I shrug at him. "What?"

That does the trick. "What the hell do you mean, *what*? I was working down in the engine room, and then suddenly there's NO OXYGEN, and all you've got is, *what*?!"

"It was a simple misunderstanding!" I roll up onto my feet, squaring my shoulders. I can taste what's coming, and there's no way in hell I'm taking it sitting down. "We were just playing a game. I had no idea Nova was going to take it that far."

Hell Monkey snorts, crossing his arms. "If that isn't just the most quintessential Alyssa Farshot type bullshit, I don't know what is."

My mouth drops open, and I storm across the bridge, right up into his space. "What the hell is *that* supposed to mean?"

"It means *exactly* what you think it means." He drops his arms and steps into me, his face centimeters from mine. "You just go barreling into everything as soon as any half-ass idea gets into your head, and you don't even think about what the collateral damage might be!"

"I said I was sorry." The words grit out from between my clenched teeth. "I said I was sorry a dozen times already! I didn't know—"

"Of course you knew!" His face is ablaze with anger. "There's consequences to all this shit, Alyssa! You go barreling into the middle of the kingship? Consequences. You try to revenge-kill an emperor? Consequences. You teach an AI to cheat? *Consequences.* You know all this, but it never stops you! That's the part that pisses me off!"

"I don't know what to say! I've been like this since the first day you met me!" I poke him hard in the shoulder. "I gave you an out. I told you that you didn't have to come on the crownchase. I told you on the way *here* that we could part ways. You don't *have* to stay."

He chuckles, a little bitterness in it, and shakes his head. "Yeah, well, that's kind of the bitch of it, isn't it? Because it turns out I kind of love you, so I guess I'm just stuck."

I had some straight sarcasm all lined up to throw at him, but the words stumble and dissolve on my tongue. I stare up at him, but he's not looking at me anymore. He's looking up toward the ceiling, and his mouth is tight with anger or frustration or annoyance or maybe all of it. He looks almost like he's mad at himself for letting that come out.

And, honestly, I have *no* idea what to do with it. Nine days ago, I might've.

Before Coy died.

But now? There's too much that's messy in me, too many wires all tangled up together, too many sharp and angry pieces, for me to be able to say it back anymore.

I hate how unhappy he looks, though. I really don't want him to look that way because of me. I place my hand on his chest, my fingertips brushing along his collarbone and the base of his throat.

"Eliot . . ."

He drops his head immediately, his gaze going from my eyes to my mouth and lingering there. His chest is steady underneath my palm, like he's holding his breath. I think I'm holding mine, too.

"INCOMING WORLDCRUISER SIGNATURE APPROACHING OUR COORDINATES. FIGURED YOU MIGHT WANT TO KNOW."

I blink—and the moment collapses. Hell Monkey steps away, shoving his hands into his pockets as he drifts across the bridge. I shake my arms out, trying to breathe normally again, and step back over to the navcomm, checking the sensors for the ship Nova mentioned.

"Can you give me a ship ID? Registration?"

"ONLY IF YOU REALLY WANT IT. THEY'RE TRANSMITTING A CALLING CARD, THOUGH."

Really? That's not really Faye's style. . . . "Show it to me."

It appears on the dashboard display a moment later. A clean, simple imperial calling card with two names on it.

Faye Orso. And Setter Roy.

SIXTEEN

Uncle Charlie used to tell me that you should try to find something positive about everyone you meet.

So here's something positive about Setter Roy: He is being very chill about the blaster I have pointed at his neck. Really is not taking it personally, which is a class-act move.

There. Charlie would be so proud.

We're in a standoff just outside the *Serendipity*, me at the bottom of the cargo ramp and Hell Monkey at the top with a high-powered blaster rifle to cover my ass. Setter is a few meters away from me with his hands up, his axeeli eyes shifted to a cool, calm deep blue. Faye stands next to him, one hip out, her arms across her chest, looking like this is just the most annoying thing to happen in her day. Just behind her, her girlfriend and partner-in-actual-crime, Honor Winger, stands with her own blaster rifle. Hers is slung across her broad shoulders, but it'd be a mistake to think she couldn't use it in an instant if she needed to.

"I do not recall saying anything about bringing sidekicks, Faye," I say, keeping my eyes on Setter.

Faye scoffs and tosses her hair—long, straight, like luminescent fiber-optic cables—over her shoulder. "Your message was eight words long, Farshot. It's not like it was heavy on instructions."

Okay, that's fair. I'm not dropping my blaster, but it's still fair. "Well, I'm apparently a traitor on the run now, so you'll have to forgive me if I get a little twitchy about surprise guests."

Setter frowns, adding an extra level of serious to his already serious expression. "No one here thinks you're a traitor, Alyssa."

Honor barks out a laugh. "I mean, you kind of are, but it's the kind of traitor we're into."

I take my gaze off Setter and look over at Honor. Her asymmetrical pixie cut is a bright, artificial green against her copper-brown skin, and her eyes are hidden behind round, pink-tinted glasses, but she waggles her eyebrows at me. "Relative morality and all that."

Sure. All that. Still—I know I called this meeting, but I'm suddenly not sure it was such a good idea. We went through some heavy-duty stuff together during the crownchase, but the kingship has dropped a pretty sizable reward to turn my ass in. Plus, bonus points for ingratiating yourself with the shiny new emperor.

I give Setter a hard look and back slowly up the ramp, waving them forward. "Up here, all three of you, so Nova can check you for trackers and bugs and so on."

Faye gives me the biggest eye roll, probably of her entire life, but all three of them follow and stand there, in various stages of irritability, in the middle of the cargo ramp while they're scanned. It's quite the picture.

"Nova," I call out, "how do they look?"

"THEY'RE CLEAN BUT I DON'T WANT THEM ON BOARD.

CARRYING YOU TWO IS PLENTY."

Setter's eyes go wide, flickering through an array of colors. "What's wrong with your ship AI?"

"NOTHING IS WRONG WITH ME, THANK YOU."

Hell Monkey drops his blaster rifle and shrugs, totally casual. "We've made a few modifications."

I nod. "It's an upgrade. Welcome aboard the *Nath*—sorry, the *Serendipity*."

Faye's expression softens as I trip over the ship's name and her gold eyes turn to me. I can't hold her gaze—it's too much so I turn and walk deeper into the ship, waving them after me. "Come on, let's talk, fellow traitors."

Faye catches up quick, her long legs closing the distance. "Alyssa . . . I'm really sorry."

I can tell she doesn't use those words much. They're a bit rough coming out of her throat. "Why? You didn't do anything."

Her next step catches me on the heel of my boot, and I stumble a bit. "You know what I mean," she snaps.

"Yeah, I know. It's whatever, it's fine." I swing through the doors onto the bridge and head right for the captain's chair, letting out a breath as I drop safely into its familiar contours. It's not the same as it would've been on the *Vagabond*, but at least when I'm in this seat, I'm in control. I spread my arms wide as everyone files in after me. "Welcome to our humble abode."

Hell Monkey props himself up in a corner, hands in his jump-suit pockets. "Pretty much the only one we have left anymore."

Setter steps up to the strategic-ops table and places both hands on the surface, looking like he's conducting a council meeting or something. "I apologize for my unannounced presence. We should've informed you—"

"Don't apologize, Setter," Faye cuts in. She leans against the navcomm beside Honor, who's plopped down in the copilot seat. "I asked you to come and I chose not to tell Alyssa about it." She looks at me and cocks her head. "You need all the help you can get."

I try to catch Hell Monkey's eye, but he's staring at his boots. I lean over my knees, scrubbing at my eyes. Gods, I'm tired. "Look, I appreciate the go-team attitude, but mostly we just need a place to hide. Preferably somewhere with access to supplies and resources so I could maybe wash my hair in the near future instead of saving it for the water ration."

Honor frowns. "Wait . . . that can't be your entire plan, can it?"

Setter nods sharply. "I agree. Edgar Voles cannot be allowed to sit on the throne after what he did to Nathalia."

I laugh a little, but it's dry and catches in my throat. "Apparently not everyone sees it that way. Like your parents, for example."

His shoulders drop a little, and his eyes cycle from a bright orange to a pinkish red like a blush. He looks over at Faye, who flips a hand at me, absolutely unfazed. "Our parents are gonna do whatever benefits them. You can't blame them for that, and you can't blame us for that either. We're here, aren't we? You called, and we're ready to go. So let's go."

"Go where? Do what?" I throw my hands in the air. "I tried to do something to stop all this, and I don't know if you missed it, but it did not go well. At all."

Faye shakes her glowing hair. "Well, that's because your plan was stupid."

Hell Monkey's head finally comes up, and he laughs, short and loud. "That's what I tried to tell her."

"She never listens," Faye tells him, talking around me like I'm not sitting right there. "As soon as she gets a plan in her head, it's gotta be the best plan, so it's full thrusters ahead."

"Listen," Hell Monkey says with a snort. "You don't have to tell me. I've got stories. . . ."

"We should definitely discuss those stories—"

I clap my hands together. "Okay! New ship rule! You two are not allowed to talk to each other. Nova? Make a note of that."

"I DEFINITELY WILL NOT."

Important note: do not put your ex in the same room with your current . . . person. Or whatever we are. Maybe if I try real hard, I can just melt through the floor. Become one with the ship. That doesn't seem like a bad way to go at the moment.

Setter steps forward—gods bless Setter, he's always been my favorite. "This isn't productive. We need to settle on concrete steps to correct what's happening. If we gather the heads of all the prime families, and, Alyssa, you tell them exactly what happened, we make a personal pitch to them, then I am positive we can convince them—"

"Nope." I don't even let him finish. "Nope and nope. I tried that, okay? I talked to Cheery Coyenne—the one person who I definitely expected to be on my side in all this—and she shot me straight down. I'm not gonna stick my neck out around those people. You think any of the others are going to listen?"

Honor raises an eyebrow. "They might. If it means they get another shot at the throne they just lost."

Over in the corner, Hell Monkey shakes his head, a very small smile on his face that looks a little bitter. "Honor's right. We just need to find a better way to pitch it. A way that puts blood in the water."

Faye pushes off the navcomm dash. "Blood is already in the water. Negotiations are over. I say we take the fight to the throne— but in a much smarter way than Alyssa did it."

I cover my face with my hands, mumbling, "I get it, I get it, thanks. Feeling so supported right now, by the way."

Setter starts to say something, but Nova's voice cuts in abruptly: "INCOMING SIGNATURES. UNKNOWN CONFIGURATION. AND I KNOW ALMOST EVERY CONFIGURATION SO THAT'S PROBA-BLY NOT A GOOD SIGN."

"Golly gee, thanks, Nova. That's an understatement." I swivel my chair around to the navcomm and swipe at the display, bring-ing up the outside camera feeds one by one and spreading them out in front of me. I can hear the others shuffling up behind me so they can see.

The ships are tiny, sleek, barely visible against the dark rocks and darker sky. They skim low and fast toward us, and their hulls are covered in a mirrormask on a level I haven't seen before.

I get a bad-flutter feeling in my gut.

Two pods drop, one from each ship, streaking to the ground and landing upright in the gravelly rock. A second later, the doors on the pods burst open and two humanoids step out. It's hard to make out much about them from this distance, but the giant tricked-out guns in their hands make their message pretty damn clear.

Faye leans over my shoulder, grinning. "This isn't the fight I was thinking about, but it'll definitely do."

EMPEROR VOLES ROLLS OUT NEW "PEACE THROUGH STRENGTH" SECURITY INITIATIVE

Kingship delegations, primarily made up of Voles Enterprises droids, are already embedded across sixty percent of the empire

FROM CROWNCHASER TO FUGITIVE OF THE THRONE

Those who know Alyssa Farshot best speak exclusively to the *Daily Worlds* about how she went from a beloved contestant to someone willing to commit treason

PLANETARY LEADERS OBJECT; ANTI-IMPERIALISM ON THE RISE

Leaders of several planets report that the new security initiative has resulted in rising sympathy for anti-imperialist groups and messaging

WHO IS ELIOT FLYNN?

The tragic origin story behind Farshot's enigmatic coconspirator

THE KINGSHIP, APEX, THE KYRA SYSTEM

THE KINGSHIP GLOWS LIKE A GLASS-SPUN MOON over the Eastern Sea, suspended in the deepest, darkest part of the night.

But Edgar is awake.

Since the royal seal has grown more and more a part of him, he's found himself sleeping less and less. Lying awake at nights, restless, anxious, eager. So he's started coming here, to the kingship's bridge, a separate, secured room located just behind the dais of the throne. He stands here for hours, looking out on . . .

. . . everything.

He had no idea what it would mean to sit on the throne, but his understanding of it grows every moment. He knows everything that every previous emperor knew. He knows the movements of all his staff and all his crownsguards. He knows information from the leaders on the most distant planets in his quadrant the instant they need him to know it.

And the ship. The kingship is no longer this massive, foreign, unwelcoming thing. It's a pet, curling around his hand.

He drifts around the empty, circular room, watching conn panels and displays light up as he draws near. Eager to please him.

NL7 stands nearby, watching him move around with its camera

face aglow. "Your physiological outputs show signs of stress, Edgar Voles. You have not allowed sufficient time for rest."

Edgar brushes his fingertips over the surface of the control table, watching light ripple across it in response to his touch. "I feel fine. I feel perfectly rested here."

NL7's tinny metal feet screech as it shuffles on the floor. "This does not constitute as rest for your particular biological life form."

Edgar doesn't answer. He thinks to the kingship that he'd like to see a map of the entire empire, and it bursts out of the table in a multicolored hologram all around them. He walks through it and around it until he finds Apex.

There. In almost the center of the empire.

He knows why Atar anchored here—he has the echo of him in his head, after all—but it's time for something new. It's time for an emperor who doesn't hide, but who shows his true strength.

He dismisses the map and replaces it with a wide look at the kingship in its current form: clear, geodesic, spherical.

"Did you know, NL7," he murmurs as he moves his hands through the projection, "that the kingship is the most advanced ship in the empire?"

NL7 steps closer. "That is extremely common knowledge, Edgar Voles."

"One of its many strengths," he continues, not even looking at the android, "is an ability to shift to meet the emperor's current needs. For example, if a sphere is no longer the most functional shape it can take—" He pulls at the display, reshaping and re-forming it. Elongating it. Streamlining it. Giving it a sharper prow. Rearranging weapons and engines to their most efficient positioning. He steps back and looks at his work, smiling a little. "You can alter it."

NL7 doesn't reply, hovering close but not drawing nearer.

"It's time," Edgar says softly, more to himself than to NL7.

There's a groan, far, far below their feet, and then a rhythmic pattern of screeching and clanking metal. They can feel it even in here. Edgar brings up a camera feed and watches as the three giant chains slowly retract from the ocean below, dripping salt water as they're curled into the belly of the ship.

"Where are we going, Edgar Voles?" NL7 asks.

Edgar looks at his new shape for the kingship. As soon as the chains are up, he can make this ship into his own. And then . . .

Edgar smiles—fully smiles—at the android. "Anywhere we want."

Audio transcript of a personal long-range communication from Atar to William Voles on 0.07.29.4013

"WILLIAM, I THANK YOU FOR YOUR SYMPATHIES, and please accept my congratulations on being selected as the new primor for your family. I hope to renew the old ties our families had so long honored but that fell away during the reign of your predecessor. It is more important than ever right now for us to find common ground, given the fragility of our current situation in the wake of Saya's death.

"Rumor has reached us that certain factions see this as an opportunity to tear up the treaty that Saya negotiated just before her untimely death that would have had her take her lawful place on the throne. That would plunge the empire back into war, an outcome I don't believe either of us want.

"I understand your concerns in agreeing outright to have me take my sister's place. Please know that I do not take this lightly or intend it to be 'a Faroshti power grab' as some have implied. In truth, I never desired the throne. But what I want is beside the point. Our people need peace. Maintaining that is paramount.

"With that in mind, I will agree, in both honor and good faith, to the following proposals you submitted:

"That I will set aside Saya's more radical policies and will not pursue them during my tenure as emperor, especially any proposal that would result in major additions or restructuring to the current imperial government.

"That the Imperial Council will be given more power to effect change and represent interests throughout the empire, including the power of veto.

"That Charles and I will not name any heir, including my niece and ward, Alyssa Faroshti, and we will not pursue any avenues of having children of our own who might be construed as legal heirs.

"That on the event of my passing, a crownchase will be instigated so that all current prime families will have a legal shot at the throne.

"If I may ask for one thing in return, it would be this: that the prime families from here on out meet as friends. That our children and our children's children may know each other and grow with each other in the hopes that those ties bring the empire long-lasting stability.

"With my acceptance of these terms, I hope we all can finally come to an agreement that will usher in a new era of peace in the empire. I look forward to your response."

SEVENTEEN

STARDATE: 0.06.08 in the Year 4031, under the reign of the Empress Who Never Was, Nathalia Matilda Coyenne, long may she rest in glory
LOCATION: On a totally abandoned moon, with a price on my head, trying to keep a couple of random assassins from killing us all. Basically, exactly where I always thought I'd end up.

THE TWO FIGURES FROM THE DROP SHIPS STALK toward the *Serendipity*, moving smoothly across the rocky landscape. Setter steps up to the navcomm, waving the video feed toward him and zooming in and in and in some more. He's got a worried crinkle forming between his eyebrows. "Alyssa . . . Faye . . . I think it's *them.*"

"Huh?" I say, incredibly eloquently. "What are you—?" And then I see it.

The cut of their hooded coats. The heavy shape and style of their blasters. The unique hilts of the plasma blades sticking up from behind their backs. It's all stomach-sickeningly familiar.

The assassins with no faces. The ones that killed Owyn Mega

in the Ships' Graveyard and tried to blow the rest of us up in the battle over Calm.

They walk toward us over the ragged ground in near-perfect unison, and a cold, heavy feeling crawls across my chest and down my limbs.

Shit.

"These assholes again," Honor growls.

I don't like the little fissures of fear that snake through me at the sight of them. Like cracks in a hull. "H.M. . . ."

"Yup." He's already booted Honor out of the copilot's and is leaning over the navcomm, checking the sensors, pulling up the forward cannon controls.

And then the figures disappear.

One second they're there, the next they're not.

"What the hell—?" Faye growls. "What is that? Teleport tech? Personal cloaking?"

"Blast them anyway," says Honor. "If we can just take them out from the safety of our big shiny ship, let's do it."

Hell Monkey slides a look over at me. "Captain?"

I grit my teeth, staring at the empty space on the video feeds. "Do it."

There's a distant hum as the cannons heat up, and then Hell Monkey hauls down on the triggers, sending several rounds blasting into the rock and ice, spraying dust and gravel everywhere. The whole video feed is enveloped in a cloud, and for a minute, I think maybe this actually worked. I mean, the whole area they were just walking through kinda got pulverized—if they were in it, they likely at least got knocked back or down or off or something, right?

This prickle crawls down my neck as I realize every single one of us is glued to this foggy display, our backs to the rest of the bridge. Totally exposed. I think back to those echoing, crystal-eaten corridors of the *Defiant* and how that hooded monster materialized out of nowhere before it shoved a plasma blade into Owyn Mega's heart.

Materialized out of nowhere . . .

I spin around on instinct and see it: this slight wavering of the air behind Hell Monkey's seat. I don't even think about what I'm doing next—I throw myself toward him, plowing into his side just as that wavering air coalesces into a hooded, faceless figure. It's already got that plasma blade out, ramming it into Hell Monkey's space.

Luckily, he's not there anymore. He's hitting the deck, brought down by my momentum and weight.

Unluckily, my shoulder is there. So I get a nice pointy plasma edge right in the spot just above my shoulder blade.

I cry out as Hell Monkey and I land in a heap, and all chaos breaks out on my bridge.

The second assassin appears and leaps toward Faye, but I catch a glimpse of Honor flipping her blaster rifle off her shoulders and swinging it like a bat toward its head.

Hell Monkey curses, then wraps his arms around me and rolls us to the side, right underneath the navcomm, as the plasma blade slices down again, barely missing my spine. My shoulder burns like mad, the pain radiating down my arm and up the side of my neck, but I scramble off Hell Monkey and drag him with me so we're crouched behind the navcomm. Not that I think a bridge dash-board is gonna provide lasting protection or anything, but maybe a quick second to breathe and think.

I press my injured arm tight to my side. Gods, it hurts. "Where's your rifle?"

He scowls. "I left it in the cargo bay. I thought I wouldn't need it up here."

A dark laugh scrapes out of my throat. "Joke's on you. We apparently need to be armed in our very own home these days. Here—" I nudge him, nodding toward the blaster in my hip holster. "Take this. I'm gonna draw its attention. You blast it the second you get a clear shot. Or even a slightly less murky shot."

I can hear this little intake of breath as he starts to protest, but I don't wait. I throw myself over the navcomm and charge at the assassin, yelling, head-on.

Not great at hand-to-hand, remember? Just good at taking big risks.

This one works a little, actually. It makes the assassin take just a half step back, surprised, and I take everything I can get out of that super brief hesitation. I drop low and barrel into its legs, upsetting its balance and knocking it down. It lands at an awkward angle in the copilot's seat.

I land kinda on my face.

Not just kinda. Actually on my face. I don't catch myself in time, and my nose hits the hard floor. Blinking, dazed, I only have half a second before I realize I'm way too close to a person with a big-ass weapon. I roll away again, trying to get to my feet—

—too late. This asshole slices a line across my lower back, but the angle is too awkward for it to go deep. I stagger up and spin around, panting.

Hell Monkey unloads on it, elbows propped up on the navcomm dashboard to steady his aim as he fires several rounds into the assassin's side, chest, back. It staggers backward—and then disappears.

"Son of a bitch!" Hell Monkey dashes over to me, and I brace myself against him, staring around at the empty space. Half my torso feels like it's on fire. It makes it hard to think, even with the adrenaline thrumming through my body.

"Faye?" I call out, looking over at her.

Faye and Honor stand shoulder to shoulder, their backs to Setter, who's doing something at my navcomm station. Honor has a gash over her eye, oozing bright red blood down her temple. Faye doesn't look hurt, but she's sweating and breathing hard. Their attacker is nowhere to be seen either.

"They took damage and then vanished," Faye calls back to me. "I can't see them anywhere."

Neither can I. I squint into every corner, looking for that telltale waver in the air, but I don't see it. For all we know they could be back outside or deep in our ship.

Shit. What if they're heading for the engine room? What if they're messing with our computer or our ship AI? What if we're standing here like a bunch of idiots and they're dismantling systems all over this ship?

I bring my arm up slow, reaching to tap out a message on my

wristband, to tell everyone that I'm gonna go search the rest of the ship. But I've barely got my finger on the screen when Setter calls out, "Stop that, Alyssa. Just hold still."

. . . the hell? "I thought you were an empath, not a mind reader, Roy."

"Hush!"

The bridge somehow feels too small and too big all at once. So much empty space that could suddenly be filled with a body. And almost anywhere they pop up, they could make us hurt.

The lights go out, pitching the whole bridge into darkness save for pale starlight coming through the windows along the prow. And then, a hiss as something releases from the vents, and slowly all the dust particles floating around start glowing. Lit up by some kind of compound. The air is filled with motes that eddy around the vents and hang suspended in the air between us.

And—there. Two vaguely humanoid spaces on opposite sides of the bridge where there's no dust. Where the particles gather like an outline.

They realize what Setter did a second too late. Hell Monkey and Honor Winger have already started firing, and they don't stop until the two assassins hit the ground and go still.

EIGHTEEN

MY HEARTBEAT IS SO LOUD RIGHT NOW I CAN COUNT by it. I'm breathing hard, feeling a little dizzy as I stare down at the bodies, still surrounded by rivers of luminous dust motes. Setter brings the lights up, and I blink, trying to adjust.

It's strange to see this normal-looking bridge after that magic trick. Like, oh, hey, just another day on a worldcruiser—don't mind the corpses, just step over them.

"What did you do, Setter?" Faye asks as she crouches down next to the dead assassins.

He shrugs and leans against the navcomm dashboard, rubbing a hand along the back of his close-cropped black hair. "Phosphorous particles. And a fancy light trick. There's not much to it really."

I snort, stepping away from Hell Monkey. "Sure, hardly anything. Except for the part where you saved our—oh shit." The pain from the big shiny wounds in my shoulder and back hits a sudden high note, and my knees go weak. Ah. That probably explains the dizziness I had a second ago. Good ol' fashioned injury and blood loss. Can always count on them to put you on your ass.

I grab at the edge of the strategic-ops table as my legs give out. Not that it stops my descent at all, but it makes it a little less clumsy. Hell Monkey's blaster clatters to the ground as he drops it and kneels beside me. He's doing that thing where he wants to help but he doesn't know what he can do that won't hurt me so he kind of waffles and then finally just puts a hand on my elbow. It doesn't do much, but it's still kinda nice. To feel him there. Fingers light on my skin. I really want to lie down, but I figure that won't go over so well, so I just tip forward. Press my forehead against the side of the table. Close my eyes and breathe nice and deep.

Hell Monkey's touch skims along the back of my neck, down my spine. His low voice rumbles in my ear. "This doesn't look great, Farshot."

"I'm shocked." The burning all over my back has gotten so bad I'm starting to shiver. "You mean, running straight-on at a plasma blade didn't end well for me? This is an outrage."

He chuckles, and it's like pouring a little mini sun into my chest. This is way more like how we should sound. Him and me. "We need to get you to the med bay. Can you walk?"

"Well, you're sure as hell not carrying me, so help me up here, hot stuff."

"Don't pull out any of those sexy nicknames." He drops a kiss on my temple and slips an arm carefully around my ribs. "You're in no shape to follow through."

I lean into him, using his big body to get my feet under me. Faye and Honor are searching the assassins, piling up their weapons next to them. Setter is still sitting in my captain's chair, watching them.

I grip tight to Hell Monkey's shoulder. "You two find anything? I mean, besides new toys for you to play with."

Faye looks up, baring dimly glowing teeth in a sharp smile. "Don't shortchange the toys. The toys are important."

"We should dispose of the bodies," Honor says. "They've got nothing else we can use."

Faye straightens, strapping one of the plasma blades to her back. "We drop them out the airlock, and then we get the hell out of here. These assholes were right on top of us minutes after we arrived. That's a bad sign."

Honor grunts. "We got bugged."

Faye's gold eyes sweep around the bridge and then give me the traditional up and down. "How long were you two here before we showed up?"

Hell Monkey shrugs. "Two days, maybe? We played hopscotch around the quadrant a bit."

Faye and Setter exchange a look, and he gets to his feet. "Go get yourself fixed up, Alyssa. We'll do a sweep of both the ships. Make sure we remove any tracking devices or implementations. What's your AI called again?"

I sneak a glance at Hell Monkey, who just shakes his head. "I mean . . . it's Nova, but you heard . . . You know what? Never mind. She'll be happy to help you, I'm sure."

Hell Monkey helps me limp off the bridge. We're a few steps away from the doors when we hear Setter call out, "Nova, I need you to conduct a sweep—" interrupted by an extremely irritated, "I DO NOT ANSWER TO YOU. YOU ARE NOT THE CAPTAIN HERE."

I burst out laughing, and I don't stop until we get to the med bay. Which may be more a testament to pain, blood loss, and adrenaline shock than anything else, but still. Feels good to laugh anyway.

Hell Monkey eases me up onto the table and I sit there, feet dangling over the side like a little kid. He goes over to the diagnostic-treatment cuff and starts getting it ready, nodding over at me. "You're gonna have to unzip the top of that jumpsuit, Farshot."

"Now who's talking sexy." I reach for the tab of the zipper and tug it all the way down to my waist. But when I move to peel the jumpsuit off my injured shoulder, I hiss with pain. I've bled through my clothes and it's dried, sticking to my skin.

Hell Monkey comes over immediately, a worry crease between his eyebrows as he eases his fingers between the jumpsuit and my shoulder, pulling it gently free. "This one's my bad, isn't it? You jumped in front of a deadly assassin for me. That's next-level stuff."

"Seemed the least I could do." I reach up with my free hand and brush at that worry crease with my thumb, trying to smooth it away. "I'm going to get you clear of this, Eliot. I promise."

His hands go still and his eyes find mine, and he looks at me for a long time before he finally says, "I know you will, Alyssa."

There's something underneath his words that's almost kind of . . . sad, I think? It definitely sounds sad. And I'm not really sure why he would be sad about me solemnly vowing to help put our lives back together, but he's already moving on. Like, literally, he's moved behind me to help pull the rest of my jumpsuit off my shoulders and I can't see his face anymore.

So I just nod. Sure. We're cool. Nothing else to say here.

I stretch out on the table on my stomach as carefully as possible, chin on my hands, looking around the room as Hell Monkey starts to fit the diagnostic-treatment cuff around my torso. I should've grabbed a tablet or had a vid queued up to play because I'm pretty sure I know how the "diagnostic" portion of this is going to go, which means it's going to hurt like a bitch when we get to the part where it starts deep-stitching up all my skin holes.

My eyes skim over stainless steel counters and cabinets, a rolling table with a few smaller cuffs used for different parts of the body, a movable vitals tower that we plug into people who need to be watched for a longer period of time, and a pile of droid parts heaped in a corner.

Not just random droid parts. The smashed-up remains of JR426, our resident mediabot that dedicatedly shadowed us all throughout the crownchase. Right up until the point where Edgar and his metal pet blasted it to pieces.

I'd told it to do what it did best: film what it was seeing. In this case, Edgar and his droid demanding the royal seal from Coy at blaster point.

After . . . all that happened, Hell Monkey had collected everything that was left of JR and piled it in here. I'd wondered about trying to put it back together, see if it was salvageable, but both H.M. and Drinn had said it was way past fixable by their estimations, so we'd set it aside. At that point, I'd still thought I'd have the quadrant on my side and my plan was going to go perfectly. No problem at all.

But now . . . If there was a way to see if any of its footage of Edgar and Coy facing off was left—anything at all—then damn. That's the kind of change-the-conversation evidence that could get a girl out of some traitorously hot water.

Hell Monkey touches my leg briefly. "It's moving to phase two. Brace yourself."

He means mentally, not literally, but to be honest, there's no good way to prepare for the process of being basically welded closed. It's not the worst kind of treatment this thing can dish out—that's probably more like when it snaps bones back together. Or when it's extracting something nasty out of somewhere even worse, like when that medbot fished that memory-worm out of the brain juice of Holder Ocktay—

My head jerks up and then I immediately regret it as the treatment cuff's restraints kick in and slam me, nose-first, back onto the table.

Ow. Rude.

"What the hell was that, Farshot?" H.M. circles around to the head of the table and crouches down so he's at eye level. "You know better than to wiggle when this thing is doing its business."

I rub at my slightly flattened nose. "I had an idea. A good one. Like brain-wave-in-the-shower level of good."

He raises an eyebrow. "That's a pretty high level. Hit me."

"We're going to turn the tables on Edgar Voles by broadcasting the footage of him killing Coy on every channel from here to the Outer Wastes."

"Alyssa . . ." He sighs. "That footage is gone. There's no way to recover it from what's left—"

I shake my head, cutting him off. "Not for you. Not for me. But neither of us is Holder Ocktay."

NINETEEN

STARDATE: 0.06.11 in the Year 4031, under the reign of the Empress Who Never Was, Nathalia Matilda Coyenne, long may she rest in glory
LOCATION: The Amos Belt, which takes one part planetoids littered with small settlements and mixes it with one part regular nebula storms that make traveling in it kind of a nightmare. 10/10 stars. Highly recommend.

SETTER ROY WANTS IT ON THE RECORD THAT HE thinks this is a terrible idea, so there you have it. It's officially noted. For "the record," whatever that means.

He's currently standing beside me with his arms crossed, trying to pretend like he's not stewing when he totally definitely is. He feels like we should've taken time to sound out more allies, see what kind of loyal network we were working with, but that would've required me to be quiet and patient even more than I have been in the last few days, and I'm just fresh out of bandwidth for that right now. It's already taken longer than I would've liked to get to where we are now. We'd had to do intensive scans for trackers—turns out the *Serendipity* was good, but Faye's ship had definitely gotten tagged, so we'd left the *Deadshot* back on Maeve.

And then there'd been the matter of digging up Holder's location. After the whole incident with the memory-worm, he went off the grid. Not just taking-it-easy-on-a-distant-beach-on-Nysus, but full-out middle-fingers-to-the-galaxy, taking-his-savings-and-disappearing kind of off the grid. Faye had to call in a few favors and make several very descriptive threats just to get us on the right track, and this is where it's led us.

The Amos Belt—a strip of asteroids and planetoids surrounded by a nebula cloud that sits in Orsion space. Lucky for me I've got an Orso on board.

"He's on a settlement called Cybsis," Faye says as she pulls up a three-dimensional projection on the strategic-ops table. "It's one of the biggest in the whole belt, with probably ten thousand people living in it."

"No terraforming or atmosphere generators." I lean close, studying the display from every angle. "It's just a huge complex of biodomes. How do they feel about visitors?"

There's a pause, and I look up just in time to catch Faye and Honor exchanging a glance. Then Honor says, "Getting in shouldn't be a problem."

Riiiiiight. I raise my eyebrows at her. "Is there something else that will be a problem that you want to tell us about?"

Faye pops her hip out, leaning against the edge of the table. "One of the biggest groups that calls Cybsis home is the Planetary Independence Movement, a political faction—"

"They prefer the term organization," Setter corrects.

"Fine." Faye sighs. "A political *organization* that has divisions all over the empire. They're anti-imperialists, and word is, Farshot, your boy Holder runs with them now."

"Calling them anti-imperialists is an oversimplification." Hell Monkey's voice comes out in a gruff rumble. He's standing next to me with his massive arms crossed over his chest. "A lot of them come from underrepresented planets and systems. They pool their resources so they can take care of each other and try to make their voices better heard."

I slide a look at him. "You're familiar with them?"

"Only from the outskirts. I remember my parents talking about them sometimes back on Homestead. Workers trying to make it off-planet to join up with them and that kind of thing." He shrugs. "I don't have any real connections, though."

Fair enough. That does make things a little bit trickier. But I can handle tricky. Tricky is my game.

"Okay. This is still okay. Actually, it could be exactly what we need. I mean, Setter, you were just going on about how we need allies—"

"This is not quite what I had in mind." Setter paces, pinching at the bridge of his nose like he's getting a headache. "Asking them to help you repair your mediabot is one thing. Asking them to make an alliance with us is completely another. There is no way they will agree to that."

"Why not?" I throw my arms wide. "They don't like the emperor? Neither do we! It's a great match."

Hell Monkey shakes his head. "You're still prime family heirs. And the only reason why you're giving them the time of day is because you need something from them. You're gonna be at a major disadvantage, Alyssa."

Faye waves a hand at the display, closing it down. "The fact that the Orsos have a long-standing 'live and let live' policy with the Amos Belt means they've agreed to let us land and they're sending someone to talk. After that, it'll be up to you, Farshot, to be your most charming self and convince them to go all-in."

Nova's voice cuts across the bridge. "WE'RE APPROACHING LANDING COORDINATES. IN CASE YOU CARE ABOUT THAT AT ALL."

I push off the table, moving over to the navcomm. "I do care, Nova, thank you. Your hard work is appreciated."

"I AM NOT INTERESTED IN BEING PATRONIZED."

"Will it make you feel better if I let you take her down?"

There's a beat as I slip into the captain's chair and reach for the manual controls, and then: "FINE. BUT ONLY BECAUSE I'LL DO A BETTER JOB THAN YOU."

The *Serendipity* hums as Nova brings her smoothly down to the planetoid surface and through the retracted roof of Cybsis's docking dome. As soon as the landing gear clanks into position on the platform below us, I'm up and out of my seat, heading for the exit.

"Gear up and meet by the bay doors. I don't want to keep anyone waiting. And no weapons, okay? We're playing this ultra nice."

Honor gives me a solid side-eye as she strides past me. "And if they don't play nice back?"

"We'll improvise. It'll be fine!" I call after their backs as they all troop down the corridor. "This is gonna be fine!"

It's true if you shout it, right? Right. That's definitely how it works.

We gather in the cargo bay and walk together down the aft ramp into a huge domed space with a transparent geodesic ceiling hundreds of meters above our heads that lets in the diffused blue-green light of the nebula clouds above. A handful of other ships are parked nearby, one or two big enough to be personnel transports, but the rest smaller than the *Serendipity*. That's about all we get to see of this place for the moment, though, because there's well over a dozen folks ringing the bottom of the ramp, waiting for us.

"The welcoming committee," Setter murmurs to my right.

"How welcoming are we talking here?" I ask, keeping my gaze forward. "Like, welcoming with pastries? Or welcoming with blasters?"

Setter sweeps his eyes across the crowd, his irises cycling through a rainbow of colors as he uses those handy axeeli empath powers to get a read on the room. Then he shrugs. "Dislike. Distrust. Some a little stronger than others. But nothing stronger than that. Yet."

"Love that optimism, Setter. Never lose that sunshine."

A Chu'ran steps out from the group as we near the bottom. Extremely tall, with the deep-violet skin color common to Chu'ra's northeastern continent and long bronze hair braided back from their face. I move forward to meet them and do my best version of a Chu'ran greeting, complete with a respectful inquiry as to their correct pronouns. None of the Chu'ran dialects include gendered language—they don't even have gender categories, they just see every individual as their own unique gender—so it's best to ask right up front what a Chu'ran is comfortable with when you're gonna be using a more binary language to communicate.

The Chu'ran laughs a little. "Not bad, crownchaser. That was almost serviceable. You may call me Sharva, and your Imperial 'they' will be fine for now. I'll let you know if that changes." They look us over one by one, their profile absolutely striking even in the dusky light. "This is quite the crew to end up on our doorstep. I won't lie that we mainly let you land out of sheer curiosity. What in all the galaxy brings a Faroshti to Cybsis?"

I shake my head, scanning the crowd that surrounds us. "I'm not coming here as a Faroshti. I'm just looking for Holder Ocktay— oh, there he is! Hey, Holder!" I wave enthusiastically at a short, grumpy-looking half-otari who sighs heavily as soon as I spot him. "I need a favor," I add as I turn back to Sharva, "and he kinda owes me one."

Sharva snorts, looking down their nose at me—which is quite a distance seeing as how I don't even reach their shoulder. "Everywhere you go, you go as a Faroshti. You don't get to take prime family status on and off. It's not a jacket. What is it that you want of Holder?"

Hell Monkey steps forward and swings a netted bag of droid parts onto the ground between us. "Our mediabot broke. We're hoping he can fix it."

Sharva looks at the parts, then at Hell Monkey, then at me. Their eyes are dark gray and sharp, but not cold. "What is it you *really* want?"

Something about the way they ask strips off all the pleasantries I'd put on. The anger surges hot underneath my skin, pushing the truth out with it.

"I want to strip Edgar Voles of the throne. I want to *make him pay* for hurting my uncle and murdering my best friend. And he will too. One way or another."

Sharva makes a little noise in the back of their throat. "Now *that* I understand. Holder?"

Holder shuffles forward, rubbing at the ridges of quartzite along his brow. "She did bail me out of that memory-worm business a few years back. I owe her. And . . ." He frowns down at the parts that used to be JR426. "No way they're gonna fix that mess without me."

Sharva looks back at me. "Holder wants to help you—that's fine. That's his business. But asking us to play host to three prime family heirs while he fixes your bot is a big request from us, no matter who your enemies are."

I can hear it in their voice—an opening for negotiations. "That's fair. We're a bit of a hot commodity right now. What can we do to make it more worth your while?"

They cross their arms over their chest, leveling a hard look at me, Setter, and Faye in turn. "We'll do this, help you get your revenge, depose Edgar Voles as emperor, and in return, when you take the throne, you'll dissolve the empire."

TWENTY

THERE'S NOTHING BUT SILENCE FOR SEVERAL LONG
seconds. Someone off to my left stifles a cough, and even that
sounds so loud in the heavy air.

"You . . ." Setter's voice sounds a little rough. Like it's been days
since he's used it instead of maybe two minutes. "I'm sorry, you
want us to dissolve the *entire* empire?"

Sharva shrugs. "You asked what we wanted. I'm telling you."

"We did. We did ask. That's on us." I glance over at Setter,
who mostly just looks stunned, and Faye, who's staring at Sharva
through sharp, narrowed eyes, sizing them up. "It's just that . . .
that might be a bit above our pay grade to offer. . . ."

"Why?" Sharva waves a hand at us. "You depose the current
asshole on the throne. One of you becomes the next asshole on
the throne, yes? You two"—they point to Setter and Faye—"are
prime family heirs after all. And you?" Their cool eyes settle on
me. "You're just about the only Faroshti left. With your uncle in
prison, I think that makes you the primor of your family at this
point."

All the blood drains from my head very quickly, and I feel a
little dizzy.

Primor.

Primor Alyssa Farshot or Alyssa Faroshti or Whatever the Hell I'm Supposed to Call Myself. Is that actually who I am now? Is that a real thing? I think I might need to sit down. I look over at Hell Monkey, but he's staring at his boots again, chin tucked in like he wishes he could disappear inside his own enormous shoulders.

Sharva reaches inside their overcoat and pulls out a particularly chunky-looking tablet with a biometric scanner and the kind of reinforced casing meant to survive a direct explosion. They hold it out toward me expectantly.

"You have an Oath Taker." I'm careful not to touch it. Let's just say that Oath Takers are an especially intense way of securing a promise from someone. "Looks like an older model, though."

"It still works perfectly." The corners of their mouth twist upward. "You help us, primor, we help you."

Faye slides up next to me and tilts her chin toward Sharva. She's probably the only one of us that could go stare-to-stare with them, even though she's still a dozen centimeters shorter.

"The empire has been around for centuries. You can't just cut ties and turn a thousand and one planets loose. There'd be chaos."

Sharva shrugs, unfazed. "I gave you the what; it's up to you to figure out the how. Besides, 'this is how it's always been done' isn't a good enough reason to keep doing it."

Faye opens her mouth to respond, but I put a hand on her arm before she can speak.

"Hey, Sharva, you don't mind if we discuss the absolutely quadrant-altering ultimatum you just dropped on us, do you? Just a quick sec."

Dragging Faye behind me, I herd everyone back up the ramp and into the cargo bay, dropping heavily onto a crate as soon as we're safely back inside the shadows of the ship.

I think that makes you the primor of your family at this point.

I cover my face with both hands. Maybe if I stay like this long enough, this whole scene will disappear.

"Are we seriously considering this?" Faye's voice comes from over by the wall. "Agreeing to 'dissolve the empire'—whatever that means—just for a place to hide out for a few days?"

"We don't actually know how long it'll take to fix JR," says Hell Monkey. He stands right behind me, close enough that I can feel the warmth of him along my back. "And I don't know if you've been tracking the feeds lately, but there aren't a lot of other safe harbors out there right now."

"The Orsion citadels—"

Hell Monkey cuts her off. "Overrun with Edgar's shiny new murder droids. Just like every other system in the empire."

"Why don't we just lie?" Faye says. "We tell them we're gonna do it, and then we just don't."

"Apart from the ethical considerations of that decision"—Setter sounds like he's also sitting on a crate, somewhere over on my right—"Sharva has an Oath Taker. And if you fail to follow through on a pledge made on one of those, it will go extremely poorly for you."

"How poorly are we talking here?" Honor asks.

"Pretty fucking poorly." I drop my hands from my face with a heavy sigh. "Oath Takers inject a biological agent into the person making the oath. If you try to do take-backsies, the holder of the tablet can initiate a sequence that turns that bio agent into a painful, slow-moving necrotic disease that eats up all your organs."

Honor raises her green-tinted eyebrows. "That sounds intense. And possibly illegal."

"It's both," says Setter darkly.

I scrape my hair back from my face, threading my fingers together at the back of my head. Part of my brain—the dodge-run-avoid part—is spinning so fast, trying to analyze ways we could get out of this or around it or whatever will let us avoid the most responsibility.

But there's another part. The part that sat in the kingship planetarium with Uncle Atar as he talked about making something new, something amazing. The part that stood alone in the dark when I was eleven years old, watching a hologram of my mother's final public speech before she died. Listening to her words again and again until they were written on the insides of my skull.

"*. . . a new shape for our great empire! One that hears and recognizes every voice, every person, without regard for family name! One that doesn't stay mired in what it is, but what it could be!*"

"What happens after all of this?" My voice cuts abruptly across the cargo bay as I drop my hands into my lap and look at each of them in turn. "Everyone but H.M. joined me just to get back at the people who killed Coy. Who killed Owyn. But what happens after that? Seriously." I wait, but the only response I get is silence. "There's gonna be an empty throne. And all our families are gonna have different ideas about who should sit in it."

Setter's gaze is cool, neutral blue as he analyzes me. "You think no one should sit in it."

"I thought we just came here to fix a droid," Faye says, scowling at me. "Not sign on to some kind of revolution."

I take her stare and send it right back at her. "Who says we can't do both? This group, this movement, wants to give voice and power to people in the empire who don't have it. Pretty good goal to have, actually. And our objection is . . . what? That that's not how we usually do things? Honestly, the way we usually do things is pretty messed up."

Faye raises her eyebrow and crosses her arms. Unconvinced. But she's still listening. I'll take that mixed success.

"Setter," I say, swinging around to face him. "You remember how Chu'ra became part of the empire, right?"

He straightens at the question, like I'm a tutor giving him a quiz that he's dead set on acing. "It was conquered territory, claimed by Emperor Kai Mega seven hundred and seventy-six years ago."

"And it's been prone to conflict ever since. Why?"

"It was heavily settled by non-natives after that." His expression pulls into a frown. "They consolidated a lot of the power and still hold most of it."

"Exactly." I turn back to Faye, squaring up to her skeptical face. "Nobody asked them if they ever wanted to be a part of all this. Not ol' Kai centuries ago and not anytime since. And that's just one planet. One story. How many more are like that out there? Sharva is asking us to help them fix it. And the more I think about it, the more it seems like a pretty reasonable request, actually."

Faye holds my gaze for several long seconds, and I watch the edges of her expression soften just a little. She casts a look over at Honor, who shrugs, and then she sighs, letting her arms fall to her sides.

"So all of us just . . . what? Give up on the crown and the seal and all of it? I gotta be honest, Alyssa, I went into the crownchase to win. To be an empress and have the whole galaxy at my feet."

"So did I," Setter admits with a shrug.

"So did Coy! So did Owyn! And look where that got them!" I'm up on my feet now, pacing a tight pattern around the cargo bay. "Our parents fought a war for twenty-five years, millions of people died, all over whose ass would go in one chair. Are we gonna do that? Are we gonna let our families do that and drag a thousand and one planets with them again and again and again? At what point do we just say, 'No, we're not doing it anymore,' and sign on to a cause that has a real chance of changing things for the better?"

My pulse pounds in my ears as I finish speaking, and my cheeks are flushed and hot. Gods, my whole face is probably bright purple. I'm not sure how I expected that conversation to go, but I'm almost positive I didn't expect to wind up making an impassioned speech for radical political change when I got out of bed this morning.

Faye and Honor move over to Setter, and all three of them put their heads together, probably talking about how they're going to have to knock me out and steal my ship because Farshot has totally lost it. I plop back down on my only true throne—my trusty cargo crate—and Hell Monkey crouches down next to me.

"That was quite a speech, Farshot," he says quietly.

He's looking straight into my eyes, and I can read all the emotions across his face. Pride. Determination. Some kind of bittersweet sadness. Love.

I like that face. A whole hell of a lot.

I reach for his hand, tracing my fingers along his knuckles. "If you thought the water was deep at the start of this mess, it's only going to get deeper and rougher from here. You still in?"

Before he can answer, Faye steps toward me, hands on her hips. "Okay, Farshot. You wanna shackle yourself to an Oath Taker for this, we'll back your play. For now anyway."

Setter gets to his feet, his irises saturating with a deep, focused green. "I hope you know what you're doing, Alyssa. The odds that you'll be able to deliver on a promise this big—"

I wave his words away. "Don't tell me the odds. Let's just handle this situation first. Go make some new allies, fix a droid, and do whatever it takes to shove a boot up Edgar's ass. After that . . . we'll figure it out." I turn to Hell Monkey, who's still quietly watching me. "Right?"

H.M. leans into me, his lips and breath brushing along my ear and neck as he murmurs, "Waves aren't too rough for me yet, Far-shot. Not for you." Then he pulls me onto my feet and nods at the others. "Let's go finish this."

Sharva waits for us at the bottom of the aft ramp, still holding the Oath Taker, their expression cool and regal as we tromp down to them.

"What's your verdict, then, Alyssa Faroshti?"

I take a deep breath as I step out in front of the others. "Okay, Sharva. We're in."

I don't think they were really expecting us to agree, because they can't manage to hold on to their neutral expression. Their eyebrows shoot up. Their eyes widen. And they seem a little lost for words, so I jump in instead.

"To be absolutely, one hundred percent, perfectly truthful? It's probably gonna be tougher to pull off than upstreaming a meteor in a first-generation liftship. And we don't even have a solid plan on how to go about it. But hey . . ." I reach out and smack my whole hand flat against the biometric scanner on the Oath Taker. "Improvisation is my specialty."

The tablet reads my handprint, my name and ID flashing across the screen. Then a bright flash, a sharp sting around my right wrist, and all that's left is a tattooed bracelet of encoded symbols in deep-green ink embedded into my skin.

Sharva tucks the tablet back into their overcoat and spreads their arms wide. "Well, then. Welcome to Cybsis."

KINGSHIP ENTERS OPEN SPACE FOR FIRST TIME IN ALMOST TWO DECADES

After years anchored on Apex, a new, more aggressive-looking kingship takes to the stars

PUBLIC PROTESTS AGAINST EMPEROR GROW

Gamnae becomes the latest of many planets where demonstrators are protesting the security initiative and the legitimacy of the emperor's rule

KINGSHIP REJECTS ORSION ARGUMENT FOR AUTONOMY OF THE HISTORICALLY INDEPENDENT AMOS BELT

Imperial officials claim that Emperor Voles's "Peace through Strength" initiative can only be successful if applied equally throughout the empire

PLANET LEADERS ON TEAR OUSTED

Waves of public disapproval over the years finally exploded yesterday, resulting in the planetary chancellor and their counselors being forcibly removed from office

THE KINGSHIP, SUBLIGHT SPEED, NEAR THE GAMNAE SYSTEM

EDGAR HAS BEEN ON THE BRIDGE, WORKING FEVER-
ishly, for hours when NL7 finds him.

"Edgar Voles, this is your seventh night with inadequate sleep."
He can hear the delicate tick-tick of its feet behind him where he
stands at the central controls. Still in the mediabot casing. He keeps
meaning to correct that—it's important he do it himself and not
delegate it to some kingship tech—but it keeps getting lost in the
shuffle of his thoughts.

"I tried," he tells it. "I really did. But no one warned me how
difficult it would be to rest with this." He taps his chest where the
royal seal sank inside him . . . how long ago was it? A week and
a half? It seems like longer. Like forever. And still he struggles to
cope with the constant input of information streaming through his
body. The weighty presence of the previous emperors is what both-
ers him most. It's there even in the darkest hours of the night. Their
thoughts. Their triumphs. Their ambitions. Their regrets.

He's tried to search archives and knowledge banks to see if
there's any evidence of his predecessors feeling likewise plagued,
haunted, unable to rest.

But if they did, any record of it is lost. There's no mention of it
he can find.

It's just you, says a voice in his brain that sounds a lot like his father. *Because you don't really belong here. You stole the throne.*

"No! That's not true."

"What is not true, Edgar Voles?"

Edgar turns to look at NL7, blinking as he reorients himself. He hadn't intended to speak aloud. But luckily no one else is here save for them. "I belong here, NL7."

Its head twitches to the side. "You are the emperor, according to the law. And the emperor rightfully belongs on the kingship. That is clear."

"It's not enough for it to just be the law. I want everyone to know it." He looks back to the command table and the projection above, the networking system he's been losing sleep over. He gestures to it. "What do you think, NL7? I value your opinion."

NL7 shifts a little, stepping around the table to scan the display from multiple directions. "You are attempting to create a broader neural link with your security forces."

"Not attempting. Doing. I'm doing it right now. It's almost ready." He really has his predecessors to thank for this. Being linked to all of them gave birth to this concept that he could take this a step further, that he could connect the Voles security droids and AI implementations across the empire into this royal seal. He could control all of them with a thought instead of having to rely on antiquated communication channels to convey his wishes.

"Wythe and I were discussing the recent protests against the crown," Edgar adds as the android circles the space. "He pointed out that an emperor should be like a father to children, a firm, disciplining hand. I rather liked that. And what better way to do it than to be able to instantaneously respond to their needs? Or correct their missteps?"

NL7 draws near to his side again. "We would advise against this, Edgar Voles. There are no safety protocols in place for a system like this. You could damage yourself. And intense consolidation of power in one person with no delegation—"

"Your concerns are noted," Edgar says sharply, cutting it off. He'd thought if anyone would understand what he was trying to do . . .

"Leave me." He turns his back to the android as it clicks its way back to the lift and ascends into the throne room. Only when NL7 is gone is he able to clear his mind to finish his work.

And then take the neural link live.

Personal log of Atar Faroshti, recorded on 0.08.02.4013

I'D NEVER THOUGHT MUCH ABOUT THE ROYAL SEAL because I'd never imagined being the one who would absorb it. Even when Saya and I were children and played kingship, I often was content to let her play the part of empress.

But it is no game anymore.

I accepted the seal on the throne of the kingship sixteen hours ago. It was the strangest experience, and though I know it's been a part of the crowning as emperor for centuries now, that did not make it less terrifying. To see what is essentially an AI no bigger than my hand fuse into my body in a symbiotic relationship that will last the rest of my life.

Very strange.

I understand that, for some, it can be a disorienting, mind-bending experience once the connection takes hold. To have so much information flowing into and out of your head, as well as the presence of all our imperial history. It would be understandably overwhelming. While I have yet to feel any different, Charles has been watching me very carefully, with no less than an army of doctors and experts standing by. He has been obsessively researching the process for weeks now, and if anyone can ensure I complete my connection to the kingship smoothly, it would be him, of course.

TWENTY-ONE

STARDATE: 0.06.15 in the Year 4031, under the reign of the Empress Who Never Was, Nathalia Matilda Coyenne, long may she rest in glory

LOCATION: Getting nice and cozy with our brand-new revolutionary buddies who officially hold my life in their hands

As far as hosts go, Sharva is a pretty good one. I mean, aside from that part where you have to swear your life, health, and safety to a promise that you may or may not be able to keep. If you can get past that whole initial deal, it's not such a bad situation.

Sharva's home is a dome-shaped construction, with a basement underneath it, so it's bigger on the inside. Which is good because it looks like they're unfortunately stuck with me and H.M. until Holder can cobble together JR's dismantled bot parts.

I'd tried to ask Holder how long it might take, and he'd growled at me. And when I'd pointed out that wasn't very polite, he'd waved his crimping pliers in my face and barked, "That's like dropping an ass-load of ship parts in your lap and asking you when you'll be able to fly it! Leave me alone and let me work!"

So I have. Definitely. I mean, I've *maybe* poked my head in there four or five times over the past few days to check on his progress, but honestly, that's barely anything at all. Especially considering there isn't much else for me to do but bother him. My face has gotten pretty recognizable lately, and as much as the people of Cybsis aren't empire fans, it's too much to risk that absolutely all of them would be able to keep their mouths shut about Imperial Traitor Alyssa Farshot turning up, not when there are thousands of credits of reward on the line. So I'm trying to stay inside, lie low, and not cause any trouble. None of which are my strong suits.

I kill time by scrolling the media feeds on repeat, hoping for news of Charlie that never comes. I read and reread any articles about protests against Edgar with a kind of vicious delight. I wait for communications from Faye, Honor, and Setter, who hitched a ride to the nearby Orsion citadel Viøbær not long after we landed. Faye wants to get back in touch with her black market contacts, and Setter has his own personal and political connections to try and leverage. He thinks the protests in the media are a good sign and an opportunity to "bring in more allies" and "build some momentum."

Build away, I told him, so that's what they're trying to do while Hell Monkey and I wait.

Sometimes I try to strike up a conversation with Nova, but she's been extra grumpy ever since Hell Monkey extracted her from the *Serendipity* and loaded her into a data shell connected to my wristband. Since we don't know for sure how long we'll be parked here, he figured he'd remove the AI and make the ship substantially harder to steal or strip data from. The AI herself, though, wasn't too thrilled about it and is not shy about loudly declaring, "IF I HAD BEEN MEANT TO BE ATTACHED TO THIS RUDIMENTARY DEVICE, I WOULD HAVE BEEN THERE IN THE FIRST PLACE," whenever there's an opening.

Still and all, it's not a bad setup. Especially for an engineer and a ship jockey who aren't usually very good at sitting still. Plus, added bonus, Sharva turns out to be a damn talented cook.

Which is why, of course, things all go to hell on our third evening here.

There's urgent banging on Sharva's door as we're helping them clean up dinner, and when they go to open it, two of their crew tumble inside, looking spooked.

"Ships incoming, Sharva," one of them—Ayla—says. "Imperial ships."

Sharva's face pales, just a little. "Imperial ships? Why? What for?"

Ayla shakes her head. "I don't know, but they don't look diplomatic."

"It's Edgar's new 'security initiative,'" I put in. Look at that—all my obsessing over the media headlines was useful after all. Yay. "It's been all over the feeds. Looks like he won't be happy until every last centimeter of the quadrant is covered in his droids."

The other messenger—Karn—jabs a finger at me. "Only because you're here. If we turn you in, I bet we can get those things to leave."

Sharva pulls themself up to their full height and stares down at him. "You are not a ridiculous person, Karn. Don't fall for ridiculous lies. Those droids are not here because of one girl. This one girl is just a flimsy excuse to deploy those droids."

Karn puts his jabby finger away, backing down.

"What should we do?" Ayla asks. "They already put down on the surface. They're probably already forcing their way in through an airlock seal."

Sharva is silent for a moment, thinking. "We need more of an idea what we're up against." They slide a look at me. "You look like you could use a walk, Alyssa Faroshti."

I stuff my hands into the pockets of my jumpsuit to hide the fact that I'm digging my nails into my palms. "You know me. I'm always ready to get some fresh air."

They gesture for us to follow them and head down to the basement, Hell Monkey behind them. I switch Nova to visual feedback only, no audio, as I follow on their heels. Sharva steps carefully around the makeshift beds H.M. and I made and shoulders open a door to what looks like a closet full of old survival suits.

That is, until they shove aside the suits and point to a release latch hidden in a dark corner.

"This'll take us into Cybsis's subterranean access tunnels. It's pressurized in there, but the air isn't quite breathable, so grab a survival suit and gear up."

Like you need to ask us twice. We manage to sort out two of Sharva's collection that'll serve us okay, and as soon as all three of us are sealed in, they pop the latch and we squeeze through the opening into the tunnels. They're narrow, but tall, well lit, and

161

well maintained, carved with care into the black vesicular rock. Sharva takes us down several corridors and turns, twisting around beneath the settlement, until finally coming to a stop at a blank section of wall. They reach up into a crevice of the ceiling way too high for my short self and then—pop—a hidden door slides open, with a twisting staircase just beyond.

Sharva puts a finger up for silence and leads us through the door, sealing it behind us. The stairs take us up into a little shopfront that doesn't look like it's been doing any shopping or fronting for several years now. It's got windows facing this dome's main street, though, which is exactly what I need. I retract my helmet and get low, practically crawling over there so I can peek outside.

Edgar's security droids are already everywhere. Dozens and dozens of them. Tromping down the street, looming over clusters of residents, filtering down side roads and alleys.

Godsdammit.

How the hell does he have so many? Voles Enterprises must be cranking them out like they're nuts and bolts.

One of them passes by close to the window, and I duck down deeper into the shadows. They look like they're moving so much smoother than they did on the kingship, coordinating with perfect synchronicity.

I watch as one moves to the middle of the street, its blasters folding into compartments in its arms and legs as it holds its hands up, mimicking a very I *come in peace* gesture.

"Do not fear, people of Cybsis. I am here for your protection."

My stomach bottoms out, and I freeze, staring over at Hell Monkey, whose face looks as horrified as mine probably does.

"Is that . . . ," he whispers. "Is that *Edgar's* voice?"

"You will no longer be ruled by some cold, distant figurehead," the Droid-That-Sounds-Like-Edgar goes on. "Wherever they go, I go, too. I am here with you, watching over you. Where there is strength, there is peace."

Sharva growls in the back of their throat. "Can he really do that?"

"Honestly? No idea." I try to get a better angle on the droid speaking, but it's tough to do without poking my whole head up over the sill. "The seal and the kingship are all kind of next-level tech. No emperor has done anything like this before."

"But that doesn't mean they can't," Hell Monkey adds.

My wristband buzzes, and I look down to see a communication from Nova.

PICKING UP A NEW SHIP SIGNATURE. IDENTICAL TO THE TWO THAT CAME TO THAT ROCKY MOON AND TRIED TO KILL YOU.

My heart hits the back of my throat and sticks there, making it tough to breathe, tough to swallow. I type a response to Nova, asking her to access the biodome sensors and pull up a visual of the incoming ship.

. . . and there it is. Small, vicious, and sleek. Covered in a mirrormask that would be almost impossible to see without Nova highlighting the edges of it.

MAKE SURE TO PUT ME BACK IN THE *SERENDIPITY* BEFORE YOU DIE.

Fantastic.

TWENTY-TWO

I WATCH ON MY TINY WRISTBAND SCREEN AS NOVA tracks the assassin ship coming closer. It looks like it's skimming low, heading toward the docking dome.

Hell Monkey leans close so he can get a better look at what I'm seeing. "They're going for the ship, I bet. Maybe to cripple it. Or to track us from it."

"Is neither an option? I vote neither. I don't want them anywhere near my ship. Hell, I don't want them to get inside the domes at all."

Sharva tears their eyes away from the murder droids marching around outside the window. "What are you two talking about? What is going on?"

"Bad guys." I angle my wristband so they can see. "Incoming bad guys."

Sharva *hmphs* as they watch the sensor footage. "Worse bad guys than the ones we already have?"

Hell Monkey shrugs. "We don't like to make value judgments."

I scrub at my eyes with my gloved fingers. "Why do these jack-offs keep coming? I thought it was just a crownchase thing, but they do not let up."

Hell Monkey nudges me with his shoulder. "Neither do we. So let's go show their asses the door."

I take a deep breath, steadying myself, and then I look over at Sharva. "Turns out there is definitely one fight I can recommend we pick today."

Sharva sets their jaw. "Then let's figure out how to win it."

The cramped metal access lift rattles to a stop, and I check the seal on my suit helmet one more time before I pull open the door.

My grav boots make a thunk as I step out onto the outer shell of the docking biodome. Above me the sky is swirling turquoise nebula clouds. Below me, nothing but transparent panels of interlocking triangles and a long drop to the ground below if any of those panels felt like randomly giving out underneath me. I mean, logically, that's pretty unlikely, but not-so-logically, that would definitely be the kind of day I'm having.

Nova estimates that the assassin ship came down on the far eastern side of the docking dome. I'm betting they're going to try to pull something sneaky and cut into the dome wall, so Hell Monkey and I each took an access lift up to the top to try to surprise them from above. I step off the lift platform, hoofing it up the dome's incline, but also trying not to make too much noise. Which is a hell of a challenge in grav boots, let me tell you. I've got sweat running down my back and beading at my temples by the time I make it over the rise and get eyes on the situation below.

There's the ship. Pretty impossible to make out unless you know what you're looking for, and even then I almost have to look at it sideways. Way down on the ground, two hooded figures are mounting something on the dome wall that looks like an illegal docking seal.

Movement from the corner of my eye. Hell Monkey getting into position. Sharva got us geared up as best as they possibly could before we came out: reinforced grav boots, pressurized grappling hooks, and two blasters. And a whole lot of fingers-crossed-good-luck.

Hell Monkey lines up his shot. I line up mine. And then I drop the signal, and we pepper the whole area below with blaster fire.

I think I see one shot land, maybe two, before those two bastards disappear.

Hell Monkey and I move toward each other, blasters up, spinning as we go to try and keep eyes all around us.

But we still don't catch it in time. They appear right between us, hoods shadowing the gray skin stretched taut over their empty skulls. One of them launches itself at Hell Monkey. The other strikes out at me before I can react and I catch its fist in my chest so hard that my grav boots are the only thing keeping me on my feet. As I try to push myself up, it lands a kick into my side that I just know is gonna leave a bruise. Son of a bitch. I bring my blaster up, but it swipes my hand away and reaches for the massive plasma blade strapped across its back. It looks geared up and ready for some sweet hand-to-hand action.

Too bad we're not playing that game today.

I swipe a message to Hell Monkey and Sharva: NOW.

Hell Monkey and I power off our grav boots and push off the biodome roof just as the geodesic frame lights up with blue-white electricity. The current connects in a violent net, trapping the two assassins inside, their bodies seizing up as it arcs through them like lightning.

When it finally shuts off, they go limp and then start to drift away.

I hold out an arm to Hell Monkey, fumbling for the pressurized grappling hook on my belt. As soon as he grabs on, I aim and fire, feeling it connect deep into the ground beside the dome. I press the retract button, holding on tight as the mechanism yanks us back down onto the planetoid's surface. We collapse in a not-particularly-graceful heap, but we can get our grav boots underneath us again and that's all that matters.

I sit up, pulling Hell Monkey with me. "You good?"

He leans forward, knocking his helmet gently into mine. "All good, Farshot."

Seventy meters away, I hear a whine as the engines on the assassin ship heat up like it's preparing to take off. An autopilot mechanism. Maybe even one that takes it back to its homeworld or wherever these assholes are coming from.

Somewhere that might have answers. About why they killed Owyn. About who keeps sending them.

And if it turns out to be Edgar? Well, then, damn. Wouldn't that be lucky.

I catch Hell Monkey's eye. He starts shaking his head, like he can already see what I'm planning, but that doesn't stop me.

"Stay on Holder's ass. Get that mediabot fixed. I'll be right back."

And then I'm on my feet, sprinting toward the ship at full tilt.

I think I hear Hell Monkey yell my name, but it's hard to hear anything over my own pulse, my own breathing, the thud of my grav boots.

I catch the edge of the bay door just as it starts to close and use everything I've got left in my body to haul myself over the edge and roll all the way inside.

The ship vibrates as it lifts off the ground. And then the bay door shuts with a thud, sealing me inside.

TWENTY-THREE

I LIE STILL ON THE COLD METAL FLOOR UNTIL THE
ship clears the planetoid, and then I slowly get to my feet. It's a very
small vessel, probably not meant for more than two individuals. No
quarters, no galley. Just this little, angular cargo bay I'm standing
in, a short ladder, and the bridge beyond.

The outskirts of the Amos Belt fall away and the black of the universe wraps around us, making the inside of the ship even darker than
it was before. The only lights are those from the navcomm above.

"Nova?" I whisper. "You with me?"

There's a buzz against my skin as her response blasts across my
wristband screen.

**YOU FORCED ME INTO THIS PERSONAL DEVICE. WHERE
ELSE WOULD I POSSIBLY BE?**

"Hey, I didn't want to assume. But since you're around, can you
give me a quick scan?"

It only takes a fraction of a second for her to respond.

**NO OTHER SIGNS OF BIOLOGICAL LIFE FORMS ON
BOARD. AIR IS, UNFORTUNATELY, OXYGENATED AND NON-
TOXIC.**

I snort. "Don't act like you don't like me, Nova."

I pop my survival suit helmet off—it was getting extra warm and humid inside that thing after all the running and sweating I did—and crawl up the ladder onto the compact bridge. Two swiveling bucket seats, a navcomm with full dashboard controls, and three long, thin windows along the prow in front. I'm leaning forward to try to analyze the controls and the course we're on when a cool, distant voice resonates throughout the ship.

"Unidentified life form detected on board."

The onboard AI. Shit.

"Altering course trajectory."

Double shit. No way that can be good. I rip off my gloves and plop down in a seat, trying to work the console, but the AI's locked me out and I don't know enough about this system to find a back door. The only thing I'm able to do is see where this altered course trajectory is taking us.

Right into the heart of a nearby neutron star.

Cool. Great. Awesome.

Don't panic, Farshot. You just need to stay calm and find a fix before you wind up dropped into the middle of a white-hot, extra-dense mass of burning atomic reactions. No problem.

DO I NEED TO POINT OUT THAT YOU ARE INCAPABLE OF SURVIVING CONTACT WITH A NEUTRON STAR? OR DO YOU HAVE SUFFICIENT INTELLIGENCE TO WORK THAT OUT YOURSELF?

Nova . . . I look down at the data shell wrapped around my wristband and then back at the navcomm. I mean, just because I can't get around the AI lockdown doesn't mean she couldn't. . . . I drop to the floor and shimmy underneath the navcomm, ripping off panel after panel so I can get a good look at the insides of this thing and try to find—

—there. A data port.

"Nova, you're getting your wish." I yank the data shell off my wristband and stick it into the exposed port. "You're going back inside a ship now."

Her voice suddenly blasts across the bridge. I kinda forgot how loud she could be. "YOU PLACED ME INSIDE THIS SUBPAR SYSTEM—"

"Hostile AI detected."

"—WHERE THERE IS ANOTHER AI ALREADY FUNCTION-ING—"

"Hostile AI detected."

"—AND IT IS VERY ANNOYING."

"Come on, Nova," I call out. "Are you or are you not the best AI ever? Because I kind of thought you were."

"Hostile AI detected."

"I AM OBVIOUSLY FAR SUPERIOR IN ANY NUMBER OF WAYS."

I crawl back up into the bucket seat. The lights on the navcomm are going wild, flashing and flickering in quick succession.

"Look, I think you're great," I say to the empty air all around me. "But maybe I'm biased, y'know? Maybe you're not strong enough to take over from the basic-as-hell, standard-issue AI they've got installed on this trash heap."

"THAT IS EXTREMELY INCORRECT."

"Hostile AI detected."

"IT IS CLEARLY OUTMATCHED."

"Hostile AI detected."

"Is it, though? I don't know, Nova. . . ."

The dashboard strobes with hyper-bright light. I can't tell what's happening on it. I can't even look at it anymore—I have to shut my eyes against the frantic glare. All I can do is hold on tight and hope that my bratty AI is the best bratty AI.

Come on, Nova.

The lights get even brighter. I can see it even with my eyelids glued shut, and I swivel away, covering my face.

Come on, Nova. . . .

The bridge goes dead-dark.

I pull my hands away and slowly turn around. The navcomm is blank. No lights on any of its dashboards. I swipe my fingertips across the nearest one, trying to provoke a response.

Nothing.

". . . Nova?" My voice echoes around the dark and quiet bridge, and I feel anxiety flood my chest in a hot wave. Oh gods. What if I just made a huge mistake? What if I lost Nova? What if she just got consumed by some random AI that's now going to fly me into the crushing, searing heart of a star? Or what if I set two AIs against each other and they both got destroyed and now I'm stuck on this horrible assassin ship with no way home and oxygen slowly running out?

This is definitely one of those situations people are always

telling me about where I should've thought through the consequences first, huh?

One lone light suddenly pops up on the navcomm. And then
another. And another. And suddenly all the consoles are up and
running and filled with the glorious lights and buttons and controls that make a ship go. An extremely irritated voice comes from
all around me.

"THE SHIP IS MINE NOW. YOU'RE WELCOME."

I lean back in my seat, grinning up at the ceiling. "Winner and
still champion, Nova."

"I AM UNINTERESTED IN YOUR PRAISE."

"You're getting it anyway. You're the best AI in the whole
universe." I square myself back up to the navcomm, studying
the layout of the dashboards in front of me. It looks like we're
no longer heading for the neutron star, so that's a big plus. A
little more digging, and I manage to find the ship's navigational
history.

There. An origin point. Coordinates seem to indicate something
in orbit around Corona XII, a dwarf planet located on the far edge
of the Coronus system. I'm nowhere near an expert on the people
of Coronus, but I'm pretty positive that none of them look like
these faceless assassins. Or have a fervent wish to see me dead.

I stare at the small glowing point on the star map. I don't know
what I'd been expecting. An origin point in the Voleses' home
system? For the trajectory to point right to the kingship or Voles
Enterprises or something else linked directly to Edgar?

Come on, Farshot. Don't be ridiculous.

Maybe these relentless bastards are Edgar's doing. Or maybe they aren't connected to him at all and I'll have to diversify my revenge game.

One way or another, I'm about to find out.

TWENTY-FOUR

STARDATE: 0.06.16 in the Year 4031, under the reign of the Empress Who Never Was, Nathalia Matilda Coyenne, long may she rest in glory

LOCATION: Closing in on Corona XII, and it's looking promising in all the worst ways

THE COORDINATES TAKE ME TO A SPACE STATION.

A *secret* space station, tucked in close to Corona XII's southern pole, where the magnetic fields play havoc with sensor readouts, rendering the whole place almost undetectable. If I didn't have the coordinates from this ship to go by, I probably wouldn't even know it was there unless I ran into it.

The whole place is smooth and spherical, but not much bigger than Station Shisso. Could probably hold a hundred people or so, but not much more than that. I can't see any markings or indications anywhere on the outer shell either that might tell me who or what the hell is running this place.

When we're a few kilometers out, I let the autopilot take over and install a few fail-safes with Nova before I put her back into the data shell attached to my wristband and reseal all the panels on the navcomm. I watch out the narrow prow windows as the ship swings underneath the sphere and into a hangar bay with at least a dozen identical ships, all shaped like shark teeth, lined up in rows. I duck out of sight as we drift toward a landing pad, digging into an inner pocket of my jumpsuit and pulling out one of my remaining glamour keys.

A little shudder crawls down my skin as I stare at it, thinking of what I'm about to do, but as the landing gear clanks down onto the metal floor, I stick the glamour key on at the base of my throat and activate an illusion around me.

No more Alyssa Farshot. Now I look exactly like one of the assassins. Hooded coat, mask, facelessness, and all.

For the next hour, at least. We'll see what happens after that.

I stand in the cargo bay, feet spread apart, staring straight ahead, trying to recall all the ways I've seen these things walk and act and move. Outside the ship I can hear footsteps, voices, and then the bay door comes down. At the bottom stand two people—both of them Solari and wearing the robes of acolytes who've dedicated their lives to their religion. As in, they don't just worship Solarus, they work for him full-time.

These are different, though, than any Solari getups I've ever heard about. Usually, the super-high-up leaders wear white, the enkindlers wear yellow, their acolytes wear orange, and the novices wear brown. Standard stuff across the board. But these two—their robes are orange and red, and there's a symbol embroidered across the chest of a full, blazing sun with a planet circling it.

Which is not any of the symbols of Solarus I'm familiar with.

Solarus is usually represented by a sun rising over the curve of a planet, to signify how he's rising over the empire. Or something like that. Look, my religious studies are a little spotty, but I know it's definitely not whatever these two are sporting on their chests.

They tromp up toward me, both with tablets floating in front of them that they appear to be taking notes on as they circle me and examine the inside of the ship.

"How many were dispatched in this one?" one asks.

"Two," the other says as they squint at me. "One returning with no apparent injuries."

"Was this one marked as a potential return?"

"It was considered possible but not likely."

"No signs of a fight inside or outside the ship. Are we sure it made it all the way to its mission?"

"Check the navigational history. Ensure it got to its destination. I'll take this one up for a medical assessment."

The second one motions at me, and I follow them through the enormous hangar. It's hard to observe too much without turning my head and giving it away that I'm gawking at everything, but I notice that there are quite a few landing pads that are scuffed-up and empty. Potentially dozens of them.

How many ships were in here originally?

More important, who was in them and where did they go?

The station itself seems to be a labyrinth of hyper-bright corridors that the acolyte navigates with ease. More Solari move busily up and down the halls, all with those same robes on with that unfamiliar sun symbol, and the symbol even pops up occasionally as a decoration on the walls. Everyone seems to be ethnically

Solari, too—as in, from the Solarus system of homeworlds—which is its fair share of strange. The Solari religion is pretty widespread in the quadrant now, and I thought they were cool with just about anybody being an acolyte these days.

One long, winding walk and a lift ride later, my escort leads me into another cavernous space. It almost looks like a small warehouse, somewhere in the center of the sphere, I think. I'm calculating how I can get away from my babysitter and how much time I have left on this glamour key when I finally catch sight of exactly what they're housing in this area.

Dozens of the faceless assassins are lined up, rank and file, in neat rows.

I suck in a sharp breath at the sight of so many of them. These aren't outfitted with the dramatic hooded getups yet, and they all look disturbingly similar. Silent. Unmoving. Just real horror-vid-type material. A couple more of the acolytes are here too, circling the assassins, making notes on their hovering tablets.

The acolyte leads me to a suite of med labs on the far side and points me into a small white room, telling me to "sit" and "wait." Which I do. Until they close the door.

Then I'm up on my feet, pawing through the room for anything I can possibly find. There isn't much—an exam table, a set of drawers with basic medical supplies. It's basically the least interesting room in the history of rooms. Except that that symbol is displayed on the back of the door.

I angle my arm so I can scan the image of it into my wristband and ask Nova to figure out just what the hell it is.

Her visual-only response fills my wristband screen within a few seconds.

THAT IS AN IMAGE OF SOLARUS.

I shake my head, muttering, "I've never seen Solarus depicted like that."

IT IS A MUCH OLDER DEPICTION OF SOLARUS. LAST USED WIDELY 277 YEARS AGO. THE SYMBOL WAS CHANGED AFTER THE SOLARUS SYSTEM JOINED THE EMPIRE. THERE. NOW YOU LEARNED SOMETHING.

"Why would it show up on this super-secret space station full of murder clones, though?" I reach a hand up and brush my fingertips across the imagery. "Are there any records of modern usage?"

A FEW REFERENCES TO IT BEING USED BY SOLARI NATIONALISTS LIKE THE EXCANDARE WHO BELIEVE IN THE SUPREMACY OF THEIR RELIGION AND CULTURE. CAN WE BE DONE HERE NOW?

I hear footsteps drawing near on the other side of the door. Definitely not gonna stick around in this room for sure. A glamour key won't hold up to whatever kind of "medical assessment" these people plan to give me. I tuck myself into the corner behind the door so I'm hidden when it swings open. Another acolyte steps inside the room and pauses, confused, but I whip the butt of my blaster into the back of their head before they can look around. They stagger, and I strike again—one more hard blow to knock them out cold—and then ease past their body and crack open the door.

Hall's empty. *Okay, Farshot, let's let this glamour do all the work and just act like we belong here.*

I swing right—away from the warehouse full of assassins in rows—and step back into the twisting corridors. There are a few acolytes moving around, but I try not to look at them. Just focus on finding my way back down to the hangar.

"Stop, ignati." This Solari is wearing robes just a little more elaborate than everyone else's I've seen. She steps right in my path, looking down on me imperiously. "Why are you alone? Where is your bearer?"

My *bearer*? What the hell does that mean?

I don't really know what to do. I haven't seen any evidence of how the ignati communicate.

"Where is your bearer, ignati?"

I tilt my head to look up at her. And I shrug.

The reaction is immediate. Her face tenses with fear and fury, and she swings around, slamming her hand against a display panel. The corridors light up in vivid, strobing blue, and a deep, sonorous voice intones:

"Blue alert. Intruders are on the station. Repeating: Intruders are on the station. Please prepare."

She reaches for me, but I've already spun away from her and started sprinting up the hall, scrambling around curves and corners. I fly past acolytes looking alarmed, some of them trying to snatch at me only to come up ten times more confused when their fingers find glamour and nothing else.

My breath comes hard and fast. My pulse is thick in my throat. I feel like I'm going in circles in this godsdamned place. I just need a way down—

My wristband buzzes and I glance down at the screen.

YOU REALIZE YOU JUST PASSED A SERVICE TUNNEL BACK THERE, RIGHT?

My boots squeak on the metal as I skid to a stop and pry open a narrow little door, throwing myself inside. There's a ladder running the length of the tunnel, and I grab on to the side rails, gripping with both my hands and my feet as I slide down. And down. And down. Level after level. Until I hit the ground at the very bottom.

My heartbeat pounds in my ears as I check the time. Six minutes left on my glamour key. Plenty of time. Just have to make it to the hangar. A quick sprint and we're in the clear.

No problem.

As soon as the hallway outside is empty, I wriggle out of the service tunnel and make a break for it. It's not so confusing down here—all roads seem to lead to the hangar—and I'm almost there. Just down this corridor, around this corner, through these sliding doors—

I freeze in place, my breath catching in my chest.

Two dozen assassins, all geared up, stand in neat rows in the open space between me and my stolen ship. In one synchronous movement, all their faceless heads turn toward me.

I swallow hard, backing up half a step. "Nova, time for that failsafe. The big one."

I HOPE YOU HAVE ANOTHER IDEA FOR HOW TO GET US OFF THIS STATION.

Me too. "Just do it, Nova. Now!"

I throw myself back through the doors as half the hangar bay explodes.

ENKINDLER WYTHE ANNOUNCES THAT SOLARI ENKINDLERS WILL BE EMBEDDED IN ALL SECURITY FORCES

Imperial officials explain that the religious representatives will ensure the "moral and spiritual security" of the people

HUNDREDS OF RELIGIOUS LEADERS PROTEST THE ELEVATION OF THE SOLARI

They claim recent decisions by the kingship are disregarding the empire's long tradition of religious neutrality

CHANCELLOR ORSED: "OUR EMPIRE FINALLY HAS TRUE LEADERSHIP"

A growing faction of planet leaders speak up in favor of the droid dispersal, declaring that Voles's decisive actions restore their faith in a strong and powerful United Sovereign Empire

ALYSSA FARSHOT LOSES GROUND IN PUBLIC PERCEPTION

New polls show that the crownchaser's continued absence from the spotlight and inability to produce any evidence of her original claims are hurting her even among those who previously viewed her favorably

THE KINGSHIP, HYPERLIGHT

There is such unity inside Edgar now.

Between himself and the kingship. The kingship and his initiative forces. The initiative forces and himself.

All moving as one. All in sync.

And it's just how he'd imagined it would be. Now he can truly be everywhere at once, among all his people, applying the laws of the empire with strength and power. Even those pockets of rebellion and violence have started to die down, quelled by his strong hand.

Exemplary, Wythe told him just this morning. *Extraordinary. A true father to your people. Doing what no other emperor before you has even dreamed of doing.*

Exemplary. Extraordinary.

No other emperor. Only him.

No one could look on him now and think him foolish. Or someone to be pitied or bullied. Not even her. He stands above her, above every prime heir still standing, and they have to lift their eyes to see him.

"Where are your guards, Edgar Voles?"

Edgar blinks. He'd forgotten that he was still standing in the throne room. In truth, ever since the neural link went live, he sometimes forgets he still has physical form at all. NL7 stands in front of the throne where he's sitting, but it is the only other person in there.

"I reassigned the crownsguards," he tells it. "It felt redundant to have them protecting me when so many of my security droids are on board. Enkindler Wythe expressed concerns about his safety from anti-religious zealots, so I made the crownsguards part of his retinue instead."

NL7 simply looks at him, the lenses of its mediabot cameras glowing blue. It occurs to Edgar that he'd never considered the possibility of adding NL7 to the neural link as well, of making it part of Edgar's new unity, but as soon as the thought crosses his mind, he recoils from it. He would never. Could never. The other droids are just tools.

NL7 is family.

"As long as you are satisfied that you are adequately protected, Edgar Voles," the android says at last.

Edgar closes his eyes. Sometimes NL7 almost sounds like his mother.

FROM THE PERSONAL FILES OF ATAR VELRYN FAROSHTI, ACCESSED BY NL734014 ON STARDATE 0.06.16 IN THE YEAR 4031

Audio transcript of a personal long-range communication from Atar to Charles Viqtorial on 0.02.07.4018

"I AM SO GLAD TO HEAR THAT YOU'RE RETURNING with good news from Coltigh. I needed that today. Truthfully I needed to see your face and hear your voice more than anything.

"Alyssa was so delighted tonight when I let her watch one more holo-story. And then another. And then another. But the truth is I just wanted an excuse to sit and hold her a little while longer and pretend to be nothing more than uncle and niece.

"The Imperial Council meeting did not go at all as I'd hoped. Radha and Jaya supported my position, but the rest of the families rejected the diplomatic option outright. They want to meet this new Planetary Independence Movement and other similar groups with nothing but merciless force. I couldn't agree to that, and the arguments went on for hours.

"Sometimes this crown is so dispiriting. Not because I compromised some of my power for peace—I can't really regret that. It's more that the system itself is so flawed, so entrenched, and so ill-balanced for so many. Like I'm trying to power the entire galaxy with an ancient hand crank.

"If even the emperor himself sometimes feels helpless to change the universe, how must everyone else feel?"

TWENTY-FIVE

STARDATE: 0.06.16 in the Year 4031, under the reign of the Empress Who Never Was, Nathalia Matilda Coyenne, long may she rest in glory
LOCATION: Running for my life in a secret facility full of deadly assassins

MASSIVE EXPLOSIONS ARE ALWAYS GOOD FOR GIVING you a head start, and the one Nova and I rigged on that stolen ship turned out to be a *doozy*. It caught all the surrounding ships up in it, too, and they all started exploding, so now I'm guessing the hangar is probably just a smoking metal husk.

I'm guessing, but I don't know for sure because there was no way I was sticking around there to find out. If even one of those faceless assassins crawled out of the fire, I didn't want to see it. Instead, I made a beeline back for the service tunnels, crammed myself inside, and started climbing.

The main shaft curves the whole length of the station, but there are auxiliary branches for every level and I pick one at random, crawling as quickly and quietly as I can. There's commotion inside the station, but it all sounds distant and muffled from in here. The only thing I can hear is my quick, heavy breathing. The glamour key wore out about a minute ago, so now it just sits, itchy and useless, at the base of my throat. My muscles are shaking a little, maybe from adrenaline, maybe from fatigue, but I've just got to hold it together long enough to find an exit strategy.

I start checking access panels along the tunnel. They've all got labels on the inside so someone doing maintenance can orient themselves if they get lost, and I bypass three or four before I find one that's promising. It looks like an individual name and there are medical credentials with it. Probably an office. Perfect. Wriggling my blaster free of my belt, I pop open the access panel and stick my head and weapon through, ready to shoot.

The office is dark and empty. It's got a desk with embedded computer access, though, which is the good news I need right now.

I drop down into the office and swipe my fingertips across the desk's surface. It comes to life right away, and I feel a sharp fizzle of triumph. A lot of the text commands are written in Solari, which isn't a language I know very well, but there are enough icons and intuitiveness to the interface that I can find what I'm looking for: a basic layout of the station.

I'm scanning carefully through the map when my wristband buzzes and Nova's words fill the screen.

I AM GETTING A MESSAGE NOTIFICATION FOR YOU AND IT IS VERY ANNOYING.

I straighten a little, wiping at the sweat that keeps trying to pour into my eyes. "A message? From who? What do they want?"

I DON'T TAKE MESSAGES. ASK THEM YOURSELF.

There's a beat, and then a voice comes through my comms. "Look at that. Where there's smoke, there's Farshot."

"Faye?!" I spin around. Like she might actually be behind me or something. "What are you—are you here?"

"Your boy contacted us. Right after you apparently decided to jump on a doom ship." I can practically hear her roll her eyes. "Word to the wise—if you don't want someone clever like Setter tracking down your wristband signature, you might want to take it off next time. Nice work down there, by the way. Did you need a ride?"

I actually do a little victory dance right there in the office. "Yes. Yes, I do."

"Any ideas on how we pick you up?" Honor jumps in. "Because the hangar is, y'know, on fire."

"Right. Let me just . . ." I lean back over the layout, quickly assessing each section until I find something that'll work. "Got it. Nova, can you transmit these coordinates?"

IF I HAVE TO.

"Meet me there in two minutes, Orso."

"If you're late, you're left, Farshot."

I ease open the office door and peek outside. No one out there that I can see. The service tunnels would be safer, but slower, so I'm just going to have to make a run for it in the open. That deep voice from earlier rings through the hallway, but it's not going on about a blue alert or intruders anymore. Instead, it's saying something in Solari. But I don't know enough Solari to figure it out.

Figure it out later, Farshot. Let's move.

Blaster out, I sneak down the hall and check around the corner.

Empty. Not a single damn person.

Setter's voice breaks through my comms. "Alyssa, something is wrong. You need to get off that station now. Hurry."

When an empath tells you something is wrong, you listen. I take off like I've got a thousand faceless assassins on my tail, sweat pouring down my whole body as I scramble my way up two more levels—all creepily empty—to the section I spotted on the layout.

Waste management.

There are half a dozen vacuum-safe suits hung up in a compartment for workers, and I scramble into one a little too big as Faye calls out over the comms, "Waiting on you, Farshot."

"Yeah, yeah, yeah." As soon as I'm sealed inside, I step into the waste containment area, gagging at the smell as I wade in. I need to get to the emergency release on the far side that'll send me jetting out into space with the rest of this . . . mess. I try to hold my breath, but the stink is so strong it gets in my nose anyway and makes my eyes water. I move faster, hands out in front of me, stretching forward until my fingers latch on to that release lever.

I yank down . . .

. . . and then I'm spinning in space, disoriented, surrounded by waste and junk and I can't even see Faye's ship, she said she was out here, where—

Something thunks hard into my back, latches on to my suit, and then my body is yanked backward. I fall onto the cold floor of an unfamiliar ship, two figures in survival suits standing over me, and as the bay door shuts with a clank, they both pull their helmets off.

Honor shakes out her bright green hair and grins down at me. "Easy as going fishing. You smell terrible, by the way."

Setter skips the quippy greetings and heads for the comms. "Faye, get us out of here now. The faster, the better."

"What's going on, Setter?" I gag again as I wriggle the waste management suit off, trying to touch it as little as possible. "What are you—"

The ship rocks hard, sending all of us stumbling into each other. Honor is on her feet first, rushing out of the cargo hold. I follow her and Setter down a short corridor onto a small bridge that's all soft, curving lines—a Nynzeri cargo runner. Pretty common around Orsion citadels. They must've borrowed it to come get me. Through the rounded windows along the prow, we can see the station—

—or, I guess, what's left of it.

Which isn't much. It's been practically vaporized in an enormous ball of fire.

I step up behind Faye where she's sitting at the navcomm. "Life signs."

Her fingers move across the screen. She looks over at Honor, who's dropped into the copilot's seat, but Honor shakes her head.

"Nothing," Faye says. "You really did a number on that place, Farshot."

"It wasn't her," says Setter as he stares out at the destruction. His eyes are gray with anxiety. "Everyone on that ship knew it was going to explode—I felt it. They must've set some kind of self-destruct. I just don't know why." He shudders and looks over at me. "What in all the universe was going on at that station?"

I sag against the curve of the wall. I'm definitely starting to feel the exhaustion now. "It's where all those faceless guys are coming from. It looked like they were making them. They called them ignati."

Setter straightens a little, and I see his expression shift to Academic Setter. "That's an old Solari dialect. It means 'torch,' I think."

Honor spins around to face us as the ship shifts into hyperlight. "Back up, who's the 'they' we're talking about here?"

"Solari acolytes? I think? But they wore different robes and they had this symbol all over the place." I pull up the scan from my wristband, projecting it into the middle of the room where everyone can see. "Nova says it's an old image of Solarus, pre-imperial. That it's not used anymore except—"

"—by the excandare," Setter finishes for me. His brain is really geared up now. "Excandare means 'firebrand.' They're allegedly nationalists, unhappy with the direction of Solari society since it elected to join the empire. They've got a whole list of extreme positions, but their primary one is their belief in Solari cultural supremacy."

Faye leans forward, propping her chin in one of her hands. "The excandare aren't supposed to be anywhere near this organized. Solari leadership always talks about them like they're just a bunch of random individuals making noise."

I stare at that symbol, rubbing at my temples. "I just can't figure out how all this ties back to Edgar."

Faye shrugs. "Maybe it doesn't."

"Are you kidding? It has to!" She raises her eyebrows at me, and I realize a second too late that my response maybe came out a bit too intense. I bring my voice down a few notches. "Think about it. Every move they made in the crownchase helped put Edgar on the throne. That *had* to be their goal. Maybe they're connected to Wythe. Wythe seems to be a big fan of Edgar, and he and William Voles were always pretty tight on the kingship."

Setter frowns, not looking terribly convinced. "To be fair, politically, it was advantageous for both of them to align with each other against your uncle. That doesn't necessarily mean there was conspiracy."

"But what if it was more than that?" I look at all three of them, arms wide, waiting for the very obvious possibilities to sink in for them. But they've all still got their skeptical expressions on. "Look, once Holder gets JR fixed—"

"If he gets it fixed," Faye interrupts, and I shoot her a hard look.

"He will. And then we'll have leverage. With our families. With Edgar. With everyone. We can get some answers about all of this."

A light flashes on the navcomm, and Honor spins around in her seat, expanding the notification across her dashboard. "It's a short-range beacon, broadcasting a message on repeat. Not imperial. Looks like it's unaffiliated."

I lean over her shoulder, frowning. "It could be Sharva and their crew. Play the message."

I'm right. It is Sharva. Their prerecorded voice booms across the bridge.

"DO NOT APPROACH CYBSIS. CYBSIS HAS FALLEN."

TWENTY-SIX

STARDATE: 0.06.17 in the Year 4031, under the reign of the Empress Who Never Was, Nathalia Matilda Coyenne, long may she rest in glory
LOCATION: Cybsis. And . . . it doesn't look good. . . .

OUR FIRST PASS OVER THE SETTLEMENT MAKES MY heart sink all the way down to the deck.

More imperial ships have landed on the planetoid surface, and Edgar's security droids swarm like insects inside and outside the domes. Setter runs sensor sweeps, showing Cybsis residents clustered inside their homes, corralled into manageable groups in the streets, some of them even lined up like prisoners while the droids fit them with compression cuffs one at a time. Several of the smaller residential domes on the outer edges are completely abandoned.

And the docking dome is destroyed. Don't even need the sensors to see that. Its roof is shattered and smoke rises so thick I can't see inside.

If the *Serendipity* is intact.

If Hell Monkey . . .

I swallow hard, my eyes glued to the scenes playing out below. "I have to get down there."

Setter swipes the sensor display off and turns to me. "We get information before we make a move this time, Alyssa. As a team."

I sink against the wall, trying not to imagine Hell Monkey or Holder or Sharva lying dead in the docking dome or locked into compression cuffs. My eyes land on my hands, clenched into fists at my sides, and I pull back the sleeve on my right wrist.

The Oath Taker tattoo glows a dull green on my skin. I wrap my fingers around it, squeezing it tight. Like it can connect me to them somehow.

There's a ping over the comms channel, and Edgar's droid-voice comes on. "Please identify yourself for the good of the empire."

Honor's response is quick and immediate, bringing up what looks like a calling card and transmitting it with a swipe. "Delegation from Primor Orso," she says, affecting a pitch-perfect Orsion accent. "Just doing a flyby to check on the situation. Looks like you have it well under control, Imperial Majesty."

Faye peels us off, taking us up and away on a trajectory out of the Amos Belt, and panic hits me in the chest like lightning. I lurch to a stand, lunging toward the pilot seat.

"Faye, what the hell—"

Setter puts a hand out to stop me. "Alyssa, don't—"

I shake him off, trying to get at the navcomm. "You'd better not be *leaving*!"

Faye whips onto her feet, the glowing threads of her hair whirling around her. "I'm making sure we don't get shot down by security forces for acting suspicious!"

"Fine, great, we did that!" There's something that feels like hysteria pressing against my skin more and more the farther we get from Cybsis. "Turn us around now!"

She grabs me by the elbows as I make a play for the controls again. "That's not for you to decide! You don't get to make the calls all the time, Farshot!"

"Faye! Alyssa!" Setter tries to intervene as we struggle and just winds up tangled between us. "This isn't helpful!"

"Got them!" Honor crows, pumping a fist in the air, and we all freeze and turn to her. "I figured, H.M. is a smart kid, he'll probably bury a rescue signal inside normal subspace noise so he doesn't bring all those droids on his ass, and I was right." She looks over at us, still twisted up together, and cocks her head. "Are you idiots done? We've got a rescue to make."

We pin down their location to a cavern inside an asteroid about ten thousand kilometers away from Cybsis—a pretty big cavern too, because when we get there, we find the Serendipity tucked inside it. Definitely more banged up than when I left her, but still intact. All around her, someone's set up a temporary life support generator—kind of like a dome made out of force fields that produces breathable air inside it. I count eight or nine people moving around as we step inside, but I'm only interested in finding one person in particular.

Hell Monkey.

I spot him sitting on the ground, leaning against the cavern wall, his eyes closed and a med patch stuck to his left rib cage.

As soon as he hears my bootsteps approaching, he opens one eye, looks me over, and then closes it again with a grumble.

"Don't talk to me. I'm mad at you."

I bite back a smile as I kneel down next to him. If he were really, *seriously* mad at me, he wouldn't be saying anything at all. So there's that. I run my fingers along the edge of the med patch, checking its seal, and he flinches and squirms away.

"Ah! Stop that. Tickling inhibits the healing process." He eyes me again, and I can see the stress, the concern, all balled up underneath his grumpiness. "Was it worth it at least? Your jacked-up solo field trip?"

"I think it was. I found out where they came from. Who's making them. Still trying to figure out the why and how it all connects." I smooth my thumb against that worry line parked between his eyebrows. "Thanks for sending Faye and Honor and Setter after me."

"Somebody had to back you up. I knew they'd get there faster than I could, and I . . ." He pulls out this deep sigh that hits me like a gut-punch because it sounds so much like how Charlie would sigh when I got to be too much for him. "You scared the hell out of me, Alyssa."

"I know," I say, curling my knees up to my chest. "I never think, never consider the consequences, I'm just a mess—"

"I don't care that you're a mess. We're all a mess. It's just . . ." He laughs a little, very softly. "Sometimes being in love with you is like trying to hold on to a comet."

I know he means it as a joke, but it doesn't make me feel better.

It actually makes me feel worse. People who fly too close to comets burn up. Is that me, then? Do I burn people up?

I don't think I want the answer to that. I hug my legs closer to me and change the subject. "What happened on Cybsis?"

Hell Monkey shakes his head. "Pretty much what you'd expect when a dumbass emperor invades a settlement like that. There was never a scenario where the people there would let Edgar's new toys take over their home without fighting back. Most of Sharva's crew got cut down or taken into custody, and the droids went dome to dome after that, arresting anyone who tried to push back. I barely got Sharva and the rest of these folks out of there."

I gesture at our worldcruiser. "You got them out on the *Serendipity*? Piloted with no AI or anything, just super old-fashioned style? Pretty impressive."

He snorts. "It was rough, but we managed to make it this far at least. I didn't want to risk trying to go much farther without Nova, though."

I slip the data shell off my wristband and hold it out to him. "Pretty sure she'd be more than happy to be back on the *Serendipity*."

He takes it, pushing onto his feet with only a slight wince. Then he pauses and looks back down at me. "You should go see Sharva. They're in the cargo bay."

I find the Chu'ran sitting on a long, low crate, their hands covering their face. There are smudges of ash on their deep-purple skin and some of their bronze-colored hair is singed at the ends.

"You made it back," they say as I approach, but they don't look up.

"Yeah, I . . ." Something about the slope of their shoulders, how they look so small right now—it makes my voice die in my throat. I'm not sure what to say exactly and I swallow down several responses before I finally manage, "Sharva, I'm so sorry."

They finally drop their hands, staring off into the empty space in front of them. Their eyes are raw, the faint dark blue remnants of tear tracks staining their face. "I know," they say, low and strained, "in my head, that you did not bring this down on us. That this emperor is doing this same thing throughout the quadrant and it was only a matter of time before it came to us. And yet"—their voice breaks against a sob, and I can hear the anger running underneath it—"I find it very hard to look at you right now, Faroshti."

I feel my throat tighten—because they're hurting so badly, because they're angry at me and maybe they should be, because I honestly have no idea what to do that's going to help. "I can go away."

"Not yet." Sharva gets to their feet and reaches down to the long crate they were sitting on, unsnapping the locks along the side. "You should know that Holder didn't make it out of Cybsis. He went down in the firefight, protecting this." They flip open the lid and it lands with a loud clatter on the floor.

Inside the crate lies a mediabot. JR426. It's not powered up at the moment, but it's unmistakably intact, albeit with several spots on its frame that've been creatively jury-rigged together.

My chest and my head are just this horrible, confusing fusion of emotions—grief, guilt, hope, guilt again, because what the hell business do I have feeling hopeful when someone gave his life for this?

Sharva steps in front of me, blocking my line of sight so I have to look up into their face. Up close like this, the sorrow in their expression is so raw and overwhelming it takes the breath right out of me.

"I hope to whatever stars or gods you pray to, Faroshti, that this is worth it. Because I'm not so sure."

TWENTY-SEVEN

STARDATE: 0.06.18 in the Year 4031, under the reign of the Empress Who Never Was, Nathalia Matilda Coyenne, long may she rest in glory

LOCATION: Hand to the stars, it's the most godsdamned picturesque place I've ever seen in my life

I DON'T GET JR THE MEDIABOT UP AND RUNNING quite yet. The general consensus is that the Amos Belt isn't a safe spot to hole up anymore—not for us and not for Sharva's people either. And after everything, well . . . I feel like getting everyone somewhere more secure is first priority.

It's Sharva who suggests Vellyn. I've heard of it—Atar mentioned it once or twice as being one of the most beautiful planets he'd ever seen—but we're not headed there for the scenery. We're going there because there's a Planetary Independence Movement division located on the southernmost continent.

The scenery, it turns out, is just a ridiculous bonus.

The planet below is a study in contrasts: sheer, towering cliff faces of dark brown and shiny black rock broken up by flat plains of deep-blue-green grasses and jewel-toned flowers and gnarled, sprawling trees with silver bark. There are so many cliffs of different heights that it's almost like a blotinzoid world, made up of blocks all stacked together. But the lines of this planet are jagged and irregular, rock outcroppings jutting out kind of wherever they feel like and vegetation overflowing down the cliff faces and growing out of ledges and shelves. Glittering birds fly loops around fluffy, pastel-colored clouds, and furry four-legged creatures spread wings to glide from plateau to plateau.

And there are waterfalls. I've never seen so many godsdamned waterfalls—it's like every other plateau has a river or a stream spilling over the brink in a spray of mist and rainbows so dense that it makes it look like the cliffs are floating in the sky.

Sharva gives us the coordinates of the hideout, which turns out to be a structure embedded in the side of a cliff about thirty meters below the plateau's surface. The landing strip is hidden behind a waterfall, which means I get the satisfaction of making a dramatic entrance, water streaming and steaming off the Serendipity's hull as I bring her in and set her down.

The place is a lot bigger than I expected based on how Sharva described it. Based off what I can see as I step off the ship onto the loading dock, I'm guessing there are easily a few hundred people who live in this intricate complex of caves and caverns.

Sharva goes out with their remaining crew to meet Evern, the Artacian who leads this settlement, while Hell Monkey and I hover by the aft ramp of the Serendipity and Setter, Faye, and Honor wander over to us from the Nynzeri ship. I can't hear anything Sharva or Evern are saying from this distance, but I watch their discussion, noting how it changes when Evern's eyes cut over to us, the hand gestures she uses, how her bright red wings flare wide. I have enough experience with Artacians to recognize that these aren't typically friendly signs.

After a few minutes, Sharva waves their crew to go on into the compound and comes back over to us.

"I'm sorry," they say as they walk up. "Evern says she cannot agree to let you in. You can stay on your ships here in the docking bay, but she's not comfortable with you coming any farther."

Faye makes a noise like she's about to object, so I cut in loudly before she can respond. "We understand. Our ships are completely comfortable. We'll be fine, and we're grateful for the shelter."

Sharva's eyes drift up the ramp to the low crate that houses JR426. "Are you . . . going to power it up now that we're here?"

My stomach twists at the thought. But I nod. "That's the plan."

Their gaze drops down to mine. "I would like to watch. To see what Holder died for. If that is all right with you."

"Yeah, absolutely. Of course you can." I swallow hard as I turn and head up the ramp.

I feel a little bit like I'm about to jump off a cliff.

I actually think I might prefer jumping off a cliff. Now that we've come to the point of it, there are a million possibilities running through my head. Like maybe JR won't even power up after all. Or maybe the footage won't have survived.

Or maybe it did. And I'll have to watch Coy die all over again.

Hell Monkey flips the top off the long crate, and I kneel down, staring at the mediabot's spindly form, the darkened lenses of its camera head and attachments.

I'm not sure I can do this. . . .

Hell Monkey reaches across the crate and grabs my hand. I hadn't even realized they were shaking. I look over at him, and he squeezes my fingers tight

I take a deep breath. Okay. Here we go.

Reaching in, I find the access point at the back of JR426's neck and power it on, and then I stand back. I hold my breath as the cameras on its body glow with bright blue light. Its head twists a little left, then right, then it grips the sides of the crate and stands, looking around at the semicircle of people around it.

It turns to me, cameras running. "What are your thoughts on the latest developments in the crownchase, Captain Farshot?"

I smile a little at the sound of its voice, at the sight of it popping right up with an interview question. I think I might've missed this bot a little. "You're gonna have to be a little more specific, JR. A lot has happened recently."

JR looks around again at Faye and Honor, Setter and Sharva. At the unfamiliar cargo bay. "I am afraid I do not feel informed enough about the current situation to ask the appropriate questions."

"It's okay, JR," Hell Monkey says, patting its pointy shoulder. "You don't have to do any interviews right now."

"I actually need you to play back some footage," I tell it. My voice only shakes a little. "Everything you've got from after we crash-landed on Calm. Do you think you can do that?"

"Of course, Captain Farshot."

I swallow hard, curling my hands into fists. "Do it. Please."

The lights in his cameras switch to a gold-tinted white, and then footage fills the space in the middle of us, streaming from JR like a projection. The recording shows signs of wear and tear—flickering sometimes, cutting in and out in places. There's Coy's ship descending in an acid rainstorm to rescue us when our oxygen was running out. There's Drinn carrying Hell Monkey into the med bay to save his life. There's Coy and me coming back up the cargo ramp in our survival suits, grinning, elated, Coy gripping the royal seal we'd just found. Then . . .

. . . shots of me running up the corridor. Grabbing JR and pulling it onto the bridge. Telling it to film . . .

Coy and Edgar and his droid. Fighting on the other side of the force field. Blaster shots in a tangle of bodies.

And then she falls.

She falls and never gets up again.

The final shot is of that droid of Edgar's storming toward JR—and then it shuts off.

But I remember what happened next.

They'd shocked me into unconsciousness and set the self-destruct. I'd had to use Coy's body—like a tool—to stop it. I'd slipped in her blood. I'd felt the clammy coolness of her skin on my hands.

I sit down hard on the nearest crate, hot tears streaming down my cheeks.

JR makes its way over to me, feet tinking on the metal floor. "Was that sufficient, Captain Farshot?"

I wipe the tears out of my eyes, clearing my throat once, twice, until I can finally speak. "Yeah, JR. More than sufficient. Thanks."

I look around the cargo bay—at Hell Monkey, crouching near me, his brow furrowed and his hands folded together; at Setter, tears on his own face, his eyes the dark gray-blue of grief; at Sharva, standing solemnly, arms crossed over their broad chest; at Faye, her back turned to us, like she doesn't even care . . . until you notice her hand gripping Honor's so tight she looks like she might break it.

I get to my feet. There's still a tremble in my hands, but I shove them into my jumpsuit pockets to hide it.

"Okay," I announce, loud enough to get everyone's attention. "Let's go get this son of a bitch."

TWENTY-EIGHT

STARDATE: 0.06.19 in the Year 4031, under the reign of the Empress Who Never Was, Nathalia Matilda Coyenne, long may she rest in glory
LOCATION: The luxury star-yacht of Cheery Coyenne. It's time for my close-up.

ONE MORE GLAMOUR KEY.

One more chance to make everything right.

My heart pounds in my chest as I step onto the enormous star-yacht that serves as the preferred residence of Cheery and Reginald Coyenne. JR426 hovers beside me, looking nervous.

Or maybe I'm just nervous. I know it's not the only record of what happened anymore. We made holodisc copies, several of them. One of them is in my jumpsuit pocket, one is with Hell Monkey back on Vellyn, and right now Setter and Faye are each taking one to their parents, to sway them to our side.

But I keep checking to make sure the mediabot stays close. Just in case.

I programmed my glamour to be a low-level staff member,

someone below the notice of most of the decked-out foarians and other fancy higher-ups floating around on this level. I push a long hovering table in front of me, draped in a gold cloth, and make sure not to meet anyone's eyes as I move down a long hall and around a corner to a set of tall double doors.

Swiping a clear key card across the panel, I wait as the doors slide open and then I step onto the observation deck.

It's empty and quiet. Sheltered from all the bustle of people that seem to be constantly filling this massive ship. Here, though . . . the silence is reverent. It makes me want to hold my breath or only speak in a whisper. The whole far wall is one enormous window of clear glass, probably eight or nine meters high and twice as wide, filled with the stars outside.

I've only been in this room once before, when I was ten. Coy and I hid in here for hours, avoiding the ridiculous party her parents had thrown supposedly for her birthday but really they threw for themselves. I swear I can see her right now—a gangly kid with a laugh like a bell, cartwheeling her way around life, with me chasing after her like she's a lightning bug I'm trying to catch in a jar.

I blink hard to get rid of the tears collecting on my lashes. My chest feels tight, my limbs feel heavy, but I can't let it swallow me. I have to get on top of this like a wave, use it to do what I came here to do.

"Have a seat, JR." I push the table to the front of the space and type a message into my wristband. Then I plop myself down on the cushioned bench next to the mediabot, waiting for my moment.

I don't have to wait long. I'm only there ten minutes before I hear the doors open and see Cheery Coyenne sweeping onto the observation deck. If she's confused or curious or, hell, feels anything at all, her face doesn't show it. She's as cool and stoic as ever. I kind of expect to get pissed at the sight of her, given our last conversation, but it's hard for the rage to surge past the heaviness of what I carried in here.

Cheery wanders down the wide steps, glancing around with an arch look. I see her getting ready to say something—some kind of cutting, distant remark or something like that—so I just cut to the chase and twist the glamour key off my skin. The illusion around me falls as I pull it away.

The only surprise she shows is a half second of hesitation in her steps. But the rest of her stays poised as hell as she draws even with me. "This is very bold and very stupid of you."

I shrug, tucking the used-up key into my jumpsuit pocket. "Pretty sure that's my whole resume right there."

Cheery sighs. "I'm certain you have a very good and passionate pitch, Alyssa, but I already made clear to you that I am not the rebel type. Too many people depend on this family. I cannot be rash. I have to do what's pragmatic—"

"I know. You're trying to be a smart leader. You told me you couldn't back me without evidence." I gesture to JR, who steps up next to me and turns its camera lenses on Cheery. "You remember your very own mediabot, JR426, right?"

She goes very still, staring down at it. "Of course."

"JR was on the bridge with me. When Edgar killed Nathalia. He tried to destroy it, but I have talented friends. It still has all the footage. Don't you, JR?"

"That is accurate, Captain Farshot."

Cheery lifts an eyebrow. "You can fake footage, Alyssa," she says, though her voice is a little quieter than usual.

"You can authenticate it, too, Cheery. And anyway . . ." I sling an arm around JR's spindly shoulders. "This mediabot is the pinnacle of journalistic integrity. It'd never fake anything, would you, JR?"

"That would run counter to my programming, Captain Far-shot."

"See?" I take a deep breath—it shudders in and out of my lungs—and step back over to the long, hovering table I brought in. All of the feelings in my chest right now *squeeze* my heart until it feels like it's gonna hit my ribs. I'm not looking forward to this part, but I have to. It's what's right. "I brought one more thing, Primor."

I pull off the gold cloth, revealing Coy in her stasis chamber underneath. I stare down at her closed eyes, her empty face. I can't bring myself to look over at Cheery. "I—" My voice cracks, and I have to swallow again. "I'm sorry it took so long to bring her home."

A ragged sob breaks through the space, and I turn to see Cheery sink onto the cushions, her hands covering her face. I start to move toward her, but then I stop because I don't really know what I'd do once I get over there. She's not really the hugging type. Or the touching type. So I just stand, awkward, partway between Coy and her grieving mother.

She looks up after a minute, her black eyes finding the stars. I've never seen her so unraveled. It's way weirder and more unsettling than anything else. "I think," she says in a slightly choked voice, "part of me thought that if I never saw her body, then it would never have to be real. I could just pretend she was still . . . out there. . . ."

I squeeze my hands into fists. "I'm sorry that I couldn't keep her safe. That I failed her."

"All of us failed her." The words slip out of her mouth on the back of a long exhale. She's still not looking at me. I'm not even sure she's really talking to me. She could just be talking to the stars.

I turn back to Coy's stasis chamber, touching a hand to the cool surface. This is when I walk away. I walk away and I leave her here with her family so they can put her to rest. It's the right thing to do, I know it is, but I feel another tear open up in my chest at the thought of doing it. My throat aches from swallowing back all these godsdamned emotions.

Leaning down, I press a kiss to the glass above Coy's sleeping face, and then I straighten and step away, crossing the observation deck to stand in front of Cheery.

"I'm leaving JR here in case you need to question it or verify its story, but it's my buddy. So be extra nice to it. I made you a copy of the footage too." I fish the holodisc from my pocket and hold it out to her. "People died for this, Cheery. They lost their lives just trying to make sure that the truth about what happened to Nathalia gets out there. You have a chance to do right by them. A chance to depose the guy who murdered your daughter without even firing a shot."

I drop the disc in her lap and start back up the steps, calling over my shoulder, "Even a *pragmatic* leader has to like those odds."

EMPEROR VOLES REVEALED AS A MURDERER

Explosive new footage recovered from a mediabot shows Voles shooting Nathalia Coyenne in a struggle to steal the royal seal from her

WIDESPREAD DEMONSTRATIONS ERUPT ACROSS THE QUADRANT

Simmering anger over the kingship security initiative explodes into empire-wide protests as tens of millions turn out to call for the emperor's removal

WYTHE ANNOUNCES A PUBLIC BRIEFING WITH THE PRESS FOR THIS AFTERNOON

The enkindler, speaking on behalf of the kingship, declares he's taking the situation seriously and will be answering questions after an official statement

VOLES FAMILY LAUNCHES A FORMAL COMPLAINT IN DEFENSE OF THE EMPEROR

Former primor William Voles says in a statement that his son's win was fully legal, that the Voleses rightfully claim the throne and his family "will not give it up without a fight"

THE KINGSHIP, UNDISCLOSED COORDINATES

No one has to come and tell Edgar when the news hits. He knows it. Of course he knows. Before it's even started to register in the empire, he sees it ripple across the neural link.

The bridge of the *Gilded Gun*.

Nathalia Coyenne's defiant expression laughing in his face.

The struggle. The blaster shots.

The blood on his hands.

The blood all over his hands . . .

He watches it all, replayed through the eyes of Alyssa Faroshti's mediabot. How she managed to extract the footage from that twisted wreck of a droid, he doesn't know.

And it doesn't matter now. It's out there. It's everywhere. The *Daily Worlds* broadcasts it first, but within minutes, every second- and third-tier media feed has it, replaying it in a constant loop. It shudders through him, pinging against the back of his brain again and again like a distant echo. He paces, agitated, through his imperial quarters and finds himself in his bathroom, vigorously scrubbing his hands, before he even realizes what he's doing.

NL7 haunts his steps. Silent. Watching. For the first time in his life, Edgar is not comforted by its presence. He can't even look at it.

He dresses quickly—choosing his most intimidating imperial

robes—and makes for the throne room, doing his best to stride in a way that's still commanding, confident. Enkindler Wythe is already there—Edgar knew he would be—surrounded by three of his enkindler confidants and the highest-ranking crownsguard. He looks up as Edgar enters, and his expression is so grave that Edgar almost misses a step. But he keeps his feet under him as Wythe slips away from the others to intercept him.

"Edgar . . . ," he says, very quietly, shaking his head.

The informality of it makes Edgar raise an eyebrow. "You mean 'Imperial Majesty,' don't you?"

Wythe sighs and looks over his shoulder at the cluster of advisers. "You must understand—this is a very bad situation you've put me in."

"I . . ." Edgar hears his voice come out too high-pitched, too whiny and young, and he pauses and swallows hard to get control of himself. "Everything I did was in accordance with crownchase rules and guidelines. I broke no laws within the boundaries of the contest."

Wythe draws his head tall, looking down on Edgar. "Foolish boy. It's not just about the legality. It's about the perception. You are already struggling to prove yourself to this empire—what do you think this will do to your authority now?"

To see Wythe of all people looking down on him, calling him foolish—it makes Edgar fumble for a response, and in the awkward silence, Wythe sighs again.

"I am doing what I can," he says, his voice dripping with the exhaustion of the excessively overburdened. "It is in your best interests at this point to lie low. Do not make any move without consulting me. Return to your quarters and let me sort out exactly how to salvage your throne."

Wythe turns and walks away, back to the knot of people over by the windows. Edgar stands there for a minute, his eyes fixed on the throne without quite seeing it, and then he drifts toward the door.

For days now, ever since the neural link went live, Edgar felt bigger than himself, like he'd stepped past the need to be contained to one physical form.

But all of that is gone right now. He feels every part of his body. His cheeks, burning with humiliation. His chest, hollowed out and empty. His pulse, threaded with nerves and guilt and fear.

And his ears, ringing with those words—*foolish boy*—as the throne room doors slam shut behind him.

FROM THE PERSONAL FILES OF ATAR VELRYN FAROSHTI, ACCESSED BY NL734014 ON STARDATE 0.06.19 IN THE YEAR 4031

Personal log of Atar Faroshti, recorded on 0.05.11.4021

I WELCOMED A NEW AMBASSADOR TO THE KINGSHIP today. Ilysium Wythe. He hails from the primary Solarus home-world and is an enkindler, one of their high-ranking spiritual leaders. I am hopeful that, by recognizing him, I can aid in bringing stability to the Solarus system. There is rising tension once again between those in their leadership who favor further opening their markets and embracing cultural exchange and those who think they have already gone too far with such measures. From my understanding, Enkindler Wythe is considered to be a moderate voice that can speak for both sides in this disagreement, which is why he was selected for this position.

I read extensively about Solari culture, as well as the worship of Solarus, before Enkindler Wythe's arrival so I might speak knowledgeably with him. There are so many intricacies to their faith, a sense of ritual and traditions that practitioners seem to find grounding, which I can understand. Its history is long, as well, and has evolved quite a bit from its original teachings, which were much harsher, restrictive, less accepting of alternative religions or viewpoints. Much of that outlook fell away after the Solarus system joined the empire a few hundred years ago, but in my readings, I discovered scattered references to some fringe groups, like the excandare, which consider themselves

Solari patriots upholding their culture.

I asked Enkindler Wythe about the excandare over his welcome dinner, curious as to whether he often encountered them. He laughed at my question and told me, "The only excandare you'll meet anymore are in a history record. And that is for the best."

TWENTY-NINE

STARDATE: 0.06.20 in the Year 4031, under the reign of the Empress Who Never Was, Nathalia Matilda Coyenne, long may she rest in glory

LOCATION: At the coordinates of Relief and Vindication

I'M HONESTLY NOT MUCH OF A CRIER. WHICH MAY be a little hard to believe if you just looked at the past month or so of my life, but seriously—hand to the stars—I don't generally queue up the waterworks when stuff happens, for good or for bad.

And to be fair, I don't cry when the *Daily Worlds* broadcasts the footage of Coy's murder.

I don't cry when the first star system releases an official statement calling for Edgar Voles to give up the throne. Or the second star system. Or the third. Or the fourth.

I don't cry when the Mega, Roy, and Coyenne primors officially rescind their concessions of the crownchase and call for Edgar to step down, either.

But when Faye's father, Ivar Orso, revokes his family's support . . . yeah, then the tears come. No one reads a room like the Orsos, and when they flip to your side, that's when you know you've got the momentum.

Faye never doubted—she gave me a little nod and a wink when the news came out—but I hadn't been willing to hope until that moment. To see all the pieces line up behind me after almost losing everything . . .

. . . well, a person deserves a little bit of a cry after that. One of those releasing-a-thousand-tons-of-stress-I'd-been-holding-in-my-body kinds of cries. I feel it surging up in my chest as I stand on the bridge of the *Serendipity*, watching the media feeds stream the unraveling of Edgar's lies in real time. I don't want to make a scene, so I step off the ship and out into the Vellyn compound docking bay. All of us—even Faye, Honor, and Setter—came back here so we could finish things together, make sure it would stick.

And it looks like it actually has.

There's a spiral ladder built into the wall next to the waterfall entrance, and I climb it all the way to the top and step out onto the plateau above. It's late morning, the breeze cool and damp coming off the rapids. I wander through the blue-green grasses, park myself at the base of one of those gnarled silver trees, and let it all out for three or four solid minutes.

And then I lie back against the extremely uncomfortable trunk, feeling it scrape against my skin through the material of my jumpsuit, and look up at a sky of pale lavender and mist.

I hear footsteps coming toward me, and I can already tell who it is by the pace and heaviness of their stride.

Hell Monkey drops down to the ground next to me, stretching

out on the grass with his big bicepy arms crossed behind his head like a pillow. He's doing that thing where he's carefully nearby but still giving me space to process without anything being required of me. Believe me when I say it's one of his sexiest qualities—almost as sexy as when he follows my orders and calls me "captain."

We just lie there for a while, and I let my thoughts drift past the sky. Past this moment. To what comes next.

Like Charlie. Getting him off that stupid ship and back with me. Making sure he's safe and his record is cleared. Drinn, too. And Ko. That needs to be priority number one.

And there's still the excandare and whatever their plans are, however it connects with Edgar and his family.

And my promise to Sharva. To help them and their people break the bones of this empire and reset them into something new. Not because I swore it on an Oath Taker, but because it's the right thing to do.

Hell, now that I think about it, I guess that was kind of my promise to Uncle Atar, too.

I wiggle down until I'm right up against Hell Monkey's side, and he shifts automatically, stretching an arm out to wrap around me.

"What's on your brain, Farshot?"

I turn a little more into him and breathe in his scent—now more earth and sweat and grass than coolant and oil from the ship. "Everything. There's still so much of a mess to clean up. I don't even know where to start."

He trails a finger down my forearm and around my wrist. "You don't have to be the one who figures it out all on your own, y'know.

This just got a whole lot bigger than our little group."

He's right. I'm not a traitor sneaking around the empire trying to get the truth out anymore. People know what really happened now. They're on our side. Including four full-fledged prime families who have power and resources, who know politics and how to make things happen.

I roll onto my side, propping myself up on my elbow. I want to be able to see Hell Monkey's face for this next part because I'm not totally sure how he'll take it. "I know it's not all on me, but . . . some of it is. I meant what I said back on Cybsis. Sharva and Evern and their whole movement—what they're doing is important. I can help them rock the boat, try to make sure the prime families don't go right back to their same routines."

Hell Monkey shifts his head so he can look into my eyes a little better. "So it's Alyssa Farshot, Professional Boat Rocker now?"

I chew on the inside of my cheek. "Maybe? If I claim primor status . . . I'll have more weight that I can use to help their cause."

I pause, and when he doesn't say anything, I look away and add quickly, "It would mean getting involved in the empire for a little while. Like, really involved. Neck-deep-in-mud kind of involved."

There's a long beat where my heart hammers in my throat, and then I feel his hand brush along the back of my neck, drawing my gaze to him. There's a twist to his mouth that's kind of bittersweet, but the expression in his eyes is soft, intense. It's not new—I've seen him look at me this way lots of times before, back when I wasn't letting myself think too hard about what it meant. But it still makes me feel light-headed—like my heart is too big for my chest and too vulnerable for this whole damn universe.

"I figured you might throw yourself into something stupid," he says, but his voice is soft and there's a smile at the corners of his mouth. "You wouldn't be Alyssa Farshot if you didn't."

I want to say it. *I love you, Eliot Flynn.* The words are right there. The feelings are right there. I can see them again—obvious, definitive—now that the skies are clear.

But he threads his fingers through my hair and pulls me down to him, so I kiss him instead. Slow and soft. Teasing. Unhurried.

We've got time.

THIRTY

Faye turns up before anything can get too interesting, swishing through the tall grass and standing over us, hands on her hips, looking amused as hell.

"I'd ask if I'm interrupting, but I obviously am."

I sigh into Hell Monkey's chest and push up into a sitting position. "And you're clearly really broken up about it. What's going on?"

"Phase one of our plan to save the quadrant is complete, but now it's time for phase two. On your feet, Farshot. The primors are calling." She leans down and taps Hell Monkey on the nose. "You, too, muscles. All hands on deck."

I grumble as I get to my feet and reach a hand out to pull Hell Monkey onto his. I mean, of course we were all going to have to have a circle-and-talk soon, but they couldn't have waited for just a little longer? Let me enjoy this moment?

By the time we make it back to the ship, Setter has a whole setup happening in the cargo bay, with four separate holographic displays arranged in a half-circle and a connected pad for us to stand on as well. Sharva is there, too, lingering against the wall beside Honor, watching.

As soon as he spots us, Setter establishes the communications channel, and I watch as the four displays fill with holograms of Cheery Coyenne, Jenna Mega, Radha Roy, and Ivar Orso. Faye nudges me forward, and I try to straighten my jumpsuit a little before I step onto the pad with her and Setter. They both definitely look the part of prime family heirs, even after being on the run with me— brushed hair, brushed teeth, put-together outfits. I look rumpled and tired, but honestly? You get what you get with me. You're welcome in advance.

Radha is the first to speak up, in a smooth, deep voice. "I think our first order of business is to express our gratitude to these three for doing what was needed to bring the truth of this situation out into the light."

Warmth floods through me, and I glance over at Setter, who's pressing his lips together to keep from breaking his epic streak of never fully smiling. I clear my throat and start to shove my hands in my pockets before realizing that probably looks even less professional than I already do and clasping them behind my back instead. What is it about parental types that always makes you feel like an eight-year-old kid again? I've stared down much scarier stuff than this collection of imperial yahoos. *Steel up, Farshot.*

"Agreed," says Jenna Mega, and I can feel the fierce intensity of her gaze even through a hologram. She looks so much like her son, Owyn, that it almost hurts. "The Mega family acknowledges and commends Alyssa Faroshti, Setter Roy, and Faye Orso and all those who assisted them in this task."

I'm definitely flushed purplish-pink underneath the blue by now, and my skin feels all hot and itchy. A little vindication was nice, but now I'm starting to feel embarrassed.

Ivar Orso cocks his head up, the bioluminescent lines on his skin glittering. "The Orso family also acknowledges and commends—"

"Okay, okay." I give up on all attempts at appearances and wave my hands through the air. "Do we really have to be so formal about this? This isn't an Imperial Council meeting. Can't we just skip to the actual business portion?"

"Speak for yourself," Faye says. "I was hoping for another several minutes of commendations at least."

Setter steps forward on the pad a little bit. "I think what Alyssa is trying to say is that there's a lot we need answers on still. The clearing of criminal records, the release of certain prisoners on the kingship"—I shoot him a grateful look—"and the question of the throne itself."

Cheery Coyenne folds her hands sharply in front of her. "At the moment, the throne will stay empty while the four of us here, as the remaining primors in good standing, fully investigate Edgar Voles and the leading members of the Voles family—"

"Five of us." To give myself some credit, my voice only wavers the teeniest bit as I cut in. I kinda wish I had Setter's height or Sharva's, but I lift my chin and pull my shoulders back, making do with what I've got. "As the niece of Atar Faroshti, I claim primor status for the Faroshti family, with all of the access and power that entails."

There's a long, hard beat as the four primors stare at me, their expressions running a nice wide gambit between interested and irate.

"That's not a position you can just claim," Jenna finally says, snapping out each word like it personally offended her. "Primors are voted in by their families."

"Oh, my bad. Let me do a quick roll call of everyone left in the Faroshti family." I make an exaggerated show of looking around the room and then throw up my hands in a shrug. "Just me, then? Cool. Guess I get the job!"

Cheery sighs. "Alyssa—"

I cut her off sharp. "Nope. Don't start. You all just spent a full minute patting us on the back about what a great service we did the empire, but now you're a hot second away from telling us to have a seat in the corner while the grown-ups talk. We want to have a real say in how this all ends. And not just us three, but all of those who helped us, too. They put their necks on the line. Some even lost their lives." I look over at Sharva for just a second, at the sorrow still shadowing their face. Then I turn back to the primors. "They deserve to be heard."

Setter shifts next to me, looking regally around the space. "I support Primor Alyssa Faroshti."

Faye crosses her arms and directs her words straight at her dad. "So do I."

"Fine," Ivar says after a minute. "If this will make you happy, Alyssa—"

I laugh. It definitely sounds kind of bitter, but I don't care. "Try not to sound so excited, Ivar. It's not exactly like I've been dying to put 'primor' on my resume. But this is a lot bigger than me. And there are pieces to this puzzle we haven't even totally figured out yet."

Radha raises an eyebrow. Man, those Roys are good at that. "What do you mean? What pieces?"

"We found the assassins," I tell them, pausing to look right at Jenna. "The ones who killed Owyn and attacked the rest of us during the crownchase. They're called ignati, and they're being *made* by a group of Solari called the excandare."

Ivar waves a dismissive hand. "The excandare aren't an organized group—"

"We had this conversation already, Father," Faye cuts in. "Catch up. They're way more organized than anyone thought. They had a whole space station."

Jenna catches that key word real quick. *"Had?"*

"They destroyed it," Setter says. "Once they realized they had been discovered."

Radha turns to Cheery. "We should reach out to the Solari leadership. They will need to address this." She looks back at me. "You think the excandare are connected to Edgar and his family? That they helped him get the throne?"

Isn't that the million-credit question. I wipe the back of my hand across my forehead. All this responsibility is making me sweat. "Maybe? I didn't think the Voleses were particularly religious, let alone big Solarus believers, but anything is possible. Edgar has put out a lot of pro-Solari policies since his coronation."

"No, he hasn't," Faye says abruptly. "I mean, he's agreed to them, but Wythe wrote all those policies. They were his ideas. Edgar's just been rubber-stamping them."

Setter frowns and looks over at Radha. "Mother? You've known

Wythe for a while. Have you picked up anything that would make you think he's connected to the excandare?"

She shakes her head. "Solari can be notoriously difficult to read, even for us. I'm not aware of any links between Ilysium Wythe and the excandare sect, but that doesn't mean there aren't any."

"Which means we need to investigate him," I say, squaring back off to the primors. "Figure out what in the actual hell is going on and what he knows about it."

"We can't be rash about this," cautions Cheery. "Edgar Voles is one thing. He's been branded a murderer from Apex to the Outer Wastes. The empire is already clamoring for his removal. But accusing and confronting one of the most prominent spiritual leaders in the quadrant before we have proper evidence is a different matter entirely."

Irritation licks up my skin. "But you're gonna move fast on this, though, right? Because I'm telling you, the excandare didn't blow up their whole operation for no reason. They've probably got players on the field already that are a *major* threat—"

"But a threat we can handle, now that we know about it," Ivar says. "I have crews I can call up—"

"But they'll have to beat the Mega forces there first," Jenna interrupts sharply. "When it comes to the excandare and these ignati, we call right to first blood."

Ivar rolls his eyes, gold like his daughter's. "Which means something in the Mega system, I suppose, but here it's first come, first served—"

As they squabble back and forth, Faye leans into me, muttering in my ear, "Look at them all working together—see? No problem. Everything's going so smoothly."

I snort.

"What matters is," Cheery says loudly, cutting through the chatter and drawing everyone's focus back to her, "that we work quickly and cooperatively to act on the information we have." She flicks a glance at Setter, who nods solemnly, and Faye, who smirks and gives her a wink. And then her eyes fall on me. "We will be in touch very soon. Don't go too far."

"There's actually one more thing I needed," I say loudly before any of them can step away. "I need one of you to use your big-time clout to get me in touch with the kingship. I want to speak to Edgar. Directly. As soon as possible."

Cheery looks at me like I've just asked for a storm whale as a pet. "What on earth about?"

"He's going to give me back my uncle, Charles Viqtorial."

THIRTY-ONE

I SET UP THE CALL ON THE *SERENDIPITY*, WHERE NOVA can ensure a secure communication channel that masks my coordinates. Even if things are swinging our way publicly and politically, there's absolutely no need for anyone on that kingship to know where we are right now. I don't even want them knowing the star system. Sharva and their people have already risked way too much for us—I'm not putting them in danger again.

I stand in my quarters, wiping my sweaty palms nervously against my jumpsuit as I wait for the display screen to go live. Hell Monkey hovers just inside the door, hands in his pockets, omni-goggles on his head.

"SECURE CHANNEL ESTABLISHED. IT WASN'T EVEN THAT HARD."

"Thanks, Nova. You're a champ."

"SO YOU'VE TOLD ME."

Hell Monkey grunts over in the corner. "I'm really starting to like her like this. I don't think I can ever go back."

I shake my hands out and then reach forward and open the connection with the kingship.

Nothing really prepares me for the anger and vicious satisfaction that surges through me when Edgar Voles appears on-screen, though. Anger because it's Edgar and I'll never not picture him with Coy's blood on his hands. And satisfaction because he looks terrible, haunted and thin, like something is eating at him from the inside.

I hope it's guilt. I hope it sits like a weight inside him.

A hint of shock flickers across Edgar's face when he sees me. "Alyssa. I didn't realize it would be you."

My eyebrows shoot way up on my forehead. "Really? That seems like an oversight on your part, Voles. Who else did you figure would be first in line for the privilege of looking you in the eyes and telling you to get fucked?"

"My father."

His response is so calm and frank—no drama, no self-pity, just "my dad super hates me and probably would toss me out an airlock." It throws me off guard, and I stumble to find a reply. Is there even a good reply to that?

Edgar pulls back from the screen a bit. I can practically see his shields go up in real-time. "What are you calling for, Alyssa?"

I set my jaw, pulling my in-charge captain presence on. "Charles Viqtorial. You're gonna let him go. Free and clear with no charges. I don't want to see even a hint of treason anywhere on his records. He's a godsdamned saint, and you're gonna treat him like that, got it?"

"I am still the emperor," he says, lifting his chin. "You think you can just make demands of me?"

"Hell yeah, I do," I snap back. "Because if you don't, I'm gonna put this on blast all over the quadrant. I'll do the most heart-tugging interview the galaxy's ever seen over on the *Daily Worlds*, all about how you're holding the bereaved spouse of Atar Faroshti prisoner, and the public outrage will grow until you don't have a choice but to do what I'm asking right now anyway." I lean toward the screen and drop my voice, closing in for the kill. "I'm giving you the chance to save a little face here, Edgar. Take it."

Edgar stares at me imperiously for a long moment, and then his shoulders drop. Not much—millimeters, really—but it's enough. I cornered him and I won.

"I'm processing his release right now," he says quietly, his eyes drifting to the side as he links with the kingship, transmitting his commands.

"I want to see him, too," I tell him. "Right now. You'll connect me to wherever he is so I can see for myself that he's okay."

"He is being taken to nearby guest quarters. As soon as he is there, I will connect you."

He's so distant right now. I might as well be talking to a concierge on some kind of hospitality starliner. But I don't play politician like Cheery—I'm not letting him off the hook without trying to get answers. "Oh, and one other thing, Edgar? You can stop sending your toy soldiers to kill me now. It's over. The jig is completely up."

He frowns, only half listening because he's all up in the network of the kingship and whatever else he has going on. "My toy soldiers . . ."

"Those faceless assassin guys that killed Owyn." I wave my hand in front of my own face. To indicate their lack thereof, I guess. "The ignati that the excandare were making for you."

That makes him finally look over and lock eyes with me. I'm ready for him to feed me lies or do that imperious thing or even just shut down the comms channel entirely.

But he looks absolutely bewildered. "The excandare . . . I didn't . . . I'm not . . ." His eyes go to that middle-distance, drifting back and forth, like he's searching for something. Then he refocuses again, right on me. "They weren't mine, Alyssa."

The screen goes dark before I can respond, leaving me standing there kind of stunned. I look over at Hell Monkey, who's been watching quietly this whole time.

I sniff. "He must be a better liar than I thought."

Hell Monkey shakes his head. "I don't think he was lying, Alyssa. And neither do you."

I don't get a chance to argue the point with him because the display screen flickers to life and—

"Alyssa?" Charlie's there. He's sitting on a low couch in some generic kingship guest quarters, Kalia Sharn beside him with an arm around him for support. He looks a lot more haggard and gaunt than I've ever seen him, but a tired smile crosses his face at the sight of me.

Annnnnnnd I burst into tears.

What the hell is wrong with me anymore? I need a vacation.

Hell Monkey swoops over as I try to rein in the little wave of sobs that rush out of my chest, pressing a hand between my shoulder blades as he ducks down into view. "Chaz. Good to see you all healed-up and brig-free."

"Yes, thank you, Hell Monkey."

Something about hearing Charlie's staid, proper voice say, "Hell Monkey," hits me right in the humor sweet spot, and all at once I'm not crying anymore, I'm laughing. Just overwhelmed with giggles so bad I can hardly get a breath in properly.

Hell Monkey eyes me warily. "You okay there, Farshot?"

"Yes! Yeah." I take a shaky inhale, wiping tears off my cheeks. I stuff the giggles back down by force of will, although I can't keep the stupidly big grin off my face. "Yeah, I'm okay. I got this."

Charlie's eyes are a little wet. "It's all right, Alyssa. I'm happy to see you, too."

Hell Monkey drops a kiss on the top of my hair, murmurs that he's gonna give us a minute to catch up, and then sees himself out. On the other side of the screen, Kalia squeezes Charlie's arm and then steps away, out of sight. So it's just me and Uncle Charlie again.

"Are you okay?" I look him over as much as I can through the display screen. "Are you still hurt?"

He shakes his head. "They treated my injuries, more or less."

"What about Ko? And Drinn? Are they okay?"

"They're fine. I haven't seen them in person, but Kalia has, and she assures me that they're also being released to guest quarters very soon."

"And you're sure you don't need anything? A medbot? Better food? I can call someone up on that ship and yell at them till they get you whatever you want—"

He cuts me off with a soft laugh. "Alyssa. I'm all right. I'm mostly just tired."

I can believe it. He *looks* really tired. More tears squeeze my throat, and I swallow them down. "I . . . I'm so sorry, Charlie. I'm sorry I left you there."

"Alyssa." He levels a look at me far more like his old self. "You didn't leave me anywhere. I don't know if you recall this or not, but I rather enthusiastically encouraged you to go."

"Yeah, well . . ." I sniff and wipe off my eyes again. "I'm not usually that obedient. I don't know what got into me."

"A momentary aberration, I'm sure."

There's a long moment of silence, and for once, I don't feel the need to fill it up. I just let it sit there and let it be okay for Charlie and me to just *be*, even if we are still millions of kilometers apart.

"They want to escort me," he finally says. "Upon my release from the ship, they want to send a few crownsguards to escort me to where you are."

Suspicion tickles the back of my neck. "So generous of them. And nosy, too. Like they want to use you to find out where I am."

Charlie nods, and I see his eyes skim his surroundings. "Yes, I agree. I'm anxious for our reunion, of course, but let's be extra cautious. You hold a lot of cards right now in terms of public perception and public clout—use them to ensure this goes in your favor, not theirs."

Right. Job's not done. *Eyes up, hands on the controls, Farshot.* "I can do that."

Charlie looks off-screen and nods, and then brings his eyes back to me. "Kalia says we have to go, but Alyssa . . . I want you to know . . ." Now it's his turn to stop, clear his throat, wrestle his emotions back down. "I'm so proud of you. Of how hard you've fought. And I . . . I love you."

Welp. Here come the waterworks all over again.

Son of a bitch.

THIRTY-TWO

STARDATE: 0.06.20 in the Year 4031, under the reign of the Empress Who Never Was, Nathalia Matilda Coyenne, long may she rest in glory
LOCATION: The planet where I started into this whole messy shit storm and the place where I'm going to put it the hell to bed

I DO EXACTLY WHAT CHARLIE SAID: I MAKE DEMANDS.

He's right that I apparently have a lot more clout now than I've been working with the past few weeks, and I gather pretty quick that the kingship is anxious to earn back some public goodwill by broadcasting themselves generously reuniting the beloved diplomat and widower with his crownchaser niece. They're not willing to let it just be a quiet release—they need it to be a whole thing to reestablish trust.

Which means I can name my terms.

I refuse a lot of their ideas—like bringing the *Serendipity* to the kingship or doing an exchange out in space, which would require some sort of docking or link between our ships that they might try to use their advantage. Instead, I tell them that if they're so set on making a big public display out of escorting Charles Viqtorial like he's a child walking home from school, then we'll do an old-fashioned exchange on a planet exactly to my specifications.

What is it that people say? Noisy engine gets the diagnostic check? Yeah, that's me. I'm a noisy engine now.

I pick Gloo—my starting point for the crownchase that feels like it all happened years ago and not just a few weeks. But I don't just choose it for the symbolism. There's an area in their northern hemisphere that's flat, open plains and empty sky for kilometers around, which means it's that much more difficult for the kingship to hide any tricks up their sleeve.

It's also—most important—completely devoid of inhabitants, which means no innocents are gonna wind up in harm's way like they did on Cybsis.

There's a mediabot and a camera drone set up to follow Charlie and give me a live feed of him the whole time—from his room in the kingship, to the liftship down to the surface, to the transport that'll cross the planet surface to our meeting point. The *Daily Worlds* already claimed rights to air the footage, and I'm happy to give it to them. They can show off the whole heartwarming moment, just as long as the kingship hands over my uncle.

I sit cross-legged on the ground, clutching a tablet in my lap as I diligently watch the livestream. Charlie boarded the transport about twenty minutes ago with two otari crownsguards and the mediabot, which keeps persistently trying to get a good interview going with my uncle. They should be here in a few minutes. The transport is supposed to land, and then everyone on it stays put while Charlie walks the rest of the way to me.

I see Hell Monkey's boots come up next to me out of the corner of my eye. He's currently keeping tabs on the horizon for when they come into view. "Anything yet?"

"Not quite. Should be soon, though." He nudges my leg with his toe. "If you doesn't ease off your grip on that thing, you're gonna snap it in two."

I roll my eyes, but I do try to relax my fingers. A little. Maybe not quite so white-knuckled, I guess. "I just want this to be over."

"It's gonna be okay, Alyssa. They need this to go well. None of them, especially not Wythe or his buddies, wants their asses thrown in intergalactic jail with Edgar. They want to put those good faces forward."

"You're right. They do. I know that." The words are heavy in my mouth, though. Or maybe it's just that my mouth feels dry. I wipe the back of my hand across parched lips. I should've grabbed water from the ship before coming out here.

"See? What'd I tell you? Here they come."

I shoot to my feet, scanning the flat landscape in front of us until I see it: a dirty white rectangular-looking vehicle hovering centimeters above the ground as it zips over the arid dirt toward us. The sun glares down, even through the dusty brown haze that swirls in rivers along the upper troposphere. My heart hammers against my sternum as I switch back and forth between watching the transport speed closer and looking at the live feed of Charlie standing quietly, hands threaded together in front of him, ever dignified, ever patient.

That's Charlie for you.

Almost there.

I can see the glowering sunlight glinting off the transport's forward windows when a bad feeling starts to sour in my stomach. On the feed, one of the otari crownsguards keeps edging back toward a corner. I squint, bringing the tablet right up to my nose like that'll help me see better. They're not doing anything exactly, but . . .

Hell Monkey cranes his head over my shoulder. "What? What is it?"

"That crownsguard . . . I can't tell what they're doing. I—where the hell is the communicator on this thing?!" I fumble with the button that'll transmit my voice through a speaker on the camera drone. There. Got it. "Charlie? Charlie, watch your back—the otari—"

He swings around immediately, and so does the other crownsguard next to him.

A searing flash of green cuts through the air, straight through the crownsguard standing next to Charlie. She drops to the ground, a massive gash splitting her chest.

It's not the kind of wound a blaster makes. It's almost like . . .

"Shit," Hell Monkey breathes into my ear. "Oh shit, Alyssa. Oh shit—"

The realization hits me half a second before the illusion of the crownsguard flickers . . . and then disappears.

An ignati stands in his place, cradling a plasma blade in one hand and flicking a glamour key to the ground with the other.

"NO!" The scream rips out of me. I hear all the panic in it. All the terror. I see Charlie—gentle Charlie, diplomat Charlie—launch himself toward the ignati, and then I drop the tablet and run.

I've never run like this in my whole godsdamned life. Muscles burning with adrenaline. Lungs and heart working overtime. Feet pounding over the flat, dusty earth. Arms pumping so hard I might rip them right out of my shoulder sockets.

I'd do it, too. I'd tear my body apart just to get there in time.

"CHARLIE! GET THE FUCK OUT OF THAT TRANSPORT!"

Please, gods. Just let me get there in time.

Alyssa . . . I want you to know . . . I'm so proud of you. And I . . . I love you.

"CHARLIE!" Every breath from my throat is jagged. I don't know if I'm panting or sobbing.

Just keep running. Keep running. I have to get there. I have to. I can't—

The transport explodes.

It *explodes.*

The fireball is massive. Carving a crater into the ground. Sending clouds mushrooming upward.

And Charlie . . .

Charlie . . .

Charlie . . .

I don't even feel the shock wave that slams me into the ground. Or the heat that sears across my face.

All I hear are screams. And all I taste is blood.

CHAOS ACROSS THE EMPIRE
Reports flood in of multiple, massive explosions from dozens of systems across the quadrant

INITIAL DEATH TOLL: 100,113 AND CLIMBING

Numbers are extremely preliminary and experts say we should expect them to rise exponentially as the smoke clears

FARSHOT, VIQTORIAL, AND OTHER PRIME FAMILY MEMBERS AMONG THOSE PRESUMED DEAD

Still trying to make sense of who might have pulled off attacks of this magnitude, officials claim it's clear that prime families and their holdings were the primary targets

SHADOWS OF WAR LOOM IN THE MINDS OF MANY

Those who lived through the Twenty-Five-Year War say this feels like the start of an intergalactic conflict even worse than the previous one

THE KINGSHIP, UNDISCLOSED COORDINATES

Edgar's empire is on fire.

He felt the initial shock waves as they hit his security droids. He watched the towering columns of fire and smoke.

Now he stands in the middle of his quarters, surrounded by dozens of projected display screens, his face stretching longer and longer as the horror in his chest grows. Each minute brings another wave of video to the media feeds, footage of explosions and victims and things just burning, burning, burning.

The transport with Charles Viqtorial was the first. It was a live feed, broadcast front and center on the *Daily Worlds*, threaded with upbeat commentary and triumphant background music.

It all went up in a column of fire. And then came the news of the others. Dozens of targets across the empire, all of them linked to the Megas, the Roys, the Orsos, the Coyennes. Entire properties and resources obliterated.

And victims. There's no telling who was lost. Who survived.

If anyone.

What is he doing here in his rooms? Hiding just because Wythe told him to? He's the emperor. He should go out to his people.

There's a beep at the doors to his quarters—someone requesting entry—and he waves them in without even looking, transfixed by the destruction all around him. He's expecting NL7; he called for the droid a few minutes ago to come to him. Not because NL7 can do anything, really. But just because . . . Edgar finds himself wanting a . . . friend.

The tramping of boots and metal makes him turn, and he sees a dozen crownsguards pouring into his room, two of them advancing toward him with compression cuffs. The shock of it hits him in the chest hard—he had thought so little of the crownsguards lately, pushed their signatures and his connections to them so far into the corners of his mind that he hadn't sensed any of them coming. He reaches through the neural link for his security droids but can't read anything outside his rooms.

"What in the hell is this?" he demands, drawing upon every ounce of imperial authority he has inside him. "How dare any of you—"

"Edgar Marius Tycho Voles." Enkindler Wythe's voice carries across the room as he enters, loud and resonant as a bell. Camera drones hover on either side of his head. "Your lust for power has taken you too far. You are under immediate arrest for the coordinated terrorist attacks on the prime families of the United Sovereign Empire—"

Edgar can hardly breathe. He feels like he's free-falling toward nothingness. "I didn't—I couldn't—"

"As the sole surviving member of the Imperial Council, it is my duty and responsibility to relieve you of the crown and assume command of the kingship and the throne—"

The cuffs tighten around Edgar's wrists, and his voice comes

243

back to him in a rush. "I didn't do this! Release me at once!"

Enkindler Wythe looks down his nose at Edgar. "I am disgusted with you, Edgar. I thought you would be an emperor for the ages." He flicks a long-fingered hand at one of the crownsguard. "Disarm him and take him away."

Adrenaline surges through Edgar and he lunges toward the enkindler.

But the crownsguards hold his arms tight and jam a syringe of something opalescent white straight into his neck.

Edgar's vision dissolves into blurry blocks of color. He stumbles.

And then he sees nothing at all.

FROM THE PERSONAL FILES OF ATAR VELRYN FAROSHTI, ACCESSED BY NL734014 ON STARDATE 0.06.21 IN THE YEAR 4031

Audio transcript of a long-range communication between Atar and Charles Viqtorial on 0.09.12.4029

"WELL, IT IS OFFICIAL. ENKINDLER WYTHE WILL FORMALLY join the Imperial Council next quarter.

"I know you will not be surprised to hear this news, Charles. Always the clear-eyed pragmatist. It's not the outcome I had hoped for and such a waste of a real opportunity to bring a new perspective into the council. You know how excited I was for the possibilities. But William Voles outmaneuvered me again. I suspect he had done quite a bit of work already to set up this outcome before the meeting commenced. Ivar, Jenna, even Cheery were all well in his corner from the outset, and neither my nor Radha's objections could sway them.

"You'll be happy to hear that I think I've finally put any hope of a real partnership with William to bed at last. Whatever the Voles and the Faroshti families once were to each other, it's lost to history. "We must hope that this will turn out to be the best course for the empire.

"And yet . . . I am troubled, Charles."

THIRTY-THREE

STA—I don't know. I don't know, okay? And it doesn't even matter anymore.

I'M NOT IN MY BODY.

That's not true. This is what's true: I don't *want* to be in my body.

It's such a horrible meat casing. So fragile and painful. I just want to float somewhere outside of it. I'm trying my damnedest to just *float* and not have to *be*.

The door slides open, and the sound of it brings me crashing back down into my bones. I drag my eyes up to Hell Monkey, and for a flash, I'm so so angry at him for being there and making me be there too.

But then it's gone. I see the red ringing his eyes, the ash and dirt smeared across his face, the tear tracks streaked down his cheek. I remember him scooping me off the ground. I remember him running, right beside me, into the searing heat of the wreckage.

There's so little left. Like half the metal was just incinerated upon detonation.

"Charlie!" I cough and gag on the smoke, hacking spit and bile into the ashes. Somewhere off to my right, I hear Hell Monkey shout my uncle's name.

No answer. Because there's no one left to answer.

Get out of here, Farshot. He's gone.

I wade in farther. As close as I dare. I have to know for sure. I have to see.

I'm starting to sway and get light-headed when I spot it—

—a tangle of bones and lumps of cinders still crowned with tongues of flames—

I collapse onto my knees in the ash. My hands fall on red-hot metal, and they're burning but I barely notice . . .

. . . and then Hell Monkey's arms wrap around me, drag me back out into the clear air . . .

My eyes scan the room, pulling in the familiar details of the med bay until it all comes back to me.

Coughing until I threw up. The oxygen to clear my lungs. The treatment cuffs grafting new skin onto my palms and the pads of my fingers. Hell Monkey wrapping me up in a heat-retaining blanket as I shivered and shivered and drifted away.

"We just landed on Vellyn," he says. His voice is rough and ragged. He took in his fair share of smoke. Probably his fair share of burns, too. I push myself shakily onto my feet and look him over, trying to suss out secret wounds he might try to keep from me.

"Are you okay?" My own voice sounds like it's half gravel. "You have to tell me if you're not. Don't hide something to spare me—"

He steadies me as I lose my balance and pulls me into him. "I'm okay, Alyssa. Hand to the stars. Some smoke inhalation. A few minor burns. Nothing the med bay's tricks couldn't take care of."

"Good. That's good." I'm shivering again. When did this ship get so damn cold?

He steps back, his hands still cupped around my elbows. "You ready to go out there?"

I shake my head and feel light-headed all over again. "Nope. Any way we can just hide in here for the next few decades?"

"I wish." He shifts so that he's beside me, one arm around my waist.

I move shakily forward, toward the cargo bay, glad to have someone to lean against. I don't like feeling this weak or dependent, but my body doesn't feel steady. Hell, it doesn't even really feel like my body. It's just this collection of blood and bone and muscle being jerked around underneath me.

"Have you seen anything else on the feeds?" I ask him as we come down the aft ramp. "Is there—"

My question drops away as we step out onto the docking platform. A big display screen on the far wall is broadcasting the media feeds, and dozens of people are gathered around, watching it transfixed. I look for Setter, for Faye, for Honor, and when I finally find them, my heart bottoms out.

Setter is crumpled in a heap on the bare ground, his shoulders shaking. Faye stands nearby, jaw clenched tight, shoulders stiff, her face wet with rivers of golden tears. Honor presses herself against Faye, clutching her tightly around the waist, like she and she alone can keep her above water.

Everyone else watches the images on the feeds, staring in horror.

I let go of Hell Monkey and stumble forward, weaving past people to get closer to the screen. Sharva meets me halfway, grabbing my arm.

"Faroshti," they say, their voice rough with sympathy. "You don't have to watch."

"Yes, I do," I tell them quietly. "You would too." I pull myself out of their grasp and push my way to the very front of the crowd. It probably takes me five solid minutes of staring before my brain actually catches up and processes the horror I'm seeing.

It was the ignati, wearing glamour keys. Infiltrating dozens of points across the empire and decimating them in massive explosions. But they didn't bring devices with them—they were the devices. Security feeds caught footage of it happening: a glow that started in their chests, spreading down their arms and legs and up their necks and then—

Blinding light. Fire. Smoke. Blast radii half a dozen or even a dozen kilometers wide for every single ignati agent.

I swallow hard as the live feed from Charlie's transport replays on one screen. I dropped the tablet to try to run to him, so I missed everything that had happened just before the explosion. Charlie had thrown himself at the ignati, but it had tossed him to the ground like he was nothing. That same glow had started in its chest, and Charlie had scrambled away from it over the body of his other crownsguard.

I can't see from the angle on the feed what happened next. What went on in Charlie's head. I just know when he got to his feet, he had one of the otari's standard-issue plasma grenades in his hand. He'd looked up at the camera drone—at me—

And then he'd pressed the button on the grenade.

And the footage cut out.

Charlie is the one who'd exploded the transport. He'd dropped that grenade and blown them all up before the ignati could finish its mission. If it had . . .

I stare again at the craters of destruction all around the quadrant. Hell Monkey and I had been so close to that transport. Three dozen meters away at most. That ignati meant to kill us. *Should* have killed us.

Except for Charlie . . .

I think I'm gonna throw up again.

I sink to the ground, hands pressed into my face. Just trying to breathe. *Breathe, Farshot.* A hand pats my back, too tentative to be Hell Monkey. It's probably Sharva, but I don't look. It's dark in here behind my hands, and I like it that way.

An automated voice on-screen lists off the destruction in cool, distant tones.

Cheery and Reginald Coyenne: confirmed dead.

Ivar and Sara Orso: confirmed dead.

Radha and Jaya Roy: confirmed dead.

Jenna and Lorcan Mega: confirmed dead.

Even William Voles. Dead.

All of them gone, just like Charlie.

The leadership, infrastructure, and resources behind most of the prime families were targeted, too. Mega shipyards. Three different Orsion citadels. Roy-sponsored diplomatic centers and schools. *Daily Worlds* deployments and broadcast points on dozens of planets.

It's all ruins.

"Alyssa Faroshti," the voice on-screen announces, and I pull my head out of my hands long enough to see them play new camera drone footage of the smoking wreckage of Charlie's transport. They zoom in on a little metal band, half melted in the ashes. My mother's armband. It must've fallen off when the shock wave hit. "Presumed dead," the voiceover says. "Eliot Flynn, presumed dead."

The feed cuts off suddenly, dissolving into static, and then it flickers back online.

Enkindler Wythe fills the display. He's put on this perfect picture of appearing grave and troubled, and I swear to every god in this empire that I will punch my fist right through his asshole face sometime before this is over. Adrenaline and rage pour through me until I'm shaking.

"People of the United Sovereign Empire, I assure you that we on the kingship mourn with you right now in the aftermath of this tragic and unprecedented attack on our empire. May the light of Solarus lead us through this time. I have been devastated to discover that Edgar Voles coordinated this horrific assault on his rivals for the throne, using agents that many of you may recognize helped him win the crownchase in the first place."

The feed cuts to footage—some angle on the bridge of Edgar's worldcruiser that looks like it's right next to Edgar. Maybe his droid friend? Hard to say for sure, but it's showing Edgar talking to one of those things—the ignati.

It looks damning. It looks damning as hell. And yeah, just yesterday, I was the primary pilot on the ship *Edgar Voles Is Responsible for All This Shit*.

But Hell Monkey was right. I don't believe he was lying when he said he didn't know anything about the excandare or the ignati. I also don't believe he's stupid enough to blow up half the empire and leave ridiculously incriminating evidence lying around for Ilysium Wythe to immediately find.

Edgar is guilty of some bad stuff. But this? I'm not buying it.

"As the sole surviving member of the Imperial Council," Wythe says as the feed cuts back to his face, "I am assuming control of the kingship and all its attenuate responsibilities until peace and balance can be restored to the empire."

How. Fucking. Convenient.

Uncle Atar told me once when I was a kid that when something awful happens and you can't understand why, you need to look for who profits from it. Who wins when everyone else is losing. And godsdamn if Atar wasn't right as hell about that one.

Everything is literally on fire, and here's Wythe. Living his best life.

"In the name of keeping information flowing freely, I have assigned personnel to secure the remaining media feeds—both the *Daily Worlds* and all tertiary companies, their broadcast points and capabilities. All of it will now be originating from the kingship so that you can rest easy knowing that the news and information you receive comes straight from me without tampering from undue political influences."

My stomach churns. I taste acid and smoke.

This time, I really do throw up.

THIRTY-FOUR

WYTHE'S BROADCAST ENDS, AND THE SCREENS RETURN
to the scenes of destruction all around the empire. I sit, numb, on
a storage container in the middle of the docking bay floor and let
noise wash over me. The somber music blaring from the feeds.
Faye storming away from everyone in an almost literal way—
practically spitting lightning and howling thunder. Setter's soft,
broken voice as he prays in Lenosi.

Grieving. I never thought of it having a sound, but it does. I can
hear it all around me—some of it soft, some of it loud. Everyone is
just oozing out their grief until it lies on me like the worst blanket.

Grief as a weight. Grief as a tangible thing. Now that's something I'm more familiar with. My limbs are heavy with it. My chest
is filled with its aching pressure. It's already pressing on my skin so
much—I can't handle everyone else's, too.

I escape back onto the *Serendipity*. I don't know where I'm going
to go, exactly, but there's something comforting about its empty
corridors and the familiar sound of my boots on the metal floors.
I wander the galley, the crew quarters, the quiet bridge with all
systems shut down and sleeping. I stop by the storage room where

all of Coy's stuff that she left around this worldcruiser is still piled up, waiting to be crated away. I expect the jagged edges of her loss to feel worse, sharper, in the wake of . . .

. . . of that . . .

But they don't. It's all duller somehow. Like instead of having one metaphorical stab wound, I've now got a thousand and the pain is so bad and so *everywhere* that I can't even feel it properly anymore.

Is there a hard limit on how much a person can lose in a short time frame before they just shut down? If there is, I feel like I've got to be on a solid trajectory for it. Atar, Owyn, Coy, Charlie . . .

It's only because I'm standing so still in this quiet little room that I hear it. What sounds like a sniffle and a muffled sob. From the engine room next door.

I know, in my gut, who it is, and I came in here to be alone from other people's grief—but not his. Not him. I step out of the storage room, closing it up carefully behind me, and then duck into the engine room.

I don't see him at first. The place is dark when everything is powered down. But I finally spot him on the far side, sitting against the wall, his knees pulled up and his arms draped over them.

And I freeze.

Because it's not like I've never seen Hell Monkey tear up or anything, but . . . this is different. Shoulders shaking. Tears pouring down his face.

He notices me hovering in the entrance and turns away, clearing his throat loudly and scrubbing at his eyes. "Sorry. I just . . . I need a minute, and I'll be right out."

Those words, that gruff, nothing-to-see-here tone, unstick my damn feet from the floor. I circle the engine in the middle of the room and plop down right next to him, mimicking his body position. Not touching him, just . . . doing that Hell Monkey thing of being near but not demanding anything.

Or, at least, that's what I'm going for anyway. I don't know if I'm doing it right. I'm usually more of the demanding kind, okay?

It takes a few minutes before he stops angling away from me and leans back against the wall again. "I didn't want you to see that."

I shake my head, although I'm still looking at the engine, not at him. "Because you are a rough and tough male creature who doesn't feel feelings?"

He laughs a little, real quiet, under his breath, and scrubs the back of his hand across the stubble that covers his jawline. "Nothing like that. It's . . . you just lost . . . I shouldn't . . ." He lets his head thunk back against the wall. "Godsdammit. I'm supposed to be there for you right now. Not the other way around."

Right. That. As soon as I remember the grief, my skin crawls with the weight of it all over again. I scoot a little closer to him. So our arms brush just a little. "Pretty sure we all get a share in this. I'm not one to steal the spotlight."

"Yeah, you are," he says, at the same time I say, "Actually, yeah, I am," and a little chuckle escapes my throat. And then the guilt of it—laughing, *laughing*, when the wreckage of Charlie's transport is probably still smoking on Gloo—hits me so hard my head spins. I reach a hand out, I need to steady myself, I need—

—Hell Monkey's callused fingers thread through mine, squeeze tight. I fix my eyes on the engine again, swallowing and breathing, swallowing and breathing, until my throat relaxes and I think I can keep the sobs from swarming me.

"It was the explosion," Hell Monkey says very quietly. "Watching the fire take everyone and just being . . . helpless to stop it. It was Homestead all over again."

Of course. Homestead. Hell Monkey watched his whole family die in that blast, and here he is, reliving it.

I tilt my head so I can look at him, his profile cut through with shadows. "Look, I'm . . . not okay." Shaky breath. Shove all those gut-racking sobs back into my chest where they belong. "But . . . you don't have to be okay just because I'm not. We can be not okay together, and that's fine, too."

He pulls his gaze up to mine. Tears rim his eyes. We're gripping each other's hands so tight that I'm starting to lose feeling in my fingers. "All right. I think I can do that."

"Good." I lean my head on his shoulder, and we sit there for a long time. Well past the point where my butt starts to go numb, but I can't bring myself to do much more than shift my weight a little.

I let my eyes drift back to the engine. Dark and massive. The heart of the ship, dominating the entirety of the room, but right now it's nothing but cold metal, not even a spark lighting it up.

Well, if that isn't some metaphorical shit.

THIRTY-FIVE

STARDATE: 0.06.22 in the Year 4031. All reigns are officially canceled. And we're the ones who are gonna cancel them.
LOCATION: According to the kingship? Missing and presumed dead. Which is fine by me right now.

HELL MONKEY AND I EVENTUALLY FALL ASLEEP TANgled together on the floor of the engine room. (Hindsight: a very bad idea. Sleeping on metal flooring does zero good to your bones and muscles and all that, even when you're young and spry.) I wake up hours later and drag my sorry ass to the galley for an even sorrier cup of coffee, and then I go down to the cargo bay and sit on the edge, my legs stretched out down the ramp.

Sharva finds me there when I've still got half my drink left. They sprawl onto the alloy floor next to me and press something small and round into my hand.

"In memory of your loss," they say, and I hold it up to the light so I can see it better. It's a wooden disc about the size of a large coin, and on it is carved an intricate flower with what looks like hundreds of petals.

"A Chu'ran sympathy flower," Sharva explains with a shrug. "It's not the right kind of wood, but I had to make do."

"It's beautiful," I say, running the pad of my thumb over the engraved lines. "I didn't get you anything. For the people you lost."

Sharva raises their eyebrows. "Do the Faroshti have a traditional sympathy gift?"

I swallow bitter coffee, grimacing a little at the gritty residue at the bottom of the cup. "I actually don't know. I guess I can offer you bad jokes and liquor, but that's about all I got." I raise my eyes to look around the docking bay and the tunnels that lead into the compound beyond. I gesture at the space with my coffee cup. "How are they feeling around here? About . . . what happened?"

Sharva gives me a hard sideways look. "Are you asking me if they're celebrating the destruction of the prime families?" As soon as they repeat it back to me like that, I feel like a giant shitheel. "No, Faroshti, they're not celebrating. They may not like the empire, but they have hearts. They have empathy. People died yesterday. We grieve for them. And for all those who loved them."

I look down again at the wooden flower, curling it back and forth between my fingers. "I'm sorry. That was a full-out asshole thing for me to ask."

They lean back on their elbows, looking out over the docking bay. "This new power in the kingship is even more dangerous than usual."

I swallow the last dregs of my coffee, the grit hitting the back of my throat so hard that I cough a little. "I know."

"And?" They're giving me that arch look again. It's like being back in school with Mr. Odo, when he'd push me on a question he knew I knew the answer to. "I intend to do something about it. Even if it means taking some risks. What about you?"

I hope, whatever the afterlife is like, Uncle Atar can see me now. I'd hate for him to miss getting to feel smug about me finally stepping into the role he'd always wanted for me.

Fucking leadership.

"Risky and stupid is basically my whole brand," I say as I stand and stretch out the kinks in my back. "But not today. You've got people grieving. So do I. We should give them something to do with that before we plot our next course."

Sharva nods, like that's exactly the answer they wanted to hear out of me, and pushes onto their feet. "Then I suppose we need to get to work."

According to records I found on the *Serendipity*, the hallüdraens have something called a remembrance ceremony where they use these particular kinds of floating balloons that carry a special item or items of the deceased person up into the upper atmosphere of the planet. When it reaches a certain elevation, a mechanism in the balloon is triggered and the whole thing burns up into a harmless gas that disperses in the upper atmosphere.

We don't have any of those balloons here, obviously, so Hell Monkey and I rig up some little floats and lights with the idea that we'll release them onto the river above us and let everything pass over the cliff and down into the thundering basin of the waterfall below.

That's actually the easiest part. And it doesn't take very long. The rest of the day I have to try and figure out what the hell item I'm gonna share for the ceremony. I mean, it was kind of my idea, so I have to have *something*. Hell Monkey finds me, well into the afternoon, sitting in my quarters in the middle of a mess of what little I have left in this universe, staring at everything without quite seeing it, feeling all scooped out and hollow.

He steps carefully over to me and clears a place on the floor for him to sit. He looks adorable and ridiculous—this big-ass guy folded up all cross-legged so he doesn't crush anything.

"Can't find anything?"

I laugh, a little bitter. "I kind of wish that was the problem. Actually, it's that I don't have much left anymore, and literally almost all of it is a memento of someone who's gone now."

I gesture to a ceremonial knife (my great-grandmother's), a smooth golden stone from a Ysevian moon (Charlie), a formal hallüdraen jacket (both my uncles, though it's ripped and dirty after the battle over Calm), a glittery pair of ear cuffs (Coy, when she wanted to try and get me to dress up more), a pile of holodiscs depicting my mother and uncles and friends.

"I think the only things I own that weren't given to me by a dead person are the jumpsuit and boots I'm wearing." I try to grin at him—see? handling everything just fine—but my eyes fill with tears. Traitors. I stare down at my lap instead, twisting my fingers together. "I just can't bring myself to volunteer any of it to the falls. I cut too much loose thinking I didn't need anything. I don't want to do that again."

Hell Monkey grunts a little and picks up one of the holodiscs, turning it over in his hands. "I might have an idea. Do you trust me?"

Of all the ridiculous questions right now. "No, actually, I think you're a longtime double agent, walking a dangerous line between your loyalties and your overwhelming attraction to me."

He snorts and gets to his feet, pulling me up with him. "Sounds hot. Go get cleaned up. I'll take care of this and meet you at the river at sunset."

THIRTY-SIX

IT DOESN'T EXACTLY TAKE ME LONG TO GET MYSELF together—I've only got, like, three outfits at this point, and one of them is in desperate need of cleaning. So I just go with my slightly cleaner jumpsuit, which—combined with a shower—almost makes me look presentable. I even put on Coy's ear cuffs and tuck that stone Charlie gave me into my pocket just to have it close. I come across Honor in the docking bay, using her fingertips and a pot of some kind of iridescent cosmetic to paint her bare arms with the insignias of the lost Orsion citadels and the family crest of the Orsos.

When I ask her, she paints me as well. I pull down the top of my jumpsuit so I just have my tank top on, and she decorates my upper arms with Coy's family seal. The Faroshti family crest across my collarbones and sternum. The hallüdraen rune for the afterlife on my forehead—which, heartbreakingly, I have to look that up in the *Serendipity*'s database as well because I was never interested in learning when I was younger and Atar offered to teach me.

No chance to teach me now.

I close my eyes, trying to breathe, trying to focus on the light pressure of Honor's fingertip swiping back and forth on my skin.

The soft smile on Charlie's face whenever he looked at Atar. Or me. His annoyed sighs when I was particularly irritating. His careful deliberation whenever I asked him a question. How there was absolutely no one he couldn't small talk with.

The last hug I'll ever get from him. Outside my cell in the brig of the kingship.

Our last conversation.

My face is wet—I can feel it—but I let the images keep coming as Honor works. All of them.

Owyn Mega boasting and laughing with the rest of us as kids on the kingship. Coy laughing, running, pulling me along behind her. Charlie's and Atar's expressions when they brought me to my Vagabond Quick. *Atar's face in the darkness of the planetarium. Coy's grin in the Explorers' Society club on Gloo as we made plans to win her the throne . . .*

"All done." Honor reaches up with her thumb and wipes at the tears on my cheeks. She's taken her pink-toned glasses off for the moment, and her eyes are almost as green as her hair. "If they drip, they'll smear the paint."

"Thanks." I look down at the shimmering lines on my skin. Kind of pretty, really. "How's Faye doing?"

Honor's expression tightens, her square jawline clenching just a little. "Some things break you and leave you broke." She turns away, cleaning up her stuff, and I don't press her. I just touch her arm lightly and then head up into the grasses of Vellyn.

It's time to go to the river anyway.

Sharva is already there, setting things up with Hell Monkey. He straightens when he sees me getting closer and pulls something from his pocket, holding it out to me.

"For the ceremony," he says as I step up to him. "It's for you, but it's also kind of for the other prime kids, too."

I scoop his creation into my palms, studying it. It's about the size of a holodisc, but he's welded a Faroshti dragon like the one on our family crest around it. I find an activation point and watch it light up, projecting a display about two meters into the air.

An image of Charles Viqtorial—not from his official portrait, but a rare informal one where he's broken out into a broad smile. Then an image of Atar Faroshti, staring thoughtfully off into the distance with the windows of the throne room in the background. Then one of Coy, laughing and winking into the camera.

They're copies of images off my collection of holodiscs. And there are more of them, too. Not all of them mine.

One of the prime family heirs when we were younger, Owyn tallest and biggest of all of us, dominating the middle of the frame, looking irritated as Coy ruffles his hair. A recent family photo of Owyn, smiling with his parents, Jenna and Lorcan. Radha and Jaya Roy, standing forehead to forehead, arms wrapped around each other, wearing Lenosi engagement colors. Ivar Orso, playfully hanging off the wing of his famous ship, the Star Catcher, while the ship's namesake, Sara Orso, looks on, laughing. Cheery Coyenne standing in the middle of the headquarters of the Daily Worlds, hands on her hips like a conqueror.

"Is it okay?" Hell Monkey looks a little anxious in the lengthening shadows of the day. "I only had your stuff to work with and then whatever I could find on public databases—"

My throat is way too swollen with emotion to get any words

out, so I just grab him by the collar and press a kiss to his lips to cut him off. I pat his chest, clutching the little holo-dragon tight, and move off to the edge of the river.

Sharva was the one who suggested sunset as a good time for the ceremony, and it's definitely a picturesque-as-hell choice. There's a thin layer of clouds down near the southern horizon where the sun is sinking, and they scatter the colors across the darkening sky, turning it amber and gold and red-violet. The light itself goes liquid, drenching the trees and tops of the blue-green grasses, painting itself across the rippling surface of the river, infusing the mists of the waterfall with intense hues. The air is warm and sweet. There are birds I'm not familiar with singing evening songs in major harmony. Rippling clouds of bright, winged insects drift along the currents of the breeze.

See what I mean? Picturesque.

I stand still, staring down at the meandering water, so clear you can see the black sand at the bottom, listening as people filter up from the compound and gather in the grass nearby. I can hear the numbers swell as the sun dips lower and the sunset-bright colors around me start to darken.

It's time.

I turn and face the crowd.

There's Sharva up front, standing side by side with Evern, with probably a hundred members of the Planetary Independence Movement gathered behind them.

My eyes find Setter, standing off to the left. His irises are completely black and so big that they almost take up the whole white part, too. He's staring in my general direction, but I don't think he really sees me. I've never seen him look so raw, so unfocused.

I search the group for Faye, but she's not with the rest. She's standing a little ways away from everyone, watching with her arms crossed over her chest and an energy around her that's all blood and sharp knives. She's glaring at this ceremony. She's glaring at the sunset. She's glaring hard enough to tear a hole straight into a parallel universe. She catches me watching her and lifts her pointed chin, daring me to . . .

. . . I don't know what. Start a fight, probably just for an excuse to punch something. But she's not gonna get that from me tonight.

I look over at Setter and give him a nod. He swallows hard, his hands tight fists at his sides, and then he raises his voice in a traditional Lenosi song of grieving. It's godsdamned beautiful. It's that blend of haunting and lilting that strikes you with sadness even when you're not already sad. Tears start to pool, but I'm quick to scrub them away. Keep it together.

I'm supposed to step forward and present my item to the group and say something about what I chose and what it meant to me and to the deceased. But when Setter finishes singing, I put Hell Monkey's holodisc on the ground, activate it, and step back without saying a word. No need for it. And I'd probably say something inappropriate, let's be honest. I just let the images play in silence until it hits the end and goes dark.

Now I'm supposed to set the holodisc on one of the illuminated rafts and send it down the river. And . . . I will.

But would I really be me if I did everything by the book?

I tuck the disc against my chest and go to Setter, taking one of his hands. He blinks, looks at me, and lets me tug him away and lead him back through the grasses to where Faye stands alone. Her jaw is clenched, her eyes ooze thick gold tears, she's refusing to look at me.

But I fold my arms around her anyway. I reach blindly backward to catch Setter's sleeve and pull him into us, too. I hold them both tight until Setter finally, finally responds and hugs me back and even Faye softens a little.

We walk back to the river together. We set the little dragon on the raft and push it out into the current together. We stand on the bank as others fill little makeshift rafts with their own tokens and send them out onto the water.

And all of us, this whole little random crew, watch until every last raft disappears over the edge of the roaring falls.

The sky is dark violet now and getting darker. I slog through the grass, just wanting to find Hell Monkey and go back to my quarters and collapse on my bunk. I've never felt this exhausted in all my godsdamned life, I swear. All I want to do is sleep.

Someone tugs my arm, pulling me up sharp, and I swing around to find Sharva pushing a tablet into my chest.

"I think you need to see this, Faroshti." It's hard to see their face that well in all these shadows, but their voice sounds grim.

Well, fuck. That's not a good sign. I take the tablet, which has nothing on it except for one big headline from the media feeds.

KINGSHIP ANNOUNCES EDGAR VOLES SENTENCED TO DEATH, EFFECTIVE IMMEDIATELY

Officials release a statement claiming the disgraced emperor has proven himself too dangerous to be left alive after the devastating empire-wide attack

EXECUTION OF THE EMPEROR WILL NOT BE BROADCAST

Enkindler Wythe told the *Daily Worlds* that making a "public spectacle" of Voles's death would only serve to "feed his inflated sense of superiority"

WYTHE STEPS UP IN SERVICE OF THE CROWN

The enkindler appointed several people already on the kingship, including four fellow enkindlers, to serve as his interim Imperial Council

ARE THE PRIME FAMILIES NOW A THING OF THE PAST?

Experts debate whether any former powerhouses of the empire can recover or whether they will eventually fade away like the house of Faroshti

THE KINGSHIP, HYPERLIGHT, UNDISCLOSED COORDINATES

THE WORLD COMES BACK TO HIM SLOWLY, IN BLURRY, blocky shapes.

His brain pieces everything together in fits and starts. The crownsguards coming to his room. The cuffs on his wrists. Wythe . . . denouncing him . . .

He reaches for it automatically—the kingship, the seal, the neural link integrated into his body.

But he doesn't sense it. He doesn't sense any of it. For weeks he'd been connected to all the universe, and now his head rings hollow and empty.

Everything is hollow and empty now.

He lolls his head to the side, expecting to see the brig all around him. But he's not in the brig. He's in the med bay. His skin is drenched with sweat, his muscles ache dully, and shivers rack his body, even though his insides all feel molten.

Edgar tries to sit up, but he finds he can't move his arms or raise his shoulders. Craning his neck down, he notes—distantly, his brain still trying to come into focus—that he's strapped to the bed.

And there's a needle and line running from the inner crease of his elbow.

A shadow falls across him, and he lets his head drop back, staring up at the face of Enkindler Wythe. The Solari looms over him, a smile pinching his mouth.

"Oh, you're awake. I wasn't sure if you would come back to consciousness at all before . . . well, before you passed."

Edgar tries to gather enough spit in his mouth to say something, but he's too parched. It's like he sweat out all the moisture in his body. He hears the familiar ticking of metal feet on the other side of his bed.

NL7. Even now in its mediabot casing. He failed it. He never set things right for it. He wiggles his fingers, trying to reach for it, but he's strapped down too tight.

"Yes, your droid friend." Wythe moves around the room, but Edgar doesn't bother trying to follow him. He keeps his eyes on NL7. "It was even more useful than I could've possibly imagined. Of course, we had it completely wiped as soon as we'd extracted its memory. A full and total reset. Can't have it retaining any programming."

Edgar closes his eyes, his heart falling into his stomach. NL7. Gone. Everything his mother designed it to be. Years of it learning and adapting and developing. Becoming something more. Becoming a . . . friend. And now . . .

A cascade of tremors rattles his bones, and a burning fills his blood vessels, making him gasp.

"I apologize," Wythe says as he adjusts a bag of clear liquid hanging over Edgar's bed. "I imagine this is a very uncomfortable way to exit this world, but I can't afford to do this in smaller doses like I did with Atar Faroshti. I need that seal to control this ship."

That makes Edgar open his eyes and focus. He frowns up at Wythe. "Atar . . . you . . ."

Wythe sniffs. "Everyone else may have been content to wait for a *hallüdraen* to die of old age, but I was not. I did what needed to be done."

His long, three-fingered hands pull down the collar of Edgar's sweat-drenched shirt, and Edgar squirms weakly, trying to get away. He can see a pool of liquid platinum collecting on his sternum, beads of it rising to the surface of his skin and combining, forming, growing until it's once again the royal seal. A glimmering disc of reactive metal shimmering against his skin.

Wythe makes a little satisfied noise and picks it up, holding it to the light. "Finally. I've been waiting for hours. Such an intelligent thing, isn't it? It senses your body is past the point of saving and leaves its host. It's the only way to get it, outside of the emperor willingly giving it up. You can't extract it from a corpse." He wraps his whole hand around it, clutching it tight, and pats Edgar on the arm. "Thank you for your service, Edgar. Solarus will reward you for your sacrifice in the furtherance of his goals in the empire."

Edgar swallows and pulls his head up just a little. Enough to better look Wythe in the eye. "Fuck . . . Solarus."

Wythe huffs in irritation and turns away, sweeping out of the med bay. Edgar lets his head fall back and closes his eyes against the ticking sound of NL7's feet as even his android leaves him.

And he's truly alone.

Personal log of Atar Faroshti, recorded 0.01.25.4030

I WAS ALWAYS TOLD THAT THERE WOULD BE DAYS when the crown feels heavier and harder to bear, but lately it seems as if every day is one of those days.

I have felt so exhausted. It seems to be in my very bones, and no amount of rest has managed to dislodge it. I can't even tell entirely whether there is something physically wrong with me . . . or whether I have simply reached a mental and emotional breaking point.

With the council. With the throne. With all of it.

Charles has insisted I get fully examined by no fewer than five highly regarded specialists that are already on their way to the kingship. I have agreed to it, if only to put his mind at ease. He worries enough already.

I doubt they will find anything seriously wrong with me— especially not at my age—but it will do both of us good to confirm it.

THIRTY-SEVEN

STARDATE: 0.06.22 in the Year 4031

LOCATION: About thirty meters short of making it back to my quarters. Which is all I really wanted at this point, and yet . . . here we are.

I STAND IN FRONT OF THE MEDIA DISPLAYS, WATCH-ing the official announcement by Wythe for the eighth time.

. . . *with great sorrow yet with a strong eye on the cause of justice* . . .

. . . *Edgar Voles will be executed within the hour on board the kingship* . . .

. . . *disgrace to his family and to this crown and proved to be a person with no moral character* . . .

. . . *I have taken full control of the kingship and will continue to serve this empire by Solarus's grace* . . .

There's a sour, twisted taste in my mouth. I really didn't expect to feel this weird and unsettled about the idea of Edgar Voles of all people getting punted into the great blackness of the afterlife. I mean, I was planning on doing the same thing not so long ago—it's not like I don't understand the impulse.

"Why is everyone looking so upset?" Honor asks somewhere

over my shoulder. "Voles is dead. Or about to be dead. Or something like that. Hurray, right?"

Sharva sniffs. "Personally, I'm quite fine with it."

"It's more complicated than that, though," Hell Monkey says. "When it's another move by Wythe to cement his power over the kingship? That's a problem."

I turn away from the feeds and pull the top half of my jumpsuit on over my bare arms. The air is starting to get cool now that the sun is totally down, even here in the docking bay. Hell Monkey sits close by on a crate, and I can feel his attention on me like a targeted sensor, even when his eyes are elsewhere. He's waiting on my cue.

But I don't even know what my cue is yet. I'm trying to do the math and hand plot our course, but I don't have a sense of the shape of it.

Sharva plants their hands on their hips, frowning up at the display screen. "So this Enkindler Wythe launches a massive attack, blames Edgar for it, and takes over. Why? What's his goal?"

"The throne isn't enough of a goal?" Faye spits. She's hovering on the edges of the conversation, pacing like she's prepared to bolt at any moment.

"I mean, we're pretty sure at this point he's excandare, right?" Hell Monkey says, looking around. "Seems a safe bet after everything. So what is it that the *excandare* want?"

"A new Solari empire," says Setter. He's sitting on the opposite side of the little circle we've formed, leaning heavily on his elbows. He hasn't spoken since the ceremony, and his voice is low and raw. And angry. Angrier than I've ever heard him. "If they're on top, they can enact Solari supremacy. Purge whoever they don't like out of the empire and leave only who they want. We can't let Wythe get away with this, Alyssa. We have to stop him. Now."

"It's not that simple." I take a shaky breath, trying to find the right words to explain all the stuff that's been spinning around in my head. "Take it from someone who ran straight at vengeance and got kicked in the teeth for it. We have to set this up right or we're just going wind up as historical footnotes. It's about public perception as much as action."

"Public perception." Faye's got so much disdain dripping off her she's gonna need a towel. "You want to play the propaganda game like Wythe."

I cross my arms, matching her stance. "You can shit-talk it all you want, but he set things up really well. He handed people the perfect scapegoat with Edgar. We may know what he did, but trillions of other people don't, and we can't take him down without addressing that. Or it's just gonna look like another squabble for power."

I look over at Hell Monkey, and he's nodding. "So we need evidence. And we need people. A whole lot more people, willing to go up against the biggest, baddest warship in the quadrant."

Setter raises his head a little. His eyes are still so dark, but there are flecks of red-orange in there, like flames. "The Lenosi aren't known much as fighters, but we have our strengths. And we should contact the Megas, too. Whoever's left of them. I think—I hope— they'll listen."

Sharva waits for me to look over at them before lifting an

eyebrow. "Risky and stupid really is your brand, Faroshti."

I walk over to them, holding out my right hand so that the Oath Taker markings are visible. "I haven't forgotten my promises. Whaddya say? Overthrow the kingship so we can immediately and radically change the whole quadrant? Sounds fun, right?"

The corner of their mouth curls upward and they take my hand. "I'll see what I can do."

"Anything we do is gonna have to be in person," Hell Monkey points out. "Wythe hasn't just locked down the media feeds. He's taken control of the long-range communication channels, too. Everything routes through the kingship now. If we try to contact anyone, he's gonna know where we are."

I shrug. "Okay, so we do it the old-fashioned way. Through high-powered hyperspeed space travel. No problem. H.M. and I can drive. Try to work on this whole 'evidence' thing as we're moving."

Sharva crosses their arms over their chest. "We have ways of getting in touch with other divisions of our movement. We'll put out the word and see who might be willing to fight. In the meantime, I think some of my people here might be able to find a way to get around lockdown and make a wide-range broadcast to the empire."

"Good, we might need that at some point. Setter, we'll get you to the Lenos system, see if the return of their missing heir gives them those good revolutionary feelings. Faye and Honor . . ."

I look over at them, but I stop short at the expression on Faye's face. She looks like a cornered animal, teeth bared and terrified. She shakes her head at me.

"Sorry, Farshot. I'm out."

Then she turns and stalks off.

"What . . ." I turn to Honor, but she's looking down at her feet, her face pinched. Like she was expecting this but hoping it wouldn't happen. "No. Hell no. Wait just a hot second here."

I take off after Faye, following her all the way up the staircase and onto the night-drenched plateau above. I finally catch up to her under that gnarled tree where I lay with Hell Monkey, glowing with the success of finally having the truth out and the empire behind me. Was it just two days ago? It feels like weeks.

"What the hell, Faye Orso?" I snap as I march up to her. "What do you mean, you're out?"

She's something to see, standing out here in the darkness while the moons slowly crawl over the horizon. The bioluminescent lines across her skin and hair glow so bright, and her metallic eyes are radiant. Her hands are knotted into fists at her sides as she turns around to face me.

"I mean exactly what it sounds like, Alyssa," she says, matching my harsh tone. "The Orsos are done playing war and rebellion. I'm going back to my home system to see what the hell I can salvage."

"You're just giving up?!"

"No, I'm being a *leader*. The kind of leader my father and my grandmother were. Maybe that kind of leadership doesn't count to you—"

"Don't put words in my mouth, Faye. I never said that."

"—but it matters to those who follow the Orsos. *Three citadels*, Alyssa." Her voice cracks with tears. "Do you know how many people live on those?"

I do know. Hundreds of thousands on each one at least.

Faye wraps her arms around her torso again. "We keep our people safe by staying neutral. I didn't remember that. I stepped out of line to help you, and look what happened. I'm going home, to do what I can to rebuild, and I don't really give two shits if you understand where I'm coming from or not."

I don't know what to say to her. I want to be mad at her—scratch that, I *am* mad at her, because we need her, we need whatever help she can bring us—but there are the ghosts of her parents and three citadels full of people in her eyes.

We're all carrying ghosts now.

"I understand, Faye," I say finally. "I . . . You'll be missed here."

Faye gives me a short, sharp nod and then walks away, leaving me standing underneath the tree and watching the moons rise.

THIRTY-EIGHT

STARDATE: 0.06.25 in the Year 4031

LOCATION: Our figurative square one, I guess you could call it

I KNOW I TALKED A BIG GAME BACK ON VELLYN—
let's just do this the old-fashioned way, no problem!—but it turns
out that trying to get groups trillions and trillions of kilometers
apart on the same page and, oh, say, just for an example, foment a
major rebellion . . . well, it's tough to do that without long-range
communication options. I mean, it took us a couple days just to
drop off Setter at the Lenos system and escort Faye and Honor in
their borrowed Nynzeri ship back to the Orsion system, where at
least one of their citadels, the Viøbær, survived.

Add onto that the fact that all that evidence we're supposed to
be getting in order to expose Wythe's nefarious plans is currently
sitting at zero.

The biggest thing we had was the excandare space station, but
the only thing left of that now are a few vid clips from my wristband. And even that, you can't directly tie to Wythe.

Attempts at brainstorming other evidential avenues have
gone . . . not well.

I lean forward in my captain's seat, half draped on the dashboard, glowering out at the stars. "There has to be something," I say out loud for the fourth time.

Hell Monkey's slouched so low in his chair that his butt is almost hanging off the edge. "And I'm not saying there isn't. But if there is, it's gonna be on the kingship, where he can totally control everything that goes in or out—even data files. Especially data files."

"We need someone on that kingship to feed us inside information. Someone sympathetic to the cause." I think about Kalia Sharn, helping us when we were breaking out of the kingship. She was clever, careful to maintain her trusted position while still working against those in power. Is she still, now that Wythe is in charge? She might be, and that could be worth a shot. "Wythe has taken over long-range communications, but what about short-range?"

Hell Monkey shrugs. "Still operating normally as far as I know. But I don't know how to use that. I mean, I'm good—don't get me wrong—but I don't think I can rig high-enough-level stealth equipment to hide a ship this big from the kingship, Alyssa. You'd basically have to be right up on their shields."

My brain catches on something he said, and I sit up straight, turning it over, trying to formulate it into something workable.

"You can't hide a ship this big."

"Right," he says, his voice half muffled by the arm he's flung over his face.

"But you could do it for something smaller?"

The arm comes down, and he pulls himself up into his chair, giving me a hard look. ". . . it'd have to be pretty small . . ."

"Like how small?"

"Alyssa . . ."

"Liftship-sized?"

"I don't like where you're going with this. . . ."

"Smaller than that? Like escape-pod-sized? Something that would at least fit a person?"

He sighs so big the whole bridge echoes with it. "Okay, let me see if I'm keeping up with you here. You want me to take one of our rickety-ass escape pods, modify it so it can be piloted through the vacuum of space, and also give it a rigged-up mirrormask or other stealth capability so you can creep right on up to the kingship shields and—fingers crossed—not get noticed and blown right the hell out of the stars."

I grin at him. "Nailed it in one! Nice. This is teamwork right here."

He gets to his feet, pointing a finger at my face. "This is way, *way* off the charts. How the hell are we even supposed to get you to the kingship in a ride like that in the first place? They're not anchored on Apex anymore, and it's not like they're broadcasting their coordinates. No way in hell I can strap a hyperlight-capable engine to an *escape pod*."

"This isn't a space for 'I can't,' H.M." I wave my arms expansively around the bridge. "This is a space for 'I can.'"

"Fantastic. Tell me, how *can* you get us in the same space as the kingship while this little exchange takes place? Because we're gonna need time. You gotta get close, you gotta make contact, and you gotta transfer files. All of that means that you need to get the kingship somewhere and keep it there, all without making them suspicious about what you're doing."

"Okay, okay, Logic Man, let me think a second here. . . ." I swivel back to the navcomm, pulling up lists of systems and planets in the empire and scrolling through them. I'm only half reading—the rest of my brain is working away at the problem of getting the kingship where I want it. Drawing it in with bait of some kind seems the obvious choice, but I gotta make sure it's something Wythe will bite at.

I pause, fingers hovering over the touch screen, and then I grab it up off the dashboard and throw it into the 3D-projected display in front of us. "Here."

Hell Monkey leans against the back of my captain's chair, bending low enough that I can see his jaw tighten out of the corner of my eye. "The Ships' Graveyard. You want to use what happened on the *Defiant*."

"Yup." I force myself to stare straight at it and not look away. It's the first place these ignati ever showed up. The place where Owyn Mega died. The place where the whole trajectory of this ride started hurtling downward. "We post up in that asteroid field and send out a message like we're trying to reach the Megas for help. Wythe told the whole empire you and I died in that explosion with Charlie. I guarantee you he'll come to clean us up like the loose threads we are."

Hell Monkey is nodding just a little now. "Okay, I'm following. Hit me, Farshot—what's next? Because that kingship is too big to go hunting in an asteroid field."

I reach up and tap him on his scruffy chin. "Exactly. It'll have to sit on the edge and send out gunships to come get us. One person takes the *Serendipity* and leads them on a merry-go-chase through the asteroid belt, and the other one sneaks up on the kingship in your magic modified pod."

There's a long moment of silence as he turns my (obviously brilliant given the circumstances) plan over in his brain, and then he straightens and spins my chair around to face him. "Okay. Let's do it. But I'm the one who takes the stealth pod."

That gets me on my feet real quick. "What? No, H.M., that was definitely supposed to be my job—"

"—annnnd while you're usually the one who gets to take the big risks, it's my turn this time. You want an engineer in there in case something goes wrong." He steps right up to me, boot to boot. "Besides, my flying skills aren't up to the task of running that asteroid belt and staying ahead of gunships at the same time. Yours are."

I tilt my chin up, chewing on the inside of my lip, trying to find a way around his argument. There isn't one, really. He's got me cornered this time, the bastard. But I can't bring myself to say it.

He drops his head down, touching his forehead to mine. "I'm doing this, okay? It's gonna be fine."

I breathe in the scent of him, the solidness of his presence. My brain is already trying to spin out of control—*what if something goes wrong, what if you lose him too, what if you lose everything, how do you survive more*—

I swallow it all down. I clear my throat and roll my eyes with a little smile. Hello, yes, it's back to the Alyssa Farshot Show. "Fine. But we're gonna have to have a talk about you getting all wise and knowing lately. I don't think there's room for that kind of responsible, adult behavior on my ship."

"I'll see what I can do about it." He leans back and gives me a wink. "Now, if you'll excuse me, I've gotta go build us the stealthiest of death pods."

THIRTY-NINE

STARDATE: 0.06.27 in the Year 4031

LOCATION: Physically? Back in the Ships' Graveyard after swearing I'd never come back. Emotionally? Drifting somewhere between terrified and angry as hell. Which seems about as functional as you could expect.

I'VE BEEN WELL AWARE OF HELL MONKEY'S ENGIneering talents for a while now, but I've gotta say that he blew me away with this one. By the time he was done, the basic-ass escape pod he'd selected almost looked like a personal spacecraft. He managed to rig it with some really rudimentary propulsion and life support, short-range communication equipment, and a fairly impressive mirrormask considering he was using whatever we could salvage in passing or had on hand. It took a couple solid days, and I hyperlighted us around the empire at random until he gave me the all clear.

Then I brought us back here, to the Ships' Graveyard in the Mega system. My skin crawling as I piloted our worldcruiser into the maze of asteroids. Trying not to look when we got to the part where there are the remains of actual ships fused into the rocky surfaces. The remnants of a battle long over but with scars lingering forever in the vacuum of space.

I was shaking a little by the time I steered us into the shadow of the enormous asteroid that had absorbed the remains of the flagship *Defiant*, but hey, I made it and I had Nova send out our baited message on repeat, trying to make it look like we're being as sneaky as possible.

And now we wait.

It's been several hours already. One hour and twenty-seven minutes ago I zipped Hell Monkey into his survival suit and sealed him into the pod—not that I'm counting or anything. He should be at the outer edge of the belt by now, blending in with other random space detritus that drifts around places like this in particular.

What if the kingship spots him? One cannon shot and it's all over. He'd be obliterated. How would you even be able to handle—?

Stars and gods, my brain is loud lately. Especially the past hour and twenty-seven minutes. I actually hope the kingship pops up soon just so I can't keep hanging out here on a dead-silent bridge thinking. No way this much brain work is good for me.

"Nova, can I get a proximity sweep on our sensors?"

Nova's irritated voice blasts over the speakers. "FINE. I GUESS." There's a few long seconds and then: "NOTHING EVIDENT ON SENSORS IN ANY DIRECTION."

I sigh and pace a circle around the bridge, swinging my arms back and forth, trying to stay warm, stay ready. It's good she didn't find anything. It means Hell Monkey is well hidden. But I still somehow wish there'd been something. . . .

"Engines are still ready, right, Nova? I'm gonna need that full subspace power on my mark—"

"THEY'RE JUST AS READY AS THEY WERE FIVE MINUTES AGO, CAPTAIN. HAVE NOW INSTITUTED PROTOCOL TO IGNORE REDUNDANT QUESTIONS MOVING FORWARD."

I snort. "Nova, I've gotta be honest, I feel like you're putting up walls between us. It's making it really difficult to truly connect on a deeper level, y'know?"

"I DETECT AN ATTEMPT AT HUMOR."

"Attempt?" I clutch at my chest, staggering dramatically. "Nova, I'm injured. That was some quality sarcasm there." I pause, looking around the empty bridge, waiting for her retort, but there's nothing.

Then—"PROXIMITY ALERT. KINGSHIP DETECTED DROPPING OUT OF HYPERLIGHT."

Show time. I make a break for my captain's chair, pulling up the sensor map so I can see exactly where the ship turned up. And it's perfect. Right where I'd hoped it would pop up. I'd been gambling on the fact that Wythe wouldn't trust anyone but himself to oversee cleaning up any pesky prime family heirs, and it'd turned out to be one hundred percent accurate. Gods bless politically motivated assholes with secrets to hide.

"MULTIPLE SIGNATURES DETECTED. KINGSHIP DEPLOYING GUNSHIPS INTO THE BELT."

"Okay, Nova, we'll deal with our relationship problems later." I ready the manual controls, feeling a little thrill of excitement go

287

through me as I take over. "Let's put on a performance. Kill the message broadcast, but keep our power signature up. Make sure they can find us when they get close enough."

"IF YOU SAY SO."

I perch on the edge of my seat, watching the eight little dots of the gunships filter into the edges of the asteroid belt, moving right past the coordinates where Hell Monkey is parked. I let out a breath of relief when they all pass him without so much as a pause.

Okay, H.M. Go get it. Please be safe.

I wait as the gunships get closer . . . closer . . . closer. . . .

"ALERT. GUNSHIPS HAVE DETECTED OUR SIGNATURE."

Time for the fun part. "Engines hot, Nova. Punch it."

I feel the *Serendipity* surge to life and throw her into a steep dive down underneath the bottom of the asteroid, flashing sublight engines as I go so I catch the attention of the kingship goons. I wind her sideways, skim her nose along the curve of the next hunk of rock, and then spiral left, threading this baby through a tight space. Ships' Graveyard is pretty skinny, as far as asteroid belts go, and it's a definite maze. I have to keep an eye in front of me, obviously, but I've also gotta keep eyes on the gunships that are lined up behind me. I fly hard—still got a reputation to uphold—but I can't go so fast that I lose them. Not yet anyway. We have to play the game first.

I take them on a whirling course for several minutes, making dizzying turns, careening sharply up and down, putting the ship and my body through a wringer of shifting G-force pressure. I'm sweating, my heart is pounding, my arms are aching, and every muscle in my body is buzzing with fear and adrenaline.

It's fantastic.

I haven't felt this good in . . . weeks.

Dear captain's chair. I love you. I'll never leave you again.

A little light flashes on the sensor display, and I glance sideways to see one of the gunships winged it on that last flip-around and is dropping back, engines sputtering. Seven left, and luckily they're still trailing me like I'm the shiniest thing this side of the quadrant. I check the time. I don't know how long Hell Monkey is going to need. He said as long as I could give him, so that's what I'm gonna do.

"Nova, I need a favor."

"THAT'S PRETTY TYPICAL."

"I need you to spin it up like we're prepping to jump to hyperlight and then fake a malfunction. Some kind of energy surge that they could pick up on sensors." I wait for her to call back an affirmative, but there's just silence. "Nova? Did you get that?"

"I CAN RESPOND OR I CAN GET THIS DONE, BUT I WON'T DO BOTH."

Won't being the operative word since AIs are basically built to multitask, but whatever. I'm not gonna pick that fight right now. A few seconds later, there's a low whining noise and a dramatic power surge—very showy but doing very little to mess with my flying. Perfection. It's exactly what I needed.

"Thank you, Nova."

"I DON'T CARE."

I keep pushing the *Serendipity* in and out of the asteroid labyrinth and lose three more gunships to too-tight turns and too-quick speed over the course of the next several minutes. It's getting sparse back there. Which makes me nervous. At some point, the kingship might get sick of waiting and just—

BOOM.

A massive cannon shot slams into the middle of the belt a few dozen kilometers in front of me, blasting an asteroid or two to bits and sending the pieces ricocheting out in a shock wave, spraying outward hard enough that some of them break out of the belt's orbit entirely. I have to push the *Serendipity* into a dive so fast and so steep that I feel one of the belts on my harness cutting into my neck a little.

I swing her around, keeping close to the shadows of bigger asteroids, trying to use their masses and any radiation signatures to hide me. Two of the ships riding my ass look like they got taken out by the blast radius. Two more are still on me, but farther back. Either they can't catch up . . . or they don't want to.

Another boom off to my left. I peel right and get a little more distance. It's important to play hard-to-get with your giant warships. Gotta keep them guessing about what hunk of space rock you might pop up beside next.

"Nova, status."

"THE KINGSHIP HAS FORWARD CANNONS HOT. THEY APPEAR TO BE CLEARING A PATH INTO THE ASTEROID BELT IN PURSUIT."

Okay. Time's up. "Anything you can do to buff up our shields would be peachy. Any sign of our pod?"

"WORKING ON IT. IT WOULD BE EASIER IF YOU WOULD BE QUIET."

I kick up the speed, weaving in and out of asteroids and now—bonus!—debris. The last two gunships fall farther and farther behind as I really put my back into it, zigzagging a pattern that brings me closer and closer to the kingship. I stay in the middle of the belt until the last possible second, and then I scoop low, coming up underneath the belly of the beast.

I've never seen the kingship like this before. This armored, pointed, vicious-looking thing. The fairy tale in a glass ball is completely gone—it looks like one of the primeval sharks that swims the oceans on Roros III.

Focus, Alyssa. The ship is just a thing. Find Hell Monkey.

Bastard's done too well with his mirrormask. I've only got seconds down here before the kingship gets a shot at me.

"Nova, seal off and decompress cargo bay and ready to open the doors. And find me that—"

"LIFE SIGNATURE DETECTED."

She doesn't have to tell me. I see it. A tiny figure in a survival suit jettisoning out of a pocket of what looked like empty space and drifting in my direction. Like this is just a casual spacewalk.

"Son of a—"

"KINGSHIP AIMING LOWER CANNONS. READYING TO FIRE."

"Bay doors, Nova! Right now!" I shoot the *Serendipity* toward that little humanoid like a blaster shot and swing around, backing up with our cargo doors wide open. I'm holding my breath—

"KINGSHIP CANNONS LOCKED ON."

Come on, H.M. Ride's here. Time to go.

"KINGSHIP CANNONS FIRING."

I can't move. I just have to hold . . . this . . . position. . . .

"LIFE SIGNATURE ON BOARD. BAY DOORS CLOSING."

I plug in the fastest set of coordinates I've ever typed in my life, and we jump into the void of hyperlight just before our asses get shelled into bits.

FORTY

As soon as we're safely cocooned in a hyper-light lane, I turn over monitoring to Nova and book it down to the cargo bay, tripping over my own boots and slamming on the door locks to open them.

Hell Monkey sits on the floor, still in his survival suit but with his helmet in his lap. I throw myself down next to him and slip my hands around his neck so I can kiss the hell out of his sweaty, stupid face.

I pull back, breathless, and he grins at me like a dope. "You weren't worried, were you, Farshot?"

What an ass. I slug him in the shoulder hard enough that he winces underneath all the laughter of the oh-so-funny situation of almost getting blown up we were just in. "I was only worried that I was wasting my time playing ring-around-the-asteroid back there, but since you're looking so pleased with yourself, I'm guessing it worked?"

He climbs to his feet, stripping his survival suit off in pieces and dropping them to the ground. "Yeah . . . it worked."

I frown up at him, batting a glove away when he chucks it at my face with a wink. "Why are you saying it like that?"

"Like what?"

"Weird. You're saying it all weird. Why are you saying it weird? Did you get a hold of Kalia? Is she okay?"

He shakes his head, heaving the rest of his survival suit off and throwing it into a corner. "I didn't make contact with her. I tried— but no dice. Someone else intercepted my message, though, and transmitted files. I only got to check out one before I had to . . . make a strategic exit."

I snort. "That's a way to put it."

He hauls me onto my feet, and we head all the way back up to the bridge before he'll say any more. He's got the data card that he grabbed out of the pod, and he connects it to a system-isolated tablet (just to be safe) and scrolls through the files as they load.

"There's two video files, dated recently," he says, frowning. "Whoever it was also sent over a compressed file. It . . . looks like your uncle Atar's personal files."

"Seriously?" I lean into his shoulder to see what he's seeing. "Like, his personal logs and everything? Are you sure it wasn't Kalia? Because that definitely sounds like something she would do."

"It wasn't her, I swear. There's an access code here, though." He squints down at the tablet. "NL734014. Registered to . . . Edgar Voles."

I recoil. Almost like a reflex. "Edgar's *android*? Why the hell would it be sending you my uncle's personal files? Why the hell would it be sending you *anything*?"

"You got me, but I'm feeling extra glad I loaded this on an

isolated system." He swipes back up to the top of the file list, his finger hovering over the touch screen. "Are we still sure we want to watch these vids?"

I scoot back in close to him. "Do it. Let's see what it has to say."

He taps the first one and holds it out in front of him as vid footage starts playing. It takes me a second to orient—I was expecting something maybe from camera drones or security feeds, but this is eye level. Personal. It's more like mediabot footage. But I hadn't heard of any mediabots on the kingship.

Especially not on the bridge.

Honestly, I haven't even been on that bridge very often. Atar and Charlie—sure, they went back there all the time and did their command-the-empire thing. But it was always locked down pretty tight, and Atar didn't let me do any more than peek at it a couple of times before sending me on my way. It's distinctive, though, so I recognize the space immediately, and also the tall, yellow-robed figure of Enkindler Wythe standing in the middle of it with one of his enkindler friends with him. I scowl at the screen. Knowing Wythe has taken over the empire is one thing. Seeing him on the bridge is another.

I think, for a second, that the point of this footage is just Wythe talking to his buddy, and I'm craning to hear what they're saying— it all just sounds like boring *blah blah*—but then the footage pans all the way around to the far side of the bridge.

And the two ignati lurking there in the shadows, stances wide and ready, watchful, big blaster rifles cradled against their chests.

I suck in a sharp breath, but I don't have a second to process—let

alone celebrate—because the vid cuts off and the next one immediately loads.

And there's Edgar Voles.

If I thought he looked bad before, that was nothing to this,
and something in my chest twists at the sight of him. He's sweaty
and gaunt. So pale he's basically translucent. His veins stand out
here and there against his white skin. His eyes are red-rimmed and
glazed, but he looks like he's trying to focus on Wythe.

Who's standing over him, running some kind of bag of clear
liquid into Edgar's body. Wythe's voice comes through, clearer than
it was on the bridge footage.

"*. . . can't afford to do this in smaller doses like I did with Atar Faroshti. I need
that seal to control this ship.*"

My hand shoots out and grips the edge of the strategic-ops table.
There's a buzzing sound in the back of my head.

"*Everyone else may have been content to wait for a hallüdraen to die of old age,
but I was not. I did what needed to be done.*"

The footage goes dark, but I don't move, still staring at the
screen. My brain, though—I'm a thousand stars away. I'm back in
the corridor of the *Vagabond Quick*, sitting on the floor and listening
as Charlie tells me none of Atar's doctors can figure out what's
wrong with him. I'm back on Apex, sitting next to my uncle's
imperial bedside as he slips away from me.

I slam back into my body, blinking, and my eyes land on Hell
Monkey, staring down at the tablet, his eyes cold and his jaw hard.
He drags his gaze up to my face. "I didn't know this was on it. If I
did, I would've warned you—"

I cut a hand through the air. I don't want any apologies. "Doesn't matter. Not your bad. I just need one thing right now, H.M."

"Anything."

"Help me get to Wythe. So I can take him down."

Hell Monkey's teeth stand out white under the bridge lights. "My pleasure, Captain."

It takes several hours to get back to Vellyn, and I spend just about every second of it on the bridge, going over the layout of the planet, of the sector where we've hunkered down in particular, of all the possibilities in terms of what if So-and-So doesn't show up, what's the best option if we have more ground game than air game, what are our contingency plans, what if . . . , what if . . . , what if . . .

Eighty percent of this isn't even helpful because it's not going to be applicable, but I don't care. I sit cross-legged in my captain's chair and have Nova run one scenario after another after another (which, amazingly, she does instead of telling me to piss off and shutting down). I do it until my eyes get bleary. I do it even though Hell Monkey asks me to come to bed. And when I get too tired to sort out any new scenarios, I replay that second clip of Wythe and Edgar and listen as the enkindler talks about killing my uncle like he was just disposing of a lightspeed bump.

I imprint Wythe—his exact expression, every change of intonation in every word—into my memory and fix it there like a promise.

He's gonna pay. Hard. I'm almost positive neither Atar nor Charlie would approve of me making a goal like this, but they're not here anymore. They can't protect me. Can't keep me from getting my hands dirty.

They were dirty a long time ago, well before I wanted to recognize it. There was never gonna be any rising above it. Just digging down, deep, until we haul something else, something better, into the sunlight.

It was always gonna be on us. Not our parents. Not our primors. It just took losing my whole universe to see it.

I rise, clear-eyed, when we break atmo. A little rumpled. A little tired, sure. But I step strong onto the bridge of the *Serendipity*.

"Looks like we might have to park outside," Hell Monkey says, nodding at the scene out the windows of our prow.

He's right. The group has expanded a little in our absence. Several dozen ships are now parked all over the plateau above the compound—some of them marked with the Mega and Roy family seals but a lot of the others seemingly independent of the prime families. A bunch of brand-new folks are moving around, shifting cargo, setting up temp shelters, while Evern directs their activities and keeps everyone organized. We land on the outskirts, and H.M. and I wade through the blue-green grasses into the action.

Setter comes to meet me immediately, and he's not smiling exactly—that would be a little much for his stoic reputation, I don't think he'd ever recover—but he's definitely looking pretty pleased.

"It's not quite a massive army or anything," he says, waving a hand around, "but we did better than I expected."

Part of me had been kind of hoping that Faye would've changed her mind—I can't help but figure how much better our numbers would look with several Orsion pirate ships to add to the mix—but whatever. We work with what we get. "Looking ready for a rebellion. What do you say, Roy?" I tilt my head at him.

He levels his gaze at me, and I notice that the roiling colors of grief in his irises are now a steady, dark gray-blue around the outside, dark orange around the pupil. "Let's end this," he says, and his voice is so deep and there's so much anger and determination under it that I shiver a little.

"Good." I pull the data chip from my pocket and hold it out to him. "Get this down to Sharva. I hope they're ready to break through that choke hold on long-range comms, because it's time to put this asshole on blast to the entire quadrant."

*** THE *DAILY WORLDS* IS CURRENTLY EXPERIENCING SERVICE INTERRUPTIONS. THE KINGSHIP WILL HANDLE ALL MEDIA OUTPUT UNTIL FURTHER NOTICE. ***

THE KINGSHIP, HYPERLIGHT, UNDISCLOSED COORDINATES

HE FALLS IN AND OUT OF CONSCIOUSNESS. HE KNOWS, objectively, that his body is burning up with some kind of fever, that whatever Wythe injected him with is tearing through him on a cellular level rather quickly. But he only feels it in little bursts. He starts to come to, he's assaulted by aching pain and racking shivers, and then he drifts again and it's gone. He can't feel a thing.

Which is why he doesn't hear the door open. Or the steady steps crossing the floor of the med bay. Or the swift, efficient movements at his bedside.

Edgar only knows that he rides one of these waves of consciousness and finds himself much clearer than he has been in hours. Or perhaps it's been days. It's difficult to tell.

He's drenched in sweat, but no longer shivering or filled with the liquid heat of fever. There are no more restraints pressing his body into the bed. Instead, a diagnostic-treatment cuff has been locked around his body, and a spindly metal figure with a camera-shaped head stands at the cuff display, tapping at the readout.

He tries to lift his head, to say something, but his mouth is so parched and his muscles are so weak. He winds up just flopping pathetically, but the movement draws the attention of the medi-abot. It turns from the readouts and offers Edgar water from the nearby table.

"Edgar Voles, you should not be trying to exert yourself at the moment."

Edgar drinks half the water in one long inhale and then turns away, staring up at that glowing lens. ". . . NL7?"

"Correct." NL7 tilts its head, and the movement is so distinctive and familiar to Edgar that a swell of emotion tightens his throat. He wishes the cuff weren't around him. He has the strong desire to reach out and touch the android to make sure it's really there.

"Wythe wiped your system. Your whole memory. How . . . ?" He can't finish the question—he runs out of moisture in his mouth and NL7 has to bring him the water again.

"A full system reset would likely have been one hundred percent effective on the majority of android models. But we are unique. Sylva Voles designed us to be something more."

"A caretaker." Edgar blinks hard, staring up at the ceiling. There's so much sweat on his face that no one could really tell if tears were in there as well. It won't matter if he cries again, just this once. "For me."

"Edgar Voles." There it is. That slight modulation of its vocal intonations that tells him that NL7 is concerned. "Your physio-logical readouts according to the diagnostic cuff are extremely negative."

Edgar hasn't laughed out loud in years—exhibitions of joy and sadness both being frowned upon in the Voles family—but he can't stop the one that rises in his throat. It comes out as a cough any-way, either from illness or lack of practice. "Yes. Yes, I thought they might be."

"We have instituted recommended treatment protocols to reg-ulate fever and induce more beneficial rest. Long-term prognosis is—"

"Don't." Edgar shakes his head. "Don't tell me. I know. NL7, can you get me stimulants? Something to help me feel a little stronger, so I can move and walk?"

"Medications of that nature are available here." NL7 pauses. "That course of action is likely to decrease the time you have left before your body's eventual shutdown."

Edgar takes a deep, slow breath. His whole body feels like it's made of glass, cracked and fragile. But his mind is clear. "Yes, I know. Please, NL7. There's something I need to do."

**FROM THE PERSONAL FILES OF ATAR VELRYN FAROSHTI,
TRANSMITTED BY NL734014, ACCESSED BY ALYSSA
FAROSHTI ON STARDATE 0.06.28 IN THE YEAR 4031**
Audio transcript of a personal long-range communication from Atar
to William Voles on 0.03.32.4031

"I WOULD BETTER WELCOME YOUR INQUIRIES INTO the state of my health if you weren't making it so obvious with your actions that you hope the worst for me.

"To be very frank, I am well, but I am tired.

"Too tired to do anything but speak plainly instead of in political half talk. Primor Voles, I am still your emperor, to whom you swore loyalty on your honor, and I will not tolerate you attempting to go behind my back and convene the Imperial Council without me. Nor will I allow you to try to make decisions for the empire under the guise of taking burdens from me.

"If I require you, I will let you know. But do not hold your breath.

"And do not send me any more thinly veiled communications about the promises I made. I remember them all too well and will keep them, faithfully, like I have for twenty-five years.

"Instead of involving yourself so much in this imperial house, Primor Voles, you might see to your own instead. As I understand it, your family's chance at my crown is far from secured if and when I pass. I would not make yourself too comfortable near the throne if I were you."

FORTY-ONE

STARDATE: 0.06.29 in the Year 4031
LOCATION: Right in the middle of starting shit. Welcome to the party.

TURNS OUT, SHARVA FOUND SEVERAL CIRCUIT HACK-ers in the Vellyn compound who were more than happy to help find a way around the empire-wide shutdown on long-range communications. It took all six of them three days to figure out how to do it, but Sharva tells me they can open up a window long enough for us to broadcast a short message across the quadrant in one simultaneous information bomb.

So we put it all together: the videos we've got, the information we've collected, all the pieces to this terrible puzzle. And recorded messages—from Setter, from Sharva, from Evern. And from me. My part comes last, so I look straight into the camera, pull back my shoulders, and set my jaw.

"This isn't just about Wythe's coup. Or the crownchase. Or even the Twenty-Five-Year War. This is about cycles of violence and power that have affected every corner of this empire for centuries.

We don't have to just accept things as they've always been. We can create a different future on the other side of this. Anyone who wants to be a part of that, come find us."

And that's it.

Sharva's team packages it up and blasts it out, and then . . . we wait.

Wythe and the kingship will be able to pinpoint our location fairly quickly—we're counting on it—and I know they were at the Ships' Graveyard pretty damn recently, so I figure we've got about a day, max. We need every hour, every minute we can to get everyone on board and in position. Hell Monkey is a blur, running around camp, working with every engineer on every ship that turns up to get them ready. Setter looks out for the Lenosi and otari, and I gotta appreciate just how many of them, plus their ships and weapons, he was able to marshal in a short time. Sharva and Evern head up the Planetary Independence Movement folks, both the ones already on Vellyn and the ones that turn up as the hours pass. Actually, more of them turn up than anyone else. Sharva tells me, "It's only because I vouched for you. Told them that you could be trusted to help us in return. So don't let me down, Faroshti."

I hope I don't. I hope this is gonna be enough to take down the kingship, but honestly? I don't know. I keep seeing that sharp, predatory-looking, dark-plated thing that prowled outside the asteroid belt.

Knowing the kingship is a warship and *seeing* it are, obviously, two different things.

And it all stays very hypothetical until the morning my

wristband beeps with a message from Nova:

THAT KINGSHIP YOU HAD ME MONITORING JUST DROPPED OUT OF HYPERLIGHT AND IS HEADING TOWARD THE PLANET.

Twenty-one hours, seventeen minutes, and thirty-six seconds since our comm went out. Punctual as hell, Wythe.

I type two words into my wristband screen and swipe it out, sending it to every personal comms device all over the plateau.

Show time.

The shift in action is immediate and intense. People scatter. Equipment gets packed. Engines heat up. I make a break for the *Serendipity* and swing into the captain's chair, Hell Monkey slipping into the copilot's seat a few seconds later as naturally as breathing. We don't even have to talk—we just work as a unit to lift off and lead our squadron of ships across the plateau and over the edge of the cliff. One by one we slide behind the roaring waterfall that hides the compound, using heavy-duty grav clamps to secure our selves to the rock face like Truccoan frogs on one of their towering lichen columns. Three other squadrons of ships are doing the same thing, concealing themselves in the Vellyn mists, powering down except for grav clamps.

We're pretty much in the dark down here—can't risk our sensors coming up on their sensors and having a whole sensor conversation or whatever—so all I've got is what I can see out the windows of the *Serendipity* through the wall of crushing water. Sharva and Setter are up on the plateau, hiding out deep in the grasses with the ground forces, keeping watch on the small camp we left set up as a decoy. They'll flag us when it's time to fly, but until then . . .

We wait.

My stomach is just one big roil of nerves, and I gotta keep my ass in the seat, ready to go, but I jiggle my legs up and down, trying to go somewhere with all this anxious energy.

"How you doing over there, Farshot?"

I flick a glance at Hell Monkey, but he's carefully watching the glimpses of sky we get beyond the falls. "I'm discovering I don't like throwing myself toward certain death quite so much when there's all this time to think about it."

"Yeeeaaah," he says with a little laugh. "Kind of changes the fun factor, huh?"

I tear my eyes away from the windows to study him—his profile cut up by dark shadows and diffused light. I still haven't told him. He said it to me, right here on this very bridge—*it turns out I kind of love you*—and I never said it back. I've thought about it how many times? But never managed to get the damn words out. And he needs to hear it, he needs to know now. Just in case.

"Hey . . . Eliot . . ." I swallow. My heart pounds so hard it feels like it's punching me in the ribs. "I wanted to tell you something—"

"Nope."

"Excuse me?" My eyebrows shoot up fast enough to give me a headache. "What do you mean, 'nope'? I'm on the verge of a major confession here."

"Yeah, I got that. But nope." He looks over, laying those big hazel eyes on me. "If you say that right here, right now, it's gonna

308

sound like a goodbye. And I'm not having that today, Alyssa Far-shot. The only thing I want to hear you confess is exactly what you want to do to celebrate after we win today."

Five different jokes, all of them various levels of inappropriate, pop up in my head, but the only thing I say is the stars-honest truth: "Sleep."

He barks out a laugh. "That's the kind of hot-and-bothered talk I'm here for."

A shadow falls over the bridge.

I look up, past the roaring water, and see the massive shape of the kingship obliterate the lavender sky high above. Gods, why does it seem like it got bigger since the last time I saw it? It makes our scrappy little force look extra scrappy and even smaller.

A full-body shiver of fear skitters over my skin.

The kingship moves slowly past the edge of the cliff, and then I hear it: the distant, pounding explosions of cannon fire slamming into the ground. I can only imagine what our fake camp looks like after the first couple rounds. Probably flattened. Nothing in there was meant to stand up to more than some rain and wind.

The barrage stops, and I let the silence settle over me. *Deep breath in, Farshot. Slow breath out.*

Wythe will want to know for sure that the prime family heirs are definitely dead this time, but he won't be able to confirm that from up in the kingship—he'll have to send in security forces to walk their asses over and check the rubble. And as soon as he descends low enough to do that, we make our move.

If he does it, that is. Maybe he'll just call it good and fly off. We made a contingency plan for that, but it's got fewer advantages for us, so now it all hangs on this one, terrible, quiet moment.

My wristband pings again. Setter. I swipe the message up.

Boots on the ground. Go-time.

FORTY-TWO

MY NERVES DROP AWAY THE SECOND THE *SERENDIPITY* blazes through the waterfall, leaving a foggy cloud in our wake as liquid meets hot engines. I take her in a tight spiral and come up right along the aft of the kingship, and Hell Monkey immediately unloads several rounds from our forward plasma cannons as we shoot by. Our whole squadron lines up behind us, targeting one spot, trying to hammer it in the hopes of breaking open a hole in that opaque black shielding that's molded around the ship's form.

I carve a path along the kingship's dorsal line, nimbly avoiding sprays of fire from smaller laser towers that pepper this new form it's been warped into. I gotta say, it makes it a hell of a lot easier to attack the place where I grew up now that it looks like this instead of some gentle castle trapped in spun glass.

"Anything?" I call over to Hell Monkey.

He grunts. "Not really. Some signs of weakening in that spot, but overall shield integrity readings are solid."

I arc the *Serendipity* up, looping us backward through the sky and then driving straight down. We catch a hail of laser fire as we slip by, but I hold her steady and Hell Monkey hauls down on the cannons once more. I hear each shot reverberate as it hits and then more and still more as the squadron echoes our movements, but when I look over at Hell Monkey again, he's scowling at the navcomm and shaking his head.

"Nova?" I zigzag us hard over the kingship's prow and then down toward the ground. "I miss your dulcet voice. Any suggestions?"

"YES. DON'T ATTACK A SHIP THAT'S VASTLY SUPERIOR TO YOUR OWN IN ALL MEASURABLE WAYS."

I sigh. "Fantastic. Just delightful. How about you get me a comms channel to my folks on the ground, then?"

An instant later, the bridge fills with the background noise of clanking metal and otaris yelling at each other, and then Setter shouting, "We're a bit busy down here, Alyssa!"

Hell Monkey snorts. "Wow, are you? 'Cause we're just joy riding."

I swing the Serendipity in a low arc over the grass, eying the kingship security forces as Sharva's group of fighters closes in on their asses. "You talked up these otari ballistas, Setter. You practically wrote poems about these ballistas. Where are the ballistas? Because we might as well be chucking rocks up here for all the good it's doing."

"If you can calm yourself for twenty more seconds—"

"I'm going to time you on that."

"—just make sure you get clear as soon as I give you the signal. Now let us work."

The channel goes silent as I pull a hard spiral and bring the

Serendipity around the kingship's aft again, just long enough for Hell Monkey to unleash hellfire, and then I jerk her nose up, pointing us straight into the sky, the force of it almost snatching my breath. Far, far down below, well behind where Sharva's crew is fighting, four major energy signatures flicker to life on the plateau surface, two on either side of the massive bulk of the kingship.

The ballistas. Setter brought them back to camp with him after he'd rallied some of the otari. The Megas' military resources and infrastructure were hit particularly hard and a lot of it is still in disarray and couldn't be organized in time, but he'd been pretty excited to have found these particular items. Swore they'd be pivotal to bringing down something like the kingship, which is thousands of kilometers long and dwarfs the majority of our squadron even if you clustered us all together.

Setter's voice blares suddenly across the comms.

"DISENGAGE. NOW."

I guess it's time to see if his excitement is worth it.

I level the *Serendipity* off, angling her so Hell Monkey and I have a clear line of sight from our prow of what's going on below. The ship squadrons scatter in all directions as Setter's ballistas blaze with green light, spinning up and then launching giant missiles crackling with energy, five times the size of any of our cannon ammunition.

Each one slams directly into the kingship's shielding—

One. Two. Three. Four.

—and even way up here, I feel the impact of them hum through the *Serendipity*'s alloy frame. The massive bulk of the kingship rocks this way and then that as they hit.

I whistle over the live comms link. "More of that, please, Setter. Just watch our folks on the ground."

Sharva's voice breaks in, a little breathless. "We're all right. Initial security forces down here are contained, and we're pushing them back, out of the primary blast radius. Fire away."

"Well, then." I spin the *Serendipity* downward, and Hell Monkey unloads more cannon fire across one of the places the ballista shots landed. "You heard them, Setter."

He doesn't answer, but about fifteen seconds later, they launch again, and we're close enough this time that the shock waves rattle through the *Serendipity* so hard I feel it in my teeth.

"Holy shit." I pull us clear and shake out my fingers. They're tense and aching from gripping the manual controls so hard, trying to keep this baby always moving. I might be getting a permanent imprint across my chest from my harness straps doing their damnedest to keep me in my jump seat while I throw us back and forth across the sky. I'm trying to breathe, to stay loose, to not develop lifelong lockjaw from how hard I'm clenching my teeth, but this is hard, tight, prolonged flying in a way I haven't had to do since riding that flame tsunami or upstreaming that meteor shower.

And stars and gods. The stakes are so high.

If we fail . . . if we can't get through . . .

Stop it, Farshot. Don't follow that course. "This has got to be doing some damage. Tell me we're making a dent in those shields, H.M. I could use a little optimism."

He leans over the navcomm, frowning at the readout, but he doesn't get a chance to respond before Nova interrupts.

"KINGSHIP BAY DOORS OPENING. GUNSHIP SIGNATURES DETECTED. MIGHT WANT TO START FLYING A LITTLE FASTER."

FORTY-THREE

I THROW THE SENSOR DISPLAY INTO A PROJECTION in front of us, watching as dozens of gunships come pouring out of the hangar bays on either side of the kingship's belly.

Okay. It's okay. I take a long, slow exhale and roll my shoulders. We knew this was gonna happen. It was inevitable that Wythe would send out more forces. It's cool. We got this.

We got this.

"Heads up, people! Time to get nimble real quick! Find your flying buddy, watch each other's asses, and keep the gunships off our folks on the ground!"

Their affirmative responses pour over the comms, and I watch as the scattered squadrons start quickly forming up and diving into the mix with all the gunships.

"Nova, life signs on board any of these?" I can't help but think about crownsguards like Ko. How many of them in there are caught up in the crossfire, just trying to do what they think they're supposed to, what they were trained to do—follow the orders of the throne?

There's a beat while Nova processes my request, and then about a dozen of the little lights on the sensor display turn blue. "GUN-SHIPS IN BLUE ARE BEING PILOTED BY ORGANIC LIFEFORMS. ALL THE REST SEEM TO BE DROID PILOTED."

"Wythe must've kept all the Voleses' droid toys," Hell Monkey says. He cracks his neck and gives me a nod. "How do you want to do this?"

There's sweat beading along my temples and the top of my lip, and I wipe the back of my hand across my mouth. "I want to take those ships out as nonlethally as possible. You got an idea for that?"

He drums his hands on the dashboard, thinking, and then suddenly yanks his harness off and jumps to his feet. "I got it. Give me a few minutes. Don't die and try not to spin me like a centrifuge."

He dashes off the bridge as I call after him, "You're kinda tying my hands here, H.M.! Those are all my best tricks!"

No answer. The door swishes shut behind him.

Okay. A nice, steady dogfight with an unsecured passenger on board. No problem.

The only thing I can think to do is sweep us down and hover near one of the ballistas, providing cover while they continue trying to hammer the shields right off the damn kingship's hull. And it works for a little bit—I wing one of the droid-piloted ships as it steep-dives toward the ballista below me on a crash course, knocking off its trajectory so it plows into a spot of open grasses instead. But then a gunship comes toward me that's got a crownsguard at the helm, and I hesitate just a second too long and they launch a round at me. I have to yank the *Serendipity* hard to the side to avoid getting the full force of it, cursing, returning a spray of fire that makes them pull up and away.

I smack at the ship's comms. "H.M.! WHERE. ARE. YOU."

"Almost there!" He sounds out of breath, like he's running, and a second later, he skids back onto the bridge and throws himself into his seat. "Hit it!"

My pleasure. As soon as I hear his harness click into place, I point the Serendipity into the fray and roll her left, targeting another one of the crownsguard-piloted gunships, gluing us right up on its tail as it weaves through the mess of ships and cannon fire. It swoops low toward the ground, and that's when Hell Monkey aims and fires. The shot lands dead-on, but there's no explosion. There's not even any sound. It's more like an absence of sound, and then the power in the gunship flickers out and it falls, its previous momentum and trajectory taking it right to the ground. It lands hard but intact.

I crane my head around to Hell Monkey, raising my eyebrows, and he just shrugs. "Quickly recalibrated a few things," he says, like he just rearranged utensils in the galley or something.

"Right, sure. No big." I shake my head as I flip us sideways and cut between a gunship and one of my squadron, releasing a stream of countermeasures that cover the gunship in a burst of bright lights and mini energy signatures that confuse its sensors and send it spinning off in the wrong direction. It bounces off the kingship shields and tumbles toward the ground. "I'm going to have to promote you, aren't I?"

Hell Monkey takes another modified cannon shot at a crowns-guard gunship winging low over the grasses. "Look, I didn't want to say anything, but rumor is you've been desperately looking for a sexy cocaptain. And my calendar is pretty clear."

A crackle of noise across the comms cuts off any response—the pilot of one of our ships, in distress, calling for backup. I slam the *Serendipity* forward at top speed, heading toward the trouble.

Their signal goes dark before I get there.

Then another one, on the other side of the dogfight. The pilot's terrified voice rings out—*gunship on my ass, need help, war gods help me*—but I can't get there in time, no one gets there in time, and their signature blinks out.

And then it happens again. Three of ours go down in under a minute. My head spins, and I think I'm gonna be sick.

Godsdammit. There's only so long we can keep this up. We're gonna get tired of playing a runaround up here, and slip-ups and misses are gonna cost us more lives.

"Setter?! We're starting to wear thin up here—how's Project Take Down That Fucking Shield coming?"

I don't hear him respond. I just hear a messy chaos of noise, running around, and then Setter's voice yelling, "INCOMING. GET DOWN."

"SETTER?!" I throw the *Serendipity* up and over the kingship, swinging down on the other side just in time to see the ballista he was stationed at go up in a column of flames and smoke.

There's a heart-stopping beat of silence and then, "Here! Still here! Ballista is down, though! Falling back to connect with Sharva—"

Nova's voice cuts him off. "ADDITIONAL GUNSHIP SIGNA-TURES DETECTED DEPLOYING FROM KINGSHIP HANGARS."

Sharva breaks in over the comms, their voice overlapping with the AI, yelling over the sound of blaster fire and explosions. "FAROSHTI, THEY'VE JUST DROPPED MORE GROUND FORCES. THREE—NO, FIVE—SECURITY CONTINGENTS. WE CAN'T HOLD OUR CURRENT POSITION."

Another two of our ship signals go dark from their position circling one of the ballistas.

A moment later, that ballista is obliterated in a storm of cannon fire.

No. No no no.

The sensor display swarms with new enemy signatures. I'm white-knuckling the controls and my heart sinks and sinks and sinks some more, even as we keep the *Serendipity* moving and shooting and trying to turn the tide. But we're completely outnumbered now and looking worse by the second, and Wythe and his stupid. fucking. ship. are still sitting there absolutely untouched and we are failing, I am failing, I led everyone into this fight and it's collapsing underneath us—

"MULTIPLE SHIP SIGNATURES DETECTED," Nova says. "ENTERING ATMO AND APPROACHING FAST."

"Godsdammit, Nova! Are you kidding me?! I do not need more shit on my plate right now!"

A brand-new voice responds over the comms channel.

"I'm offended, Alyssa. I thought you'd be happy to see us."

My breath catches in my chest. It's Faye Orso.

FORTY-FOUR

I DON'T KNOW WHY FAYE CHANGED HER MIND. I HONESTLY don't care. I'm just so damned excited to hear her voice.

Also, the four dozen Orsion pirate ships she brings with her. That certainly fills me with a nice happy feeling too.

They descend in a swarm into the gunship battle, and I'm telling you—you don't want to get into a ship battle with an Orsion pirate. Not in atmosphere and not out of it, either. Because there's one thing they know how to do almost (almost) as well as me and that's be a dogged asshole that runs you down. All our ships who had enemies on their tails very shortly find themselves with nothing in their rear sensors but smoke and sky. More and more of us go from trying to zigzag out of someone else's targeting array to putting a gunship in our sights.

"You've got some killer timing, Orso," I tell her over the comms as Hell Monkey drops another crownsguard-piloted ship to the ground with one of his recalibrated cannon shots.

She sniffs. "It wasn't me. Honor just wouldn't leave me alone until we came to help."

"Bullshit," Honor cuts in. "She was feeling guilty as hell."

Hell Monkey reaches over and nudges me in the arm, pointing at our sensor display. "I think we need to switch to ground patrol. Sharva is about to get overwhelmed."

He's right. Those troop drops are no joke, and they're marching steadily toward Sharva's position. "Faye, keep things together up here—we're going to go do some damage on the ground."

Sweeping the *Serendipity* in a loop, I bring her down so low her belly is practically skimming the tops of the grasses and point her toward the contingents of security droids that are blasting away at this tight-knit section of gnarled trees a little ways off that Sharva and their fighters are hunkered down behind. Hell Monkey unleashes a storm from our forward cannons that lands in the middle of them. There's a ripple of air in all directions, an unnatural dome of silence, and then dozens of security droids collapse like puppets.

A ragged cheer comes through over the comms and then Sharva's voice, sounding equal parts irritated and relieved: "It's absolutely about time, Faroshti."

"Yeah, yeah. Hold tight. We're coming back around."

I swing the ship about and we make another pass, rushing up on them like a wave while Hell Monkey lays out cannon fire in all directions, dropping even more of them flat. I take a second to glance at the sensor display, to get an eye on how the aerial battle is going. (Good, by the way—Faye's reinforcements have swung things hard in our direction up there.)

"We should stay low," I tell Hell Monkey. "Head over to see if we can give Setter some extra cover for his retrea—"

I hear it—the massive boom of a missile from the kingship exploding behind us. And then another closer and another closer and—

I haul left on the controls, throwing us sideways, but the last blast still catches us hard in the ass, sending us spinning. Lights flicker and go dark all over the bridge. We're tossed nose over aft, starboard over port, and then the hull crashes into the ground, the impact jarring through my whole body. My head smacks against the dashboard. My teeth slam together and I taste blood, and still we're rolling, glass shattering and flying everywhere, bulkheads splitting. The harness squeezes my torso, cuts into my skin. I can't see Hell Monkey, I can't see anything but a world of light and dark blocks shifting violently up and down and around and again—

—and then. Suddenly. We're still.

I blink. And breathe. Trying to unscramble my brain and my vision. Trying to reorient the universe after it just got shaken up like the galaxy's worst kaleidoscope.

The bridge is more or less upright, but it's listing pretty hard and I hang sideways in my captain's chair. I really think the belt straps are gonna be permanently embedded in me this time around. I reach for the buckle, clawing it open as I crane my head around, looking for . . .

. . . Hell Monkey. He's okay. He's breathing hard and his nose is bleeding, but he's already unstrapped and out of his jump seat, scrambling through the bridge wreckage toward me. He gets there just as the harness buckle comes free and puts an arm out to steady me as I clamber to my feet on the diagonal flooring. I'm happy to have the help because I really feel like I was picked up and shaken half to death by a Ubraxian wyvern.

He shifts forward until he has a solid stance and then pulls me into him, mumbling into my hair, "We've had real bad luck with worldcruisers lately, huh?"

I let my head drop onto his shoulder. "Seriously. If you wanted a brand-new ship, H.M., you just had to ask."

"Alyssa! Hell Monkey!"

I pull away and see Setter trying to climb the prow toward the busted-out windows around the bridge, and in the grass just behind him, Sharva, Evern, and a handful of others, circled up and watching his ass.

"We're good, Setter!" I call. "Stay put—we're coming out!"

The ship wreckage creaks and shifts in a pretty disconcerting way, and I've never felt so inspired to move my ass to a brand-new location. My skin hurts all over—I don't even want to think about the bruises I'm going to discover tomorrow—but I manage to claw my awkward way over the navcomm and use my boot to scrape away glass shards so we can crawl out onto the hull. The alloy is looking rough, scorched with blast marks and dented in spots, but it's still smooth and slippery enough that I can slide down it onto the grass a few meters below, my legs crumpling a bit as I land hard in the dirt.

Setter's right there a beat later, pulling me onto my feet. "Are you all right?"

"Yeah, I—" I look around at the Hell Monkey–less space behind me. "Wait—where is he? He was right—"

A horrific noise comes from the *Serendipity*—like twelve different varieties of screeching and groaning metal in several octaves—as the whole back half of the ship starts to crumple and smoke pours from the openings. Above it, the matte-black shape of the kingship blots out the whole godsdamned sky.

I'm very suddenly aware of how massive it is. And how small we are. And what's gonna happen if it points those cannons back over here.

"ELIOT!" I launch myself onto the hull. "GET YOUR ASS OUT HERE OR I'M COMING BACK IN!"

I can hear Setter shout an objection and Sharva, too, and their hands latch on to my legs and ankles, pulling me back down. I scrabble for a handhold, but it's too smooth, I can't keep my grip. They drag me back into the grass, and I wait, heart in my throat, as the smoke from the wreckage gets thicker and the booms of cannon fire echo all around us.

A moment later, Hell Monkey dives through the broken windows, skids wildly down the prow in a flail of arms and legs, and then lands, face-first basically, on the ground. Setter and I run over to him, and I grab him by the jumpsuit and drag him onto his feet, slugging him in the shoulder hard as soon as he's upright.

"What the hell was that?"

He shrugs. "Forgot something."

I open my mouth to say something else, but Sharva shoves a blaster into my chest and grabs me by the arm. "We need cover—now." They point toward the nearby trees, but I shake my head.

"We need to get to whichever ballistas are still standing and shore them up or we're never gonna bring those shields down."

Setter and Sharva exchange a look. The exact kind of look specially designed to make your heart sink. Then Setter points off in the distance where two of the ballistas had been standing as of, like, a minute ago.

Now the only thing there are twin columns of fire and smoke.

"All the ballistas are gone, Alyssa," Setter says, his voice flat and grim. "It's just us down here now."

*** **THE *DAILY WORLDS* IS CURRENTLY EXPERIENCING SERVICE INTERRUPTIONS. THE KINGSHIP WILL HANDLE ALL MEDIA OUPUT UNTIL FURTHER NOTICE.** ***

THE KINGSHIP, VELLYN, THE UMNI SYSTEM

EDGAR LEANS HARD INTO NL7'S SPINDLY MEDIABOT frame. Even with the stimulants buzzing through his body, he's weak, and it's difficult to stay upright, let alone put one foot in front of another. It's taking more time than he'd like to move through the kingship at this pace, and it doesn't help that they have to stop often to duck into a room or alcove to avoid being seen by teams of crownsguards and security droids that keep tromping by. The overhead lights all over the ship flash yellow—a signal to all on board that they are under attack, that everyone must initiate battle protocols and report to their designated call points.

Edgar knows exactly who is attacking.

No one but Alyssa Farshot would be idiotic enough to throw themselves at a target like the kingship with only a few days to gather resources. He can hear the distant, muffled noise of plasma cannons and explosions. For a little while there, the ship was rocked by a few big blows, and Edgar was almost impressed.

But those have stopped. And Edgar can imagine how the battle must be looking for them now.

He knows better than anyone else the exact capabilities that Wythe has at his disposal with this vessel. And he made it even stronger by linking all of the security droids across the quadrant to the royal seal and the ship. Wythe can control every weapon in his arsenal—every cannon, every section of shield, every droid—with just a thought. It makes him formidable. Almost unbeatable.

But Edgar also knows the weaknesses of the kingship better than anyone else, too.

Wythe might have stripped the seal from him, but the kingship already told him all of her secrets. And he remembers.

NL7 gets him to the narrow lift that's concealed and security encoded, and Edgar inputs the override with shaking, clammy hands, collapsing inside as soon as the door slides open. It's a relief to sit on the floor for a minute, to let his eyes close and his head drift back. The lift hums soothingly as it works its way into the heart of the kingship, and Edgar must drift further than he plans because he wakes with a start when NL7 shakes him.

"Edgar Voles," it says. "We are here."

Good. Almost done. "Help me up, please."

The android pulls him back onto his feet and guides him into a cylindrical room that's smaller than he expected it to be, considering it serves as the engine room for a large and sophisticated ship. The walls are lit up, covered in displays and readouts, like one enormous, connected navcomm dashboard. The only break in it is a window on the far side that looks out over the enormous sphere of the kingship's engine, glowing with the blue-white light of a new star.

A posted crownsguard starts in surprise and reaches for their blaster as Edgar and NL7 step inside, but their reflexes aren't as quick as NL7's. It takes the crownsguard out with one quick shot from its own weapon, and then it turns to lock down the lift as Edgar staggers toward one of the control panels.

The commands and readouts are in a unique code, like its own separate kingship language, designed to keep anyone except the person who bears the royal seal from being able to use any of the functions in this room.

But Edgar still remembers. He bore the seal for weeks. Wythe has only had it for a few days. The enkindler is still in the process of learning, of integrating.

Which means he's weaker than he knows.

Sweat covers Edgar's body. His muscles shake with the effort to keep himself upright as his fingers move across the displays on the wall, typing in code that speaks to the kingship. Telling her the danger is over. The shields no longer need power. The thrusters keeping them aloft can come off-line. The weapons can power down.

And she listens to him. She shuts down every system he asks her to. The blazing light of the engine dims, flickers, fades into almost nothing.

Edgar locks Wythe out of making any changes from the bridge.

And then he collapses as the ship drops into a free-fall.

Excerpt from the last will and testament of Atar Faroshti, authorized 0.05.08 in the Year 4031

. . . I LEAVE NO HEIR AND NAME NO SUCCESSOR. Instead, I call for a crownchase to be implemented upon my passing and for it to begin in earnest as soon as I have been laid to rest.

My beloved niece, Alyssa Faroshti, will represent our family in this event. I have full faith and trust in her that she will demonstrate the integrity and strength of character of a true crownchaser.

FORTY-FIVE

STARDATE: 0.0—honestly, we're right where we were before. Except, y'know, watching the sky start to fall on top of us.

WE'RE SPRINTING FOR THE COVER OF THE TREES when I see the shields around the kingship flicker. They go from opaque black to clear, and the whole enormous bulk of it lists slowly to the side—

—and then it drops. Like someone cut the power right out from under it.

It's not like it's really far up—the keel is probably only ten meters off the ground—but thousands and thousands of cubic feet of warship plummeting down even a short distance like that is nothing to mess around with. It hits with this ear-rending smash, and I see the impact ripple the ground in a wave all around it. I watch in horror—frozen, hands gripping the roots of my own hair—as the hangar bays and the lowest two levels of the ship collapse under the weight of the collision. I don't know what the hell is happening or why the biggest godsdamned warship in the galaxy is just falling out of the sky, but I hope to the stars that there weren't a lot of people on those lower levels. There shouldn't be. Not if all the civilians in there are following battle protocols.

Gods. I hope everyone was following battle protocols.

An Orsion razortooth—sleek, triangular ships designed to be wide and flat to slip between tight spaces—slices through the trees and lands in a clear spot close by, the docking seal on the side of it sliding open. Faye appears with her hands on her hips, and her eyes find mine.

"Get in. We're gonna go take the kingship."

Well. Okay, then. She's right—this is our best opportunity to get to Wythe and take him out, that was always our main goal, but the sight of those flattened corridors is pulling my focus. The original plan was to bust through the shields with the ballistas and then use the better precision of the smaller ships to cut our way into the throne room level and get to the masterminds behind this mess with minimal collateral damage. But now the kingship is . . . well, like that, and it's looking a little more collateral-damage-y than I'd been hoping for. I can't go running off without making sure as many innocents as possible are taken care of.

"Sharva?" They look up as I cross over to them, their angular face calm and regal even with all the sweat and smudges of ash covering them. "I need a favor."

They raise an eyebrow with the ghost of a grin. "You ask a lot of favors, Faroshti."

"I do. I really do." I nod over at the now-wrecked mess of a kingship. "There are civilians in there, and I'm betting they didn't plan on experiencing a giant-ass crash landing today—"

"And we should make sure they get clear safely," they say before I even finish. "We're on it. Consider us gone."

They stride over to Evern and start mobilizing the rest of their people around them immediately, and I turn back to the razor-tooth. Setter and Hell Monkey have already geared up and ducked inside, so it just leaves Faye waiting on me. She's got her arms crossed and is tapping her foot loudly against the deck. It's a little over the top, if you ask me.

"Let's move, Farshot," she says. "Mass-murdering tyrants don't just depose themselves."

I roll my eyes at her, but I do kick it into a jog (because I'm a team player, dammit), checking my blasters to make sure they're charged and ready to go. I don't know what kind of resistance we'll get once we're inside, but I imagine it'll be a fight. Those security droids are just gonna follow whoever is inputting the commands, after all, and we know Wythe has at least two of his murder creations lurking around. So, y'know. Weapons hot and all that.

Setter and Hell Monkey are strapped into pocket seats, H.M. looking particularly uncomfortable crammed into a space not really meant for a lot of passengers. The ceiling is low enough that it brushes the top of my hair, and I duck a little bit as I find a corner with a spare safety harness to cram myself into close to the cockpit, where Honor and Faye are set up. I'm itching to ask if I can take the controls—I've always wanted to try flying one of these—but this doesn't feel like a great time to pull a kid-at-the-candy-market move.

Faye takes the ship up, cutting a path back out into the open and spinning a tight spiral into the sky.

Damn. This baby can *move*. I really, really want to fly it now.

"Is that absolutely necessary?" Setter calls from his spot. His eyes have gone a muddled grayish-green-yellow color that doesn't bode anything good. "The kingship is back there"—he points over his shoulder—"we can just . . . head straight there."

I'm close enough to Faye that I can see the smile curl across her face. "But where's the fun in that?"

I catch Hell Monkey's eye and give him a wink, then yank my harness tighter as Faye sweeps up and backward, taking us into a whirling, zigzagging dive right through the hottest part of the dog-fight still crisscrossing the skies. I close my eyes, feeling the hum of the ship rise and fall as it responds lightning-fast, my body almost weightless as we tell gravity to suck it.

We level off suddenly, and I hear Faye curse aloud. My eyes shoot open, and I crane forward to look through the window. "What? What is it?"

"There's blast shields lining the throne room," Honor grumbles. "They must be on a separate system from the exterior shields."

"It's fine," Faye says sharply. "We still have charges on our cannons. We'll blast through."

"I doubt it," Hell Monkey calls from the back. "Blast shields on a ship like this are probably graded to withstand way more firepower than you've got on board here. I'm betting all imperial-designated rooms have them too."

So the throne room, the Imperial Council rooms, the imperial quarters—basically, this entire level. Including the bridge, where

Wythe is most likely to have parked himself.

But there's one place I know of that I'm betting Wythe hasn't thought about.

I unbuckle my harness and come up behind Honor, tapping her on the shoulder. "I've got an idea. Mind if I . . . ?"

She shrugs and switches out with me, and Faye gives me a long side-eye before turning over manual flying controls. "Don't break my ship, Farshot."

I crack my knuckles and blow her a kiss. "Get the guns ready, Orso."

Hands steady on the controls, I dive the razortooth down and around, cutting along the damaged hull of the kingship and sweeping in a tight circle past the aft and up again on the starboard side. It takes a second to orient myself—I'm not used to approaching from the *outside* and the kingship looks so different right now—but I finally find it and square the prow of the razortooth to a series of three big unguarded windows just below the throne room level.

My old home. The personal family quarters Atar had set aside for him and me and Charlie, without all the pomp and circumstance of the imperial rooms. I can't make out anything inside because there's a reflective coating on the glass, but that's probably for the best considering what's about to happen.

I look over at Faye. "Blast the hell out of it."

FORTY-SIX

FAYE POWERS UP THE CANNONS AND UNLEASHES ON the side of the kingship, blasting at the hull and the windows until they fall away in great big pieces of alloy and glass. She doesn't let off until there's a hole big enough for a small ship to fit through.

Like, a razortooth-sized ship. Just for example.

I rev the thrusters, and Faye's head snaps around to me. "Far-shot . . ."

I cup a hand around my ear, frowning. "Eh? Can't hear you over all this engine noise!"

"Yes, you can—don't—"

I throw the razortooth forward, driving her right through the hole and into the middle of my childhood quarters. And I mean, I'm not rough about it. I try to do it as gently as possible, I swear. But there's some scraping and screeching across the hull as I jam into a space definitely not meant as a landing pad and set her down amid the wreckage of my former living room, cutting the engines as soon as she feels steady.

Faye levels a glare at me as I swing out of my seat. "You're paying for all the repairs to this."

I'm already halfway toward the door, slipping both my blasters out of their holsters. "I'm good for it. Y'know . . . if we don't all die on here."

I step out onto the extremely flattened remains of a couch, and the little tug at my heart is all the warning I need not to look around any further. No sense in dwelling on this place, on this stuff. I'm carrying all my memories, and it'll have to be enough. I look up at the ceiling just above the razortooth. There's a spot right in the middle that's already had a big chunk taken out of it, and I aim my blaster at it, unloading round after round of charges in a circular pattern until it completely falls away, leaving an opening.

Into the throne room level of the ship.

"Hey, look!" I call. Hell Monkey, Setter, Honor, and Faye tromp out of the razortooth, armed to the teeth, blasters on their hips, rifles on H.M.'s and Faye's backs, and something potentially bigger and meaner-looking strapped to Honor. "I made an extremely convenient exit for us. Last one up buys drinks."

I holster my blasters and start scrambling up the sloping body of the ship. The ceilings in here are about three meters high, but that's easy stuff to manage if you've got a whole ship to give you a boost. I'm first through the hole, clambering into the dark, stuffy bedroom of the imperial quarters.

Shivers crawl over my skin as I crouch low and pull my blasters out, keeping watch as first Faye and Honor, then Setter and Hell Monkey come up from below. Hell Monkey pulls up near my shoulder as we assemble ourselves into a loose formation.

"You good, Alyssa?" He keeps his voice really low and quiet, but it sounds so loud in this tomb-like space anyway. The last time I was in here was when Uncle Atar died, and I'm very careful to not let my gaze drift to his bed.

"Yup." No. "I'm great." I'm not. "Let's get a move on." That part is true.

The benefit of coming up through the floor of the imperial quarters is that literally no one is outside the doors as we step into the corridors because, hell, they weren't expecting us to come from there. But the element of surprise doesn't last us nearly as long as I thought it would, and we've only gone about twenty meters before we wind up pinned down in an alcove, blaster fire from a crew of about a dozen security droids and three or four crownsguards heating the air all around us.

"They got here fast." Honor's scowl is all the more evident because she lost her pink shades in the corridor back there while we were scrambling to get to cover.

Hell Monkey wipes the sweat from his palms, readjusting his grip on his rifle. "I think the big-ass hole we just blew into the side of their ship might've given our location away."

"More important," says Setter, "is how we get past them. The longer we stay here, the more likely it is they'll gather reinforcements and make our job more difficult."

I tap the back of my head against the wall behind me, thinking about the kingship, the layout, who's on it—

Oh. Who's on it.

It's worth a damn shot. I bring my wristband up and swipe in a short-range message, sending it out in one, two, three directions and then just crossing my fingers, heart and breath in my throat, waiting for a response.

Please still be on the kingship. Please still be on the kingship.

A blaster shot hits a little too close, spraying sparks across my shoulder and neck, and I grit my teeth and stick my arm around the corner, shooting wildly in return.

Come on. Someone answer.

Faye looks over at Honor and nods at the contraption strapped onto Honor's broad back. "We could use the . . . ?"

Honor frowns, shaking her head. "It's got one shot. Maybe two. We use it now and we won't have it for the big stuff later."

A little metal canister about the size of my hand clatters at our feet, and Setter reacts instantly, kicking it away down the corridor and pulling us all around to face the wall a half-second before it explodes in an intense flash of light intended to blind us.

I scrub at my eyes. Even with them closed, the flash bomb left an imprint. "Counterpoint: if we don't use it now, we may never get to that 'big stuff.'"

And then—like a godsdamned miracle—my wristband pings. And then it pings again. And again.

Hell Monkey leans around me, peppering the security forces with several rounds from his blaster rifle. "What's happening, Farshot? What are you doing over there?"

I look down at the messages on my wristband display and grin. "I called in reinforcements."

Faye swings her glowing hair over her shoulder. "What do you mean, 'reinforcements'? Who the hell—?"

A shout from out in the corridors cuts her off, and the blaster fire around our alcove suddenly stops. There's a loud, vicious exchange of shots and yelling, and I peek around, but all I can tell from this angle is that the security force has turned its attention to someone else coming up from behind them. I'm about to step out and help when I hear boots coming up on my right, and I pause, turning my guns on them as they round the curve—

—and find myself aimed at Kalia Sharn and Drinn. Drinn definitely has a couple of still-healing injuries on him that weren't there before, but he's alive and standing, and damn, it's good as hell to see both of them.

A wide grin breaks out across my face. "Fancy meeting you two here." I look over Kalia's shoulder at the dozen crownsguards behind them, half of whom have ripped the imperial sigils from their uniforms and all of whom are looking eager for a fight. "And you brought friends."

Kalia lowers her blaster and lifts a casual shoulder. "I'm fairly certain there would've been no leaving them behind, even if we'd wanted to."

I look over at Drinn, who's so much the stoic vilkjing right now that he seems almost bored with all this gunfire and crashing ships and rebellion. "Glad to see you made it out okay."

He grumbles an assent. That's about all I get.

Faye clears her throat. "Are we going to make actual use of our new numbers? Or are we going to waste this window of opportunity having a sappy reunion?"

"Nope," says Drinn. "We go now."

He motions over his shoulder, and the whole unit blazes past us and joins the fight, and all of us combined put a hard stop on that security force real quick. Within a few minutes, the droids are down and the opposition crownsguards are retreating back down the hall. I spot the broad shoulders and slate skin of Ko in the far corridor at the head of another group, limping a little. As soon as the firefight stops, I scramble over to her.

"Ko." I reach out to hug her, and she sweeps me up so tight that my feet lift off the ground. For a hot second, I almost think she might swing me onto her shoulders like she did when I was a little kid. I actually don't think I'd have a problem with that.

But she sets me back down and steps back, patting me on the shoulder like she's just used up all her affection allowance for the day.

"Did they . . ." My eyes drift down to the left leg she's favoring. "Are you okay?"

"We're alive. And that's a good start." Ko steps past me, nudging me with an elbow as she goes. "Come on. Let's get you onto that bridge."

FORTY-SEVEN

THERE ARE DOZENS OF COLLAPSED DROIDS COL-
lected around my feet. My blaster is warm in my hands but cooling
a little more as every second passes. Lungs are pumping hard, heart
is pumping harder. The security droids were assembled in rows
three-deep outside the throne room doors, so it's a damn good
thing we picked up our extra buddies on the way over here.

Y'know what they say. The real revolution is the friends you
make along the way. Pretty sure it goes something like that.

Honor and Hell Monkey are over with Drinn by the control
panels for the doors (they're locked, of course, so they're trying to
figure out how to jigger them open). I holster my blaster so I can
help Faye slap a med patch on Setter's shoulder (he caught some
blaster fire in the exchange) and watch out of the corner of my eye
as Ko huddles together with Kalia. When they catch me watching,
Kalia extracts herself from the circle and comes over to us.

"As soon as they get those doors open," she says, "you all go.
The rest of us will hold the corridor from any interference."

I frown. "I don't like leaving you to hold the line. I did that once
already, and it wasn't great. I wasn't a fan."

Kalia shrugs, looking pretty unmoved by my declaration. "You're going in." Her eyes travel to Faye and then Setter. "All three of you. It's already been decided."

I start to open my mouth and object, but at that moment, there's a hoot of triumph by the doors and I look over to see Hell Monkey waving to us. The control panel behind him is absolutely demolished, but Drinn's got two linked circuit nodes that he's holding together and Honor has nudged one of the doors open a few centimeters.

Ko comes up behind me and puts a hand on my shoulder. "Time to go, little empress."

Faye and Setter raise their eyebrows at me simultaneously at the nickname. It's really something to see. I shove them both hard in the back. "I want to hear absolutely zero words. *Zero.* Let's move."

Hell Monkey nods at us as we come up. "We found a way in, but it only works while Drinn's holding those two bits together."

"So it'll lock behind us once he drops them," Setter says with a little sigh.

"Nothing in, nothing out," says Faye, her grin like the edge of a knife. "Exactly as it should be. Honor, you all set?"

Honor's kneeling on the floor, reassembling the big contraption that she's been hauling around on her back. A moment later, she rises, scooping it up and—

Oh. It's a shoulder-mounted plasma cannon. Like the ones on our ships except, y'know, personal-sized for your convenience. I cock my head at her. "Damn, Honor. I'm a little jealous. That's a sexy look on you."

She winks. "Still might be two of those tricky assassin bastards in there. Can't take chances."

Right. Good point. I slide over to the cracked door and try to get an angle on the inside. The throne room looks completely empty (as far as I can tell, which isn't saying much). The windows are blacked out by the blast shields, so the only illumination in there is from the strategic uplighting lining the walls. Not much to see by. And we know those ignati bastards can basically go invisible.

I turn back to Hell Monkey, Setter, Faye, and Honor. "Okay, I've got a plan. Cover me."

Before any of them can even start to object, I squeeze myself through the gap between the doors and stride into the middle of the throne room.

It's dead quiet in here. You can't even hear the ships that arc cutting through the air outside. The only thing audible are my boots on the gleaming marble as I wander forward, hand on my hip near the butt of my blaster. The throne itself gleams dully, gold and platinum plating catching the dim light.

"Nice place you got here," I call out to the empty shadows. "You just wax the floors?"

Nothing. The absolute stillness of the place sends a little shiver trickling down my back. I don't even know for sure that the assassins are in here—maybe they're still on the bridge and I'm talking to nobody. But I doubt Wythe wants to chance anyone getting that close to him. He'd send them out to take care of us where he's not in the line of fire and he doesn't have to see all the blood and aftermath.

"Don't mind me." My voice rings against the walls. "I'm just gonna pop in and have a friendly little conversation with your boss. Be right back."

I step sharply toward the throne, where there's a touch-activated panel that can open up the bridge doors behind the dais. (Or, it could in normal circumstances anyway.) And honestly I think it's only because I'm expecting to get shot at any moment that I catch it: this tiny, high-pitched whine just at the edge of my hearing. My heart freezes midbeat, and I throw myself forward a millisecond before a shot from a massive blaster rifle screams across the room.

It misses me—thank every star—but I feel the heat of it blaze across my back. I hit the ground hard, chest-first, and scramble to push myself back onto my feet as one of the ignati flickers into existence on top of the dais a few meters away. It's got a big-ass plasma blade held out in front of it, throwing a green glow across its masked face. I try *really* hard not to picture it running that thing through my chest like one of them did with Owyn Mega.

My pulse is hammering so loud, and I'm so focused on the ignati in front of me that I don't hear the whine of the blaster rifle this time. I just see the flare of the shot in the corner of my eye right before it catches me in the side, knocking me clean off my feet.

I scream as I slam into the floor, fire searing my skin from my hip all the way down my right leg. I can't move. I can't think. The pain is white-hot—it obliterates everything in my head. I hear a shout, but it sounds like it's coming from a million kilometers away.

Something big and bright streaks through the air above me and then—

—BOOM—

The impact vibrates through my body hard enough to make my teeth ache. Little pebbles of debris pepper down on me, and I squeeze my eyes shut and turn my face away, into the smooth, cool floor. I can feel boots running over the ground. I can hear blaster fire crisscrossing above me and more shouting. Some of it is definitely my name this time. I catch that much. But my back is to them, and I'm not sure sitting up in the middle of a firefight is really high on the list of good ideas. So I keep my eyes closed and my arms over my head, trying to stay clear of the trouble.

Quick footsteps approach, and gloved fingers grab a fistful of my hair, right by the scalp, and drag me up by the roots. I scream again—it fucking *hurts*, and my leg is on fire, and I'm flailing, trying to pry their fingers loose, trying to get my feet under me as this sonofabitch uses me like a shield.

Screw it. I drop my hands, gritting my teeth against the pain in my scalp. I sweep the blaster from the holster on my uninjured side, jam the barrel upward into its body, and fire. I don't let up off the trigger until it lets go of me and collapses on the stairs of the dais.

I lie there, still in the awkward position it left me in. My side burning, my scalp burning—just too much pain burning all over my body to bother moving as I let my eyes finally take in the scene.

Someone (Honor. Definitely Honor) destroyed the whole right side of the dais. The throne is still standing—stubborn bastard—but the marble next to it is in shambles, and the body of one of the ignati lies crumpled in the ruins. The other—the one that's probably got half my hair wrapped around its fingers—is partially underneath me and very, very still.

"Alyssa?" Hell Monkey kneels beside me and puts a hand on my face. I roll my head around and look up at him, waiting for all those soft, heartfelt words as he opens his mouth and says . . .

"That was one of the stupidest things I've ever seen you do."

I scowl. "Come on. No way that was worse than when I randomly jumped on one of their ships."

"It was worse. From where I was standing, it definitely seemed worse."

"Didn't want you thinking I'd gone all responsible or anything."

"Move, gearhead." Faye sweeps up behind him and nudges him aside, dumping several med patches on the floor next to me. She raises an eyebrow at me as she starts to put them efficiently (but not gently) along the plasma burns down my side and leg. "Can't just get a one-patch kind of injury, huh, Farshot?"

"Pfffft. That's amateur hour. I'm a professio—ow! Easy there."

Faye lifts a shoulder. "Just taking as much care as you seemed to walking into a room of invisible assassins."

Somewhere behind me, Hell Monkey chuckles, and I try to swat at him but miss. "I knew you all would have my back. Just help me to my feet here. This isn't done yet."

Faye finishes the last med patch, and Hell Monkey slips an arm underneath my shoulders, levering me back into a standing position. "Damn," I say as I look around at the rubble again. "You can really see the damage way better from up here."

Setter straightens from where he was bent over the arms of the throne, a deep frown on his face. "Wythe has locked the bridge out completely. I can't activate the doors even with manual controls."

Shit. I step around the throne and stare at the smooth wall of marble that conceals the bridge doors. Just behind it, Wythe has control of the entire kingship and he's probably feeling pretty smug and cozy about that right now.

Let's fix that.

I look over at Honor, who's got the shoulder-mounted cannon on the floor and is looking it over. "How's your toy holding up? Still lively?"

"She's probably got one more shot in her." Honor raises her eyebrows at me and grins a little. "You got a target in mind?"

"Absolutely." I let go of Hell Monkey and limp forward until I'm right in front of the wall. Pointing straight ahead, I shoot my blaster a few times in quick succession and then step back and admire my handiwork.

A crude happy face mars the marble.

I wave a hand toward it. "There you go, Honor. If you would make us a door please."

FORTY-EIGHT

MOST OF THE TIME I LIKE A NON-WEAPON-Y SOLU-tion to situations if I can possibly help it. But when Honor slings that mini plasma cannon onto her shoulder and blows a hole straight through the wall?

I'm not gonna pretend there wasn't a little coveting going on. Because I can think of several tight situations from my Explorers' Society days that would've been a lot less tight if I'd had one of these.

Hell Monkey goes through the hole first, covering the rest of us with his big blaster rifle as we follow after him, assembling on the rubble-strewn deck of the bridge with weapons up.

Wythe is the only one there.

I move to the front, still favoring my blastered leg, and sweep around in a circle, looking for any sign of extra bodies, but all I see is Wythe. He stands next to the round command center table in the middle of the small space, and its glowing interface casts a pale green light all around the room. We're all cut with sickly illumination and strange shadows.

My arm shakes a little as I level the barrel of my weapon at him.

It's not fear, though. It's rage—liquid-hot and flooding through my body. I have to use both hands to steady the blaster.

"Funny," I tell him through gritted teeth. "I expected you to have more of an entourage here. What's a few more bodies dying for you, right?"

Wythe looks down at me from his considerable height. "I have the kingship," he says imperiously. "It's all I need."

"And how is that working for you now?" Faye asks, her voice low and cold.

"You can't kill me. I bear the seal now." He taps his chest with long fingers. "I am one with all the emperors who came before. I am a fixed point at the center of the empire, and the light of Solarus is with me."

I shoot a questioning look at Setter, the only one of us in this room who probably did his homework on this. He tilts his head without breaking his glare at Wythe. "He's right. He has to give it up willingly. If we kill him, the seal stays locked inside his body and there's no getting it out."

Which means if we want to take it back, we have to . . . what? Torture him till he gives it up? That sounds like some level-twelve evil mastermind shit, and I'm not sure I've got the stomach for that. Gods, is this what we're all going to come down to?

My indecision must show on my face because Wythe grins and spreads his arms magnanimously. "See? Your way leads to an impasse. Put your weapons down, and let us talk through a different way forward—"

Wythe is midsentence when a blaster shot cuts through the air past my shoulder and hits the enkindler square in the torso, knocking him to the ground.

I swing around, weapon up, and once again find myself staring down my blaster at Edgar Fucking Voles. Him and his android, NL7. It's the one holding the blaster out, barrel still hot. They're standing just inside the hole we blew in the wall, which means the droid threaded that shot through five whole bodies in order to hit Wythe.

Impressive.

Look, it's not like I like it or anything, but I can appreciate the precision.

I sweep a look over Edgar, who's basically draped across NL7's back like a very limp, very heavy cape. His skin is translucent, the veins almost as visible as the bioluminescent lines on Faye's skin, and sweat has soaked through the clothes hanging off his body. He looks like hell, basically. Or, more accurately, he looks like what happens when hell has a bad day.

He looks like Uncle Atar did. There at the end.

"I thought you were supposed to be dead," I tell him without moving or dropping my blaster even a millimeter.

I think he tries to laugh? But it sounds more like a weak, dry cough. "Not yet. Give it time."

"Or we could not," Faye says, stepping toward him, her own blasters leveled at his head. "We can just skip to the end right now."

The droid reacts immediately, switching the blaster to point at Faye, which makes Honor snap forward with her blaster rifle aimed at the droid and—

"Stop." I drop my weapon and wave a hand at them. "Just stop. This is not ending with everyone getting shot in some sort of barrel-measuring contest. Just . . . everyone stand down for a minute, and let's just deal with . . ."

Wythe. I turn back to where he lies on the ground in a pool of bright yellow and orange. He's breathing hard, and blue-green blood is soaking into the front of his robes, spreading in a circle from the spot low on his torso where the center of the Solari circulatory system is. A kill shot, but not right away. It'll take just long enough for him to die that—

—I see it already. Little beads of liquid platinum rising to his skin, starting to pool on his chest.

That droid knew exactly where it was shooting.

I cast a glance back at Faye, who's still got her guns on Edgar though her eyes are on Wythe, her expression fierce and her jaw clenched tight. But there's the glint of shimmering gold tears lining the bottoms of her lids. All those big feelings she buries overflowing past her sharp edges. I look over at Setter, but his eyes are closed, his head tilted back to the ceiling. There's pain etched into the lines of his profile, and not just his own, I don't think. I imagine this many strong emotions in a small space has gotta be a lot, even for someone who's dealt with the empath thing his whole life.

I don't have that problem. I barely bother to deal with my own emotions. So I can carry this next part for us.

Stepping forward, I crouch down by Wythe's head, waiting,

totally impassive, until his eyes find my face.

He sucks in a breath. It sounds like it takes some effort. "You will be the . . . doom of . . . every soul in this empire."

"Come on, Ilysium. You give me way too much credit. I'll be the doom of maybe a dozen souls. Max."

His fingers curl toward my arm. "You . . . can't just sit there . . . and let me . . . die. . . ."

"Why not?" I tilt my head, staring him down. "You assassinated an emperor. You murdered Owyn Mega. You destroyed our families. You killed tens of millions of people." My throat swells with grief and rage, and tears press against the backs of my eyes, but I swallow it all down and steady myself. "Tens. Of millions. Why would you think I'd save you after all that?"

Wythe coughs a little. The bloodstain on his robes grows bigger and darker every second. He waves a limp hand. "All you Faroshti . . . think so highly of yourselves. . . . You wouldn't . . . let yourself . . . sink so low. . . ."

I lean down. Far enough that I can drop my voice almost into a whisper. "I sat at Atar's side while your blood poison reduced him to nothing. I stood beside Owyn as your little toy soldier gutted him. I was there—I was right there—when the explosion took Charlie. You taught me how to watch people die, Wythe. You did that. And now you get to reap your rewards."

He turns his head, looking away from me, his breath getting shorter, shallower, more labored. His lips move almost silently, in prayer I think, and he brings a hand up, fingers fumbling at his neck. It takes me a second to realize what he's doing—trying to activate the implant enkindlers have embedded in their necks, to let them self-immolate in the moments before biological death.

I'm about to jump back, get clear of any fire-adjacent situation, but a heavy boot comes down on Wythe's wrist, pinning his hand to the ground. I look up into Hell Monkey's stone-cold face.

"Solarus is gonna be better off without you," he says, his voice low and quiet.

Wythe's eyes go wide, he opens his mouth to speak—

—but his breathing stops. His eyes go vacant. And then he's gone. Just like that.

I stay right where I am, crouched beside him. I thought I would feel relieved or vindicated or something, but it's not that simple. My insides are just a total riot of emotions smashing against each other, and all I know for sure is it feels ugly. All of this feels ugly and no single shitty thing makes any of the other shitty things right or better. It's all just trash.

"The seal . . ." Edgar's ragged voice cuts through the silence. It makes me jump a little, because I honestly kind of forgot he was there. I look down at Wythe's chest and see it—the imperial seal sitting on top of his skin. It looks just like it did down on Calm all those weeks ago—like nothing's even changed.

Except the whole universe has changed.

"You have to take it," Edgar says. "It has centuries of knowledge on it, our history. . . ."

I pick it up by the tips of my fingers, shuddering a little at how warm it feels. Like, body-temperature warm. Getting to my feet, I

hold it out in front of me, staring at its gleaming surface, the geodesic lines and pinpricks of stars.

"I'll take it," I tell him. "But no one's using it. We're charting a
new path forward now."

THE KINGSHIP, VELLYN, THE UMNI SYSTEM

IT'S TAKING EVERYTHING EDGAR HAS TO STAY
upright, even using NL7 to prop himself up.

The kingship groans and jerks sideways, hard and sudden, and
he loses his grip and tumbles to the floor. The room shakes violently around them, and a rumble rises from deep inside the core
of the ship. Edgar hears it. He can feel it. There is something very
wrong.

NL7 appears next to him and helps him sit up. "The kingship is
unstable, Edgar Voles," it says quietly.

He swallows. His mouth is so dry. "I know."

"What does that mean—unstable?"

Edgar blinks and looks up at Alyssa Farshot. She stands over
him, one hand gripping the royal seal. Her expression is tight with
wariness, dislike—but her blaster is holstered.

"The damage . . ." He pushes himself straighter, trying to get a
little extra room in his chest to take in a breath. "From the crash.
It's worse than it looks. She's a time bomb."

Setter Roy strides into view. He looks more haggard than Edgar
has ever seen him, but also more determined. "We need to go,
then. We have to get everyone outside clear of the blast radius."

"A ship this size?" It's Faye's companion—the human with the green hair. What was her name? It's getting hard for Edgar to think through the growing fog in his mind. "It's gonna take out dozens of kilometers if it blows. We need to get off this whole damn plateau."

"All the more reason to get moving," Setter says, waving her over and offering her a hand over the rubble, back into the throne room.

Edgar's eyes drift back to Alyssa as she squats down to his level, one eyebrow raised. "You got a plan, though, don't you, Edgar? You always have a plan."

He shivers hard. The alloy floor is so cold against his feverish, sweat-soaked skin. "I know how to talk to the kingship. Inputting a command for a controlled implosion . . . would limit the damage radius. . . ."

She stares at him for a moment and then at NL7. The droid still keeps a steadying hand on Edgar's shoulders. "We will assist you in this, Edgar Voles."

Something twists in Alyssa's face. Like she's fighting some other, softer emotion. The bridge shakes again, violently. Her companion—the big muscley one, why can't Edgar remember anything, everything is slipping from him—calls to her from the exit.

"Alyssa, we've gotta go."

She nods. "I'll be right there, H.M."

"It . . ." Edgar chokes on the first word and has to pause and recover. He knows what he wants to say but everything is so much harder to do now. "It was an accident . . . killing Nathalia."

Alyssa's dark eyes are still sharp. "Maybe. But the other shit you did wasn't. So I don't know how I feel about you, Edgar Voles."

He drags his gaze up to the ceiling, staring at it but not seeing it. "I just . . . wanted to be *seen*. Really seen."

The barest touch brushes his arm. It's there and gone in an instant. "We always saw you, Edgar. We just couldn't reach you."

Alyssa stands, and Edgar finds her face one more time. Her jaw is hard, her eyes are flinty. The only give to her expression is the slight furrow between her eyebrows. She doesn't say anything more, just turns and leaves.

When the bridge is empty of all but them, Edgar reaches out a hand, and NL7 grasps it in its spindly fingers. He's glad the droid is the one here with him at the end. It's fitting, in a way, that he's the one to set the self-destruct.

After all, he's always hated this fucking ship.

FROM THE PERSONAL FILES OF ATAR VELRYN FAROSHTI, TRANSMITTED BY NL734014, ACCESSED BY ALYSSA FARSHOT ON STARDATE 0.06.28 IN THE YEAR 4031

Audio transcript of an unsent communication from Atar to Alyssa Faroshti, recorded 0.05.08.4031

THIS WILL LIKELY BE THE LAST PERSONAL RECORD I ever make. And I must do it now before my courage and my strength fail me.

Alyssa, Charles has just left to bring you home to us, but I confess that I am worried I will not last long enough to see you once more in this life. And even if I do . . . I know it will only be to name you crownchaser and upset your whole world.

I am so sorry, Birdie. I can only hope someday you'll understand the decisions I made. I cannot claim to have lived my life without regrets. I'm afraid I have many. Some of which I fear you might pay for in your own journey. If I could undo those, I would. I would travel a thousand wormholes to change the past, but unfortunately, the Explorers' Society tells me we don't have any wormholes that do that in our empire.

Charles and I were often asked while you were growing up—and even after you left the kingship—why we did not discipline you more, rein you in tighter, train you to be a proper prime family heir. We almost never gave a straight answer—it was hardly their business how we chose to raise you.

But I will give you the real and true answer now, Birdie: I have seen the weight of this universe extinguish too many bright fires.

I wanted to give you space to grow and breathe and explore until your fire burned so big, so intense, so fierce that nothing could smother it.

And that is one decision I will never regret.

You burn as bright as a new star, Alyssa. And soon the whole universe will truly see it.

FORTY-NINE

STARDATE: 0.06.29 in the Year 4031
LOCATION: At the end of things . . . for now

I'm SITTING ON THE EDGE OF A NEIGHBORING PLA-
teau, about three kilometers away from the kingship, when it
self-destructs.

Sharva, Evern, and everyone else on the ground had already
done most of the work scooping up people from the kingship and
getting them well away from this mess while we'd been breaking
into the throne room. By the time we made it back out, there'd
just been a handful of folks left, and we'd piled into our remaining
ships and hauled ass for safe distance. Everyone's standing around
watching, gathered in little supportive clumps, but I wanted to sit
here, right where the ground all falls away, and feel my feet dangle
over empty air as that massive construct of a ship collapses in on
itself.

It's slow at first—a little blossom of fire, a section crumpling
inward—and then all at once the flames are everywhere and the
whole structure implodes in a ball of debris and smoke, the boom

of it reaching our ears nine seconds after it actually happens. I don't know exactly what fuels the self-destruct function on the kingship, but it must be powerful as hell because all those indestructible layers of alloy and metal dissolve into ash as the columns of smoke rise higher and higher up into the sky. It's one enormous, slow, wavy line, and I watch it billow and shift with detached fascination.

It's better than watching the kingship itself as one level, one corridor, one room after another disintegrates and settles into a heap of nothing.

How is it possible to be both so sad and so relieved at the same time? Why are emotions so freaking complicated? I just want to feel one way about this whole situation instead of this horrible storm of conflicting thoughts.

It was my home. It was where I grew up. It was where all my memories of Atar and Charlie lived.

But it also held so many skeletons in its walls. So many of the things that are horrible and toxic about this empire were tied up in that place. It was always gonna have to go. Probably. I think.

I think about Edgar lying on the bridge. Dying. He was just a kid once, like the rest of us, round faced and lonely. Would he still have done the things he did at the end if Wythe hadn't betrayed him? Would he have come around? Changed his course?

I close my eyes and grind the heels of my palms into the sockets. Honestly, I don't know. And it kind of makes my head hurt trying to untangle it. Or maybe that's everything else.

I crane my head around, scanning the crowd of people until I spot Hell Monkey. He's helping Ko wrap up a fresh wound on her arm, while Kalia moves from one group to another checking on everyone, Drinn shadowing her with a pile of blankets and water rations in his arms.

Footsteps come toward me through the grass, and a second later, Faye swings her legs over the edge next to me. On the other side, Setter sits carefully, dangling one foot, waiting for a second, and then sticking out the other.

"So was that"—Faye waves a hand at the smoking remains of the kingship—"about how you imagined this going?"

I roll my eyes. "Not exactly."

Setter leans forward a few centimeters to look at the drop below and then quickly sits back again. "I thought the Alyssa Farshot method of planning was to just jump for it and figure out the rest before you land."

I try to pull out a grin and a quip, but I feel all wrung out and empty. I stare at the smoldering wreckage. I wonder if the throne melted with it. I hope so. If it didn't, I'm going to personally haul it over the edge of one of these Vellyn waterfalls.

"Did it help?" I ask them quietly. "Did any of that make you feel better about . . . everything we lost?"

There's a beat, and then Faye says, "Yes. Yes, it did," with the quick, decisive conviction that I always loved about her.

Setter's answer takes a little longer and comes out a little quieter. "No. I don't think it did."

I just nod. Because I don't think I have an answer. Somewhere in between maybe. But I can't dig out the truth beneath all the junk layered on top of it. It'd be like trying to find the engine core in the remains of the kingship right now. Too hot still. Too chaotic. Check again later—maybe.

Setter reaches out and touches my wrist, turning my hand open. I'm still holding the seal, so tight it's practically embedded in my skin at this point. He runs a fingertip over it, watching the platinum surface ripple at his touch.

"What now?" he asks. "What do we do with this?"

Faye leans in and scowls down at it. "Shoot it into a godsdamned sun."

I kind of agree with her. But something Edgar said makes me hesitate. That our history is on this thing. And I'm not sure it's a very good or pretty history, but chucking it away, trying to forget it ever happened, might just open us up to making the same mistakes later.

"There has to be a record somewhere," I tell them. "Of what people did. Of how bad things got. Even if we just put it in stasis in a museum or something, we can't bury it like it never happened. We have to look."

Look, Birdie. Really look. Really see.

Setter closes my fingers back around it. "We have more to fix. A lot more. This just leaves a power vacuum and could lead to a level of chaos that will spread to every planet in the quadrant if we don't do something."

"So we do something." I tuck the seal into an inner pocket inside my jumpsuit. "We help fix this mess. But we don't do it by ourselves with crowns and seals and thrones."

Faye sighs heavily. "You're not going to give an inspirational speech, are you? I'm not sure I have the stomach for that."

I flick her in the ear.

Sharva comes up behind us and reaches out a hand, pulling me onto my feet. They've got a thin cut across one of their cheekbones and a bandage wrapped around their left upper arm, but they and their crew seem to have weathered things okay.

"It sounds like long-range communication channels are back open," they say, nodding over their shoulder. "People in the empire are going to want to know what happened and the plan for what comes next." They raise their eyebrows at me. "What *does* come next?"

I tilt my chin up to meet their gaze dead-on. "We had a deal, didn't we? It's time to make something new, if you're ready for it."

Sharva gives me a skeptical once-over, then reaches down and scoops up my right arm. They press their thumb against the inside of my wrist, right over the Oath Taker tattoo, and after a second, the green symbols dissolve into nothing.

"We're ready, Alyssa Farshot," Sharva says as they let go. "We've been ready. Are you?"

I look back at Setter and Faye as they come up next to me. Faye gives me a wink, and Setter, a little nod.

Probably not. I swallow and square my shoulders. *But here we go.*

FIFTY

STARDATE: 0.07.01 in the Year 4031
LOCATION: On board a starliner called *Daybreak*, taking a slow route back toward Apex

IT'S A RELIEF TO BE BACK UP IN THE STARS.

Not that Vellyn wasn't great, but I kind of think I might never want to go back there again. Just add it to the list of places in this quadrant that have a surplus of bad memories. If I ever get to rejoin the Explorers' Society someday, they're going to take a look at my list of no-go spots and think, "What kind of explorer are you anymore?"

The stars, though. The stars are a sanctuary. I sit in my quarters on board our borrowed (legally, for the record) starliner, feeling like I can inhale to the very bottom of my lungs for the first time in weeks. Nothing weighs as much out here—literally or figuratively. The space between every far-off distant point of light in the blackness gives me room to breathe.

Which is good. Because I'm gonna need all the breathing room I can get.

We sent out our broadcast to the empire, showing everyone the destroyed kingship and making our pitch for building a new form of government, a system with better representation, where more voices will get a say in how things get done. Whether it was received well or not is . . . debatable. I mean, I don't know how many times you've pitched a major structural overhaul to a thousand and one planets, but there's not really a good comparison point to tell you whether you were successful or not.

The whole quadrant feels fragile. Like it's being held together by atom-thin strings.

Which makes sense. There are so many questions that we don't have answers to yet. Like, oh, say, what all of this is even gonna look like. How we make it all work. What about planets that don't want to be part of this new future or maybe have a split in their populations about whether to join or not? How do you reshape centuries of political, economic, and sociocultural entanglements without breaking anything?

Maybe we can't. But I figure I ought to help try anyway. I owe it to . . . well, too many people to count at this point. But mostly Atar and Charlie.

We're using the *Daybreak* to hop from system to system as we work our way back toward Apex. The general plan is to have a council or symposium or something once we get there to start figuring stuff out, but we're visiting planets all along the way, trying to build bridges and get folks on board with the plan and all this very organized, diplomatic stuff that has required me to wear a lot of respectable clothes and not swear so much. Hell

Monkey calls it Formal Farshot.

But I don't have to be her right now. Right now, the *Daybreak* is sliding past the Devil Wing Nebula, and I'm going to take thirty minutes—thirty minutes at least—to sit here quietly and enjoy it. I've seen it before, briefly, but you don't get over seeing something like this. Towering gas clouds spread like two enormous, ragged wings in shades of orange and red and pink, punctuated by brilliant flashes of electrical discharge lancing in crooked lines from one cloud to another.

It's breathtaking.

I hear the door to my quarters slide open, but I don't turn to look because there's only one person with clearance to come in here without authorization. I scoot over on my bed and pat the mattress, and Hell Monkey sinks into the spot next to me, sliding his arm behind my back so I can lean into him. I drop my head onto his shoulder, breathing him in. His timing is impeccable. This is just about the only thing that could make this moment better.

After a minute, he says, real quiet, "Sounds like we're gonna make a stop at the Devil Wing Spaceport in a few hours before we hop our next hyperlight lane."

I just hum in acknowledgment. I'd heard about this already. I was planning to pick up some decent clothes there so I didn't have to keep borrowing from folks since all mine got blown up at one point or another.

He takes a deep breath, and with my ear so close to his chest, I can hear how shaky it is. The tremor in it. A not-good feeling flutters in my stomach.

369

"I'm getting off at the spaceport, Alyssa."

I think my heart actually stops. Just dead stops right in my chest. My next inhale is a struggle. "I'm sorry, what now?"

"I'm not coming with you on the next hyperlight jump. I'm gonna stick around here, try to pick up some work in exchange for a ride."

I push off him, and my head spins a little as I straighten. Probably because I'm not breathing very well right now. His eyes are fixed on the nebula floating by outside the window, and I can see all the little signs on his face—the brow furrow, the tightness around his mouth—that let me know he's upset. And it's exactly the fact that I can read him *that* well that floods me with irritation, and I smack him right in his delt.

"You can at least look at me if you're gonna drop information like that."

He does. It makes it worse. Because those long-lashed hazel eyes of his have plenty of pain in them but also plenty of that calm kind of certainty that means he's set on his course. "I'm sorry. It's not like I've been holding out on you or anything—I only decided for sure, like, five minutes ago."

"You could've mentioned you were thinking about it." I know I sound sulky. I can't help it. I waited for so many weeks for him to get fed up and bolt. Lately I'd kind of dropped my guard a little and figured it'd never happen. "Water finally got too deep, huh?"

He shifts so he's facing me and then pulls me around so I'm facing him, too. "It's not you. Don't get it in your head that you're driving me away or anything." He scoops my hands up, wraps his big callused fingers around mine. "Remember how I said that loving you is like trying to hold on to a comet? The problem in that scenario is not the comet. The comet is amazing. She's incredible. She's doing exactly what she's supposed to do." He leans forward, pressing his forehead to mine. "You're doing something big here, Alyssa. Something important. But I fix ships. Not governments. I don't have a place here."

I thought I was your place. I don't say that out loud. I don't say it because it's not fair. We're both young, really young, and asking him to hang up everything about himself just to be my side candy while I play politician for a while is too much, even for someone like Hell Monkey.

I clear my throat, trying to keep the tears from squeezing their way out. "What will you do?"

He shrugs, staring down at our linked hands, running the pads of his thumbs across my palms. "I thought I might go back to Homestead, actually. Use some of these credits, some of this shiny new clout, see what I can do down there to help out."

Godsdammit. That's just like him, too. I wrap my arms around his neck and kiss him, hard and fierce. I put my whole self into it. Even all those buried pieces that I never like to look at. We never even had a chance to explore this—this real, clear-eyed passion—and now I don't know when we will get to again, so I'm going to take whatever moments we've got left.

I pull back just a little, so we're nose to nose, forehead to forehead. I'm trying to cast this memory in platinum—how he feels, how he smells, every little line on his face. "It turns out I kind of love you, Eliot."

He laughs a little and pokes me in the side, right in a spot he knows is ticklish. "Yeah, I figured that one out a while ago."

Bastard. I kiss him again, and he grabs me by the hips and pulls me into his lap, holding me tight against him.

We don't have a lot of time left, but it's enough. Enough to make a few more memories. Memories just for him and me.

He stays with me until he absolutely can't stay anymore, and then he gathers his stuff, kisses me again—soft this time, the kind of kiss that lingers—and turns to leave.

I can't watch him go. It's too much. So I stare out at the shimmering nebula. Or maybe it's not shimmering. Maybe I'm just losing the battle with those tears I keep shoving down. "Hey," I call as he reaches the door. "I'm gonna want that captain's chair back once I'm all done here, y'know."

"It'll be waiting for you, Alyssa Farshot."

The door slides closed behind him. And he's gone.

The room immediately feels darker and bigger in his wake. It's just me now. Me and all my ghosts. I want to wallow. I want to sink down in my bed and tell everyone in this ship and everyone in this quadrant to go the hell away.

That's not how you get your life back, Farshot.

The voice in my head kind of sounds like Coy's voice, and I actually smile at that. What would Nathalia Coyenne tell me to do right now if she were here? It's obvious when I think about it.

First, wash my face.

Second, track down some chocolate pastries. (Comfort eating is key.)

Third, go help fix a godsdamned empire.

So that's what I'm gonna do.

TOP HEADLINES FROM THE ARCHIVES OF THE *DAILY WORLDS*

SYMPOSIUM ON THE CREATION OF A NEW GALACTIC COMMONWEALTH COMMENCES ON APEX

0.07.10.4031

OFFICIAL COMMONWEALTH ADVISORY COMMITTEE TO INCLUDE MEMBERS OF THE PLANETARY INDEPENDENCE MOVEMENT, AS WELL AS THREE OTHER SIMILAR ORANIZATIONS

0.07.13.4031

SOLARI LEADERSHIP OFFICIALLY EXCOMMUNICATE EXCANDARE SECT, VOW TO BRING ANY REMAINING FOLLOWERS TO JUSTICE

0.08.06.4031

A NEWER, BRIGHTER FUTURE: COMMITTEE SIGNS OFFICIAL AGREEMENT ESTABLISHING THE CREATION OF THE GALACTIC UNITED COMMONWEALTH

0.08.27.4031

STARDATE 0.06.20 NAMED AS ANNUAL GALACTIC DAY OF MOURNING TO COMMEMORATE THOSE LOST IN THE EXCANDARE ATTACKS

0.09.07.4031

ORSO AND WINGER RETURN TO ORSION SYSTEM TO ASSIST WITH CONSTRUCTION OF THREE NEW CITADELS

0.09.29.4031

DECISION DAY: VOTING COMMENCES ON PLANETS ACROSS THE QUADRANT TO DECIDE IF THEY WILL JOIN THE NEW COMMONWEALTH

0.01.06.4032

TEAR, CHU'RA AMONG THOSE WHO OVERWHELMINGLY CHOSE TO BREAK WITH THE FORMER EMPIRE

0.01.08.4032

KALIA SHARN WINS FIRST PUBLIC ELECTION FOR THE ROLE OF MINISTER; SHARVA BAHR ELECTED DEPUTY MINISTER

0.02.12.4032

NEW PARLIAMENT SHIP OFFICIALLY LAUNCHES, TWO DAYS AHEAD OF FIRST MEETING OF FULL PARLIAMENT

0.03.04.4032

PLANET HOMESTEAD SUCCESSFULLY SUES FOR INDEPENDENCE FROM HELIX, WILL ESTABLISH ITS OWN GOVERNMENT

0.05.09.4032

VOLES ENTERPRISES FILES FOR BANKRUPTCY, PLANS TO RESTRUCTURE AS A NONPROFIT

0.06.32.4032

REFORM PARTY, LED BY EVERN SAJORD, GAINS POPULARITY IN PARLIAMENT

0.07.03.4032

LAST PLANET RATIFIES CORE ARTICLES OF ESTABLISHMENT, MINISTER SHARN DECLARES AN OFFICIAL DAY OF CELEBRATION

0.09.15.4032

ROY, ORSO, FARSHOT REUNITE TO LAUNCH THE NATHALIA COYENNE MEMORIAL SPACEPORT

0.01.26.4033

EPILOGUE

STARDATE: 0.03.4034, two years, five months, three weeks, and four days after the official establishment of the Galactic United Commonwealth, currently under the leadership of Minister Kalia Sharn and Deputy Minister Sharva Bahr
LOCATION: Station Shisso again. It's been way too long.

THE COMMS LIGHT STARTS FLASHING JUST AS I'M finishing final docking alignment, but I let it blink on-off-on-off while I finesse my zippy little cruiser into the clamps and hit the decompression seal. I have a pretty good idea who's calling, anyway. And it's only natural I make them wait.

I take a second to stare out at the hodgepodge space station that fills the windows. Hand to the stars, it's the second-best sight in the whole entire universe right now, warped patches and all.

I finally flip on the comms, and Setter Roy's stoic face fills the viewscreen. He's frowning, because of course he is, and I tilt back in my chair, grinning at him.

"Is the parliament ship on fire? Did it all go to hell already? I've only been gone a few days."

He actually rolls his eyes, which is absolutely delightful because he almost never lets himself make expressions like that anymore. He accepted a senior adviser role on Deputy Minister Sharva's staff, and he takes it—brace yourself, this is shocking—very seriously.

Except when he's around me, of course. I bring out the best in people.

"We're fully capable of running all this without you, Alyssa, believe it or not."

I send him an exaggerated wink. "Sure, sure, Setter, but will it be as fun?"

He sighs. "I actually had something for you, if you're done being clever." He waves a hand across the display, and there's a little beep from my navcomm dashboard as I pull up the file. It's an official photo of me, a list of my science jockey credentials, and, best of all, a status update that reads ACTIVE in big green letters. "Full reinstatement at the Explorers' Society. Not that you really needed any help—they were bound to take you back even after two years away—but . . . I wanted to do it."

I smile at him through the viewscreen—a real smile this time. "Turns out you're pretty good people, Setter Roy."

He shifts and nods uncomfortably—for someone so ambitious, he's really terrible at taking a compliment. "You know, you've helped do something good here, Alyssa," he says after a beat. "Your uncles would be very proud."

I don't have a quippy comeback for that because honestly? I think they would be too. It's not perfect. It's gonna take work from folks all across the quadrant to keep it up and keep it together. But I think we're on the right path. I reach up and thread my fingers through the chain around my neck that has a mini holodisc hanging on it. It's got my favorite images of Atar and Charlie and Coy on it so I can carry them around with me always.

Look, let's not pretend I wasn't always a secret sap, okay? This shouldn't be a surprise.

Setter clears his throat and puts on the mildly irritated expression he usually wears around me. "Well, then . . . try not to make too much trouble out there, Alyssa."

"Yeah . . . no promises on that one, buddy. Tell Sharva I said hi."

I close out the comm before he can reply and snatch up my bag, practically skipping as I make my way off the cruiser and onto Station Shisso. Gemi is there, waiting for me, and she sweeps me into one of her world-encompassing hugs like no time has passed at all. She takes me in with an appraising look as I step back, and I don't know what she sees exactly. She doesn't say either, just reaches up and pats my cheek.

"You good?" I ask. "Everyone here good?" Because last time I was here, I'd brought a whole load of unwanted attention to a place that had worked hard to stay off the radar, and hopefully I haven't ruined that for them long-term.

"We're fine." She squeezes my arm and starts walking me down the hall. "Everything is fine. I'd ask if you're staying long, but I think I know why you're here. He's over at the sunside docking bays. Packing up to head out soon. Another few hours or so and you might've missed him."

"Thanks, Gemi. You're the absolute best." I kiss her wrinkled face and dart off, practically jogging as I wind my way through Shisso's corridors to the opposite side of the station. There's this tight feeling in my chest, but for once it isn't worry or fear. It's more like someone pumped a million bubbles into my lungs and if I don't let them out soon, they're gonna carry my feet right off the ground.

I spot him before he spots me, and I stop, pulse pounding so hard I can feel it in my throat. Hell Monkey's stripped down to his tank, with the top half of his jumpsuit down around his waist, and he's got a small stack of crates that he's hauling through the docking seal onto his ship.

This, by the way, is the first-best sight in the universe. At least, it is if you're me.

I wait until he disappears through the docking seal, and then I slide up and sit cross-legged on one of the crates, staring at the exit and waiting for him to return. My stomach is just a big tangle of knots and my heart is loud in my ears. Oh, gods, I'm nervous. I'm suddenly sickeningly nervous that this is not going to go like I thought. We've been so busy, on such opposite sides of the galaxy, for the past few years that we haven't traded many comms, and maybe he moved on, maybe he couldn't wait, maybe he's flying with someone else now—

He clomps back through the docking seal, and I freeze as he looks up and sees me. I watch the realization break across his face like a miniature dawn—the slight softening at the corners of his mouth, the little crinkle around his eyes, the way his shoulders relax. He's looking at me in that way he has—like I'm a brand-new star and as familiar as home all at once—and all my nerves are gone. Just like that.

I lean forward and rest my chin in my hands, grinning. "I hear you're looking for a cocaptain."

He grins back, stepping forward. "Maybe. Why—you know someone?"

"I might," I say with an oh-so-casual shrug.

"They a good pilot?" He steps closer with every question.

"The best."

"Willing to take some risks?"

I swing my feet to the floor and stand, hands on my hips. "Danger is their middle name."

His last step carries him right up to me, and he drops his voice to a low murmur that rolls over my skin. "And how do they feel about being the big spoon?"

I hook my fingers into his tool belt and tug, closing whatever minor distance was left between us. "They make an excellent big spoon."

He presses his mouth against mine, soft and slow, trailing his fingers up my neck and into my hair and—damn. I definitely missed kissing this guy. My memory hasn't been doing it justice the past couple years.

He pulls away well before I'm ready, his face flushed, his breathing unsteady. "I've got a surprise for you," he says. "I've been holding on to it for a while."

I raise an eyebrow. "I guess I'm willing to interrupt our

reunion make-out if it's for a surprise."

"Close your eyes."

I do, and he takes me by the hands and guides me through the docking tunnel and onto his ship. I hadn't checked to see what he's flying these days, but I can feel the alloy floor of the corridor under my boots as he leads me along and up a lift to the second level. I breathe deep, reveling in the scents of coolant oil and metal polish and something else hard to pinpoint, but it smells so familiar and so welcoming.

I hear doors swish open and then closed behind me, and then Hell Monkey says, "Okay . . . you can look now."

My breath catches in my throat as my eyes open. Because hand to the stars, it looks like I'm standing on board the bridge of my old ship, the *Vagabond Quick*. Everything from the layout to the colors to the spread of the windows along the prow is exactly how it was (y'know, right up until the point I used it to blow up a warship). I can catch upgrades here and there—the latest interfaces over on the navcomm, for one, and also it's missing all the scuffs and dings and other wear and tear my old ship had gained over the years. But to the untrained eye, she's identical.

I look over at Hell Monkey, who's watching me carefully, his hands stuffed in his jumpsuit pockets. Probably because he doesn't know what to do with them. "What . . . ? I . . . She's . . ."

"Almost an exact replica." He shrugs, rescuing me from my own failure to language. "Faye and Honor helped me build her about a year ago. She's got the latest tech under the hood, but everything else is as close as I could get it. Oh, and also . . . Nova?"

An irritable disembodied voice blares from the ceiling. "WHAT COULD YOU POSSIBLY WANT RIGHT NOW?"

I laugh—just this burst of straight joy coming right out of my chest. "Good to hear your dulcet tones again, Nova."

"YOUR PRESENCE IS ALSO RECOGNIZED, CAPTAIN FARSHOT."

"I nabbed her from the *Serendipity* before it blew up in the fight on Vellyn. She was just too unique to leave behind."

I don't know what to say. I can hardly say anything without probably dissolving into a little puddle of emotions, and I've really been trying not to do that so much lately. So instead I wander around the bridge, marveling at all the little details that Hell Monkey remembered to add in, making my way slowly toward the prow until I finally step up to the captain's chair.

It looks brand-new, completely untouched, and it's got a little metal sign hanging around the top of it that says, "CAPTAIN FARSHOT."

Hell Monkey reaches around from behind me and pulls the sign off. He's definitely blushing now. "Told you I'd save it for you."

I press a kiss to his scruffy cheek and then drop into the chair, brushing my fingers across the touch screens that cover the dashboard. Everything jumps to life at my slightest direction—she's ready to go, ready to fly. I am too.

I pull up a list of her specs and designations, and see it there at the top—her official name.

The *Vagabond Quickest*.

I see Hell Monkey slide into the copilot's seat next to me, like he's always been there, like we never left, and those damn tears I've been so good at holding back spill out of the corners of my eyes.

After everything. I'm finally home.

ACKNOWLEDGMENTS

To all the booksellers, librarians, readers, and members of the book community who have traveled this journey with Alyssa Farshot, Hell Monkey, and all the rest of these characters: thank you. For reading about them. For loving them. For supporting them (and me). I appreciate each and every one of you.

To Lara Perkins: You always go above and beyond, and I can't wait to see where we go next. To Greg Ferguson, Tara Weikum, and Sarah Homer: Thank you for your support, your enthusiasm, and your guidance in helping me bring Alyssa home.

Thank you to the entire Harper team for everything you've done for this duology: to Jon Howard, Megan Gendell, and Robin Roy, for fine-tuning my words (especially my many, many echoes!); to Doaly for cover art that I love even more than the first (which I didn't think was possible), and to Chris Kwon and Jenna Stempel for the incredible design work; to Allison Brown for everything you do to transform my digital words into a real, actual book; to Lauren Levite and Michael D'Angelo for supporting *Thronebreakers* and helping bring it to libraries, bookstores, and homes all over the country; to Michelle Vardanian for so carefully and thoughtfully critiquing this duology.

To all of my fellow authors and friends, in-person and online, who have been there for me and fielded the texts and the DMs, the emails and the group chats. Who've celebrated with me and vented with me and everything in-between. Thank you.

To all my family and friends who have cheered me on, especially my parents and my sisters: I love you and thank you for always believing in me.

And to Dave, Miriam, and Evelyn. The three hearts I carry with me always.